A Pimp In The Pulpit

A Pimp

IN THE PULPIT

God Ain't Sleep   A Novel

ROD PALMER

Black Wren Press
Columbia, SC

BLACK WREN PRESS LLC

Copyright © 2022, by Rod Palmer
No part of this publication may be reproduced, stored in a retrieval system, or transmitted in any form or by any means, electronic, mechanical, photocopying, recording, scanning, or otherwise, except as permitted under Section 107 or 108 of the 1976 International Copyright Act, without the prior written permission except in brief quotations embodied in critical articles and reviews.

LIBRARY OF CONGRESS CATALOGING-IN-PUBLICATION DATA

Names: Palmer, Rod, author.
Title: A Pimp In The Pulpit 2nd Ed/ Rod Palmer
Description: [South Carolina] : Black Wren Press [2022]
Identifiers: LCN 1-11433773181 | ISBN 979-8-9864282-2-2 LCC PS
LC record available at https://lccn.loc.gov/
LC ebook record available at https://lccn.loc.gov/

International edition ISBN

Printed in the United States of America

This is a work of fiction. All characters, organizations, and events portrayed in this novel are either products of the author's imagination or are used fictitiously.

Where did your Christ come from?   From
God and a woman! Man had nothing to do
with him.~ Sojourner Truth

Chapter 1

Lynn pulls her long-handled luggage case of books down Carter Street. Across the narrow one-way, the barbershop has eyes. Among the men watching, is Pastor Stewart at the window chair, eyeing Lynn's high-heeled stride as his cut hair falls like black wool.

Stewart is bewildered by her beauty, seeing continents unite in her face – lips hinting Africa, eyes whispering Asia, but if beauty is more than an ensemble of well-formed features, she has that other thing too: a feline grace, a quiet intensity that could stop a heartbeat.

"Breathtaking, ain't she," says Calvin, his barber.

Pastor Stewart shrugs nonchalantly. He can't admit perking up for a random woman no matter how her legs glisten in the sun.

Calvin, isn't having it. "Now *reb*..." Calvin ceases all work to appraise the pastor's indifference. "You was lookin' just like we was lookin'."

Stewart, refusing to be categorized, replies, "Our *eyes* was on the same thing but not our minds. I thought she looked familiar."

"You ain't seen Lynn before? Dr. Lynn Cummings–"

"–Doctor?"

"Professor. And author. She drops by here every week this same day and time. The girls sell her novels on the other side."

Stewart comes in on Saturdays as religiously as church on Sundays. If his routine were not thrown off for his upcoming birthday, Stewart and Lynn's paths would've forever missed by two days. Stewart feels a sermon budding, where he'd challenge the idea of a small world, claiming that what's small is our routines, like self-imposed borders, blocking us from blessings laying just outside of our comfort zones.

Although Lynn has disappeared, Stewarts squints, as if still watching her in his mind. "*Missus* Doctor Lynn Cummings?"

Calvin's eyes turn leery. "Naw, she ain't married... But I thought you wasn't studying her like that though."

Junior, the kaki-colored man plucking boiled peanuts from a damp paper bag, nods at Stewart, "Ole white Jesus got you thinking it's a sin to admire our women?"

Calvin glares. "Chill, Junior."

Junior's arms spread in open protest. "If we can't air it out in the barbershop, where can we go, brotha?"

Stewart welcomes the smoke. "Jesus only said don't look if you can't control your lust."

A heated debate ensues, each man in a barber's chair or waiting chair taking their shot at the megachurch pastor.

Lynn, leaving the hospital gift shop, now crosses over Carter Street to the beauty salon adjacent the barbershop.

As Lynn enters she's hit with the rankness of lye. Lynn's head of glorious ribbons, her loosed Bantu knots, makes raw scalped women rethink their decision. The beauticians light up when they see Lynn. Tia, the shop's co-owner hugs her former English professor, hands Lynn her skimmed profit, then unlocks the glass case for Lynn to restock her novels.

They hear a commotion on the men's side. The instant Tia rolls her eyes and assures, "They always get like that." The men get louder, barking like a kennel of dogs. Tia goes to the adjoining door. Lynn and the other women gather behind her to see.

A young rapper type, in a ball cap and baggy pants, is the center of attention with Junior egging him on. He is up pacing and laughing, but his laughter is angry, manic; his sights trained on the pastor. "What you're not understanding is this: my wife is mines! Shouldn't we be able to go there when *we* say go?" This stirs the male patrons. They rally behind the young up and comer as logically, he puts the reverend's back against the ropes.

Stewart is noticeably peeved. "Did *I* say abstain while fasting? Did *I* write the bible?" Peeved, but shielding himself with the bible.

The young man jerks away, frustrated, but holds Stewart in the corner of an eye. "But did the bible order the fast last Sunday? On *your* call, I can't be with my own wife?"

They're debating in questions, which feels silly to Stewart; he tries leveling with him. "I understand where you're coming from, ok? Look… You *can* have sex with your wife–"

The young man howls and snatches his baggy crouch – the best he could do to keep from jumping fresh on the pastor's behind. The young man just can't get past the semantics. "Are you granting me *permission* to be with my own wife?"

"No that's not what I'm saying," Stewart asserts. "I was *saying*," but then the young man is *say-ing* too, so their argument boils to a point where Calvin has to pull the lid.

"C'mon, yall! Chill! Chill!"

It works a few seconds, until the young man notices his wife standing in the doorway. "Look at my wife!" A stiff hand aims at the young lady with a tattoo peeking out of her low-rise jeans. "Look at huh. My wife is setsy. If she looked like Deacon Bacon's wife, heck I'd be *glad* to fast." Pockets of laughter flames; his wife blushes; both charmed and embarrassed. The young man adds, "Even when we decide to go ahead and do our thing, she's laying up feeling disloyal because she's broke the fast that *you* ordered! So, *your* name comes up in our bedroom, and I don't near appreciate that, pastor."

The debate escalates. Everyone wants in. The men chuck to the edge of their seats and volley their opinions. The women pool in from the parlor, denying fingers waving like wiper blades. Even level heads who try to find common ground, has the ground split beneath them, falling into the fray.

Junior springs to the center of the floor, promising to *break it down* for everyone. First, he is pointing up to the moon that man walked on, next he's shelling out invisible money as he muses about perpetuating systems, cohorts, henchmen, ranked and filed under a grand scheme in the hierarchy of Christianity. Finally Junior ends with, "But y'all don't hear me though!"

Baffled looks finds other baffled looks. Calvin, the shop owner, speaks for everyone with, "Maaaan, sit your dumb butt down."

Lynn raises her hand like a student. "May I interject?"

Junior bows aside, "My queen."

"What my friend Junior here is trying to say is that the *word of God* is the authority – not the *man* of God. No man – pastor or no-pastor – should put a wedge between husband and wife."

"*Thank* you," Junior cannons.

Lynn adds, "First Corinthians chapter seven says husband and wife should fast only by agreement." She then addresses the young rapper, "Did you and this beautiful young lady agree to fast?"

"No Mam."

"Well, then, the bible says you 'should not deprive each other.'" The husband checks his wife to see that she is getting this. The young lady scoffs back. Lynn adds, "But it also says that you should honor your wife's desire to fast by finding a time where you *do* agree, amen?" The wife sticks out her tongue, teasing her husband with her newfound privilege.

Amens go around the shop while the young rapper nods in consent. Lynn then ribs him, "You've got to hand it to him, though. Takes a big man to admit that when he's in bed with his wife, he doesn't have what it takes to keep her mind off the pastor." The shop explodes with laughter, all but the young man in the ball cap, and Pastor Stewart, who cuts an eye at Lynn but also smirks. Lynn pets Stewart's hand for being a good sport.

Stewart is so in awe of Lynn that he wants to talk to her and possibly get to know her but he couldn't attempt to charm her in the presence of men who saw him deny his attraction. Not knowing if he'd ever see Lynn again, he lets her walk out of the shop, savoring the touch of her hand on his. Stewart says, "Now, a woman who knows the word of God, that's what I call attractive."

The young rapper chimes in, "But what if she know the word of God but looks like Deacon Bacon's wife; is she still attractive then?" The men chuckle in response.

When Pastor Stewart's haircut is done, he goes over to the adjoining beauty salon and purchases the novel that the beauticians rave about: *Don't Pray For Love.* The bio on the back cover says Lynn is a professor of literature and women's studies at the University of South Carolina and that she is an activist for Women's Rights.

Her portrait is stunning. She's sits sideways on a park bench at dusk, hugging her knees. Her clasped hands hold a two-piece copper telescope as old as wooden freight ships. Stewart sits parked outside the barbershop with the book spread in his hands.

He is awestruck by the characters' wit and the narrator's depth. The prose is as gorgeous as Psalms. Stewart drops the book on the console as if it's volatile. He snatches it up again, as if *he's* volatile. He gazes at the back cover in mind-bending confusion. Her writing skill makes her beauty more compelling; her beauty makes her writing skill more compelling, and yet there is something extra lifting out of the pages though, some pattern formation coming forth like a hologram puzzle, although the author's secret isn't visual; it's intellectual, spiritual. The narrator's word choices, the angles of logic from which she speaks. The wisdom feels brotherly – feels eerily familiar. Stewart is blown away, when he recognizes: *Jesus.*

Chapter 2

*L*ynn could fill a drawer with all her rejection letters had she kept them. Publishing houses imply that Lynn's stories are good, however, they are cylinders that won't fit into the square slots of genre. Lynn refuses to make her art conform and as a result, her novels sit on the bookshelves of hospital gift shops and in beauty salons next to bootleg DVDs.

The only way she could suffer all the rejection and keep on writing is to insist that she *is* a great writer, only waiting to be discovered. So, when Lynn arrives on campus in her office and finds an email requesting stage production rights to her novel, *Don't Pray For Love*, she feels somewhat discovered.

She's elated, in fact. She replies with interest, and just minutes after clicking send, a reply comes back, requesting a meeting today, at a coffee shop not far off campus, which Lynn quickly confirms. The signature on the bottom of the email says Pastor Stewart, whom she met in person at the barbershop. She suspects this meeting might be a coffee date in disguise. The pastor is so tall, handsome and well-mannered that, in any event, that either way, business meeting or coffee date, is be worth her time.

Her workday becomes nothing more than a prequel to this meeting. By the end of her last class, the meeting time drawing nearer, Lynn is so excited that it's hard to stay in character when returning a batch of dismal papers.

Lynn leans against her desk, takes a weary look around the room and sighs. Their analytical papers are so red with marks, that while grading them Lynn had felt like the villain in a slasher movie. Lynn shoves off of her desk and begins walking down the rows, turning the papers down on each student's desk. "I assigned *Their Eyes Were Watching God* as a gift because I know that most of you have read it already in lower level classes, and some even in high school. And before anyone asks, no. I will not be curbing the grades." Lynn pivots at the end of one row and goes up another, drill sergeant style. "Have you been spoon-fed by the introductory levels? Absolutely. They encourage any interpretation as long as it seems as though you're trying to think critically. The training wheels are now off, ladies and gentleman," she says as she drops another dismal paper face down. "At this level, we let you know that it is possible for your assessment to be... baseless." Even here in a three hundred level class, it would break some cardinal rule by uttering the word *wrong*. "The evidence is not in your heads; it's in the text. Lynn takes the book off a student's desk and turns to a passage. As it reads:"

He ain't kissin' yo' mouf when he carry on over yuh lak dat. He's kissin' yo' foot and 'tain't in uh man tuh kiss foot long. Mouf kissin' is on uh equal and dat's natural but when dey got to bow down tuh love, dey soon straightens up ...

Lynn adds, "As you can see, Hurston isn't ambiguous nor cryptic about her message. She hands you the juxtaposition of gender roles and romantic love, and yet you all go and write papers about whatever irrelevant thing that may have stood out to you personally – and tried to pass it off as scholarly. Our job is to interpret, on a deeper level, what the author is trying to convey, by how they use story structure, narrative voice, language... how the author deals out fate. The author is God of their fictional world..." On that note, class time expires, and Lynn's next stop is her meeting with Pastor Stewart.

When Lynn arrives at the café, she lets the door close behind her as she scans for the pastor. She stands by the newspaper rack, just now feeling self-conscience, wondering only now, if she's dressed too casual for this business meeting, in her linen skirt and her strappy Herculean sandals.

Lynn spots Stewart as he gets up, his tea brown complexion; his thick lashes seem to outline his eyes like a pharaoh. He slips her book out from under his armpit and holds it under his chin like a mugshot plate. "I've finished reading it *already*," he says.

Below that sunny smile, in San Script font is the words, *Don't Pray for Love* – hopefully not an omen, Lynn thinks, as she notices a wedding band, but on Stewart's right hand and not the left. It would be quite pretentious to ask so soon, so Lynn tries not to let the ring distract her.

"Pastor Dana Stewart." Their hands shake and then let go, not knowing what to do next. Stewart ushers Lynn to the counter where they order lattes. They pepper the wait time with small talk. "So, you're an English professor. My twin sister is an English professor."

Lynn smiles and nods. "Twin sister…"

"She lives up north. Connecticut."

"Ok." Lynn squints. "So, you say you've read it. I was about to say, because… The word *pray* may be in the title, but I wouldn't exactly call it Christian lit – hardly fitting for a gospel play." The main character and her love interest have premarital sex, which is an automatic disqualifier for the religious genre; Lynn's rejection letters says so.

Stewart replies, "How is it not Christian lit when Christ Himself is your narrator?"

Lynn's brow lowers. The man speaks as if he knows. "You're *sure* of this?"

"If it is unintentional, I am all the more impressed."

They take their lattes. Stewart very gentlemanly offers his forearm, butler style, which Lynn takes as he guides her to a booth. He sits across from her, holding this glazed over, waiting look that makes Lynn look out the window to avoid smiling and seeming flirtatious.

Lynn says, "I've seen your sermons on television in the early mornings. First Baptist Church." Lynn spies his nod, adding, "Isn't that the *huge* church over on–"

"–Big church, but with a small-church feel." One of their slogans.

The size of the church makes Lynn wonder about the size of the play. "Have you considered a venue? Longstreet theatre or Trustus? Certainly not the Township auditorium, right?"

Stewart wants to impress her, to out-imagine her wildest imagination, to guarantee that she'd accept this business proposal so he'd have months to court her – to *work with* her, he meant to think. "How about the Colonial Life Arena?" Five times grander than her loftiest guess.

Lynn flops back, quitting like a poker player folding a measly pair. "Our ball games don't even fill that arena."

Stewart defers to scripture, "'And God said unto Pharaoh, even for this same purpose have I raised thee up, that I might shew my power in thee, and that my name might be declared throughout all the earth.'" In his own words Stewart says, "It's a charity play and the 'purpose' that would declare God's name, throughout South Carolina, at least, is to build a Christian Academy, as the community's response to the Abbeville versus South Carolina board of education decision." Lynn gasps in agreement, as Stewart continues. "They made their ruling that textbook shortages, plaster caked ceilings, sinks backing up with raw sewage, and more drip buckets than students on a rainy day, is *not* unconstitutional. I aim to show them that where there is a church doing what it's supposed to do, the community will never be at the mercy of their ruling."

"Amen," says Lynn. "That is so admirable of you. And ambitious." She smiles and kids, "Are you aware that we're in the middle of a recession?"

"God don't know the meaning of the word recession."

Lynn smiles. "You quote Romans nine and seventeen. You're pharaoh, in this scenario?"

Stewarts leans back, wanting no part of the comparison. "No, *you*. It's your book."

Lynn rests her chin on her fist. "You'll say anything to flatter me, won't you?"

The man seems so pleased with himself, Lynn lets him have it, and changes the subject. "Do you have a date in mind?"

The word date splashes him in the face, as their meeting begins to feel like one. "Keep in mind that this is still in the infant stages. The board of trustees gonna meet in a couple days to debate whether or not they approve funding."

"How is it that you have to get approval? You the pastor."

"At a church where the trustees technically have all the power."

Lynn says, "Actually, I did my homework. The church website says it owns a credit union. So how is funding a problem when your church owns a bank?"

"Octavia, who is the Chief Financial Officer is the first person I brought this to—"

Lynn lights up. "A woman as your CFO? Tell me more."

Stewart smiles modestly. "I got into a lot of trouble appointing her. There were a number of brothers expecting to have that role handed to them."

"But you stood up to them. Whew." Lynn lays back in her booth and fans herself. "You just don't know, pastor. Stuff like that kinda turns me on—" Lynn freezes, suddenly, her eyes wide. "Did I just say—"

"—Yes you did." Pastor Stewart smiles with all of his teeth, adding, "Better mind. The Lord's still working on me."

They chuckle together and then sigh together. Stewart clears his throat and picks up where he'd left off. "Not only is it a small bank, it's a ministry in and of itself. For the surrounding community, we offer a lifeline for foreclosures, low interest loans for distressed local businesses – things like that. Octavia will never do anything that would put a strain on lending for those initiatives, so we're at the mercy of a board of trustees that don't like me very much because I ignore their rigid traditions. But they too are under the hand of God, so just know that the funding is a given. You can go ahead and start working on the script, and I'll handle the rest."

Lynn's mouth falls open, spilling word, "*Script…*" She gathers her hands. "I came here to negotiate the production rights, pastor, not to be employed by you."

The man's sigh deflates him. "Well… You see–"

"–I have obligations outside of teaching… I'm a key member of a Women's Rights organization." Lynn pauses. "Must sound like a dirty word to a southern Baptist preacher, huh?"

Stewart with an uneven brow asks, "Do you support abortion?"

"No. That's where we differ with most organizations like us. We don't campaign for it – but we don't campaign against it, either."

"Hmm…" Stewart nods.

"I've wrote a proposed bill of legislation that we're trying to get onto the senate floor: The Fair Wage Transparency Bill. Although we have the Equal Pay act of 1963, there's no checks and balances. All the time it takes for a class action lawsuit to come about – or not – companies get away with decades of discriminatory pay and even if the suit is settled, the only ones who truly benefit are the lawyers. We want large companies to make available are their wage statistics per job title, categorized by race and gender. We're trying to get this bill before the senate, which is no easy task. So, you see, pastor. I'm stretched thin; I don't have time to create a script for a play, nor do I know how." Lynn sinks in her booth, her face sullen.

Stewart smiles paternally at her disappointment. "I'll work it out. I'll hire someone to write the script. It's ok to step wrong, as long as we keep taking steps. But I must admit, Lynn. I am thoroughly impressed you. You wrote a bill of legislation…" Stewart's lips tighten as if he wants to say more.

Lynn folds her arms to reaffirm her disappointment on top of what he'd just said. Not a detail was worked out prior to their meeting. The emails seem like he had it planned out like an architect, but come to find out, he doesn't even have a blueprint; he's just a big dreamer, albeit a handsome one.

The big dreamer's dream sits across the booth, vivid and stunning even in her displeasure. "I know how to build," says

Stewart. "I know how to get feet moving behind a purpose, Lynn. I've been doing this since age twenty-two, when I took over as pastor, back when First Baptist was the size of a corner store..." The church is now the size of a community college campus, its sanctuary now a domed mountain with an evening shadow blanketing a stretch of highway next to it. "Believe me when I say that when this play hits the arena, I will have twenty thousand people waiting at your feet."

That line seems premeditated, as Lynn could tell by Dana's proud smile. Still the words cut through to her. An indescribable chill swims through Lynn. She feels like she's being offered a small kingdom. Lynn's negotiation posture melts; her poker face breaks into blushing. Even if it's rubbish, she let herself believe, for a moment, that all the countryside might pour in from far and wide because of her writing.

To break the silence, Stewart asks, "That day at the barbershop. How were you the only one who could make sense of what Junior was trying to say."

Lynn shrugs. "I didn't... Even *Junior* couldn't make sense of what *he* was saying." Lynn and Stewart laugh like old friends, the blinds laying stripes over their booth table.

As the sun dips behind Columbia's stout buildings, their conversation wanders; words no longer matter. Conversation is simply the rhythm for the dance of body language. They could sit there reciting The Preamble and convey their attraction with the rises in their eyes, the listener's giddy interest, and when there are no words, their shy look-aways veer out the café window only to send back targeted glances. They sum up their lives in tourist brochure versions, covering the landmarks of their careers while skipping over love like a flat rock skipping through the lakes of their past.

Already, Stewart is envisioning a castle around himself and the beautiful princess now sitting across the table. Lynn snaps him out of the daydream with the question, "What's with the ring?" Lynn nods at the band on Stewart's right hand. "Divorced?"

"Never married." Stewart twists the ring nervously. "About twenty years ago, I was engaged."

Lynn successfully prevents a reaction. *Twenty years ago, and he still wears the ring,* Lynn notes. "What happened?"

"Inoperable brain tumor."

"I'm sorry," Lynn says, painfully. "Must've been devastating."

Stewart's head shakes. "I even had a little falling out with God over that one."

"Never found love again?"

Love. The man's heart flutters. "Yes. But she didn't love back; I wasn't her type."

"If tall, Godly, and handsome is not her type…" Lynn, blushing as he blushes, continues, "… then what *is* her type?"

"Women."

Lynn gives a shocked, but silent oh.

Stewart then turns the tables. "And you? How has a woman as beautiful and intelligent as you escaped marriage for so long?"

"For so long? Are you calling me old?" Her lips wrestle a smile.

"Oh no." Stewart's hands try to scrub his words out of the air.

"I'm kidding." Lynn captures his waving hands and places them on the table. The touch of hands feels somewhat loaded. "Marriage," Lynn sighs. "I've been asked twice… I'd love to tell you all about it, but would you look at the time." She rolls her wrist to show her watch face.

Stewart assumes she's kidding, but she is actually pulling her bag strap over her shoulder and getting up. "So, you're going to leave me hanging just like that?"

"If you knew my story, you'd know there's not enough time to tell it. Besides, I've got midterms on my plate."

Stewart follows her out into an evening that is dimming and turning brisk. He throws his suit over her shoulders. Lynn secretly sniffs the jacket's cologne. Stewart walks her to a sapphire blue, boxy European car. Stewart holds her door open for her.

Lynn stops just inside of the door; they're now face to face. Lynn says, "Forgive me for acting all flirtatious, pastor. I'll be more professional next time."

Their close proximity turns them serious; the pastor is seething with intent. "Naw, keep that same energy," Stewart replies. "Brotha like me, struggles to make the first move."

Lynn smiles slyly, "Looks like you're making it now."

They inch closer, ever so slowly, eyes dancing, lips parting.

A squinting Stewart pauses to inquire, "Too soon?"

"Shshshsh..."

Their eyes close. Their lips merge and press; their bodies following suit, as they inhale and grip one another. The kiss is brief, but, loaded with a desire that is as urgent as greed. But this is a business meeting. This is a pastor. Lynn comes away smoothing Stewart's tie down the front of his body, smiling, and kidding, "Alright, passa."

Stewart bites his lip as if he was stopped short of more mischievous intentions.

Lynn warns, "I'm saving myself. Do me a solid, and don't make it hard for me, okay?"

As Lynn lowers into her car, Stewart struggles to keep eye level and ignore those beautiful legs drawing into the car. "You're too gorgeous for this ugly car," he jokes as he shuts her in.

Her driver's side window lowers and she feeds Stewart's jacket through. "I love my ugly car. Maybe it's not the pricier models like *you* drive," she says, as she periscopes for the nearest Cadillac or Bentley that southern pastors are known for. Seeing nothing, Lynn asks, "Where *did* you park?"

"I'm right in front of you." As proof, Stewart points his key chain. A Toyota Camry chirps and Lynn looks on in amazement, as if staring at Jesus's mule. Pastors of smaller churches drive cars three times the value of Stewart's, advertising the material life that is supposedly attainable through their ministry. It is infinitely more impressive for Lynn to see a pastor living the creed that the only true, transcendent wealth is to be rich in spirit. "Now *that* is impressive," says Lynn.

She tickles a wave out of the window as she drives off. Stewart stands rooted to the spot until Lynn's red brake lights disappear in the distance. Stewart then celebrates with a fist pump.

Lynn's ambitious side and her romantic side are two warring factions, fighting for territory in her mind. Lynn doesn't realize, until she gets home to her city condo, how many business details they failed to cover. She didn't even get around to negotiating the fee for the first-time production rights, and with someone else writing the script, she hadn't clarified how much creative control she'd relinquish. But on the other hand, she laughs at her blunders in business because it only proves how enamored she is with this fine, gentle mannered man.

She still wears the glow from their latte table. Within the mint green walls of her bedroom, she lies belly down, her legs scissoring behind her as she watches her cell phone, waiting for it to ring while a fact so obvious dawns on her, but means something so incredibly new: *But he's a pastor*, she winces. A relationship with this man would tie her to his church. Her love for God is rooted solidly in her heart, but when it comes to Sunday worship, she's a free grazer. She'd squat at one church for months, but then run off as soon as they mistake her for someone she's not.

Chapter 3

Stewart sneaks out of the office after half a day to pick up a tailored suit that he gifted himself. His staff has tricked him into believing that they've honored his wish to treat his birthday like just another day. Little does Stewart know, twenty some-odd folks wait at his home with the blinds shut and the lights off; a surprise party is gathered at his home.

Levi, the associate pastor, mans the window. He peers through the scrunched blinds, natural light glowing on his bald head. He looks back and asks Stewart's quote-unquote friend, "Bianca, have you called him yet, or what?"

She eyes Levi as if he has no business asking her. "*You* call him."

He thumbs at Bianca for the other guests to take notice. "Y'all see how she do?" His scowl deepens like Mr. T, but his sharp suit makes him look like an Ivy League twin. Levi makes the call, and in just a quick exchange with Pastor Stewart, Levi lowers the phone. "He's on his way," he says, with his eyes landing on Bianca, Stewart's quote-unquote friend who bought a pricey outfit for this day as if it were Easter. Surprisingly Bianca seems disinterested, as if she were not the party's fretful organizer who'd all week long, demanded perfection from charity hands.

She goes for the kitchen in small linear steps, her stride strangled by her pencil skirt. She finds Nay, Levi's wife, in the kitchen refreshing the seafood salad with a lemon squeeze. Bianca pouts, "I'm fixin' to go, Nay. I don't feel too good."

Nay sniffs something peculiar, as she appraises the same woman who'd been driven nearly to blows over her infatuation with the pastor, now backing down to a mere tummy ache on the man's birthday. "So, you're leaving," Nay browbeats.

Bianca should have guessed Nay's reaction, as any stranger might guess just from Nay's aggressive blonde hair, short and bristled back like a badger. "Girl get yourself somewhere and sit down. You done got all dressed up. At *least* let him see you."

Bianca is like milk and honey, with her light brown complexion wearing all white, a tight pencil skirt and a Chiffon blouse, her push up bra boasting cleavage, a ponytail spilling to the middle of her back. "I'm just not feeling it, Nay."

"Which one is it: are you not feeling *well*, or not feeling *it?*"

Bianca bites her lip to punish herself for not following her first mind to slip out in secret. Of all people, she checks in with Nay, who's known to strip her excuses down to the trifling truth. Bianca leads Nay to the patio, but not without swiping a bottle of champagne.

From her patio chair, Bianca gazes in the distance, her doom playing out on the horizon. "One day Pastor Stewart had an emergency situation, and um… He sent me here with his house key and security code. On the way back I stopped by the hardware store to cut a copy of the house key – just in case something came up again, I'd be prepared… But I forgot to tell him." Her face tightens; her smile is bent, as if laughing through pain.

"You ain't no forgot, Bianca. You *chose* not to tell him because you knew he wouldn't go for it, Amen?"

"Think he'll be upset?"

Nay leans back and crosses her ankles. "When we was going in and out this man's house, I *asked* you if everything was good, and you made like I was crazy for asking. Unbeknownst to me, you've got all up in here, trespassing."

"Slow your roll, Nay. Nobody has to answer for this but me."

"That may well be, Bianca, but what I'm getting at is this: the law is the line between infatuation and obsession. Breaking into this man's house crossed that line."

Bianca now wonders what possessed her to think that breaking into a man's home even to throw him a surprise birthday party would make him open his heart again. Bianca just wants to leave before Stewart arrives. "I'm for real, Nay," Bianca says. "I'm not feeling good. We can talk about this later."

"You owe it to us to at least call him, instead of leaving us here to deal with this."

Her eyes widen. "I don't owe him anything."

Nay's head shakes. "It's like Groundhog Day with you two. You make folks think you two are an item. And when he embarrasses your lil behind, all he's doing is setting the record straight. If you don't *put* ideas into people's minds, he won't have to remove them."

"Whatever, Nay. Me and Stew is closer than you think."

Nay's hand drops on the patio table like a cat's paw pinning a mouse by its tail. "I'm through talking to you, Bianca. That's why folks 'round here calling you crazy now."

It's the first Bianca's heard the claim. "What folks," she asks, as if ready to place their Polaroids on a dartboard and map out their assassinations. "Child, I counsel crazy people. I'm qualified to know that there ain't nothing crazy about me, honey."

Nay squints, crushing Bianca between her top and bottom lashes, "Says the woman with stolen keys."

Someone comes out to the back deck to alert them that Stewart just pulled up. Nay goes along, shaking her head. Bianca mopes behind her.

Everyone shuffles to the living room and faces the door. Bianca, figuring she may as well act normal, pushes her way up front, shimmies her skirt and fluffs her breasts.

Their *surprise* jolts Stewart into a defensive stance; his quick scream is more geese's than mans'. Peeking out from his boxer's guard he realizes that the intruders are his church family, with Bianca taking dibs on the first hug. Stewart rears back and frowns, examining Bianca as if he were a baby passed to a strange hand. His senses are still calibrating after the scare; Bianca's *Happy birthday, boo-boo* sounds liquid.

His mind rushes to identify the upload of faces: Reverend Tucker; his secretary Mrs. Winnie, Nay Ginyard and others, including Elder Rutherford and more. He hugs each one and poses for selfies. Stewart shakes a fist at his associate pastor and best friend, Levi, for luring him with the false emergency.

Levi swoops in with a handshake that folds into a shoulder bump, "I got you good, brother. You alright?"

"I'm alright… just confused," Stewart says, noticing that his parents, sole possessors of his spare key and code, are absent. "How, on earth, did y'all get in here?"

Levi's head tilts curiously and then he offers nothing but his weary departure, pleading the fifth. Stewart asks again with a little more heat.

The attendees' laughter seems cued like a live studio audience, but their eyes roll toward the perpetrator, Bianca, who stands in front of Stewart, her back to him, but facing the attendees, shushing them with low hand signals.

Stewart comes up behind Bianca with a show of strangling hands, but it's hugging arms that fall around her shoulders. He refuses to spend the day upset; it's his birthday, a happy occasion.

Bianca laps her arms over his, gratefully. She cranes back, searching for subsurface anger. This open, blatant show of affection feels like a reunion, until Stewart ruins it with, "Wish I had more friends like Bianca here."

Bianca gives an animated wink as if to assert a more covert spin on the friendship Stewart refers to. She spins out of his embrace and lands in a diva's pose. Through a pearly smile she says, "If you had another friend like me, I'd have to kill her."

Stewart shudders and walks away. He realizes how foolish he was to ever have put his house keys in Bianca's hands.

Stewart settles in near the kitchen where the pranksters Levi and Deacon Bailey try to convince him to try their special punch. Nay intercepts Stewart's cup, swirls it under her nose and becomes enraged at the smell of liquor. Stewart tries to tell Nay she is overreacting, but her hand fins out and wiggles, "Naw pastor, ya don't play like that – bringing hard liquor with all these eyes and ears up in here."

She dashes the punch bowl in the sink. Deacon Bailey has the biggest reaction, his face frozen in horror like a kabuki mask. Nay pushes Bailey's forehead with her fingertips. He commissions her husband to handle his *light work*.

Nay confronts her husband, Levi, the man who's supposed to handle Deacon Bailey's light work. "Am I light work, baby?"

Levi answers, "How can you be light work... *Heavy* as you is." He gives her pumpkin butt a wallop, and the party erupts. Nay is as tall as a model, thick, but with a small waist; she pours out of everything she wears. Nay leaves the kitchen, switching her prized pumpkin from side to side. That's the way the party goes for the next hour, minor blips fall in rhythm with the fun, like a vinyl record's needle-bump inventing a jerky new dance. Even a carpet spill might've taken on the shape of Jesus.

They're having such fun; the birthday boy is able to slip out to the deck unnoticed.

Levi soon finds him. He sits down and looks out at a pond the size of a football field, as still as a mirror, reflecting a perfect sky. "You should've never put no key in that broad's hand."

Hindsight's perfection makes Stewart wonder how he hadn't seen this coming. "I don't know why she try, Lee. She know I ain't got nothing for her."

Stewart's naivety makes Levi feel old. "I just can't figure you, bough. That's a *good* woman. She fine. She can cook. And believe it or not, she *ain't* crazy. You're making her crazy by leading her on."

"That's where you're wrong, Levi. Look, if I wadn't no pastor, Bianca wouldn't be on me like that. What I found out about her, is that she ain't crazy over me; she's obsessed over the idea of becoming a first lady," Stewart says. He then slides the book across the table with the back portrait facing up, saying, "Here's the other reason why I ain't studyin' no Bianca."

"So, this the lil' writer who got you going crazy." Levi backs off the photo, stunned by some revelation, "Know who she favors?"

"Not Fiona."

Levi turns away and tugs his suit closed as if he'd quit, on account of such foolishness.

"I was with her when you called." Nostalgia flickers in Stewart's eye. He and Lynn were huddled over a laptop at the same café where they met previously.

"I'm telling you; that's first lady right there, bruh."

Levi swats the claim. "Let you tell it… So was Jasmine. So was Savannah."

"But this ain't Jasmine or Savannah."

Examining the back cover, Levi agrees, "Shole ain't. Says here, she's one of them activists… And a Baptist *preacher?* Sounds like the first line of a bar joke."

Bianca appears. They stash the conversation like it's dope. She stands in the sliding door frame, barefoot, twiddling her long ponytail over her shoulder. "Hey Pastor Levi," she waves. "Hey friend," she says to Stewart. She wobbles a little as if she's had too much champagne. "It's time to cut the cake *friend,*" she says, dropping the message and retracing her path like a carrier pigeon.

Because of the second *friend,* Stewart and Levi swap high beam looks before going in, Stewart whispering, "She broke into *my* home, but *she's* the one upset?" He'd long since given up on the whys and has settled for the whens.

When Bianca feels wronged, she studies revenge with the level of dedication that goes into a life's work. She's not above acting out at someone else's party. She is the product of a father over-loving his daughter in order to raise her standards above the reach of the hormonal young men who chased her through high school, but instead of Bianca demanding the love her father modeled for her, she adopted the model for herself. Bianca's unconditional love is her handicap in love's negotiations with men who have endless, rotating conditions.

When it's time to sing happy birthday, Bianca, the church's top singer refuses to employ her vocals; she sings like a four year old along for the cake. As the party wears on, Bianca is increasingly antisocial. *Not feeling well,* is how she curbs the concerns of others. Music plays but she doesn't sway or hum, when normally she's a lightning rod for melody. She only moves when Stewart moves, migrating with him, but keeping her distance like a safari tour.

Their eyes meet. One side of Bianca's upper lip spikes upward, as if Stewart has the cooties. Stewart looks away, which somehow offends Bianca. She pops out of her chair and confronts him in the middle of his living room floor. "May I have a word with you, please?" Her words broke like glass. Heads turn. Above the crest of her ponytail, Stewart plays eye games with their audience, giving it over to comedy. "Oh, you wanna dance," he jokes.

Those are good folks at the party, masking the awkwardness with Christian kindness *Dance with the girl, pastor, you know she sweet on you. That girl loves her pastor – nothing wrong with that, I love him too.*

Bianca folds her arms and taps her bare foot on the wood floor. They're becoming the scene Stewart wanted to avoid. Blood rises in Stewart's eyes as he realizes that in order for he and Lynn to have a chance, he needs to be out from under the leverage that Bianca has over him. Stewart looks at no one but Bianca, but his words are for everyone except her. "Everyone… May I have your attention?" As if he doesn't have it already. "Bianca and I have been friends for quite some time now…"

Bianca's objection stalls; her hand cups breast level. She is experiencing déjà vu, a re-run episode of a dream where Stewart kneels before her with the silliest of questions. Bianca holds her concentration to keep from waking.

Stewart continues, "…But I'll admit that we've been more than friendly on a few occasions–" Levi, who is standing behind Stewart, realizes that what initially sounded like a toast is really a confession, so Levi covers Stewart's mouth. Bailey helps Levi corral the pastor toward the porch. Considering how Bianca crowds the pastor in public, antagonizes any woman who'd campaign for his attention, and has a key to his home, Bailey and Levi have their own ideas about what *more than friendly* means.

While Levi and Bailey constrain Stewart and try to speak sense into him, Bianca stands rooted to the center of the living room floor, looking heavenward, hands on hips. "Really? Really?" Prayers she'd sent up had asked for better than what's going down. The party has become a scene; the astonished group looks to Bianca, for her response? For clarity?

Bianca takes the opportunity to chastise those who assumed that affection only went one way between she and Stewart. "Y'all hear that, right?" She's obviously had a few too many glasses of champagne. She spins around, peering into each onlooker, her pointed finger whipping at each head count. "*More than friendly,*" she asserts. Elder Rutherford approaches as if to muzzle her too. Bianca snaps. "Get *away* from me!" She backhands the man in his gut. Rutherford gulps, on impact; his eyes bugged, as he lowers to one knee. The party turns into a mess, with voices raising over voices, their cries for peace and order, becoming the chaos they're trying to prevent.

Stewart slips past Levi and Bailey and rushes into the living room clapping for attention, "It's not what you all think! This is not no scandal!" The group returns a concert of *Oh*s.

Bianca interjects, "Yall! If you must run and tell... before you start talking about, *Oh, he's dating the teen choir director — carrying on in the church?* No." Her long fingernail pops an imaginary bubble. "If you *must* talk, talk about how two unsuspecting individuals intertwined spiritually–"

"–Girl hush with that mess," Nay says to her human project. "You ain't *deep*, no matter how many big words you try to throw over this mess; it's still a mess. I'm disappointed in you – both of you."

Bianca sulks while counting her costs: time, spiritual drain, and how she's turned down potential relationships while waiting on Stewart to commit. She adds, "He may not have had my body, but he has my spirit and he won't let it go."

Stewart covers his mouth in mach fright. "So, you're the victim? Because I'm a pastor? *You're* a trained psychologist."

"A *child* psychologist."

"*You're* the victim, though? The same woman who whispered in my ear that you can unhinge your jaw like a snake and swallow me whole?"

Bianca comes after Stewart with claws drawn, but Levi gets in the way, telling her it isn't worth it and to just get over him.

Next Bianca let Levi have it. "Get over it! Get over it? Who are *you* to tell me to just get over it. You're married and settled. You don't know what it's like," she says, her neck winding and her long fingernail skywriting in front of Levi's face.

That's when Levi's wife, Nay, cut in on the dance in grand fashion, saying, or rather, singing, "Waaait a minute!" Her blonde cropped head carries the note on a rainbow from shoulder to shoulder, her head landing cocked, viewing Bianca laterally. "Let me tell you one thing heifer. All *this—*" she mimes Bianca's neck rolling attitude. "—Ain't gon' work up in *my* husband's face. See, that's when I just sliiide right on in and bus' you in your face." On *slide* her head cranks up erect, like a bully adding style points to intimidation.

Bianca humbles instantly. Her mouth smiles only to clear its frown. "Chardonnay? Chardon*nay*," she calls, for the friend, Nay, hiding inside this monster. "You know I would *never* disrespect you or your husband. My anger is for the fool standing behind him. You just want to find a reason to get in somebody's face." Bianca cries miserably, tears darting down her cheeks.

"That's your one time, heifer. That's all you get." Now that Nay is understood, she goes off to the sidelines, mumbling threats.

Bianca smears her tears with the heel of her hand. A hush of pity descends for her. She hunts for her shoes. The others scatter from Bianca like a dorsal fin scatters a populated beach.

The party is over. They depart seemingly in the order of importance. Levi, the associate pastor is last, his wife waiting in the idling car. Levi drops a hand on Stewart's slumped shoulders, "Don't overdo it Stew. It ain't like you boonked her over, or nothing, so the board shouldn't have much to say."

"Don't tell that lie, bruh." With Stewart outing himself, power is taken from Bianca, but given to the board. "They'll *make* it into something in order to justify denying funding for the play. Watch…" Aside from his issues with the board, Stewart has issues of the spirit to contend. He believes he is a bad pastor; lust burns inside of him like flames. "Bianca and I may not have had sex, but we were surely sex-*u-al* with one another."

"So, you're human." Levi hesitates and then asks, in a lower tone, "Would she have been your first?"

Stewart removes the promise ring from his finger. "Virgin? You already know about Jasmine and Savannah. Virgin? C'mon, now."

Levi asks, "Anything before Savannah?"

Stewart returns a glare and a mouth twisted in ridicule; not an answer. The two pastors touch fists and Levi leaves the head pastor to himself.

Stewart's tailored suit, fit for a casket, sits on the couch next to him like a departed brother. Night is falling outside, the living room dimming around him. Under the soft light casting from a drooping lamp, his eyes ride the lines of immaculate prose from Lynn's novel *Don't Pray for Love*.

Bianca has a delayed meltdown. She cries herself to sleep, but it's a rather subdued cry. She sends a few rapid-fire texts to Stewart, all insults, but it doesn't truly hit her until morning when she's getting ready for work, dabbing her makeup brush in the color pallet and leaning into her vanity as she brushes in the light base for her smoky eye. She dabs her brush into the darker grays, smearing and blending upward. She turns left and right in the mirror, her face floating around stationary eyes, verifying all angles, and suddenly something comes over her, like what she'd imagine an asthma attack to feel like. Her breathing climbs high in her throat. She looks down, eyes darting as if finality is sweeping in around her ankles and billowing upward like stage fog, like when she starred in the gospel play, *A Woman Possessed*. But then she snaps out of it. In stillness, she catches her breath, and then returns to the work of her makeup, as if nothing happened. With her soft brush, she finishes the left eye. She rises from her stool, renewed, confident, regal. Next, she snatches up the stool, screaming, and crashes it into the vanity mirror. She stands there seemingly expanding and shrinking with each breath. Her face: angry, muscular, watching until every scattering thing stops. Anger bleeds out and her public face is restored. Bianca swings her purse over her shoulder and goes to work like any other day.

Chapter 4

Lynn and her women's rights organization's founder, Gayle, ambush Senator Kelley as he exits the statehouse. Lynn trots sideways down the steps to keep pace and eye contact with the senator who refuses to get behind their bill.

Lynn gives Senator Kelley the grilling of his life. "When's the last time you've gotten out front on anything senator? You sit and wait on the benefit of public opinion, from which you form your own opinions; is that prudence? Or are you afraid of being wrong – afraid of being put out to pasture… Prove that your legacy is more than just your *tenure* in your senate seat – and cement your legacy by actually putting that seat on the line!"

Shane Kelley halts, red blood rising in his face as one damning finger rises, but no words issue. He turns and walks away fuming.

Even Gayle is taken aback by Lynn's fire. Lynn smiles and asks, "Think I got to him?" In no less than an hour, they learn that she had. Senator Kelley's wife, Beatrice Kelley calls to set up a meeting.

Later on in the day, they await Beatrice's arrival at Gayle's home, a tall, colonial style, porch heavy, home that's Indigo with four white pillars supporting the upper deck.

Beatrice Kelley is an honored guest. She's been the topic of articles and even a book in the early eighties, when she, as the lone black chemist for a fertilizer company, broke into a storage locker in '85, uncovering decades of payroll documents proving that white males, at all levels within the company, were paid up to forty percent above their minority counterparts. She hired a law firm that leveraged a settlement for minority employees, past and present. The lawyer who headed the case, later became her husband.

Beatrice Kelly's courage had earned her the kind of popularity one could build a political career around, so her lawyer husband, Shane Kelley, used it to win an election. Her husband has since grown old in his senate seat, turning from a Burt Reynolds to a Colonel Sanders. Having a political career catapulted by an issue of unfair wages, Gayle and Lynn couldn't fathom how Senator Kelly could thumb his nose at a wage bill.

"We're having tea with Beatrice Kelley," Gayle announces while staring at nothing. She's as nervous as a bride; the known fact still so incredible it bears repeating.

Lynn throws out a diversion, "I'm seeing someone."

Gayle stops, looks, and then returns to nervously polishing a tea kettle that she has squeezed in a headlock, knowing that the "someone" to which Lynn refers, is none other than the happy-go-lucky pastor, making a cameo appearance in Lynn's life. "Feminist and a Baptist preacher? Ain't no romance, hon... Epic tragedy, I believe, is the correct genre. Let the pages keep turning."

"He's progressive," says Lynn. "He'll surprise you."

"No, he'll surprise *you*, as soon as this Ultrasound Mandate bill comes down the pipe, and you see what side of the protest barrier *he's* on." Gayle goes back to trying to polish blood out of the tea kettle. This is their chance to make history. The pressure of history is what knots in Gayle's belly as they await the arrival of a local icon.

They hear a car outside. It's Beatrice. Lynn and Gayle go out in the yard to usher her in. She's over seventy, but her black hasn't cracked yet, except slightly around her eyes, while the rest of her face is pulled tight as plum. "You ladies make me feel important." Because they're overdressed. Beatrice came with her gray hair in house plats. She wears casual lime Capris and a white blouse. "So, *you're* Lynn," she says, and then laughs.

She carries on about the delicious tea, the aristocratic tea set, and Gayle's interior design, right out of the pages of a Southern Living magazine. They relocate to the porch rocking chairs, facing the Saluda River breeze. Beatrice praises their organization's work, how they'd come out of nowhere and cleared a space for themselves on the lobbying floor.

"Now about this bill," Beatrice says. "When you approached Shane, what did he have to say about it?" She's ready to laugh like she already knows.

"He said we should light a match to it," Lynn tattles.

Beatrice laughs again. Gayle laughs and nudges Lynn to make her laugh too. Beatrice adds, "What he honestly believes is that this bill could be the single most important piece of legislation towards *real* equality since the voting rights act. He believes this is legislation that must pass, but he can't come out and say it publicly. Not yet."

Gayle claws Lynn's wrist in excitement as they listen.

"The problem with this bill is that it's a political landmine. This is the south. Labor." Beatrice names the two like conjoined twins. "The only way to get a senator behind this bill is to first prove that the public demands it, that way it doesn't seem radical. You'll need thousands of signatures. To achieve that, my husband believes you're gonna need some help – a *non*-political face with some clout, to draw citizens to this cause."

Lynn and Gayle strain to think of options before realizing the one staring back at them, Beatrice Kelley, sitting upright and smiling as if posing for a portrait, "How about *this* face?" Each woman looks at the other two, and then they celebrate with a toast.

Chapter 5

While Pastor Stewart goes before the board of trustees concerning funding for the play, Levi stays in his office because he already knows the outcome. The men on the board of trustees are his close kin, so he'd already heard that they would deny funding for the play, citing Stewart's recent fraternization scandal with Bianca.

Levi is in his office, busy updating his calendar when two board members barge in. Elders Rudy Ginyard, who is Levi's uncle, and Otto, the one they call Catfish because he's all head and mouth. They look like suited goons from the 80's. The mere sight of the two would draw bets that there's a tinted Cutlass parked outside.

Levi asks, "How'd he take it?"

His uncle Rudy answers, "Well, he *didn't* take it. Pastor Stupid came back with an offer we couldn't refuse."

Levi tilts with wide eyes, "Oh?"

"The nigger guaranteed us he gone sell out that big ole Colonial Life Arena – and that if he *don't* – he gone step down; give up his robe."

Catfish adds, "And I'll be right there to take that robe right from his hand, then turn around and wipe my behind with it."

Levi plants his hands on the desk as if to get up. "Don't go nowhere, yall. Lemme get Stew back here so we can straighten this out. The man wadn't thinking straight."

Rudy says, "He was thinking as straight as that finger he pointed at us and said that God will prepare a table before him, in the presence of his enemies."

Levi flops back in his chair and sighs. "This ain't right y'all."

Rudy comes forward with a calming hand. "That's where you're wrong, Lee. Let me tell you why we're here. We come to you as family, brother – not administrators," says Rudy. "You and me both know ain't no way he finna fill that arena, so the door is open. It's time to get a Ginyard back behind that pulpit. Out of respect for Pappy, we come to you first."

Levi jerks away like a baby's no to a spoon of pureed peas. "You don't want me. You'll hate me worse than him. *I* sure won't let you fatten your wallets at the expense of the ministries' budgets."

"Nothing wrong with growth; the budgets will get so much more on the back end."

"While we're on the subject of back ends, you can go ahead and kiss mine."

The men look at each other and then back at Levi, smirking. Rudy says, "So, you gone buck up at me like that, Lee? What about family first?"

"Family first? That's nepotism idn't it?"

"As I was saying, the founders laid out for us–"

Levi's hands fly out like shooing yard chickens. "There you go. Every time you want something you say it's what the founders would've wanted." Levi, counting off on his fingers, names their wish list, "You wanna franchise the ministry, company cars, increased profit share, church funded family vacations for leaders…" the gist of their wish list.

Rudy's gathered hands scrubs circles. "Save all that, Lee. You've been singing that song so long; you actually believe the words. This is about priority one: a Ginyard pastor at the helm." They blame Levi for breaking the eighty-year string of Ginyard pastors because he was serving in Kuwait when Pappy Ginyard, Levi's biological father, had to let go of the reigns. "Your daddy knows the importance. It's why he was willing to drag an oxygen tank to the pulpit. Killed himself trying to keep the pulpit held up for your return."

Levi is one of two children bore outside of Pappy Ginyard's marriage; there are six children in all, five girls. Levi is the only boy, therefore the only possible successor to the ministry. He didn't know he was a Ginyard until age six when he met his father at an inner-city playground under the watchful eye of his chain-smoking mother. Young Levi, with only an inkling of what a father was, learned that the straight-backed, wide-nosed, preacher man was his. He'd always been a shadowy, distant figure who showed up with bags from the butcher to stock his mother's freezer, who stuffed cash in her purse, who would slip into his mother's room and tickle her crazy, but never played with Levi, only stared at him and asked him questions about school. That day, at the playground, within five minutes of acknowledging his son, Pappy told the boy he is going to be a preacher, that he already had a seminary school picked out for him; his own alma mater. All of this, he'd painstakingly planned for his son. Levi's growing up was, in part, learning how things were *not* about him, but about his father and his father's family. They want success for Levi, only so he could better serve them, so with this in mind, Levi poses a question to the men standing in his office. "So, Pappy killed himself holding the pulpit up for me? My enlistment in the Army didn't kill him; I believe that was Emphysema." Levi's coolness about his father's death stuns the two leaders. Levi says to the goons, "You say you need a pastor, but you mean puppet. And I'm offended that you see me as one."

Catfish taps Rudy with the back of his hand. "*This* negro say he don't wanna be no puppet. What do you think you are now but Pastor Stupid's sock puppet? Why do you think the sissy's afraid to franchise the ministry? It opens opportunity. *Talent* flocks to opportunity, but your little Pied Piper sees talent as competition. He'd rather surround himself with clergy like you: men who make him feel comfortable."

Levi is entertained as if he were at the theatre. "So, you came to me first? Who next?" The mere thought of the available Ginyard options makes Levi laugh and pound his desk. Fate could not have been more brutal on the clan. Of the other four Ginyards who actually went through seminary, Tyrique Ginyard turned from religion and became a mixed tape rapper with tattoos up to his throat; Lester had half his tongue bit off in a car accident, and Vincent Ginyard is now Vivica Ginyard. Levi wipes his glasses, sniffling while coming down from his laughter. "Should've started that Ginyard seminary scholarship twenty years sooner."

The men huddle, Rudy asking, "Should we tell him, Cat-o?" Rudy goes for it. "Ain't you forgetting about Lamar?"

"Lamar…" Levi doubletakes, observing that they're serious. He laughs again.

"He's cleaned up, bough." Catfish insists. "He's got his own church again. Turned down an offer to be an associate pastor of a prestigious Memphis church and started his own." Catfish tells Rudy, "Unlike your nephew here, Lamar ain't fixin' to be nobody's backup singer."

"Even if it means preaching out of a storage unit?" A known lie, but Levi uses it as shtick anyway. Truth is, Lamar has cleaned up his drinking in recent years and he's on the comeback trail.

Catfish challenges, "First of all, Lee, don't take this as an offer. This is a warning. Keep following up Pastor Stupid; you'll follow him right on out the door when the hammer come down."

Levi says, "The people is more powerful than the pen."

"When *your* time comes, the people is precisely who'll spearhead your demise. No one will have to show you the door, you'll be running to it." Catfish is as sure as if summarizing a movie he'd seen many times over.

Levi replies, "There be but one God. Surely He don't tell me one thing and you another."

Catfish rubs the back of his neck, as he does just before getting disrespectful. The negotiations have already soured, with nothing left to salvage. "I *know* why you're so loyal to Pastor Stupid."

"Why, Otto? Tell me why?" Levi gets up from his desk, anticipating fighting words. Levi approaches, a finger peeling his ear forward, "I'm listening, Catfish. Tell me why?"

Uncle Rudy wedges himself between them, his arms out, hands planted on their chests as if holding back the clap of thunder.

With a daredevil's glare, Catfish launches the stunt, "Pastor Stupid bought your loyalty, with the woman you now call your wife!"

Levi lunges for Catfish's throat. The skirmish, amounting to nothing but a missed punch and an overturned lamp, draws more attention than it's worth. It ends with Stewart rushing in and shouldering through the others who had busted in before him. Stewart hugs Levi's neck and pep talks his ear while steering him out to the parking lot. It is lunch time anyway. They go down the highway en route to Big Daddy's food truck.

Stewart has never seen Levi so angry, and for some odd reason, Levi won't say why. By the time they reach the rundown shopping center where the food truck is stationed, it's Stewart's third time asking, "What'd Catfish do or say to set you off like this, man? Was it about your daughter? Your wife?"

"Go on, now," Levi says, finally. "I'm hot just thinkin' 'bout it."

Stewart insists, "Whatever it is, man, don't take it to heart. He'll say anything just to get under your skin; it's not like he meant it."

Levi's head jitters no. "If *he* don't mean it; *they* mean it. He's their attack dog. He don't bite lest they sic 'em."

Stewart sighs. "Just try to calm down, man."

Levi looks over. "*You* telling *me* to calm down? Was you calm when you made that dumb bet?"

"I made a bet but it wadn't dumb."

Levi swats the air, but then adds a smirk. "Man gone and get me a fish sammich, Stew. And fries… Bringing me here, knowing I'm on a diet… It be your friends," Levi giggles for once.

"Nay is the only person who thinks you on a diet," Stewart says as he gets out of the car.

Levi is eleven years Stewart's senior with diabetes. His wife, Nay, is constantly on him about his health. Stewart has witnessed times when Nay was on Levi's heels and he's ducked around corners to get rid of the evidence, fisting fries in his mouth, even one time stuffing cake in his pocket.

Stewart returns with the contraband, fried cod and sugary coleslaw between a mattress of buttery Texas toast wrapped in tin foil. They pick from a community basket of crinkle fries on the console.

With Levi's anger now dissipated, he goes back to explaining what happened in the office. "My own kin say I'm going down right along with you. That's what I was saying just the other day: you can't up and make moves like that because it affects more than just you." Levi throws a finger up between them. "And *don't* say that skirt didn't have nothing to do with it either. Normal people just ask a woman out on a date. *You* have to invite them into ministry."

"Lee," Stewart says as he periscopes to his friend. "When has that ever been the case, man. You talkin' nonsense."

Levi's eyes widen. "Oh, I'm talking nonsense? You sure?"

"Jasmine was the only one."

"Didn't the board just give you an earful about Bianca?"

Stewart's eyes roll. "Lee, you said *invite* to ministry. I hadn't exchanged two words with Bianca until *after* she'd became the teen choir director."

Levi licks his fingers and says, "Ok, let's see what excuse you got for Octavia."

Stewart shrugs. "We went on a couple lil dates, but she confessed that she had been married before, which was a dealbreaker for me, and that was *prior* to me campaigning for her to run the bank, Lee, so try again."

Levi says, "You ain't gotta try to prove nothing to me. What you need to do is talk to Catfish and them to undo what you did. Cause ain't no way you finna fill that big ole arena with no chitlin circuit play."

Stewart gives a daring side-eye. "Watch me."

"I went on their website just yesterday," says Levi. "Of all the events they have lined up future and past there ain't one theatric play on the list. Ya got concerts, ya got Cirque du Soleil, even a professional wrasslin' tour came through there, but I couldn't find not one play. Guess why I couldn't find a play. Because you're the only one fool enough to *attempt* to fill that huge arena with a darn chitlin circuit play."

"But you should know that, with me, there's always more than what meets the eye, Lee; I got a secret weapon. You'll see when I unveil it next Sunday in front of the congregation." Stewart says nothing for a while and then he says, "What do you think of her?"

"Who, your little writer? How can I think anything? I only saw her once – yesterday as a matter of fact – when she stopped by the church to see you."

"How many times does it take for a first impression, though?"

Levi takes a bite to occupy his mouth, but Stewart waits on his appraisal. "A'ight, just remember you asked for it," Levi relents. "The impression I get: she holds her nose a bit too high for my taste; umma leave it at that."

"You don't like her because she's political."

"So, you're a mind reader now?" They take a break from words while they eat, then Levi adds, "The bible says a man findeth a good thing when he findeth a wife, but every woman ain't a wife. Ask her when the last time she actually cooked dinner, a *real* dinner."

Stewart keeps on eating as if he'd heard nothing.

"So, what's this secret weapon," Levi asks, with finger quotes.

Stewart swerves away, saying, "I ain't messin' with you, Lee. You'll tell Nay, then Nay get on the phone with her sister in law and mother in law, next thing you know, the whole Ginyard clan knows. I hope you understand, bro, but I really need to see the shock on their faces when they lay eyes on what I got planned."

"When? This Sunday?"

"Next Sunday, when you're preaching.

"Why when I'm preaching – so you and your lil girlfriend can worship together."

Stewart swivels a little. "I figure it's time."

Levi giggles. "So, who's gonna stop Bianca from popping her head off?"

Stewart's secret weapon insists that he isn't one. D'mitri Dalton, the playwright who sells out venues along the south eastern coast from Georgia to Virginia, said that no stage play known to man can fill that arena. He's the bronze-colored version of the artist formerly known as Prince, minus the perm, a soup can taller than Pastor Stewart and impeccably dressed in a slimming grey suit decorated with a paisley handkerchief tie.

Despite his sharp dress, D'mitri is a man in dire need of a lifeline. His company folded after being robbed by his accountant, which also led to a six-month tax evasion stint in a federal jail. Also with mounting personal debt, he didn't have the money to dump into a venue, staff, props and wardrobe and bet on ticket sales to cover the investment. He had just finished a three-city tour of a one-man play, just to pay the bills, so when he got the call from Pastor Stewart, offering to cover all up-front expenses, and even advanced pay, D'mitri jumped at the offer, to get back to heading a cast, but now looking over the plans, his enthusiasm dims as he and Stewart wait on Lynn's arrival.

Lynn enters Stewart's home, saying, "I must say, pastor, you sure have a curious taste in settings for business meetings. First, latte shops, now your home?" She's scans like a building inspector. "Mansion is more like it." She's in awe at the sheer size and the vintage look. Stewart is also in awe as guides Lynn toward the kitchen because she'd just left yoga. All the question marks left by her usual flowy linens becomes explanation points by the skin tight yoga attire. Her hips curve like parenthesis – not eye-popping, but noteworthy. The impressive part lay between the bottom of her sports bra and the waist line of her yoga pants, eight inches of taut self-motivation, abs flat and stitched like a mattress that Stewart can't stop glancing at. He manages conversation distractedly, like a third grader in class, contemplating recess.

D'mitri gets up from the island kitchen counter to greet Lynn with air kisses and flattery, calling her a genius and *even more* beautiful in person.

Stewart set down a pitcher of lemonade and finger sandwiches so neatly arranged, that he obviously did not prepare it himself.

To begin, D'mitri huddles next to Lynn to bring her in on what he and Stewart were arguing about before she arrived. He drops a rigid finger on one line item, the venue, his smile wooden like ventriloquist's puppet. "*This* is a problem." D'mitri rattles off more feasible alternatives, like Hawthorne Theatre, or The Township Auditorium.

Stewart doesn't budge. "They don't have enough seats. We are trying to build a school, not a chicken coop."

D'mitri looks off, mumbling with the devil on his shoulder. "The *worst* kinds of fools are the ones who don't know it."

Pastor Stewart grins, loving the challenge, "Faith looks foolish in the beginning; it *takes* a fool to pull off a miracle."

D'mitri raises one pledged hand. "I was just about to discourage you by telling you it would take a miracle, but you actually prefer those odds?"

"Gentlemen, please…" Lynn sighs in disappointment. She can't figure out where else she fit into the discussion besides keeping the two civil.

D'mitri takes two drinking glasses. "Watch here," he says. He half-fills one glass with lemonade, saying, "This glass (the glass half-full) represents Columbia's theatre going population." He then lifts the empty glass. "This *empty* glass represents the Colonial Life Arena's twenty-thousand seats." He then pours the theatre-going population into the arena's twenty-thousand seats and only fills it halfway. "So, now what do you have? A half empty arena." D'mitri's eyes stretch and his puppet smile tightens. "You see, sometimes a fool is just a fool. This is math, pastor. This is based on projections I've always used and I ain't left a ticket unsold yet."

Lynn caresses Stewart's arm, as if D'mitri's analysis is the eulogy to Stewart's great expectations. "Consider the source," Lynn says softly. "He does this for a living."

Stewart's eyes go begging heavenward as if Lynn and D'mitri are the ones who needed schooling. He says to D'mitri, "All you're telling me is that the reason why your shows sell out is because you're dumbing down the venues – like shutting down a lane at a grocery store. Longer lines don't mean more customers."

D'mitri again transfers the lemonade from one glass to another. "Your boy here is about to spend *all* that money on that humongous arena and wind up taking a loss. How do I get thirty percent of revenue when there ain't fin'na *be* no revenue?"

"Are you done?" Stewart confiscates the lemonade pitcher for his own demonstration. D'mitri holds his objection to let Stewart bait his own trap. From the pitcher, the reservoir of potential ticket holders, Stewart pours, filling the arena's twenty-thousand seats.

"Oh, I see. You just thirsty. You parched," D'mitri giggles. "Gone get you a drink. Take ya time passa," D'mitri says with a holy hand raised.

Stewart continues. "The theatre community won't be the only community filling those seats. With this being a charity event, expect the community of philanthropists to step up to the plate. I didn't get to where I am without some very important friends – friends who'll buy hundreds of tickets and pass them out to their employees just to get their name on granite plaques."

Lynn gives Stewart a slanted look. "Earlier you called it *faith*. Now you're saying it's rich *friends*."

"*Thank* you," D'mitri says as he reaches for a high five. Lynn taps his hand reluctantly, while miming apologies to Stewart. D'mitri adds, "You say thirty percent, but we need a bottom figure to ensure I walk away with something. Waste your *own* time – and when it comes time to write the checks don't you get arthritis on me." D'mitri then slides a stapled stack of papers in front of Lynn, "That's your plot summary right there. It's what your novel looks like on stage – no narrator, your twelve settings reduced to four, okay." With that D'mitri leaves. Stewart leads him to the front door.

Lynn stays put while looking over the plot summary. Stewart returns to the kitchen with Lynn's anger halting him. "If that man thinks he's adding a big momma character to *my* script… Over my dead body."

"Don't even worry about it," Stewart says. "He ain't putting up the money, so he don't have a say. We go with what you want."

Lynn then swats Stewart with the rolled-up plot summary, "And you!"

"Me what?" Stewart attempts to block a second hit that never comes.

"Your little Camry is just a 'front. Look at this… this… *palace*." She springs up and walks, her head on a swivel, eyeing the size, but as if the size is a deformity, like gigantism disease.

The fiction writer, Stewart guesses, perhaps prefers quaint cottages over castles. "The church didn't do all of this," he defends. "I have a lot of investments."

Lynn goes further into his home, with the righteousness of the duped. "You have an elevator in your home?"

He shrugs. "For my old age."

Lynn keeps her self-guided tour on the first floor. Stewart waits in the living room, unable to withstand the shame. Lynn spots a fitness room as big as three rooms combined. He has an actual home theatre. Lynn presses her hand on a bed so soft it makes ghost prints. She lay down, her head on a goose-down pillow in a satin case, her sneakers hanging off the bed. It feels like lying on a large marshmallow, so heavenly, she nearly dozes off just that quick.

They rendezvous in the living room where Stewart waits. She looks out over the platform floor, the recessed center, a rink of marble. "So, you're paying D'mitri an advance." Stewart nods yes as he guesses where this is going. Lynn adds, "You project twenty-five thousand dollars in book sales for me, but before my first sale, that's six thousand dollars needed to supply the inventory on the front end."

Stewart has had money for so long, he forgets that a few thousand dollars is a tough swallow even for working professionals. "But D'mitri has to cover wages for his *staff*."

"And for himself, am I right? But you get my one-time production rights for nothing more than a promise?"

Stewart grows a prankster's smile as he offers his empty hand, waiting for grasp.

Lynn bypasses him and goes down to the recessed marble floor with her arms folded, a sneaker tapping the marble, which looks like frozen rain clouds or curling smoke. "I just want to be treated fairly. For that, I shouldn't have to ask."

Stewart approaches her, pointing. "If you would simply turn to that mirror, I'll give you your advance."

"What are you talking about," Lynn protests even while she locates the mirror and goes to it. Stewart says, "I can't give it to you. I have to place it on you." He goes behind her, reaches into his interior pocket and lowers, in front of Lynn, a diamond drop pendant so perfectly cut, it twinkles every color of the prism.

Lynn leans toward the mirror, overcome with emotion. "I can't take this."

"Either I write you a six-thousand-dollar check, or you can take that. If you sold it for half its value, it'll still get you well over the six thousand."

She turns in the mirror, her eyes never leaving the sparkling jewel. "You're full of games aren't you… You know I wouldn't sell it because it's a gift. But I can't accept it because it's too expensive."

"Well, if it's too expensive, you can pay the difference with a dance." Stewart points a small remote from his pocket and suddenly instruments play softly. Lynn rolls her eyes and goes with it. The song is familiar, an old Stevie wonder love ballad fills the room.

Over time, I've been building
My castle of love

Just for two, though you never
Knew you were my reason…

One hand grips the waist, the other hand meets out at the side as if, together, they're drawing back a large bow and arrow. Eye contact turns gravitational, bringing them into orbit, coalescing around this sparkling diamond. Stewart feels Lynn soften against him, her eyes lit with motive; her motive leaps inside of him, and Stewart descends. Lynn catches his face in her hands. Four lips slip into each other, massaging, pulling, cresting over, receding. They go climbing skyward to a summit where the air is thin, so they pull back to catch their breath, their eyes tangling, searching constellations in the cosmos of the other's face.

Stewart's heart bobs in his chest; he's never felt so stirred. Ever. All of life's trials were preparation for the woman staring back at him, just as dizzy and astounded as he, over what just took place. She forbids him from speaking. Her two fingers touch his lips and then she seals them with another kiss. Stewart thinks maybe his heart is confused, some calibration gone awry because after knowing Lynn for only weeks, his heart feels years: years' worth of belonging, years of verification, already a full-fledged affinity deeper than family.

Chapter 6

Pastor Stewart is shining. Levi sees him kiss a baby like a politician, but knows Stewart only cares about one vote. He is impersonating his twenty something year old self, the young pastor's grass roots approach to winning the confidence of his flock. He's not so different in present day. He's giddy without reason and cordial, but always in passing, while barreling forward in a hurry to somewhere, head down like shielding against the wind. Now he leans back on a cool strut, elbows hooked with his demure lobbyist. Stewart wanders around like a visitor in his own church, introducing her, making acquaintances like he's trying to make a nest for her.

Bianca and Nay enter the church together, the sight of the couple brings Bianca to a standstill. Nay advances a few steps before realizing she's lost a friend. Bianca flicks her head at the sight. Nay echoes Bianca's thoughts exactly, "Oh no he didn't." This is where their paths split with parting waves, Bianca heading off to group with the choir. She takes the long way around the vestibule just to avoid Stewart and his 'lil girlfriend.

Bianca watches from high up in the choir as members pool into the sanctuary. She burns at the sight of Stewart introducing his little armpiece to any and everybody – how Lynn puts on this fake looking, squinty-eyed laughter. Bianca hates watching another woman walk in shoes that rightfully belongs to her.

Stewart's own shining dims by the end of devotional. He seems worried that there's still no sign of D'mitri. Stewart becomes obsessed with his watch. He needs D'mitri to be there in time for announcements.

Stewart leaves the sanctuary to call D'mitri, his secret weapon, the game changer, the board's object of reckoning. For weeks, Stewart has been living for this day, to see the shock on the faces of the board members in attendance when he reveals, during announcements, his partnership with the star playwright, but again, there's no answer.

Stewart returns to his seat with a stiff neck. "Still no answer." He complains to Lynn, "How does he call himself a business man when he can't keep engagements?"

Lynn studies him; she is seeing him upset for the first time. And then the thought hits her: *first time*, meaning some girlish part of her believes, already, that there will be many more times, like she's learning his signals, his triggers, learning to recognize what is not readily offered, learning how to be the man's partner. "Are you upset?"

"No." He offers a made-up smile as proof. "Hardly nothing upsets me; I'm just saying…"

Stewart just happens to look up into the choir and his eyes land on Bianca, whose scrutiny from up high in the choir, burns Stewart like a magnifying glass over an ant. At the end of announcements, Stewart takes the floor podium, unable to announce D'mitri as the play's creative director. He announces the funding for the play, for the building of the Christian Academy, for which the congregation gives a standing ovation. Next he introduces Lynn as the writer and business partner; nothing more. The slim beauty is captured on flanking monitors standing and waving, at the sound of her name, surprised by the sudden spotlight.

When it's offering time, Bianca closes out with the second song, giving a solo so soul-stirring that it would make Levi's sermon anticlimactic, an afterthought. She showcases the full, wide rainbow of her voice. She carries suicide pitches seemingly with ease, feeding the furnace of her diaphragm as if all the air in the sanctuary is at her disposal, which explains how she takes the congregation's breath away. When the choir runs the chorus, she stares into nothingness, caged, tapping the side of her thigh until it is time to unleash her beast. Her highest range makes ears pop, makes Lynn dig nails into Stewart's knee before she rises to her feet and let praise have its way. Near the end of the song, two words sung over and over – *God Is* – takes on many hats, moaning in agony and then overjoyed; exhausted and then renewed. She carries the final note so long, closed eyes open, confused and then amazed.

By the end of the song, the congregation is stirred for the preached word. Levi's sermon entitled, *The Christian Way*, is a referendum on scripture spitting church folk to lead by walking rather than talking. He preaches like a grizzly bear. He rumbles rants of alliteration, calling Christians a fraternity of peculiar people, whose purpose, reflects God's perfect presence. He asks them how they could they expect to be fishers of men when they act like fish themselves. If you don't conduct yourself in the Christian way, you're just another negro who's memorized scripture for style points. He goes on about how church folk use scriptures to insult, taking aim with scriptures that reference the fool and the serpent and the blasphemer, and turn them against those we should be saving.

Stewart, as always, is his biggest cheerleader. Lynn is right there with him, punctuating the man's points with praise. She squats with both fists tight under her chin as she let out a whoop. Stewart fans Lynn and then watches her praise, delighted, with his fists on his hips, the flaps of his suit spread back behind him as Levi's gritty voice sings his sermon into a peaceful landing.

After the service, the congregation pools out of all doors, high on the spirit. Most of God's well-dressed children scatter to their cars. Stewart and Lynn are among those who take the breezeway to the banquet hall. Lynn sits with Stewart at the table designated for the pastor and his circle. Lynn looks around and then nudges Stewart. "Do you think it's obvious to them that we're dating?"

Stewart says, "Well, we *are*, so…"

Stewart's radar picks up Bianca's voice in dangerous proximity. He spies her halfway across the room, in conversation with Nay. He could tell they're talking about him, how they pretend to look elsewhere, but send careful glances at his table.

Nay and Bianca are a tandem in the middle of the banquet, red carpet style, flashing waves. People stop by to thank Bianca for her solo and their blessed tears.

Bianca, talking through a tight smile tells Nay, "Do you see how Lynn praises? Looks like ballet at the Special Olympics." Bianca gives a three second, phone booth skit that is spot on. "Now what kind of praise is that…"

Nay's laughter is too big, like giant's voiceover. "Girl you is a *mess!* Ballet is not no Special Olympic event."

"Somebody needs to tell *her* that, then."

Nay put a hand on Bianca's shoulder, "*Girl…* Don't do that again, because if she sees you, she'll see a mirror."

Bianca accepts the dare, and mocks Lynn' praise again. Her arms flap slowly at her sides like deformed wings, her head withers sideways, her eyes close like she's performing this while asleep.

Nay slides to provide cover. Heads turn, some amused, some looking only to whisper back to their circles what they see. At the sound of Nay's loud laughter, Levi comes out, with the kitchen's stainless steel double doors flapping behind him. His hands flip out at his sides. He doesn't like his wife being loud or whoring attention. Nay, as if her husband is not already headed her way, calls him to her, "Come here baby, let me show you something."

When Levi stops in front of her, Nay thumbs the corner of his mouth then tastes it to determine what he was doing in the kitchen. She cites the violation of his diet, "Is that pecan pie I taste?" The tables turn on Levi, so he goes away guilty.

Lynn and Dana watch from their white clothed table. Stewart laughs and shakes his head. The humor misses Lynn by a mile. "Levi seemed really angry, like he was about to yell at her."

"But at the end of the day, you see who's *really* boss."

"That's the singer next to her isn't it?" Lynn's eyes draw shut. "Lord. That woman is truly anointed." Lynn almost gets up to compliment Bianca, but Stewart stops her with a hand on her thigh.

"Skill doesn't necessarily mean anointing."

They both notice the hand on her thigh. Lynn pets the hand to let it know that it's welcome there.

Lynn says, "Anointed or not, that sister can blow."

Stewart nods in agreement. "That's what the guys say."

Lynn squints and calculates, The guys... blow... Lynn frowns.

Not quite looking away, Stewart says, "She's got a reputation."

"I know what you meant."

Stewart can't imagine that Bianca, the woman whose *reputation* of which he'd just enlightened Lynn, would approach their table and throw an arm around Stewart, greeting him like a visiting aunt. "Stewey! How are *you* this afternoon?"

Stewart draws stiff like he'd been sitting in a freezer in that pose with only his eyeballs thawed loose. "Good. Good." He looks like he is deciding whether to hide under the table or hightail it out of the banquet.

"I need to have a word with you," Bianca says. "That's alright isn't it?"

Lynn wipes her mouth and tosses her napkin, anticipating an introduction, but the alleged whore is purposely avoiding eyes. Bianca only glances at Lynn to pose the question, "Can I borrow your man for a minute?"

Lynn's eyes lock on Stewart, invoking a death sentence. Stewart gives a plea-bargaining shrug; how quickly he's become a line drawn in their sand. "Be right back, ok?" He is at Bianca's mercy. Complying with her request is the only way to avoid a scene; separation of the two women, the only remedy.

The moment they are out of the banquet, Stewart unloads, "What. Do you think. You're doing?"

Bianca pretends to be blindsided by his anger. Her hand leaps to her crucifix medallion. "Why are you yelling at me?"

Stewart knows she is laughing inside, behind this act. "What's so important that you have to drag me out here for?"

"Suit yourself, if you'd rather we have this conversation back at the table in front of your little girlfriend." Her arm floats out, showing him the welcomed way.

They are in the U-shaped hallway, a beltway hugging the dining area. The building front is mirror tinted glass. A well-dressed family is closing in on the entrance. Stewart, wanting a more secluded location, abouts-face and marches, disappearing around the bend just as the family enters. Bianca resists running after him so not to make a scene. The family comes through the door, the boy asking Bianca, "Girl where your shoes?"

Bianca: "In jail for killing my feet." She waits for them to enter the dining area, before skating after Stewart. She finds him waiting in the connecting hallway to the fitness center where no one would likely venture since the fitness center is closed on Sundays. His back is against the wall, a leg up; he rubs his chin in thought.

She strides toward him, her arms floating out, modeling the inevitable. "Dark corridor… You, me…"

"You better make this quick."

"I only want to talk business, though."

"*Talk*." His hands twirl around each other, hurrying her.

"The moment you called D'mitri to direct the play, he called me for the lead role." Bianca raises both palms in innocence. "Now, I tried to turn him down, but he wouldn't take no for an answer."

Stewart had forgotten that Bianca is also an actress and that she used to brag about starring in D'mitri's plays when he was just a startup. Stewart counters, "But D'mitri can't give you the lead role. Money makes decisions," Stewart says. "I'm the one putting up the money, so it's *my* decision–"

Bianca's head shakes. "D'mitri ain't goin' for it. He's trying to rebuild his company. He has to put the best product out on stage."

Stewart thinks maybe he's arguing a lie. "How do you have the role when we haven't done auditions, yet?"

"Auditions are for the *supporting* cast, boo-boo. D'mitri's got a stable of go-to actors for the main roles."

Stewart sighs as he takes out his phone to call D'mitri, but Bianca beats him to the punch. The man who Stewart couldn't reach all morning answers Bianca's call in one ring, with a spirited, *Hey Bianca,* coming through speakerphone. Bianca says, "D'mitri. Pastor wants to ask you something."

Leaning toward the phone sitting in Bianca's palm, Stewart asks, "What's this I hear about you handing out roles before the auditions?"

"Auditions are only for the supporting cast," D'mitri says, confirming Bianca, whose eyes flair wild at Stewart.

Bianca, in exasperation, watches the ceiling and taps an impatient foot while the two men get into a brief back and forth about talent, risk, investment, and why D'mitri was a no-show. D'mitri adds, "Bianca told me what happened between you two and I didn't want to be anywhere near that."

"Anyway, we can't get back the past," says Stewart. "…But we can do something about the future. I'm putting up the money, D'mitri, and I'm telling you, you need to open up the auditions. There's other talent out there. You could be selling yourself short. You could be selling *me* short," Stewart says.

D'mitri fires back. "There's gone be singing in the play, pastor. Name a better singer than Bianca." D'mitri waits and then says, "That's what I thought." The argument that Stewart started, D'mitri finishes with, "Don't misunderstand me, Pastor. This is not a debate. I'm simply telling you what it's gone be. I can't let you kick my legs out from under me."

Bianca thanks D'mitri and hangs up. "Heard enough?"

"You can say no, Bianca. I'll pay you triple what you'd make."

"It's not about money. It's about me getting my talents out on front street. Ain't no telling what kind of doors that can open for me. This is not about you–" Bianca stops talking because Stewart is laughing.

His laughter dies with a sudden change in demeanor. Stewart checks his periphery, licking his lips. "Something about dark corridors, huh," Stewart says. He approaches, as if going for a kiss.

"What are you doing?" She wants his advance, but doesn't trust this sudden turn of events; she doesn't know how to take him.

Stewart says, "What if I *want* it to be about me, Bianca? Think I can just drop my feelings like a stack of books?" He eases up to her. She doesn't trust his words, perse; she only trusts the pattern, their relationship playing out in shadows. Stewart stops to appraise her: her Bambi eyes, her plump, berry lips, his eyes burning as he closes in for a kiss. This is what Bianca wants more than she wants him, to have the love she gives re-gifted back to her. Her starvation for his embrace has been too long to play hard to get and chance missing this opportunity. She let him lift her chin. Her eyes fall close. Her lips part.

And then nothing. No fireworks. A dead fuse. Her eyes open. She sees Stewart, a prankster backing away, hands up like he'd beat the buzzer in a timed contest. "Now," he says. "Repeat what you said a minute ago... *Tell* me this is strictly business. *Tell* me there's no ulterior motive."

Bianca feels as if a clean sword is driven through her heart – shocked by the idea of life itself ending, and melancholy, feeling so undeserving of this fate, but with the dealer of this fate still in arm's reach, she spazzes – punches his taunting mouth.

Stewart stumbles back against the painted cinderblock wall. His tongue rolls over a cut inside of his lip.

Bianca rubs her elbows; regret feeling like a chilly breeze. She's sorry for her actions, but not for its victim. "I'm sorry," she says, as if she's put up to the apology.

Realizing how he'd hurt Bianca, Stewart apologizes, but he prays that there's no swelling.

Her head shakes no. "Just leave me here," she requests. "Go!" She is on the verge of breaking down. She's panting as if going into labor.

Stewart offers his pocket handkerchief. Bianca stares at the handkerchief as a sign of Stewart's audacity, thinking he could be both the source and the soother of her pain. She goes off again, charging at Stewart and swinging for his face. To trap her blows, Stewart hugs Bianca and holds her to his chest, where she breaks down and cries miserably. Bianca finally pushes Stewart away. She pushes him again when he tries again to console her. Reluctantly, and regretfully, Stewart walks away, leaving a crying Bianca alone in the low lit corridor.

Stewart stops in the men's room wets a paper towel and begins dabbing the makeup stain on the breast of his suit, but when Stewart leans into the mirror, he notices that his upper lip is swelling. "Aw naw," Stewart agonizes. "Naw, naw, naw, naw!" He nearly loses it. He dips his head under the faucet to try to run cold water over his lips but ends up clunking his head. He staggers away then returns to the mirror, and it looks. It's even worse. The knot on his lip is swollen tight like a little bicep. It's the same lips that not long ago kissed the woman of his dreams, the same woman who held his hand to her thigh under the table just minutes prior. How could he return and tell Lynn nothing happened between himself and the woman he called a whore, who dragged him away from their banquet table; his swollen upper lip would call him a liar.

Stewart has no choice but to return. He comes into the to the dining room, hurrying as if late to a meeting. Levi and Nay has since joined Lynn at the table.

How Stewart knows that they all know something's awfully wrong, is that no one says a thing; three pairs of eyes watch Stewart lower in his chair.

He tries to sip ice water, hoping to help the swelling but picking up the glass only shows how badly his hand shakes, the ice cubes rattling like dice, so Stewart sets the glass back down.

Lynn looks at Stewart. "What happened," she asks, although she knows; Stewart has some loose ends with the woman he described as a whore. Lynn wants to scream at him, but she waits, judiciously, for the report.

Stewart says, "Bianca's got the lead role in the play."

Lynn spots the wet ring on the breast of Stewart's suit where he'd tried to clean the makeup stain. Lynn slides her chair back, gets up, and asks the party, "May I be excused." She doesn't wait for their reply nor does she react to Stewart calling behind her.

"Wait, Lynn." Stewart hurries after. "I can explain."

Stewart's flock watches him speed-walk after Lynn, knowing full well which woman led him out of the dining room prior to this one. Stewart follows, brisk and stiff, like a tin man after his heart.

Nay leaves the table to check on Bianca. She finds Bianca coming out of the lady's room after padding her makeup. Nay can tell that Bianca had been crying. Nay hugs Bianca and escorts her out, saying there's something she'd been wanting to show Bianca since she and Stewart's relationship was exposed at his party.

They go into the deaconess's meeting room where Nay digs into a trunk of memorabilia. Nay pulls out an old, large scrapbook compiled from many years before Bianca joined First Baptist Church. Without a word, Nay blows dust from its cover and flips through the pages, stopping on a picture of a young lady, and asks, "Who does she look like?"

Bianca frowns. "Lynn used to be a member here?"

Nay sighs. "That ain't Lynn. This is a picture of Fiona, Stewart's first love. They were going to marry, but before the wedding, Fiona died of a brain tumor."

Bianca's head shakes. "You sure, Nay? Because I swear this looks just like a younger Lynn."

Nay looks over with lazy eyes. "Do I look like I'm stupid? I'm telling you what I know. Fiona and me were best friends. I mourned her just as hard as Stew did." Fiona holds the mysteries of the man's heart. Nay tells the story, how Stewart did find love again, with a gorgeous young woman named Savannah who succumbed to the pressure from everyone encouraging a relationship with Stewart. Savannah and Stewart were together for two years. Just when everyone expected First Baptist to finally get a first lady, Savannah and Stewart's relationship ended abruptly. "Turns out, Savannah was misleading Stewart all along; she likes women." The betrayal of Stewart's second love deepened his yearning for his first; Fiona, who died still young, still innocent, still perfect. Stewart remaining unmarried late into his thirties and now forty, along with the purity ring on his finger are memorials to the death of his first love, and evidence of prolonged, subconscious grieving. Stewart never made a serious attempt at another relationship. Stewart's relationships ever since, were no more than casual experiments, too long distance to stick, or too brief to blossom. Stray too close to Fiona's plot in Stewart's heart and he'd scare off.

Bianca holds the floppy picture of Fiona and still can't get over the resemblance. Like Lynn, Fiona has bronze cheeks and a small mouth, some kinship around the brows. Fiona is posed with her hands clasped in front. Her hairstyle says it's early nineties. They're presenting her with some sort of recognition that she awaits' she's glancing and smiling at someone beyond the photo's edge.

Nay pats Bianca's shoulder, saying, "His rejection of you, Bianca, is not about you. Him falling head over heels for Lynn isn't really about Lynn either. You see the resemblance. Pastor Stewart is trying to raise the dead."

What is clear to Bianca, is now that he's found a Lynn, an age-progressed Fiona walking this earth, Bianca would never have a chance at becoming Stewart's first lady.

Chapter 7

No one knows the extent of Stewart's heartbreak. Lynn ended the relationship. She had so swiftly and decisively cut Stewart's heart out of his chest, that he couldn't even fashion a response. The man who makes a living with words, was no verbal match for this activist who, with regularity, puts heads of state to shame.

At first, there is no communication between the two. Lynn let all of Stewart's calls go to voicemail. Their only hope to communicate is concerning the play, as Lynn and D'mitri co-author the script.

The more at-odds Lynn becomes with D'mitri's ideas, the more hands-on she becomes with the script, which causes heated arguments and hot emails landing in Stewart's inbox.

D'mitri would email Stewart with his frustrations about the script and Lynn would do the same. Lynn would email Stewart her copied exchanges containing D'mitri's insults in caps, D'mitri calling Lynn's ideas boring and Lynn calling D'mitri's suggestions buffoonery.

Since Lynn wouldn't answer Stewart's calls, he would have to play mediator by email only. No matter how many times Stewart would try to call Lynn she wouldn't answer. So, it surprised Stewart to one day get a phone call, out of the blue, from Lynn. Her call comes in at the worst possible time. Stewart's in his office mediating a shouting match between two men, Deacon Bailey who heads the transportation ministry accusing one of his drivers, Clifton Moss, of inappropriate use of the gas cards. To get the men's attention, Stewart has to make a T of his hands and yell, "Time out!" He tells them he has an important call to answer so the men hush.

Stewart answers his ringing phone with a quick, "Yup."

Lynn asks, "Are you busy?"

"Nope." Stewart takes a seat in his chair and swivels around, putting his back to the men who're fuming as they wait to resume their argument.

"I happen to be in the area," Lynn says. "And thought maybe I could drop by to talk about a few things – about the play, meaning," she says before Stewart gets any ideas.

"Of course, 'course...'"

"I'll only need a few minutes of your time." Lynn realizing the shortness of Stewart's replies, says, "Are you sure this isn't a bad time?"

Stewart looks back over his shoulder. "Everything's just fine."

As soon as the call ends, Deacon Bailey resumes, "I don't know what else to call it but stealing!"

Stewart rubs his forehead in distress as the argument continues. Finally, Stewart rises out of his seat and says, "Y'all got to go!"

"Say no more," says Clifton who hurries out of the office.

Deacon Bailey hangs back, protesting, "Ain't you the one called this meeting?"

"C'mon, Deek," says Stewart. "You're the head of the ministry. You got the authority to handle things like this without me."

Slowly, Deacon Bailey heads out but stops at the door. He looks back over his shoulder and asks, "That was Lynn on the phone, wasn't it?"

Pastor Stewart looks away to hide his smile. Deacon Bailey leaves the office, shaking his head.

It's high spring, so Lynn comes by, fresh from a pedicure and wearing a tennis skirt, her navel peaking from under a blouse without shoulders, looking like gauze wrapped around her torso. Stewart holds his composure, but Lynn could see the thought bubble above his head, reading *Good Lawd.* Under his strong brow, those brown orbs are busy in the milk white of his eyes, zipping up and down, gathering information.

Lynn sits in the leather, buttoned chair in front of his desk and crosses her legs. Between Lynn's complaints about D'mitri, Stewart tries to coax conversation out of her. He asks how she's doing and How's the semester going, but it is all disruptions to her cause. All she's willing to discuss is the play.

When Lynn is ready to leave, she pulls a jewelry box out of her purse and tries to hand it to Stewart; it is the diamond drop pendant that Stewart gave her. Stewart's hands go up like she is handing him porn. "Don't do this, Lynn," he says. "*Don't* twist the knife in my heart."

Lynn's head shakes. "Knife in your heart… You do have a flair for the dramatic…"

"You know whatever there was between Bianca and me was over well before you and me. How could you expect me to see that coming? How am I being blamed for being hit in the mouth?"

Lynn rolls her eyes. They've had the argument before. "That's not the issue. One: you kept me in the dark. Two: you should not have left my side that day. And then you: coming back to the table with that almond on your lip, acting like nothing happened. No matter who hit who, if you're a party to that kind of dysfunction that gives me pause."

"Well *pause* then. Don't stop altogether." He pushes the boxed pendant back to Lynn. "Is Bianca the only one?"

"She wadn't *one* to begin with."

"You know what I mean, pastor." Lynn gets out of her seat, with a glint in her eye. She plants both hands on Stewart's desk, as if she'd crawl over, a leg lifts playfully behind her. "Is this where it all happens? Where your clients come in for counseling and the next thing you know, they're sitting on your desk." Lynn demonstrates by sitting side saddled on Stewart's desk. She watches him bite down, flexing his jaws. Stewart knows it is a game, but any affection from this woman he'll take, real or pretend. The door pops open and Lynn nearly falls off the desk.

Levi gives a quick *oops* and shuffles back into the hallway pulling the door shut. Lynn tries calling him back to explain herself, but Levi is gone.

Stewart folds over prostrate, anchoring his desk. Lynn reams him, "Don't just sit there go talk to him. Tell him I was just playing!"

Stewart, drying his eyes, says, "The man know what he saw."

Lynn stamps out of there angrier with Stewart than she was before, but she leaves, however, with the diamond pendant.

Shortly after Lynn leaves, Levi returns, impish. "I see you had a lil' visitor today."

Stewart is a mess. He pulls his head out of his hands like uprooting a turnip. "I can't figure her out man. She came in here looking good, smelling sweet, just to punish me."

"Boy nose so wide open you can park a car in his nostril."

Stewart just looks down in his lap as if there are scattered puzzle pieces there.

Levi says, "How could anything as simple as a woman be so confusing."

"Tell *her* that."

"No woman gets dressed up for a man she doesn't want, so it don't matter what comes out of that mouth of hers." Levi leans in. "What does she do for a living?"

"Teacher. Professor."

"I ain't asking; I'm reminding. What do she teach?"

Stewart's head swings away and returns. "C'mon with all the breadcrumbs, man. Where're you leading me?"

"She teaches fiction. She writes fiction. The whole point to fiction is to make it immersive and interesting." After a long pause, seeing that Stewart still can't follow, he adds, "Such is life for someone like her. She's the author, weaving her plot and you're just a reader, immersed in her story, struggling to make sense of things. That's how she likes it."

Stewart stares blankly until a refusal so convicting rises up inside of him it is comical, "Where do you get this stuff?" Stewart laughs, not only at the man's words but at the man himself.

Levi could be so profound at times, but also he'd go too deep in his mind and resurface sounding aloof.

Levi is undeterred by Stewart's skepticism. "Even fairy tales must have dragons. If you want to be her hero, you'll have to slay her dragon."

"You've been out of the dating game too long Levi. If you had to start all over, you'll be like a trout in a sandbox."

"It's being married this long that makes me wish I could re-do the past now that I know better. I'll tell you this and then I'll leave you. For ninety-nine-point-nine percent of all women, the dragon is doubt. The way you beat doubt is with trust. You build trust with *consistency*."

Chapter 8

The script is only half done. It is D'mitri's idea to go ahead with rehearsals anyway. Lynn decides to be present at rehearsals to make sure that D'mitri doesn't get to crazy with her script.

D'mitri welcomes Lynn's presence at rehearsals, thinking it would give her the opportunity to see how boring her novel looks on stage and may influence some much-needed changes to the script before it's set in stone. The actors are given stapled copies of the first half of the script. They rehearse in the banquet room after hours. Lynn assumed she'd be a distant observer, but to her surprise, she's hands-on at rehearsals helping the actors hone her characters.

D'mitri is cruel towards his cast. Bianca would shield them from his wrath, and when that fails, she'd follow the insult with encouragement.

Day one, Bianca stands up to D'mitri when he shouts at the youngest cast member, Ashton, a happy-go-lucky college sophomore. Bianca pulls Ashton close and lashes out at D'mitri, asking him why he had to be *such a diva*.

The whole thing turns comical when D'mitri gets up from his director's chair in his polka dot shirt and turquoise bowtie. "How dare you call me a diva. Heifer, I am a prima donna. Know the difference."

Nay Ginyard graces the second rehearsal, her church status as the de facto first lady, earning her a spot in the room as a bystander. When employees and ministry members who are around after hours, crowd at the doors and even crash the rehearsals for phone pictures and autographs with the celebrity, D'mitri Dalton, Nay runs them off like a guard dog, so D'mitri asks Nay to stick around.

Nay loves her role. She sits at D'mitri's side, chuckling at his insults, and even egging him on, but when eyes appear in the door's rectangle window, she'd bolt to run them off. Nay loves D'mitri's company. She alone greets him with hugs and air kisses. Nay, speaking to be heard, says to D'mitri, "You're what's been missing in my life, honey. Every diva needs a gay male friend."

D'mitri's shoulder swims one back-stroke, throwing Nay's hand off. "Tell me where you see a gay male at?"

Nay, never to be outdone, pats his back in condolences. "Poor thing, still in the closet… But I wonder who you think you're hiding from in them sherbet color pants, hurtin' my eyes."

Bianca stops in the middle of her lines, her hand flicking at her throat as she vouches, "He's not, Nay. Trust me, he's not."

Nay's hands draw to her hips. "How you know? Is he married, divorced, got a girlfriend?"

Monique steps forward, her emphatic *Yes* is pecked out of the air in a quick neck jerk.

Nay leans back, her eyes inflating, taking in a hideous sight, the rail thin, starving artist in a cowl neck blouse and flowy bell-bottoms. "Miss, you look hongry. Wearing them big witch boots in this hot weather." Nay then let loose her big bonfire laugh at her own comment, but then she stops, abruptly. "No kidding though? You? And y*ou?*" Her pointing fingers crossed, wrists limp like dog paws, pointing at sherbet pants and witch boots. "When they say there's somebody for everybody, they ain't *never* lied."

Lynn is the overbearing mother at rehearsals. There's little difference between Lynn's rehearsal role and her classroom role: helping students (and actors) get on the same page as the author, except with rehearsals, the author is herself. She helps the actors channel her characters, recovering what is lost in translation through their interpretation of the script.

According to the staff, having to deal with D'mitri is enough in and of itself. They argue that there is one too many chiefs, how D'mitri and Lynn tag team the stage. Lynn's interjections often draws gasps. Even when Lynn withholds her objection, they feel her hesitations. Bianca characterizes it best when she finishes a set of lines and then immediately turns to Lynn, asking, "What is it *this* time, Lynn?"

Lynn flashes palms, pleading innocence. "I didn't say a word."

"But you're thinking it."

Lynn gets out from her banquet table and approaches the stage, apologizing for the intrusion, "Bianca… dear… You come across as if your character is oblivious, but she is well aware that the day she prayed for love is the day she decided to use God as an excuse to lower her standards. She's complicit in her denial." From then on Bianca plays her character differently. Bianca pretends to be irritated by Lynn, but knows her insight produces brilliance, so she often pumps Lynn for more insight, and before they know it, a bond forms between Lynn and Bianca, over the imaginary character in which Bianca sees so much of herself.

They have fun at rehearsals. Ashton, the twenty-year-old college junior playing the role of Miriam, is at the center of it all. She calls D'mitri daddy, Bianca mother, and the other adult women aunties. She'd call Kevin uncle to his face, but behind his back, puts the adjective "crack-head" in front of uncle. Bianca, in confidence, tells Lynn that Kevin, though a gifted actor, has more than his share of demons; cocaine, apparently being one of them.

Lynn soon witnesses another one of his demons – pride – when she interrupts Kevin's line. It is the scene where the main character and her love interest meet. He and Bianca are alone on the empty stage, where she pretends to serve him in a make-believe bistro. It is Kevin's very first line. "Girl you sho' got some lips on you," his character says to Bianca's character.

Lynn stops him. "Have you read the script, Kevin? He's not flirting; he's antagonizing. Her happiness irritates him because he's miserable."

"But is that my failure or the script's failure? How is he talking about her lips and not flirting?"

"He can't be flirtatious out the gate, Kevin. This is an enemies to lovers trope. He has to start out being mean."

Kevin's head shakes as if he'd heard it all before. "This character is on paper. I'm a living, breathing man, an artist just like you. Actors have leeway for their *own* artistic interpretation."

Siding with Lynn, D'mitri adds, "Don't tell me about artistic interpretation. If you haven't read the script to know what's there to interpret."

Kevin holds the papers up like pinching the tail of a dead rodent. "You mean this *half* of a script.

"That's how I want it. Not knowing your characters' fates should keep you all in the moment," D'mitri says to Kevin. He then says to everyone, "By next rehearsal, let me find out that any of you have not read the half script that you *do* have. I've got a stack of applicants who would love to take your job."

To D'mitri's ultimatum, Kevin stares at Lynn in fury, as if she'd authored this result too. Kevin proceeds with rehearsals, waiting to be stopped, itching to be corrected again while, in effect, projecting the bitterness that his character feels.

Right after his evening workout, Pastor Stewart walks through the rehearsal in a sleeveless t-shirt, his arms veined in the front and lumped with muscles high on the back side. It is the first time Lynn gets a look at Stewart's arms. While on stage with the actors there is a moment when she forgot how to breath.

Stewart stops by and talks to D'mitri for a progress update. Lynn feels gravity pulling her head in Stewart's direction; she has to concentrate to keep from looking. Bianca whispers in passing, "Girl, you's so shook, it ain't even funny."

Lynn's next opportunity to talk to Bianca is after rehearsals. She walks up alongside Bianca in a comedic confrontation, "Let me tell you something, Bianca, I was not shook. Not in the least."

"Could've fooled me," Bianca replies flippantly.

"What about you?" Lynn's waiting glare says her question is whole point of bringing this discussion.

Bianca stops, looks Lynn up and down, and then laughs. "Girl please. I've moved on."

Lynn glows. "You're *dating* someone. I knew it," Lynn says.

Bianca folds her arms at Lynn's insolence. "And how could you possibly know my business?" They're standing in the parking lot by Lynn's car under a starry night, thick with humidity. Around them car engines are cranking, low beams swinging through their three-point turns.

"I can tell by the way you two look at each other."

"*Who?*"

"It's the guy who stands one row up from you on the choir. The one with the thick beard."

Bianca waves a limp hand. "Brice? Child, he ain't nobody. What would I look like, dating a retail manager? It's not like he's a *pastor* or anything." Bianca's fingers rustle like dusting cracker crumbs, the thought filthy, the idea of dating a commoner, pure blasphemy.

"But what if that's who you happen to fall in—"

"—No." Bianca's makes a hand puppet, her fingers coming together like a shutting mouth.

"So, who *is* the lucky guy?"

"We're not dating just yet. We're kinda in the seduction phase." Bianca's nose wrinkles, scandalously.

"*Seduction* phase…"

"Yeah. Everything's casual as far as conversation, but at the same time, I'm putting my moves on him. I'll have him eating out of my hands before you know it."

Lynn is highly intrigued. "What moves?"

Bianca demonstrates and Lynn mimics, intensely, as Bianca talks her through the details. "First you stare directly at him. If he's not looking at you at the time, he will. But you hold the stare. Not too intense," she taps Lynn. "Look at him like you're not even aware that you're looking at him." Bianca, uses two fingers to direct Lynn's eye focus. They're side by side staring straight across the highway, cars swooshing by. "The next step is very important. When he sees you looking at him, you look down as if maybe you've lost your train of thought. You then slick your hair behind your ear and then you walk away. It's that simple. No tongue action or licking lips. The idea is to convey relationship interest, not sexual interest."

"You just walk off? You don't wait for him to approach you?"

"Once you give a man that look, trust me, he will find you and he will come see about you."

Stewart comes up with the idea to feed the actors at rehearsals. He brings food to keep everyone focused and productive. He comes in with an assistant rolling in a steam table to the center of the banquet, with Stewart, musing about Imhotep, famine, and grain silos, a biblical explanation for providing the grub. The banquet normally closes after lunch, but one staff member would return. Stewart is actually *his* assistant. The chef lifts silver lids presenting his take on chicken and waffles, crispy fried chicken and sand dollar waffles with a caramel and bourbon sauce.

After the meal, Stewart goes around collecting dirty dishes. Lynn and Ashton, at a table of their own, are having a lemon challenge using their iced teas' lemon wedge garnish to see whose face would go bitter first. Stewart reaches their table as Lynn's face puckers like she is blowing a saxophone, one eye blaring wide open. Stewart jokes, "Ooh girl, don't make that face."

Ashton jumps in for Lynn, saying to Stewart, "No *you* don't make *that* face."

Stewart, sacrificing himself as the girl's punch line, offers a clueless, "But I'm not making a face."

Ashton, in mach terror, checks Lynn. "That's how he really looks?" Lynn looks away to hide her laughter. Stewart walks away smiling.

The next rehearsal, it is flat bread pizza with roasted arti-choke topping and side salad. Ashton hugs Stewart from the side, pinning his arms, as she apologizes for calling him ugly the last time. "I had no idea you were the pastor of the church. Look at you, you're working and getting your hands dirty. What are you *doing*," she says, with her palms flipped out at her sides.

Lynn, her pretend auntie, interjects. "That's what *good* pastors do." This is her first compliment to Stewart since his swollen lip.

Ashton can't refer to the head pastor as a mere uncle; she gives him the nickname Big Poppa. Bianca, in passing, let go of a cold, what-*ever*, like a blown scarf and Nay laughs in a way that makes a room stop laughing just to watch her laugh.

Stewart knows what he is doing; he's taking Levi's advice to heart. If this fair maiden's dragon is doubt, he has to build him-self up, in her eyes, as a knight wielding the sword of trust. If bringing food and staying engaged with the cast; in addition to backing Lynn on every dispute over the script would win her back, then Stewart plans to deliver without fail.

Stewart becomes aware that his plan is working the day Lynn comes out of her cold shell. They nearly bump into each other when Lynn is coming out of the ladies' room as Stewart is headed towards rehearsal after a workout. Lynn bypasses hello, or good afternoon and goes straight to, "You know what... I think you're delirious."

"Delirious..." The claim invokes Stewart's inner parakeet.

"I fail to see how you would simply brush off a woman like Bianca." Lynn is heated, actually. Her pointed finger jabbing Stewart in the chest for each quality she'd observed in Bianca. "She's beautiful, she's intelligent, she's humble, she's Godly, she's the glue that holds the *cast* together, I can tell you that much." Each jabbing virtue slowly backs Stewart against the wall.

Stewart smirks in confusion. "Are you for real? Or is this just an excuse to touch my chest?"

Lynn turns and walks away fuming as if she is so done with him. She ignores Stewart as he follows her down the hallway, claiming he was only kidding.

Stewart returns to serve the cast dinner. Nothing much is said between them. Stewart makes no effort to initiate conversation nor even look Lynn's direction. It's Lynn who initiates. While Stewart pays the banquet chef cash in hand and let him leave early. Lynn swells with admiration at the pastor volunteering his own labor to breaking down the steamtable and wash the dishes himself.

The lunch break is over, rehearsal is resuming. The actors are taking their places; Nay is seated next to D'mitri, shucking and jiving already, and amidst all this, Stewart catches Lynn standing stock-still and gazing at him. When she realizes that Stewart is aware, she looks down as if she's lost her train of thought. She then slicks her hair behind her ear and walks away.

At the end of rehearsals, while D'mitri and the actors are on their way out, Lynn lagging behind, when Stewart, remembering how their eyes met, comes to see about her.

He comes over, wiping his hands in his apron.

Lynn pretends not to see him coming, but all the while, she's thinking, *Well I'll be… Bianca's advice worked.*

Stewart doesn't know quite how to begin. "Hey, Lynn, umm…"

"Hi," Lynn says.

Stewart asks, "You got a minute?"

Lynn checks back toward the exit. "Actually, I think Bianca's expecting me. It seems like after every rehearsal we end up chatting in the parking lot."

"I see," Stewart says in disappointment.

"I just wanted to thank you," says Lynn. "For your consistency, being here every day. The food – which you really don't have to provide – is such a treat, I mean, rehearsal can be pretty intense sometimes, and… I just want to thank you, Pastor Stewart."

Stewart waves it off. "It's nothing," he says. "So, maybe we can talk later, then, when you *do* have a minute?"

"Absolutely," Lynn says. "Bye now." She tickles a wave and leaves to catch up with Bianca outside.

Stewart returns to the kitchen, whistling while he works because he feels like he has won himself another chance.

He calls Lynn later on that night. Whatever enchantment Lynn was under at the banquet is rubbed off by the time of their phone conversation. Stewart lowers the phone, crushed and confused. He thinks maybe his magic only works when they're face to face – even better, away from church grounds, like their coffee shop meetings, the dance in his living room, and even the day they met at the barbershop. Stewart rubs his chin, remembering Calvin saying that Lynn comes by the barbershop every Thursday around the same time. Today is Wednesday, he thinks.

The next day, Stewart comes into the barbershop, again two days sooner than usual, hoping to run into Lynn. Calvin says he just missed Lynn but he points to the corkboard thumbtacked flyers and business cards thumbtacked to it. He pulls one of the flyers and hands it to Stewart. "You can probably catch up to Lynn here."

Stewart leaves the shop with the flyer in hand, his haircut fresh, the sun on his face. It says there's a rally being held to get signatures for the Fair Wage Transparency Bill.

Chapter 9

The multi-county rally ends at home, in the city of Columbia. They're at Finlay Park, near the state house. Their petition is far short of the projected signatures. There're discussions already about extending the tour a few more weekends. A bill without support is merely a suggestion, says Senator Kelley, their silent partner. In its truest form, a bill is a call to action, but so is free food. They plan a free hot dog rally to draw a daunting two thousand signatures in one afternoon. They leave hopeful, but when they arrive at a desolate Finlay Park, their enthusiasm takes a blow.

They're around the amphitheater setting up the sound system. Gayle is on dog duty. She has Mrs. Kelley's terrier on a leash, sniffing at every pair of feet that happens by. "We need those signatures *to-day*." Gayle is on the brink of insanity. "I can't stand another day of that woman." The pup tucks its rear end and trembles; Lynn and Gayle look away in disgust. Gayle is sick of her idol, Beatrice Kelley, who requires more catering to than a teen pop star. She's not the great woman Gayle thought her to be, but actually a fussy, arrogant woman characterized by one great act.

It is a beautiful day to be at the park, the sky, blue, clouds are large and fast; ominous shadows pass overhead. The park is sparsely peopled with the homeless, some frisbee tossing families, and a few dog walkers.

A good day to slay a dragon, Stewart thinks, as he strides across the carpet of grass, spotting Lynn in the distance in a knee length blue dress, her hair held back out of her face by a blue wrap. "What are you doing here," Lynn asks, smiling at Stewart's cargo shorts and satchel.

"What am I doing here? How about: why didn't you tell me about this rally?"

"Because…" Lynn's shoulders hop. "I didn't want you to feel obligated."

Stewart's eyes search Lynn's. "That's not the reason. You were afraid I'd disappoint you."

"This is not your job."

"Aren't we friends?"

"*Friends…*" She emphasizes.

"Today, I'm a volunteer," Stewart announces. "How can I be of service?"

One member, named Iris, presents Stewart with an apron and a pair of tongs and escorts him to the grill.

Lynn spots the church busses arriving and it feels like Christmas. This is Stewart's surprise. Lynn leaves a huddled conversation, waving the group to follow her. "They're with us! Welcome them!" She hugs the church members as they step off the buses and they love her back. She ushers them to the long table with the petition and information pamphlets. Lynn blows grateful kisses Stewart's way. Members sees her kisses land fifty yards away to their pastor who works the grill, a towel keeping the sun off the back of his neck. Stewart's blush tells them, better than any skywriting plane, that he is crazy about her. Myrtle, a tall, smiley, woman, her hair in a Geisha's bun, touches Lynn's face and sums up the pastor's choice for everyone. "*Do* pastor!"

Stewart is the most enthusiastic volunteer. Although in the role of follower, he leads – modeling, for his members, the embodiment of God's grace and zeal. He is jovial with stragglers who wander in and takes their plates as if purchased with their signature.

A red headed family trails in behind the father, the parents with sunshades resting on their crowns, the mother tending the inquisitive boy and girl. The dad learns what his signature would mean, so he refuses the food. The son wails and has to be dragged away by one arm. The mother, struggling to comfort the children, calls their father a dick, appealing that the kids cannot yet comprehend the lesson he tries to teach. Stewart chases them down with a tray of hot dogs, chips and soda, insisting that he didn't have to sign anything. Stewart then sends them on with hotdogs and his blessings.

Lynn's colleagues seek her out to report high praises for her *friend* Dana – his meekness, his enthusiasm, his kindness. Their approval rating boosts Lynn's.

By midday, their title changes. When she introduces a latecomer, a biker woman her thumbs hooked in her belt loops. Lynn says, "This is *my guy*, Pastor Dana Stewart." After the introduction, Stewart folds his arms. "Your guy?" He has the diploma in hand, without any recollection of the graduation ceremony.

Lynn, neck rolling, replies, "Oh? Did I misspeak?"

They giggle like stoners. Lynn hugs him and then pushes him. "I ain't messin' with you today."

Just after walking away from Lynn, Stewart runs into Levi and his wife, Nay, in their matching tight T-shirts. They're arm in arm shaking their heads pitifully at the flirty skit. Nay says, "That boy so gone, I can see the love birds chirping around his head."

Levi stares Stewart down like a drill sergeant disgusted over a messy bunk. "Up here grinning like a Cheshire cat."

Stewart mocks, "'Up here wearing shirts so tight, it look like body paint." Stewart pokes Levi's swollen gut, and the tough-as-nails drill sergeant shuffles back and giggles like a boy of dough.

Nay browbeats her husband, likely to yank his ear, "Watch this one, now…"

All afternoon Stewart and Lynn are connected by a ribbon; they never lose sight of one another. Even thirty feet away, one admirable gaze tugs the other out of their conversations just for a glancing smile. Lynn approaches Stewart at the grill, her upper lip beading sweat. She throws an arm around his waist, snuggles into him, and tries to convince him to take a break, "… before you monkey in this hot son," she says. Since he's *her guy*, she now has an invested interest in his wellbeing.

Stewart refuses. "This is what I love. Community is life." The community: the home outside of his already made mansion; community is the home they could both have a hand in building.

After a few preliminary speakers, Lynn, the face of the organization, and author of the bill, is up. Stewart finds Levi and nods at the stage to steer his attention toward what is about to take place.

Lynn opens methodically, giving the nuts and bolts of the bill.

"… this bill would require mid-sized to large corporations to publish wage statistics, per job title, as it pertains to race and gender. A little more ink on their year-end financial reports is all we ask..."

Lynn references the bible for moral alignment; Matthew twenty, the vineyard parable where workers felt cheated for being paid the same although they worked longer hours. Stewart observes with admiration.

Lynn references the Unequal Pay Act signed by Kennedy, offering a single note of criticism, "It demands no burden of proof, which means corporations who are discriminating against you pretty much have to tell on themselves. You have this illusion that the world is becoming more and more free because you have the right to bear arms and free speech… Well, I've got a seed for you and I'd appreciate if you would just open your minds for a moment let this take root. In biblical times, vineyard workers had the freedom to *know* if they are being paid fairly. They had the information necessary for which to form their complaint, while roughly twenty centuries later, not only are you kept in the dark, but you will be terminated for even *discussing* pay. And you call that freedom? You don't have a sling shot's chance against corporate Goliaths. And yet you are satisfied?"

Lynn smiles, her head shaking at the madness. She leans over the podium, getting personal with her audience. Her brows go up, "So, you're *not* satisfied? Name the last major South Carolina strike… Nine-teen-sixty-nine!" Lynn begins counting on her fingers, but it's only theatre. "The Charleston Hospital Worker's strike. Many of you weren't even born… You say you're *not* satisfied…" Lynn stares blankly, "If you're lying down and taking it, you *are* satisfied — in a passive sort of way, but satisfied nonetheless. Strikes occur mostly in the north: why? Unions. Unions inform *them* when they're not being compensated fairly. But we've ran unions clear out of the south. But no! We're in a Right to Work state." She stops like a soldier coming to a halt, posing in mach pride, but then turning on that pride, noting how foolish that pride is. "*Right* to work… Did we *not* have the right to work before this bill? It's called Right to Work because it's afraid to say what it really is: it's an anti-union bill. Because the south doesn't want outsiders looking in on how it conducts business down here."

Helpers roll in two nearly identical maps of America, each showing a divide of red and blue. Lynn enlightens, "These are not political party maps, if that's what you're thinking." The first map is a pre-Civil war polarization of slave states versus free states; the other, a present day Right to Work states versus union states. Lynn explains how today's contrast illustrates that the old Mason Dixon line is still intact, only now the verbiage on either side have changed. A massive cloud covers the sun, its shadow floating over the park like a large cloak.

"I ask you, today," Lynn peers out over the crowd. "Are you *really* free?"

Stewart is a believer. He checks Levi's reaction; the man just watches, his arms folded, a hand climbing out of the fold to cover his mouth, the forefinger hooking his nose.

By the end, Lynn receives resounding praise. She smiles like a clam, downplaying the idea that something special had just taken place. Stewart says to Levi, "She's got a way with words. Wonder what she'd do with *the* word."

Levi doesn't face Stewart. Levi drops his hands and says, "Nigger you done lost your damn mind." Levi walks off. Stewart's hand, half raised in objection, is left hanging.

Senator Kelley comes by, scoops up the hand that Levi left hanging, then Kelley says to Stewart, "You alright, partner? You look confused." Senator Kelley sports shorts and knee-high socks, like Colonel Sanders at a ping pong tournament.

"It's nothing," Stewart replies while looking the man up and down.

Kelley's head dips like a horse, "Thank you, man. Without you and your folks we didn't have a puncher's chance to reach the signature goal. Why don't you go on up and add a few words?"

Stewart declines. "Sometimes adding is really subtracting. This is Lynn's time."

"And that's what I admire about you. You don't just *preach* humility, you live it."

Lynn walks up and ducks in under Stewart's arm.

"*Best* speech I've heard all year." Kelley kisses his fingertips like a French chef. Next, he asks the immediate crowd, mostly minorities, to gather round, since the camera crews had folded up and gone. He began, "Those dead set against the bill will never admit knowing that if it'd pass, it'd give you all (minorities) a pay raise, and fact is *they* don't like you all very much. They'll pretend it's a whole 'nother reason when really they're afraid that, once you all can afford to, you'll flood *their* neighborhoods." The crowd watches him in awe – not by the ideas, when six blocks from the park where they stand, the Confederate flag waves boldly on the statehouse grounds. No, they are in awe over *who's* delivering the message, as if Colonel Sanders, himself, is divulging his secret recipe.

With all eyes on Senator Kelley, Lynn and *her guy* sneaks away together, holding hands as they stroll by the naturalized fountain with shallow algae-green water, busy with slow moving orange fish the size of pickles. Stewart leans against the rail. Lynn backs into him. He wraps his arms around her, both looking forward. Stewart says, "I now know why you kept this event under wraps." Lynn says nothing. She cozies in his embrace. Stewart slants his head to avoid hair in his face. "You didn't want me to see your... talent. I know people like you. It's why you hopscotch from church to church. How long have you been running from God?" Still, Lynn says nothing. It is the weirdest thing, Stewart thinks, how she pretends as if she can't even hear him. "I guess you're not ready to talk about it," Stewart says. "I'll leave it alone, for now."

And *then* Lynn spins around to face him, her smile ready for adventure. "Got plans for dinner? I'm cooking." Their hands clasp in front; she spread their arms to bring them closer and kisses him.

Stewart realizes that when Lynn failed to respond, her back was turned. He wonders if maybe Lynn is deaf. Ya can't read lips if you can't see them.

A little later when the head of the Women's Day committee approaches Lynn and asks her to be the keynote speaker. Stewart calls Lynn from behind to see if she could hear. "Hey babe," calls Stewart.

Lynn hears him easily. She turns, smiling. "What's up *babe*?"

Chapter 10

Stewart can't wait to tell Levi. He hurries into Levi's office, saying, "She cooked."

Levi leans back in his chair, his hands joined over his belly. "Cooked what?"

Stewart smirks. "Squash casserole."

Laughter pulls Levi upright in his chair. "And how was it?"

Stewart considers lying, but offers the truth. "I'd say mushy – but tasty." Levi laughs harder. Stewart laughs at Levi's laughter.

Levi comes down sniffling. "You'll have to get better at lying or you'll see many nights on the couch, messing with this gal."

"Nay puts *you* out on the couch?"

"Who me? What I look like, some kinda chump?"

Levi's answer is so ridiculous, Stewart waits on it to change. "Bruh, you stuff chicken in your pockets, pie under your hat…"

"Don't misunderstand me, brother. I give her say over a few areas in our marriage. Outside of that, my word is law."

For the real reason he's come to Levi's office, Stewart says, "I've gotta ask you, man. What's your problem with Lynn? I get the feeling you had something against her before you ever met her."

Levi let out a groggy sigh. "Sometimes people's spirits don't agree; I'll leave it at that."

"You say y'all's spirits don't agree, but you don't know her spirit. All you have is an impression. What is it? Does she seem shifty? Pretentious? What? You seem to know so much about women, give me the heads up so I can look out for it."

"This is ridiculous," the whole conversation, meaning. "You *ought* to know me by now…"

Stewart's head shakes. "I can assume and make an ass out of me, or you can just *tell* me."

"Do you really want to do this?" Levi's brow lowers in disinterest. "Didn't I give you relationship advice to help you get her? So that should tell you that my problem isn't with her."

"You're spending an awful lot of energy telling me what it *ain't*. Tell me what it *is*."

Levi's hands come together, his forefingers forming a triangle. "All these years I sat up here and watched you campaign for women to head all kinds of ministries. Did I say anything?"

"I only campaigned for a woman when I knew they were best qualified."

"If *beauty* is a qualification, I'd see your point. Ministry is one thing, but when you talk about some broad preaching the word of God, I hope you meant just Women's Day. I heard Lynn's gonna be the Women's Day keynote speaker. I'm all for it."

Stewart shrugs. "*Just* Women's Day?"

Levi stares at Stewart for a few beats. "You ain't talking about grooming her to be an actual minister on the roster, is you?"

"I was pointing to her potential, not about grooming her for anything. But I will tell you this: it *is* high time for this church to come out of the dark ages."

Levi's open hand side chops in front of him. "You show me a woman in a preacher's robe and I'll show you a Halloween costume," Levi says. "There ain't no such a thing as a woman preacher."

Stewart is dumfounded. "Over the years, *all* these visiting female evangelists and preachers, and never a word outta you?"

Levi's head shakes in denial. "Near one of those women ever preached at the pulpit. The do it from the lectern, where they give a speech, or an exaltation – not no sermon."

Stewart looks at Levi as if he's seeing him for the first time. Levi is a Ginyard after all, Stewart thinks; cut from the same cloth as his brethren. Stewart wonders how he missed all the signs over so many years in ministry together. Stewart squints. "You're kidding."

"I got an appointment coming in directly."

Stewart challenges, "Directly, as in what time?"

Levi gets up. In silence, he goes next to the entrance and stands there like a doorman, a hand resting on the knob.

The revelation washes over Stewart. "So, you're kicking me out of your office?"

"I'm not kicking you out, brother. I'm welcoming you to the hallway."

Calmly, Pastor Stewart walks out with his tongue rolling under his lip as he advances down the hallway, his head heavy, eyes to the floor watching his stride, razor sharp pant creases over oxblood wingtips tossing forward with alternating steps. The man who has always been Stewart's greatest ally is now an enemy. The proverbial line drawn in the sand between them, is Lynn.

Bianca didn't attend the Finlay Park political rally, so she must've heard about how Stewart and Lynn were acting as a couple because throughout rehearsal, Bianca gives Lynn the silent treatment. Lynn doesn't jump to conclusions. She figures maybe Bianca is lost in-character or deeply involved in her work, but then the silent treatment holds up throughout the lunch break.

Stewart hands Chef Maurice his pay and tells him, "I'll take it from here."

Maurice blocks Stewart from the steamtable cart. "What are you talking about, pastor? This ain't your job, man; it's mine."

Stewart peels off another forty dollars and stuffs it in the breast pocket of Maurice's chef's coat. Maurice gets the hint. Without asking any questions, he expeditiously takes off his apron, tips his hat and skips out of the banquet a free man.

Stewart, from a distance, tries to make eye contact with Lynn, but she's trying not to flirt or blush in the presence of Bianca.

After rehearsals is the first time Bianca speaks to Lynn. She politely mentions that she doesn't have time to chat after rehearsals – something about an auntie needing help with a sew-in.

As everyone files out, Lynn hangs back.

Stewart moseys out of the kitchen.

Lynn says, "I thought you might need some help."

"If that's the only way we can be alone."

"May*be*, after that mess you pulled the other night."

"But you loved it."

The door closes behind the last person and they embrace. Lynn looks up at him with sly eyes and a smile. "I gave you an inch and you tried to take a mile. I *had* to shut you down."

Stewart smirks. "I let you."

Lynn leans back. "Let me?"

"I had you right where I wanted you."

"My mind hasn't changed. I'm still saving myself. I let my guard down because I thought you were safe... because you're a pastor, but..." Lynn draws back, her head shaking. "I should've known since the first date. I *never* kiss on the first date, but there I was, bringing my lips to yours without any inhibition whatsoever. And the other night over at my place, I was naïve enough to think that holding hands would've been as far as things would go, but... You're so crafty; so... skilled... It makes me wonder if you really are who you say you are."

Stewart says, "I'm only this way with you. You are the woman God has for me, so it's frustrating having to behave like girlfriend and boyfriend while waiting on what's already done in heaven to manifest here on earth."

Lynn brings a pointed finger up between them. "There it is... It's your words," she says. "You just don't know what you do to me." Lynn backs away as if to gather her composure. "But can I trust you? Not long ago, another woman punched you in the face. How do I know I won't be the next."

Stewart reaches out and pinches her cheek. "For one, I've been practicing how to duck."

They laugh. Lynn swats his shoulder.

Their laughter cuts when they hear Nay returning through the banquet entrance, clearing her throat in the most exaggerated way imaginable, "Uh, hummm!" She walks so fast she's liable to throw out her hip. "Won't get far without my keys… Don't y'all work too hard, ya hear…"

Stewart and Lynn keep their hands to themselves as they watch Nay swipe her keys from a chair in front of the stage, and head out as fast as she'd walked in, but stops at the entrance to say, "Pastor? Lynn? Have a blessed night. I'll pray for you both."

As soon as door closes Lynn says, "Did you see that?"

Stewart freezes. "What?"

"She didn't leave any keys. She took it from her purse and pretended to pick it up." Lynn squints. "Was that…? Jealousy?"

"Don't even start," says Stewart as he places his hands on Lynn's shoulders to turn her towards the kitchen.

Lynn says, "I'm a woman. We *know*. But it doesn't mean, necessarily that she wants you… Maybe I'm in the way of something."

Stewart looks back with weary eyes and keeps on walking. Lynn follows him into the kitchen, under the cold bright lights. Lynn looks around and can't find anything to do. There is only one rack of dishes, which Stewart slides inside of the machine, lowers the hatch and begins doing the only thing there is left to do: wipe the counters down.

"So, where were we, before Nay interrupted?"

Stewart loosens his apron and tosses it in the linen hamper. "I was just about to tell you that the reason why Bianca and me are not together has nothing to do with any sort of commitment issues on my end. We was never officially in a relationship yet I found out that I was not the *only* one–"

"–So, she betrayed you, then hit *you* in the face? That's odd. And another thing… After working with Bianca and getting to know her, I don't believe what you said about her; she doesn't give off any ho vibes at all."

"Because she only lifts her dress for pastors. In her twisted mind, it's a form of worship."

Lynn points as if she's onto something. "That explains Brice – who is tall, charming, fine... Bianca treats him like he's a peasant."

Stewart confides, "When Bianca and me were seeing each other, she was also seeing another pastor. The person who told me made me swear not to say anything about it, or Bianca would automatically know who told me, so I ended it with Bianca without even telling her why. All that acting out was because she was never given a reason," Stewart says as he removes his chef's coat.

With Stewart's jacket removed and he's standing there in only a V-neck cotton t-shirt, Lynn shakes a finger at him. "You know what you're doing."

"What…" Stewart catches it late. "Oh…" He takes her in his arms. "Can I spend the night?"

The mere suggestion makes her tingle. "You're a pastor. You should be saving yourself too."

"I am," replies Stewart. "It's just that I'd rather play dangerously than not play at all." They're flirting in an industrial sized kitchen that's all tile and stainless steel, the walk-in refrigerator hums in the background.

Lynn replies, "We gonna *play* around and do something we can't take back."

"If so, we'll pray it out." Stewart kisses Lynn's neck and she swears it sizzles. She backs away, her wagging finger, a nonverbal *no-no*.

She pulls Stewart by the hand, leading him outside. T h e y round the corner, horseplaying like teens in love without a care in the world, until they spot Bianca sitting in her car, alone in the parking lot, the interior lit.

The interior light flicks off. Headlights flick on, the bright granular light glows on the front of Stewart and Lynn while dashing their stretch shadows across the courtyard and folding up the side of the building. They keep walking. Stewart mentally prepares himself to throw Lynn out of the way if the car were to peel off and bank towards them.

Bianca backs out in a two-point turn, her headlights swinging like a lighthouse beam; she'd seen all she needed to see.

Bianca's car disappears in the distance. Lynn stands there holding her heart. "I thought she was gonna run us over."

Stewart seems so unsure when he says, "She ain't crazy."

They hug each other in relief; very different from the embrace they had in the banquet. The moment of fearing for their lives kills the mood and they kiss and go their separate ways for the night.

When Lynn calls to announce that she's made it home safely, Stewart pretends that he's also home, 'dog tired,' and fixing to shower and turn in for the night.

After they end the phone call, Stewart gets out of his car and walks toward the apartment building, under a dark night sky, the chalky moon tinted sickly yellow. Stewart listens to the sound of his feet hitting the pavement, questioning every step right up to the apartment door upon which he knocks. Bianca answers; mascara stains the wells of her eyes and dried tears contour her cheeks like black ink.

PART II

Chapter 11

Lynn couldn't even guess how Bianca changed overnight, from perhaps contemplating mowing Lynn over with car, to now acting it never happened. Lynn was called for the fitting. Monique has gotten the measurements of all the actors, but now she's come to the church to get measurements for Lynn, who doesn't have a role but will appear at curtain call to give a short speech. Monique is also getting measurements for Nay, whose constant politicking in D'mitri's ear finally paid off and earned her a role as the play's opening narrator, so a dress will be made for Nay, as well.

Bianca had just happened to be on the church campus that day. "Hey girl," Bianca says, with a wide smile.

Lynn tries to act as normal as possible but still can't shake her confusion. "Hey Bianca, um… Everything okay?"

"Blessed and highly favored."

Lynn says, "I mean, is everything okay with us? I feel like we need to talk."

"No, we really don't," Bianca replies. "I'm good. I assure you."

Lynn frowns. "What are you doing at the church at this hour? The teen choir's not rehearsing today are they?"

"Came by to holler at my girl Monique, then tinker on the piano a bit… composing a new song."

Bianca follows Lynn to the banquet where Monique takes Lynn's measurements, wrapping her with measuring tape and using the pencil from behind her ear to record the numbers.

Nay comes late, from some activity with the wellness ministry, so she's wearing a t-shirt, spandex and sneakers. Monique begins taking Nay's measurements. Nay winks as the tape goes around her. In triumph, Nay yells, "Fifty inches! Read em and weep."

Lynn rolls her eyes. Monique nearly gags. This pastor's wife's principal object of pride is her rump.

Maybe Nay sees the reaction out of the corner of her eye because she immediately focuses on Lynn. "I keep asking myself what pastor doing with a ole scrawny somethin' like you." Nay starts walking, to nowhere in particular, but simply pacing as an excuse to switch her butt from side to side. Lynn ignores the comment. Nay tries harder to elicit a response. "Pastor done got them cookies yet?"

Lynn considers telling Nay to mind her business, but fears that it would be taken as a yes. "Cookies… Child, we haven't even made the dough yet."

Nay laughs too loud and throws up a high five, which Lynn obliges. "Girl you is too much," Nay says. "But I know that man long time, honey – *long* time. He ain't into cookies, baby, he's into *cakes*." Monique rolls her eyes and marches off. As Nay leaves the room, she flips up the tail of her t-shirt, revealing what cakes (Stewart's preference) really looks like.

Lynn looks wide-eyed at Bianca.

Bianca laughs then says, "Don't pay Nay no mind, ya hear?"

Nay's gesture leaves a bad taste in Lynn's mouth. Nay seems to be flaunting more than just her rear end. Lynn recalls Nay pretending to lose her keys just to look in on them, and now she seems to be flaunting, perhaps, some shared past with Stewart. Lynn turns to ask –

Bianca stops her. "Don't… She only spoke on what Stewart likes. She said nothing about where he's actually been. That ain't nothing but a setup."

Lynn's brow goes uneven. "A setup?"

"That woman's got some wicked ways. She *wants* you to misconstrue something, or maybe talk behind her back just so word can get back to her. That'd be all the justification she needs."

"Justification for what?"

"To come for you. And I wouldn't wish that on anyone."

"To come for me?!" Lynn hands slap her thighs in disbelief. "The de facto first lady, a bully?"

"Just keep your head down. It'll pass over," Bianca says, like the counsel of an elder slave. "Nay has a lot of pull. If she wants folks to hate you, they'll hate you because women won't disagree with her. She gets away with murder because she's pastor Levi's wife, and nobody can put her in her place *but* Levi. Not even Pastor Stewart."

Lynn seems unmoved. "What's the worst she can do? Nay ain't near as scary as what I've been through."

"Yeah, it's easy to sound tough," Bianca replies. "A couple years ago, Felicia sounded *real* tough… until she was on the floor with a busted lip and half naked because Nay ripped off her blouse in the tussle." Bianca cuts a warning eye. "Play wit' it," she says, and gets up to go chase down Monique, leaving Lynn sitting there in disbelief.

It's not the end of issues between Lynn and Nay; it's only the beginning. They can't get through the very next rehearsal without fireworks.

The last pages of the script is finalized and each actor learns their characters' fate. The play's leading man, Kevin is the first to confront Lynn. He stands centerstage, his is head down, reading. The hand that holds the script drops down to his side as he glares at Lynn and says, "This ain't right."

Lynn who sits in front of the stage answers, "What's not right?"

"I feel like my character is neutered, man."

Lynn twitches and frowns. "How so?"

Kevin strokes his big beard. "It's like he wants what Shannon wants. He don't have no desires of his own? He ain't tryna get the draws or nothing."

Lynn stands from her chair and gently tries to reason with him. "Sex isn't all there is to a man," Lynn says.

"Only a woman would say that," counters Kevin. "You only get to see how manhood is *presented* to you. I know it from the inside. Even when we turn down sex, it's with the hopes of securing it later. Every platonic relationship you ever had with a man, started because secretly, he wanted you."

Lynn sighs and rolls her eyes, but before she could get a word out, Ashton pushes her way in front of Kevin, holding up her copy of the script in protest. "I die?! *Miriam* dies?" Ashton makes praying hands under her chin, asking. "Don't do this to me, Lynn. C'mon, now."

The complaint catches Lynn off guard. It's surreal, having a character she created, praying for her own sake. "Look," says Lynn. "As D'mitri and I were working on the script, we had a long talk about that. Have you talked to D'mitri?"

"I did that. And D'mitri said come to you," Ashton says with a neck roll.

D'mitri interrupts from behind. "I tried to tell her. It goes against my brand to have a character pour their heart out to God and have that prayer go unanswered–"

"–Really, D'mitri?" Lynn smiles. "Are you really throwing me under the bus right now? I see how you do."

D'mitri doubles down. "She even sic the pastor one me about her artistic integrity," D'mitri quotes with his fingers.

Kevin points at the words fresh out of D'mitri's mouth and Kevin says, "See what I was talkin' about. That Pastor Stewart is the perfect example, struttin' 'round rehearsals in his muscle shirts. Tell me, Lynn, do you really think Stew is worried about some artistic integrity or is he worried about getting' in yo drawls?"

The cast takes off laughing and running in every direction, leaving Lynn standing alone, a hand covering her mouth as she fails to hold back her laughter. "Touché, Kevin," says Lynn.

Nay walks in just as it happens. Nay asks, "What'd I miss?"

Bianca whispers. Nay takes it in and doesn't crack a smile. She announces, "This is still a church, y'all. Don't get beside y'self!"

Ashton greets her with a hug. "Hi, Auntie Nay."

Nay coldly dismisses her. "I ain't up for it today. Play witchya mammy."

Bianca gives Lynn a subtle side-eye, warning that trouble is brewing. Nay changes the entire mood of the rehearsal. D'mitri calls a fifteen minute break so the cast can review the script's ending.

Ashton says, "Lynn, I gotta side with D'mitri on this one. Pray is in the title, but for what, if her prayer isn't answered?"

"God answers *every* prayer," counter's Lynn. "But it's not always the answer we want. This play is about maintaining unshakeable faith, in the face of one of those times that God doesn't answer in the way that we want Him to."

Nay yawns loudly, and then mumbles under her breath, in obvious shade.

Ashton kids, "So basically, you're playing God."

Lynn says, "Like I tell my classes all the time, the author is God of their fictional world."

Nay uncrosses her legs and feints as if ready to hurry to the stage. "What that heifer say just now?"

Lynn's swivels with wide eyes. "Who me?"

"You done bumped your head or what... talkin' 'bout you God."

"It's an expression," counters Lynn. "If you're talking about who creates the characters and decides their fate. The author is God of their fictional world, Nay. Not the material universe."

Bianca is all protective grins as she steps down off the stage bringing calm. "That's not how she meant it, Nay."

Nay's blond cropped head shakes. "Don't matter what she *meant.* Talkin' bout the author is *God?* No creature should put those three words in that order, not even for play-play. That's blasphemy!"

Lynn becomes agitated, insisting, "I'm telling you; it is *just* an *expression.* Get over it!"

Nay's head jerks up at Lynn's forceful tone. Nay asks, universally, "Who she think she talking to?"

Lynn is fearless. "I'm talking to *you.*"

Bianca impedes Nay, vigorously. Nay can't get around her. Nay's hand makes a finger a pistol, pointing up over Bianca and down at Lynn who realizes just how large and solid Nay's arm is. "You good, talking that mess from yonder. You walk up in my face; bet you'll limp back." Nay is nearly two Biancas. She could easily toss Bianca aside, but Nay let Bianca coax her out into the hallway, Nay, yelling back, "I'll run that heifer up outta this church, talking crazy like that!"

Soon after, Pastor Levi walks through the banquet on his way to get Nay together.

Pastor Stewart comes in to have a word with Lynn, but Lynn is smiling. "I'm ok. It was nothing." They have a brief conversation, Stewart kisses Lynn's forehead and leaves. Nay doesn't return to rehearsals. Soon everything is back to normal and Ashton is her playful self again, pretending to come to terms with her character's fate, "So, that's it. I *die*." She glares at the responsible party. "Huh, auntie?"

Lynn turns coy, unsure if the young lady is kidding as she always does. "Death is literature's greatest teacher. Your character's death is far more useful than her life."

Ashton, pretends to cry on Lynn's shoulder. Lynn rolls her eyes and says, "D'mitri put you up to this didn't he?" Remorsefully, Lynn hugs Ashton and says, "How could I bring death on a face like this? I'll change the script."

If only Nay were still there to see Lynn answer Ashton's prayer, granting fictional life, it would've cleared the controversy.

Chapter 12

Levi follows the music down the hallway. The singer's voice is unmistakable, but maybe *Levi* is mistaken to think that this young, beautiful woman was shining for him. The other day, after the altercation between Nay and Lynn, Bianca seemed to admire the way Levi brought calm to the situation. Levi feels like he's not much to look at, but he also feels like a man's leadership and anointing makes him desirable to a woman who desperately needs a man at the head of her life. So after calming Nay down after rehearsals, and he found Bianca's glare cutting through a crowded room and targeting him, he believed it. Their twenty year age difference and Levi's marital status makes him unbelieve it. He's ninety percent sure that Bianca's shining was accidental; it's that ten percent possibility pulling Levi to come see about her.

Levi stops in the doorway and listens. She is alone, sitting at the piano, playing, singing, stopping after many false starts, and then straining the song through varying chords, feeling around for some undiscovered melodic pulse.

Levi clears his throat.

When Bianca turns, her hair arcs out like a curtain to a breeze. "Pastor Levi." Her smile shines. "Spying on me?"

"If that's what you wanna call it." He comes forward, his hands massaging each other. He has to concentrate to not lick his lips. Levi asks, "Can we talk for a minute?"

Bianca's hands pounce the piano keys and she sings, better than Tevin himself. *Can we talk… for a minute… Girl I want… to know… your name…* Bianca swats the air and laughs. "Couldn't help it, pastor; that's my song. Won a middle school talent show with it."

Levi's head drops and hangs. "You was in *middle* school when that song came out?" It played at Levi's wedding reception.

Bianca looks away, rolling her eyes. "Anyway, pastor. What's on your mind?"

"Well… Trying to gather some facts on that dust up between Nay and Lynn."

Bianca sighs. "I don't know, pastor. I think it's safe for me to keep Nay's name out of my mouth. We just became friends again after what happened at Stew's surprise party."

Levi replies, "I don't give up my sources."

Bianca leans to the side, looking past Levi. She waves at a passerby. "Hey sis… Fine and you…? Alright now…"

Bianca turns her attention back to Levi. "Sorry, about that," she says, then squints. "Actually, can we talk somewhere more private? Too many eyes up in here."

Levi shrugs. "Cool. Where 'bout?"

"Now, you know I don't like people up in my business. *My* safe space is my home."

Levi hooks a finger in his collar. "Your home?"

Bianca's head shakes in all seriousness. "Don't do that, Pastor Levi. Don't do that." She gets up from the piano bench and pats his shoulder. "I'll call you." Bianca leaves him leaning against the piano as if it's the only thing holding him upright.

Bianca hurries home. She cancels all her plans so she can have the day to prepare.

Later, when Levi gets the call from Bianca, she doesn't give him room to object. She gives her address, and hangs up.

It's all happening too fast for Levi. Before you know it, he's sitting in his car parked at Bianca's apartment complex arguing with himself. He consults the angel on one shoulder. *Don't do this Levi.* The devil on the other shoulder counters, *What Bianca's got for you, it's for you!* His angel warns, *Remember all the drama she caused Stewart?* The devil urges, *But that young thang finer than a mug though ain't it?* Levi feels like a terrorist, his hand on the door handle like a detonator. Once he gets out, there's no turning back.

A knock at the driver's side window nearly ejects his ghost. It's Bianca, her palms flipped at a startled Levi, his eyes bugged in fright. Levi gets out of the car, holding his heart.

Bianca chides, "Sittin' up here talking to y'self. Come on in this house."

Bianca ushers him up to her apartment. Suddenly Levi can't help feeling like he's walking in the footsteps of his father, leaving a whole wife at home, and visiting a young, single woman in secret.

Just as Levi is ready to change his mind and turn around, he's hit with the aroma of downhome cooking, coming from Bianca's kitchen. Levi asks, "You entertaining guests today or something?"

Bianca's head floats east and west. "I'll get you a plate." While she's in the kitchen taking up his fried chicken, collards, potato salad, Bianca throws her voice as she reminisces to a time when she was a little girl and the pastor would visit her family, during times of hardship. "Ma would have the house spic and spanned and all of us dressed in our Sunday best, simply because the pastor, the man of God, was stopping by for a few minutes. That's old school, ain't it pastor?"

Mmhm, Levi says, his mouth watering as the meal is being spooned for him.

Bianca comes around with his plate and sits it on the coffee table in front of him, along with a tall glass of iced tea. "Daddy would get so jealous," Bianca continues. "Because momma never really catered to him like that. He'd say, 'The pastor is a man just like me.' Momma would say, 'How many souls have *you* saved lately?'"

Bianca sits up in the couch, her arms folded tight under her breasts, her legs together, lying along the couch like a mermaid. She pinches her skirt downward and watches the pastor while he eats.

Levi keeps the compliments flowing as he enjoys food that violates his diet; food from which his palate has been deprived.

Starting from the beginning, Bianca starts explaining the altercation between Nay and Lynn, which she believes was a carryover from a prior argument Lynn had with Kevin.

"So, Lynn been picking fights with everybody, huh?"

"I wouldn't say that. *Kevin* is the one who gets into it with everyone."

"So, what made Lynn fly up at Nay?"

Bianca squints and asks, "If I'm not mistaken, it sounds like you're trying characterize Lynn as a problem."

"I wouldn't say all that."

Bianca's eyes widen as she's hit with an epiphany. "You don't want her as the keynote speaker for Women's Day, do you? Is it because she's an activist?"

"I actually have no problem with Lynn being the keynote speaker, as long as she ain't going around calling herself God."

Bianca purses her lips at the ridiculous claim. "I remember when Nay told you that," says Bianca. "I didn't want to say anything in front of Nay, especially since you were already there, trying to calm her down, but in all honesty, Pastor Levi, those words never left Lynn's mouth. She said authors – meaning every author who has ever put pen to paper – is like a little God over the fictional world they create."

Levi points. "See, that's why I came to you. Nay lies. She lies for no reason." Levi's head shakes.

Bianca says, "Pastor Levi… Forgive me, but has it dawned on you that if you *were* to stop Lynn from speaking on Women's Day, it would put you and Pastor Stewart on bad terms?"

"With me, I don't operate in those realms, when ya talkin' about good and bad terms. I'm on terms with the word, so if anybody split paths with the word, they split paths with me."

"*There* you go, pastor." Bianca performs an overhand toss of an imaginary ball.

"In fact, lemme tell you what Pastor Stupid's been up to–"

"–Hold up!" Bianca blurts out in laughter, "Pastor *Stupid*, you say? That's what you call him?" Bianca covers her mouth and chuckles. "Guess y'all not in a good place right now, anyway."

"Right," Levi agrees. "Anyhow… you know, on Women's Day, how the keynote speaker – the woman – delivers their speech from a lectern, right?"

"Uh huh…"

"Stewart is pressuring the board to get rid of the lectern and have his lil' skirt preach from the actual pulpit."

"Nuh, uh…"

Levi says, "Doesn't first Timothy say to not permit a woman to teach or to exercise authority over men? That's why you have a lectern; it is a platform of no authority. It's merely a speech, an exhortation. But when you place a woman behind the *pulpit*, it asserts that she's giving a sermon from God and has authority over men. It ain't my word. It's God's word. And I'm not about to go against it."

"Amen," Bianca cheers, with Sabbath day enthusiasm. She then inquires, "So, what did the board have to say."

Levi swallows a mouthful and says, "Now, I wasn't there to see it for myself, but they say Catfish bout cursed him out. Told Stewart they fixin' to make *him* preach from a lectern."

Bianca covers her laughing mouth. "Oooh, no!"

"Catfish with that sharp tongue… He killed that *real* quick."

"Pastor Stewart – I mean Pastor *Stupid*, sho got some nerve. By Women's Day he won't even *be* the pastor anyway so…" Bianca covers her mouth.

Levi cuts an eye at her. "Only leadership is supposed to know that. Who told you?"

"Pastor Stupid put so much pressure on D'mitri to make this play a success… and for that very reason, D'mitri sorta vented to me about it one day." Bianca licks her lips and says, "Question: So… when this play fails and Stewart is out the way, *you* gone be the pastor, ain't it?"

Levi nods proudly. "Yes I am. Truth be told, it should've been me all along. Pastor Stupid ain't nothing but a glorified fund raiser. As far as biblical scholarship, he ain't on level with me – and he *can't* out-preach me," Levi exclaims with a wide-eyed finish, but then he starts up again, as if catching a preaching spell. "It's in my blood, *ha!* It's in my lineage," Levi growls.

"I ain't new to this! I'm true to this. I've been groomed for this, *hah!* Since the uterus!"

Bianca spazzes with a praise-break shuffle.

Levi eggs her on for laughs, but they soon quit the game, returning to their seats and coming down off the laughter with sighs. As quick as Bianca sits down she gets back up. "Why don't I get that plate out of your way." She uses Levi's napkin to scrape scraps off the edge and onto the plate. "On a more serious note, Pastor Levi," Bianca says. "You know what they say: Heavy is the head that wears the crown. But a heavy head needs a soft pillow." Bending over the table gives Levi a closeup of her cleavage, so pillow takes on a new meaning. "What I mean by that, Pastor Levi, is that you must be sure to keep counsel with folks who *truly* love you." Bianca then turns and walks away.

Levi had noticed a flicker in Bianca that's so fleeting, so noncommittal, that he could only grasp at it. Like trying to catch steam in his fist, it's gone quicker than he's able to study it, but was undeniably there, Levi thinks, as he watches Bianca switching her hips on into the kitchen.

He's left alone, staring at the space where she had been, trying to place his desire. It less to do with her youth or beauty. What Levi feels – stronger than his desire *for* Bianca, is that *through* Bianca, he's reliving his childhood. His own guardedness reminds him so much of his father and Bianca's reverence reminds Levi of his mother. Dwelling in Bianca's apartment feels like a family gathering. The third person that would've been dwelling in the apartment would be himself, as a child. Levi almost projects himself on the other side of the wall listening in on his mother having company with the man who had really soft hands.

These are Levi's thoughts, as he stares at the opening to the kitchen until Bianca's legs, in sheer stockings, returns to view, walking toward him to set down a bowl of desert and a tin cup of toothpicks.

At the sight of banana pudding, Levi lights up like Christmas. "Girl you ain't nothin' but the truth."

Levi takes a mouthful of banana pudding, then licks the back of the spoon. "This is *so* good, Bianca."

Bianca eyes him with mischief. "Mm-hm… You like being catered to, don't you? You're a good man, Levi. You deserve it."

There it is, Levi thinks: that shining, that nonverbal invitation; her targeted glances, the body language like she's modeling for him and how even her words are spoken ever so succulently. But so quickly she switches back to normal that it makes Levi wonder if he'd imagined it.

Levi figures his loyalty to his wife Nay is about to be tested. He feels trapped like an animal, having let down his guard with an entrapment as abundant as food. This is the woman who said she could unhinge her jaw like a snake, yet he agreed to meet her in secret and enjoy her food while she sits across from him with her arms folded under her dew-kissed breasts.

After conversing with Bianca a few minutes more, Levi gets up to leave, thanking Bianca for clearing up what happened between Nay and Lynn at rehearsals.

"So soon?"

Levi rubs the back of his neck. "Before there's any misunderstanding, let me just say, Bianca, that this isn't right."

Bianca pouts, "Pastor *Levi*…"

"I'm a married man," he says, even as he looks at her with longing. "We shouldn't be meeting like this."

"This is innocent, pastor. And I'm offended by what you're trying to imply."

"Regardless." Levi taps the bevel of his watch. "I don't want to have my time so badly unaccounted for, that it urges me to lie."

"Here." Bianca reaches over the side of the couch, picks up a gift bag and hands it to him. "Take this."

Levi frowns in confusion. "What in the world? What is this?"

"It's a gift for Nay. If she has any questions about where you were, tell her you were out getting her this gift."

Levi reaches a hand into the packing tissue but stops to look at Bianca in disbelief. "If you did this, in advance, to buy us time together…. What were you really planning?"

Swerving with sass, Bianca says, "To tell you, Pastor Levi, that while you're sitting up here worried about meeting *me* in secret, Nay has been meeting Stewart in secret."

The news kicks Levi in the chest. He drops on the couch. "I'll kill 'em!"

Levi listens as Bianca tells him about the night Pastor Stewart showed up at her door unannounced, saying he felt responsible for her rage, and Stewart thought the only solution was to finally give her the reason he ended their relationship.

Levi listens, following along with a mm-hmm and uh-huh, his anger building.

Bianca continues, "No one knew that me and Stewart were together in the first place. Nay, just by being my friend, she knew by the way I was acting that I was seeing *someone*. She *suspected* that it was Pastor Stewart, but she didn't know. You should see how Nay kept badgering about Stewart… I had tell her something, so finally, I told her about this *other* guy I was entertaining, which me and him wasn't even dating, all like that. He was a very persistent man so, for his efforts, I let him take me out twice. But my thing is, why is Nay so concerned about Pastor Stewart? Ain't she married to you? Here it is, she badgering me about Stewart as if she was trying to catch him cheating on *her*."

Levi grabs his head and shakes, as if given a terminal diagnosis. He needs time to process the information. "I gotta get outta here, Bianca." Levi stands and starts backing towards the doorway.

Bianca gets up and comes forward, picking up the giftbag that Levi had forgotten. "It is unbecoming for a first lady to be out here behaving like some single man's groupie. A first lady should be a mark of excellence…"

Levi keeps shuffling back, nodding through Bianca's soliloquy until Levi's back hits the door; he's cornered.

Bianca adds, "A first lady should never be the loudest person in the room, nor is she *ever* to sit with her legs uncrossed. Why: the first lady is the flock's glimpse into the pastor's house. Forgive my saying, but Nay gives the impression, Pastor Levi, that your house is *not* in order." Bianca shoves the gift bag into Levi's gut and says, "Go home to your wife, Pastor Levi."

Heading to his car, Levi, now outside, struggles to wrap his head around what transpired inside. He thinks back to when he called Stewart a fool for being confused by something as simple as a woman. Now Levi is more confused by Bianca than Stewart was with Lynn. Standing inside of his open car door, Levi stops to gaze at the apartment he'd just left. While lowering into his seat, Levi mumbles, *Crazy ass.*

Levi is deeply troubled by his wife's investment in Stewart's affairs. Levi thinks perhaps he wouldn't be so suspicious if Stewart and Nay hadn't dated in the past.

When Levi joined the military as a way to escape the burden of becoming the head pastor, he couldn't bring Nay overseas to live with him because Nay was too young to marry. In fact, Nay was too young for legal consent, so Levi couldn't reveal their relationship to anyone, much less the military. When he deployed and was chaplain for desert-worn soldiers protecting American oil rigs used in the grand theft Middle Eastern oil, Nay's perfumed letters gave Levi life. Some years later, when he returned to Columbia, SC, stationed at the nearby Ft. Jackson base, Levi returned to First Baptist Church to take his rightful place at the pulpit. Stewart, although he was an interim pastor, had become the first non-Ginyard pastor in the church's eighty year history. Stewart's darling Fiona had already passed away and the young woman at Stewart's side was none other than Nay.

Just recently, Catfish and Levi came to blows because Catfish rehashed an old rumor that Levi and Stewart made a bargain: the pulpit in exchange for Nay. Those on the outside looking in, saw how quickly Nay seemed to change hands from Stewart to Levi, and how Levi, all of a sudden, refused the pulpit, so a bargain between the two pastors didn't seem so farfetched at all.

True or false, remaining loyal to a deal, sounds like a better reason than Levi running from the responsibility of being at the head of the flock.

Levi had driven the long route from Bianca's apartment to his home. He needed the time to sort things out in his mind. He's in his driveway taking a few deep breaths before going in.

When Nay enters the den, she stops in her tracks, but her focus is on the gift bag. Nay smiles and points. "Aw, honey, is that for me?"

Levi smirks and nods.

She approaches him for the bag, saying "Thank you baby." But Nay doesn't realize, until within arm's reach, that Levi isn't himself – that the evil, diabolical version of him is risen to the surface. Knowing that ducking or blocking him, would only stoke more abuse, Nay just stands there and waits on it, her eyes glassy with tears. Levi slaps her with the back of his hand, and Nay crumbles at his feet.

Chapter 13

Lynn staggers at the thought of being relegated one stair-step below man. Before she goes off on Stewart, she tries to clarify, "So you're telling me they set up this little box to the left of the pulpit for me to speak from?"

Stewart huffs, "It ain't no box, Lynn. It's a five by seven platform. It has a decorative guard rail going around it."

Lynn cuts her eye at Stewart. "And here, I thought your church was progressive." Lynn had failed to make the distinction because First Baptist looks no different than many churches along the Bible Belt that *do* allow women in ministry: an all-male clergy anyway, and majority female congregation. The difference is the choice – that women *can* join the roster of ministers if they want to, versus First Baptist's *can't* even if they wanted to. Lynn looks across the white clothed table, staring down the shepherd of such injustice. They are at a posh uptown restaurant; Stewart's idea to butter Lynn up before dropping the bombshell.

"I met with the trustees, suggesting they ban the use of the lectern, but it didn't go over so well." Stewart gathers his hands on the table and sighs. "I did a lot to change the culture of First Baptist. Before I became pastor, women had to have their hair covered during worship. The lectern is just one of those issues they won't budge on."

Lynn, with her fork sawing across a lamb chop, pauses to say, "The issue isn't the lectern, it's gender. It's the reinforcing ideas of inequality. It's the men hoarding power, which ultimately leads to abuse. Starting at the administration level, trickling down into the congregation, infiltrating marriages… not to mention that it's just plain insulting."

"I *figured* you wouldn't want to do it," says Stewart. "Although, we've had some powerful women speak at that lectern, including names like Judy Gadson, Cynthia Harding, Judge Hatchett… They're all about the empowerment of women…"

Lynn takes over. "Being made to stand in a place of lesser, I'm sure they made you witness greater – just like I'm about to do."

Stewart lights up with surprise. "Oh really?"

"I'm preaching from Exodus. And I'm about to set that little lectern on fire. By the time I fold that bible closed it will be apparent that *no* man can hold a light to me."

Stewart smirks with a side-eye. "*No* man?"

Lynn pulls her fork from between her lips, savoring the flavor. She puts up a number one, letting Stewart know that she's getting around to a response, after she's done chewing.

"Don't worry about it," says Stewart. "I was just messing with you, anyway. I love the confidence."

Lynn swallows and then picks her teeth with her pinky nail as she says, "Not that I'm competing."

Although Lynn doesn't agree with a ban on any one race or gender, First Baptist's ban on women actually gives Lynn personal relief. Every church Lynn would settle into, she would eventually leave because of the pressure to take up the cloth, running from her call to preach.

No matter what church, big or small, and no matter how hard Lynn tries to hide, the spotlight finds her. When she was offered to be the Women's Day keynote speaker, she only said yes under the pressure of dating the pastor, but alas: the spotlight, nonetheless. People see her as a lightning rod for God's word. She sees herself as just a woman who spent years in the word to strengthen herself against her own suffering.

Aside from her ex-husband beating her with his fists, he also beat her with the word; his control, ever increasing. He eventually forbid Lynn from working. She spent her days in God's word, reading The Holy Bible from cover to cover. As Lynn grew stronger in the word and began beating her ex-husband's skewed interpretations of the word, he increased his physical attacks.

Lynn took on the abuse like her personal cross, testing God's word, growing in the word to where her spirit gained power over the flesh. As she grew more power*ful,* his abuse became power*less.* Lynn believed that God wouldn't give her a burden she can't bear. But the one time in her life where Lynn is sure she heard the voice of God is when she was lying beaten nearly unconscious on the bathroom floor, ready to face death, and God, in a soul-curdling voice, said: *All burdens are not mine.*

Regardless of how many people have told her, simply because she speaks eloquently, that she, by all appearances, is chosen of God, she knows that she is a woman who had only heard five words total from the Master.

Chapter 14

There is now a black president and first lady in the White House. His brand-new administration is met with a live recession, the worst economic downturn since the Great Depression. The moment Obama's hand lifted off the inaugural bible, the auto and banking industries threw themselves at the foot of the White House steps, begging for a bailout, and yet the fearless president maintained, *Yes we can.*

America's new mantra, *Yes we can*, is also Stewart's and D'mitri's, and everyone involved in the play, as ticket sales go live, but in the first twenty-four hours, only a dismal ninety tickets are sold. It takes three days to sell ninety more.

The board of trustees salivate at the inevitable demise of Pastor Stupid and his fancy pants ideology. The Ginyards can't help taking their shots. To Stewart's face, and with an audience of Ginyards around, Catfish gets his dig, "There was I was really convinced of what they say about this man. They say Stew got the Midas touch, but instead of everything he touch turn to gold; everything he touch turn into a building. But not that Christian Academy building." Catfish laughs. "Stewart's *Midas* touch done turned into the 'Arth*ritis* touch,' says Catfish, as he makes his hand look deformed, imitating a chicken foot, awkwardly curled into his body.

The recession became society's scapegoat for every shortcoming. Every holiday showed percentage drops in consumer spending. Christmas of 2008 is the first to suffer; Valentine's Day of 2009's showed record lows in consumer spending. With the play *Don't Pray For Love* falling on the next holiday, the day before Mother's Day, the expectation is that the trend would continue, and for the play to sell out, Stewart would need a miracle.

Outwardly, Stewart could not blame the recession where there is a sea parting, globe flooding, resurrecting God. The Christian Academy is no different than the other lofty ministries, with its design to help those who governments won't, include those that legislation carves out of its equations. All Stewart knows, is that the Christian Academy's purpose and its success would proclaim the word of God throughout the land, and for this, he believes wholeheartedly that God would bless the endeavor. But as the weeks go by, and the deficit of ticket sales grows, Stewart wonders if maybe his overconfidence angered God when he wagered a bet for the pulpit. Looking back, he thought of himself as a poor man's Noah, daring to build a multimillion-dollar structure at the height of a recession, like an ark in a desert.

Inwardly, as Mother's Day draws nearer, even Stewart's prayers seem void. At times he feels like hanging up his robe prematurely just to deny the Ginyards their opportunities to rub it in. In his private time with Lynn, he painstakingly counts down the weeks. Out of nowhere in the middle of conversation or in the quiet of each other's arms, Stewart would shake his head and announce *four weeks* to hanging up his robe; *two weeks* to his head-hanging departure, and yet Stewart hasn't contacted any other churches in need of a pastor; he has enough savings and income streams to sustain him. Stewart actually considers life as just a man, a husband and father. He even finds himself staring down into glass cases at engagement rings.

Chapter 15

Ticket sales spike just before that Mother's Day weekend. There's a digital billboard outside the arena counting down the number of seats; the dwindling availability becomes a call to action, forcing people to buy tickets ahead, for fear of being stuck on the outside of a sold-out arena, but it is still uncertain whether the play would sell out.

On the day of the event, Stewart goes back and forth into the service elevator, hauling Lynn's books on a dolly. Lynn is with him, chatting nervously and pretending to help.

On one trip going in, Stewart stops in front of the door to secure the stack of books. They stop and stand at the foot of the arena, the grit of asphalt underfoot. They look straight up the back of structure, which seemingly presses up into the belly of the sky. The moving clouds above give the illusion that the mountainous structure is slowly tipping towards them. Lynn is overwhelmed with ecstasy. For her, the turnout already makes this undertaking not only a success, but a landmark among the other successes over her lifetime. For Stewart, however, having a packed arena won't quite cut it; every seat must be sold. Stewart flexes his hands to remove the jitters. He's more nervous than he was for his first sermon, a teenager stepping up to the pulpit to impart spiritual wisdom in the presence of elders. In just hours, he'd either hand over his robe or secure the building of the Christian Academy that God showed him once in a dream. To have two thousand seven hundred walk-ins on the day of the play would take a miracle. After helping Lynn setup her vendor booth, Stewart disappears into the restroom and vomits in the sink.

The outcome goes down to the wire. It's just ten minutes before curtains when the ticket booths start turning folks away. The arena is sold out. Lynn's play, *Don't Play For Love*, is not only the first stage play to ever sell out the arena, it is the first stage play daring enough to try.

Deacon Bailey dodges his way through the crowded walkway to deliver the news. Pastor Stewart, who is with Lynn inside of her booth, loses the uses of his legs. He drops into a metal folding chair and holds his heart. Deacon Bailey reaches over the counter and grabs the hand Stewart had placed over his heart, saying, "We did it man! We did it, pastor! We gone break ground on the Christian Academy." Bailey shakes him and laughs. "*Breathe* brotha!" It takes Stewart a few minutes and more than a few deep breaths to recover.

Lynn nudges Stewart as a group of trustees and elder Ginyards, walk through the turnstiles. "A feast before thine enemies," she says through cherry red lipstick, a flower tucked in her hair. Stewart gazes at his love, withstanding a breaking wave of certainty that, looks aside, Lynn is everything that Fiona would have been.

The arena is bustling like a large convention. A line grows in front of Lynn's table with those who are willing, as Stewart predicted, to buy the outrageously priced autographed copies from her table versus the standard editions being sold by the arena staff. Pastor Stewart wanders off to go shake hands with the big wigs: Mayor Steve Benjamin, Attorney and Councilwoman Tameika Isaac Devine; CEOs like Ed Sellers of Blue Cross and Jim Apple of First Citizens Bank.

Stewart comes back by Lynn's table giggling and shaking his head, swearing that Governor Mark Sanford farted as they shook hands. Lynn can't get over the fact that these men who carried the aura of importance and influence are on first name basis with her boyfriend.

The arena walkway begins to clear. The bustling convention becomes an abandoned star ship with natural light casting structural shadows over the grey painted floors and walls. Lynn locks the register and books in her fiberglass locker while Nay's voice flows through the sound system, reciting the prologue.

Stewart guides Lynn into the dark arena, down the illuminated steps to their seats. Lynn's rotating gaze studies the party of twenty-thousand hushed men and women, the orange lit stage glowing back on every pair of glasses like flyspecks in the night. Bianca is joined on stage with this fictional world's population of twelve, carrying out their destinies in a world half the size of hardwood basketball floor that the stage is raised above. Bianca on stage, is now Fatima a waitress receiving a lewd comment from the handsome football player who also scribbles his hotel room number on his receipt. Lynn, having foreknowledge of every outcome on stage, spends more time studying the audience as her world slips over them.

Lynn grips Stewart's hand. "This has to be the happiest day of my life," she whispers, although the day doesn't feel like a day at all; it feels like a dream. Holding hands with the pastor she discovered at the barbershop arguing with a rapper, who later said he'd bring twenty thousand people at her feet, and has done it. The day Stewart's ex-girlfriend gave him a swollen lip, Lynn couldn't Lynn foresee this man becoming the love of her life. Lynn looks over at Stewart and wants him, *really* wants him, beyond her ability to express – wants him like she could pull him down between the seats and do it like dogs.

Stewart agrees. "It's the happiest day of my life too." He thinks about the jewelry box sitting in his breast pocket, and knows that he isn't out of the woods yet. This 'happiest day' could soon come crashing down.

In the dark arena, Lynn turns, chin over shoulder, to look directly at Stewart so he knows it's no mistake when she places a hand in his lap. She then looks forward, eyes fixed on the stage as she feels Stewart grow inside of her hand.

Stewart bites his lip and slowly lets it pull from under his teeth. They don't even look at each other again until prior to intermission, when Lynn gets up to return to her vendor booth to set up her register again. She scales the steps with a swagger that knows that Stewart is watching.

Her table is stormed again, her cash register already stuffed. The magnetic debit card swipe attachment on her smart phone is giving her fits. Amidst her overflow of success even the monster, stress, is reduced to a darling kitten. Everyone at the arena knows her name. She feels discovered. She feels levels higher in the social pyramid. She can't count how many phones now had selfies with her, traveling around in pockets and purses. Stewart comes by smirking, his hands joined behind his back. After being groped by Lynn, it's like he now has her chastity in hand, like a canary hidden behind his back, "How's it going?"

"Don't be casual with me," Lynn kids. "Make yourself useful." She handles the register while Stewart mans the card reader until intermission is over and they're back sitting next to each other. Lynn watches the audience more than she watches the play; they seem to be immersed in it; their disbelief suspended as shock spreads throughout the arena when the identity of Miriam's kidnapper is revealed. At the end, when Bianca fires the blank gun into the chest of Miriam's captor, the audience seems to fully believe that he man is dead – until the curtain falls and later the actors return, the shot character returns to bow in his ketchup-stained shirt.

Even D'mitri is overwhelmed by the size and energy of the standing ovation that made him delay his thank you speech, unable to get a word in for a full minute.

Coming in behind D'mitri, Stewart and Lynn go up to the stage hand in hand to say a few words. With his arm around Lynn, cupping her shoulder, Stewart leans over the mic and lets the audience know they had reached their goal and that the Christian Academy would break ground before the end of the year. He then slides out of the way as he slides Lynn in front of the microphone. After a few lines of Lynn's misty-eyed gratitude, she turns to whom much gratitude is owed, but Stewart has vanished. The audience's reaction tells her he is behind her, misbehaving, making rabbit ears, perhaps. She turns to scold

Stewart, but finds him down on one knee with a ring that sparkles like a cluster of stars plucked from the night sky.

Lynn staggers back, nearly knocking over the microphone stand. She'd just spent the last two hours, watching her play, seeing everything in advance, which doubles the impact of now being so blindsided.

Hair stands wherever there are follicles; she feels fuzzy all over. Disbelief and reality take turns crashing over her. Looking out over the audience, astounded, Lynn spots her mother in the front row, reserving excitement, no more than documenting what is happening before her eyes. Lynn feels like a contestant on a game show, too nervous to think for herself, so she goes with the audience's advice and says, "Yes." Stewart slides the ring on her finger and they kiss under the beaming spotlight. The cast surrounds them all except for Bianca. Stewart's parents appear and then Lynn's parents come out on stage to exchange hugs and kisses. Stewart had asked Lynn's parents for their daughter's hand in marriage a week earlier. Lynn could tell by the look on her mother's face, "You knew?"

Her mother replies in a whisper, "Does *he* know?"

Lynn shakes her head no, meaning no Stewart does not know, nor does she know if this engagement would hold up once she tells him.

Bianca is the lone soul out of twenty-thousand who is not happy for them. Solemnly, she goes backstage. Stewart sees Bianca's exit and his heart dives in his belly. The red velvet stage curtains rushed towards each other. Stewart and Lynn dip out of the way of the curtain and find themselves backstage, in the darkened make-believe set, so eerily false. Lynn runs her hand back through her hair, speechless behind velvet curtains.

Stewart asks, "Are you ok?"

"You're my future husband. Just like that, huh?" As if she would've preferred an open-ended question rather than be boxed into a simple yes or no.

"I've always been your future husband." He slides his hands around her waist. "Wanna get out of here?" He asks, with every intention to fornicate with his fiancé.

Lynn looks away from his naughty proposal, remembering, "I've still got books to sell." Lynn slips out of his embrace, apologetically. Stewart's head drops in acquiescence. Lynn stamps his lips with another kiss before slipping through curtains.

Stewart goes backstage or rather downstage because the production area is below the arena floor. It feels like a warehouse with its humming florescent lights, naked eggshell walls and exposed networks of beams and ductwork. Stewart navigates what feels like the hull of a giant ship, a system of tunnels labeled with pairings of numbers and letters for each corridor. From there, Stewart struggles to assess which hallway would take him to the service exit where he is parked. He pauses at the intersection of four corridors, hearing sniffling, crying, echoing possibly from any direction. Stewart turns in the direction opposite of his best guess, unwittingly running right into the person he was running away from.

Bianca glares from behind the barrel of a gun. Stewart's hands rises on instinct, as if being robbed.

Bianca says, "You don't give a damn about me do you?" Her mouth is a miserable, trembling frown. "You proposed to her right in front of my face, Stew? Really!"

"I figured you'd be ok. I thought you were over me."

"I *am* over you." Bianca tightens her grip. "That doesn't mean I'm not offended. Don't you think it's rude, what you did?"

"I'm sorry, Bianca. I wasn't thinking. And yes, it is rude, Bianca. I just don't see how you're gonna solve anything by pointing that prop gun at me?" He drops his hands.

Bianca places both hands on the gun, ensuring her aim. "I assure you this gun is real. Blanks were used in the play, but it's got live rounds now lover boy, where do you want it?" The gun drops two levels from head to chest to balls.

Stewart pleads, hands up again, flinching at Bianca's every move. "Bianca, don't do something you know you'll regret. If there is still a chance for us, I guarantee you this is not the way."

Bianca remembers how Stewart tricked her once before in another dark hallway by the fitness center. "Child please. Don't nobody want you. I just want you to hurt like you just made me hurt." Bianca closes her eyes to brace for the gun's power and she squeezes the trigger, Stewart sees a bulb of fire, the sound deafening like thunder claps around his head. Stewart sprawls back, yelling for help, and falls in a sitting position, frantically patting his body as if he were on fire, his mouth fizzling dry. He is disoriented, his ringing ears unable to make out Bianca's words as he begins fading out.

It isn't long before Lynn sells her last book in the slow emptying arena with all exits stuffed with people like sands of an hour glass drizzling through a tiny neck. The gun shot is heard out in the lobby as a loud bang echoing through the ventilation system, but with so far for the sound to travel, it lost its impact, sounding no more serious than minor accident by the staff breaking down the structures on stage.

Stewart's body is not leaking. Bianca lied; the gun still had blanks. She shakes the gun, laughing despite her tears, "You shoulda seent yo bitch-ass face!" She advances while Stewart is still down on his butt, scooting back in retreat. Bianca tries to kick him in the chest, but he catches her foot and stands with it. "*Now* what," Stewart taunts.

Bianca throws the gun with a toss so telegraphed; Stewart is able to he let go of her foot and still catch the gun against his chest, but not quick enough to block her second strike – the slap that sends his world blurring by, lights streaking as his head spins a full ninety degrees, the heavy-handed blow, stinging and clammy against his face as if he is slapped with a sizeable raw fish. Stewart nearly loses it. He sticks one, aggressive hoof in the ground to stop his backward momentum, but also to spring forward, his chest puffed out, before decency reminds him that his attacker is a woman.

Bianca flinches at his aggression, but makes up for her show of weakness by confronting him again, stomping forward and throwing her chest into his like an angry baseball umpire. "What! What," she challenges. Two of the actresses find Bianca and with little effort pulls her back. Her damage is done. It is more than Stewart's ears ringing; his body is ringing. He looks down at his hands with concern, how they flutter like tuning forks, as they cradle the gun.

Chapter 16

They chose Stewart's home. They were brave at the arena, but alone, they sit on opposite ends of the couch like cowards. Their entrance is not the entrance either had envisioned – no cyclone of kissing and groping, raking the counter. Ever since Stewart saw the blast from the gun barrel, he'd been shaking and it won't go away. He makes small talk like nothing is wrong while, internally, he is a bee swarm; he has to concentrate hard to stay in tight, bunched in the form of a man, or the swarm would scatter, pulling him apart in a thousand different directions.

Lynn wonders why Stewart is suddenly quiet and rubbing his hands so nervously, perhaps that verbal commitment to marriage is just now weighing on him, but then again, maybe… "What did my mother say to you?"

Stewart is looking down at his fists, as if he'd done something awful with them. He looks up. "Congratulations? That's about it." His answer doesn't iron out Lynn's wrinkled brow so Stewart insists. "Seriously that is it. Were you expecting something else?"

"No…" Lynn gazes emptily. "After the play… while I was out front waiting on you…"

"I can explain." Stewart jumps like he knows; thinking maybe Lynn learned about altercation with Bianca, which is why Lynn now sits far away from him like a stranger on a subway.

"Explain what?"

No, Stewart realizes that Lynn is clueless. "Hold up – I thought – you were – never mind…" He gives the floor back to Lynn.

Lynn asks, "Have you ever noticed anything strange between Levi and Nay?"

"Like what?"

"I saw something today that literally blew me away. Nay: she walked up to Levi while he was talking with some gentleman. He's tall, big gray beard–"

"–Smitty."

"Nay walked up, with something to tell or ask Levi, but he was clearly ignoring her. Does he tell Smitty to hold on a sec while he sees what's bothering his wife? No. Levi kept on talking with Smitty like his wife was nothing more than a lamp post. I'm there at my table, working, chatting with people in the lobby; I keep checking the situation and I swear to you, like, five minutes go by… Nay's still standing there, waiting. Finally, Levi acknowledged her, but when she tries to tell him whatever she needed to tell him, he wouldn't let her get it out. He kept saying, 'bye-bye, bye-bye,' dismissing his wife like a child – *worse* than a child."

Having just agreed to marry, Stewart assumes the story is somehow related to him. "I would never do you like that."

Lynn's look turns fiendish, daring him to *dream* as reckless. "Do you know why she waited that long, why she didn't walk away and come back later, or yank his freaking ear? She's paralyzed by fear – fear of being punished."

"When you say punished…"

"Does she wear sunshades often? Have any unexplained injuries or bruises. Is she chronically late for events?"

Stewart, wincing harder at each question, answers, "You've been around Nay for quite a while now, putting this play together. What have *you* seen?"

"Incidents of abuse can have months, even years in between."

"I'm sure you know the data, Lynn, but I know Levi; I know the *man*. We may have had our differences lately, but I doubt he would harm his wife. He dotes on her."

"To overcompensate for bashing her ribs probably. Abusers, after an episode become really generous and romantic. It's called the honeymoon phase. It's never over, it's just a phase in the cycle of abuse."

"Nay is the director for the domestic violence ministry, Lynn."

Lynn's head shakes as she remembers her personal experience with the domestic violence ministry she sought out to help her escape her abusive marriage. "You show me a church domestic violence ministry and I'll show you nothing more than some propped up excuse for an annual fancy hat luncheon. No battered woman seeks help from church folk and risks becoming the topic of gossip."

Stewart's arms spread in grandiose sarcasm. "Your smoking gun is Levi ignoring his wife and then dismissing her? Off of *that*, you're convinced he's dishing out body blows? *How*, with so little evidence?"

"It's not what I see on the outside; it's what I see inside of Nay. When you've been through it, you can spot it a mile away."

Stewart nods while the information sinks in. "So, you were in an abusive relationship?"

Lynn gulps, and answers with the thing that might make Stewart take back his engagement ring. "An abusive *marriage*," Lynn says.

Stewart turns heavy; his shoulders slacks; his brow lowers, as if gravity turns up the wattage right under him. He speaks, not to Lynn, but to an imaginary consultant, "Did this woman just say marriage? Knowing good and hell, well that I'm a pastor, and just *now* got the presence of mind to tell me?"

"If I had any idea you would propose..." Lynn shrinks, her question comes out small. "Do you want the ring back?"

"I need to know more about what happened."

Lynn huffs. "Our future hangs on the technicalities?"

"A divorce settled in man's courthouse doesn't mean it's settled in God's." Stewart seems heartless, still focused on the technicalities rather than his fiancé's hurt.

"He's dead. Is that settled enough for you?"

Stewart huffs and looks down and away. Death breaks the marriage bond; she is free to re-marry, in God's eyes. "Look at you," he says. "You're awfully puffed up for someone who raked me over the coals for hiding something from *you*, while all along you were hiding this from *me*?"

Stewart hadn't provided any empathy so Lynn provided her own, mocking what Stewart should have said. "I'm sorry to hear, *Lynn*, that you nearly lost your life at the hands of a man, *Lynn*. I couldn't imagine you living four years in perpetual fear every waking hour, *Lynn*." Even as Lynn watches Stewart drain of anger and fill with remorse, she holds her blood glare. Stewart reaches for her and misses. Lynn darts away like a school of fish, not wanting to be touched.

She paces as her story trembles out of her. "I was nineteen." Her past swallows her whole, she is there again, nineteen again. Bloody in her wedding gown, lying on her back, blinking in and out of consciousness. She woke with her hand stuck to her face. She pulls the hand back to see blood drying thick like ink, stringing between her fingers, under the popcorn ceiling. This marriage she thought would fix the abuse only escalated it. She wasn't carried over the threshold – she was pushed; she went sprawling and then face planting at the foot of the hotel bed, all because her groom didn't like the way she danced with her step father at the wedding reception. Somehow this experience is the worst because it happened on her wedding day, in her wedding dress, but she's had broken ribs, a punctured lung, and a pistol in her mouth. Although skeptical of Stewart's sincerity, Lynn let Stewart hold her then. Stewart spends all night apologizing and reassuring Lynn that he would've married her regardless.

Chapter 17

Small stages make big stages. Lynn is a big proponent of the theory and Stewart agrees. First Baptist's Women's Day, however, is no small stage; it is like a royal wedding at the palace, the entire countryside in attendance, dressed in ceremonial digs. Inactive church members show up. Members of other churches cheat on their home churches for First Baptist's annual event. There're enough magnificent white hats migrating into the building to be spotted from a space station, equal to the North Pole's effective albedo. The main sanctuary fills from the front pews back to the entrance. Overflow spills into the old sanctuary, outfitted with large display monitors. The only thing small about Women's Day is the apparatus from which the speech is delivered.

Lynn, the lobbyist who could wrangle a hostile lobby floor and shame heads of state, now feels nerves growing inside of her like an inflating ball, as she sits in an honorary clergy seat, awaiting her moment. She is riddled with nerves as if Jesus Himself is a celebrity judge waiting to grade her performance.

From the microphone at the lectern, Stewart gives Lynn's elaborate introduction, listing more accomplishments than even Lynn knew she had. As an icebreaker, when Stewart gives the podium over to Lynn with a kiss on the cheek, as he turns to leave, Lynn gives Stewart a hearty slap on the butt like an amped football coach. Stewart yelps and scoots, his slick church shoes slipping on the auburn carpet as he covers his buns. The congregation erupts with laughter, applauding Lynn's spunk, loving her already.

After an elaborate thanks to church leadership and the Women's Day committee and others, Lynn scans her arranged papers and recites the burning bush passage from Exodus. She looks up from the text and repeats the question Moses asks God, "Who am I that I should go unto Pharaoh, and that I should bring forth the children of Israel out of Egypt?" Again, Lynn poses the question, releasing it like a freed bird, an albatross, flying about the sanctuary, *Who – am – I…*

Lynn says, frankly, "You already know that by the end, I'll be dropping you in Moses' shoes, issuing that same question to God. I already know you reject the comparison to the great Moses, am *I* right?" Lynn raises her hand as a way of polling her audience. As expected, from the floor to the cathedral balcony. The show of mass facing palms waivers like wind rustling through fields of barley.

"Are you telling me that you don't compare to the murderer who is slow of speech and by birth, a slave?" Applause cranks slowly, stymied by this slight woman's audacity to insult Moses, but with the brilliance to pull it off by tying her audience more intimately to him.

"Moses could not, under his own authority, command Pharaoh to let go of his people and expect success. *You* cannot go confront Pharaoh under *your* own authority and expect success." Playfully Lynn says, "When I say Pharaoh, I'm not talking about Ramses. Pharaoh is but a metaphor for the great adversaries of *our* time; adversaries that hold *many* hostage; adversaries too big for you to confront under your own power: the streets that won't let our children go; an education system designed to funnel us into the prison system; generational curses that keeps families in turmoil." The fist that had pounded out each item on her podium remains tight in front of her, her eyes deep with conviction. "The reason why I'm talking about saving those around you, is because in order to invite God into your life the way you want, it can't be just about you." She picks up the bible, weighing it to show how heavy it is. "Out of everyone in this big ole book, who has God poured His authority into for their sake alone?" She then lowers her voice, like she's letting them in on a secret. "You can pray for money all day long, but if it's for the purpose of blessing your*self* and not *many?* Don't hold your breath. The contemplations of your mind and your heart must include more than just you. But your spiritual work… that has to *start* with just you." ▌

Lynn repurposed the SOS distress acronym, starting with S: Submit – not your wish list, but your *will* to the will of God. "People…" Lynn's head shakes with pity. "Let me tell you something about people… They will sit here and lie to your face… They'll give you every reason why they won't come to Christ except for the real reason. They doubt that living for Jesus would give them the same thrill that sin does." The congregation lifts like a carpet, nearly everyone stands in agreement, cheering her wisdom.

Lucky for us, God is a God of direction, not distance. Doesn't matter how long you've been set on the spiritual path, as long as you *are* on the path, Amen? You can be a crack prostitute on the streets, but the *moment* you step off of that corner to live for Christ, your slate is wiped clean – in that – very – moment!" Lynn's arm slashes each word in a Z formation. A woman with all the appearances of a former addict, the smoky complexion, the sickened frame is picked up and shaken by the Holy Ghost; a group joins hands in a circle around her. The woman's energy spread like wildfire and gets the whole left side of the church going. A slim man with hollowed out eyes, pedals in place, pinching up on his pant knees as if he is sloshing in a puddle, then takes off galloping sideways toward the front of the church.

The band gets hyper; the pianist, hit by a thousand volts, stiffens and jolts, his eyes amazed at his hands which takes on a life of their own; the drummer goes rapid fire like a turret gunner, and the Holy Ghost dominos through the sanctuary, like the world's largest flash mob. Lynn is one of the biggest culprits, her praise, in her small, railed off lectern, taking on the form of the funky chicken.

No one realizes how spent they are until it dies down and they're fanning themselves and their neighbors, shell shocked, surprised that they hadn't blown the dome clear off the building. There's heaving and crying out with surrendered hands. When Stewart takes the mic and offers salvation, thirty-six women and seventeen men come down the aisles to join the church.

After worship there is a line at the front desk, ordering DVDs of the afternoon's service. Lynn would go on to sell more DVDs than any guest speaker in First Baptists history, more than the renowned Bishop A.C. Gomes and more than Reverend Al Sharpton's Men's Day sermon.

Later, in the banquet hall, Lynn sits in front of steaming hot tea with a lozenge dissolving in the bottom of the cup, Stewart's post sermon recipe to restore a strained voice.

Stewart has to catch up to Catfish, so he kisses her forehead and promises to be right back. With this being just the morning after the successful play, this was his first chance to have a discussion with the board members. Lynn looks up from her tea, at the sound of her name. It's Bianca calling her over to join herself and Nay. Before going over to join them, Lynn takes a deep breath. She'd been worrying about how last night's onstage proposal had effected Bianca, plus Lynn and Nay hadn't been on the best of terms since their altercation at rehearsal, and yet it's Nay – to Lynn's surprise – who steps in front of Bianca and greets Lynn with a hug and air kisses. "There's my sister in Christ," Nay announces. "What an insightful and mighty word you delivered this afternoon, Lynn."

Bianca, concerning the proposal, says, quite genuinely, "I'm so happy for you, Lynn." Bianca leans in for a look at the engagement ring. "I still can't stand your fiancé, girl, but I'm certainly happy for *you*."

"Thank you, Bianca."

The length of Bianca's false lashes slow-bat under its own weight. "I've got something to show you, Lynn. You not gone believe it." Bianca digs in her purse and pulls out a newspaper clipping. It's raves from a columnists who Bianca insists is respected critic. Bianca reads the highlights. "… *Don't Pray for Love* unwraps the heart like a gift… loftier than mere genius…"

Lynn's jaw drops. "Lemme see that?" Lynn snatches the clipping and scans it. One comment in particular catches Lynn's eye: *The adaptation of a brilliant novel Don't Pray For Love, by Lynn Cummings, may be D'mitri Dalton's ticket to finally avoiding a snub at the Homer Awards.*

Lynn asks, "Homer Awards?"

"It's the Oscars for theatre, basically."

Nay injects, "They name it after a cartoon character?"

"Not Homer *Simpson*, Nay," Bianca balks. "Homer, the epic poet: The Odyssey… The Iliad?"

Nay gasps, "Homer, Oscar, Tony… you let me know when they come up with a La 'Quisha award, then maybe I'll care something 'bout it." Nay rolls her eyes and turns away from the conversation, as she spots Levi in the distance, wandering into the kitchen. "Time I turn around," Nay says quietly as she leaves to try to catch Levi in the act.

Lynn leaves Bianca midsentence to catch up to Nay. Since their altercation, Lynn and Nay have walked a fine line; a line that Lynn now crosses as she catches up to Nay and loops her arm to hold her back. "Nay, do you *ever* give that man a break?"

"He don't give me no breaks so I don't give him none."

"When you say he don't give you no breaks, what do you mean? I don't see him calling *you* out in public? Or maybe it happens in private?"

Nay stops, knuckles on her hips studying Lynn like a misbehaving child. "Girl, who is you to be concerned about my marriage when all you got is a ring and a promise," Nay laughs.

Lynn also laughs but persists, "What I'm asking is: does he go off on *you?* And that's why you go off on *him?* Why so truculent?"

Lynn draws back with Lynn fixed her gaze. "Honey, I don't know what truculent means, but if it's good, I'm that," Nay says, as she goes switching after Levi.

Lynn watches as Nay continues onward toward the kitchen.

Being that Nay is a bully among women, she is the last person Lynn would would've suspected as a sufferer of domestic abuse.

Stewart comes up from behind, slips his arms around Lynn and whispers in her ear. "Just had a little meeting with the board." Even now he struggles to contain his laughter.

Lynn, coming out of deep thought, cuts a playful eye at him. "What'd they have to say?"

"They spent less time talking about me and more time talking about your sermon," Stewart giggles. "They got a preview of what their future first lady and it got 'em shook."

Lynn just smiles. She and Stewart go to the pastor's table where they have their meals and entertain everyone who approaches the table to visit the pastor and future first lady. Lynn finds herself getting irritated because no one seems to care about Stewart spending time, uninterrupted, with his new fiancé – Stewart included. It's as if any woman who feels like cutting in to have facetime with the pastor has a greenlight to do so, but Lynn doesn't say anything. With a lifetime ahead of them, she has plenty of time yet to complain, but with her anxiety mounting, she leaves Stewart's side without even announcing her departure. She heads for the ladies room.

The moment she's away from the situation she begins to reason; he's a pastor. Sharing him with the flock is a part of the assignment, but to have the meekness to sit there and take it with a smile is something Lynn makes a mental note to later ask for in prayer. Lynn touches up her makeup in the mirror before leaving the ladies' room. The moment Lynn exits, she's startled by Levi waiting by the door with his back to the wall.

Lynn says, "If you're waiting on Nay to come out, there's no one in there."

Levi rubs his chin. "Who says I was waiting on Nay?" With that comment, a darkness falls over their interaction.

"Where is she," asks Lynn.

Levi comes off of the wall and towers over her. "You sure got a lot of questions. Curiosity killed the cat."

"I don't see no cats around here."

Levi's jaw grinds. "Stay outta married folk business, ya here?"

"Keep your hands off of her and I won't make it my business."

Levi grins. "It's a dangerous world out there. Better worry about your *own* safety."

Lynn looks him up and down, observing this act of intimidation, the threatening nature of his posture, and the gloom in his brow; his mask is off. "You don't scare me, Levi."

Levi lunges! Lynn's hands fly up to block, but there is no attack. It was only a jab-step and feint. Levi walks off with wheezy laughter, looking back over his shoulder at a Lynn who stands there trembling. Her eyes are teary, but she is defiant nonetheless.

Lynn returns to the ladies' room and stands in front the mirror. She grips the sides of the sink and bears down on it as she breathes deeply, as tears run down her cheeks. She looks up at her reflection and sees her younger self. The incident has taken her back to a time when the fear of a lover's fist was as ever-present as the air around her. Lynn closes her eyes and tries to hold it together. Still gripping the sink, she takes another long, deep breath in an attempt to harness her courage. Quietly, and with few words, she mumbles a prayer of protection and discernment. Lynn opens her eyes again and sees her true self, the woman who God has already brought through everything man can of dish out.

Chapter 18

Lynn is running. No treadmill. School is out, so she has time to enjoy the run along the River Front Park trail. On her return trip back over the antique train trestle that had been made into a landmark walking bridge, she checks her pulse, two fingers on her throat as she slows to a brisk walk for the quarter mile cool-down from the park to her city condo. A nondescript sedan idles in the parking lot, a man sitting inside with the car door open, the sun's glare on the windshield blinding his face. Lynn stops to stretch, pretending not to notice him. He gets up and stands behind the open car door, his face pointed at Lynn like a hunting dog spotting a rabbit. He is too far away for his facial features to come into focus, but Lynn observes that he is broad shouldered and coffee black. He calls Lynn as he approaches, skip-walking and showing his badge. "I'm Claude Davis, Federal Bureau of Investigations." He appears to be late thirties, early forties, but with deep creases in his face that makes him look noble beyond his years.

Lynn is still catching her breath. She lowers, hands on knees.

The man says, "Congratulations on the success of your play."

"And I can assure you, I have every intention of reporting the income on my taxes."

His head bobbles, drowning in exasperation, "Well, that's very patriotic of you Ms. Cummings, but that's not what this is about. I'm more interested in your business partner. Shall we?" He motions toward his car.

Lynn wouldn't take one step toward his car as if it is an animal cage. She is already spooked from being approached by an agent and to find out that she's somehow tied to an investigation of D'mitri, who had already spent some time in jail for tax issues. She leads the man upstairs to her condo. He declines her refreshment offer. She pops the cap on a spring water bottle and takes a seat on the couch. She starts talking as soon as she lowers the bottle. "I'm not too clear on D'mitri's financials. I know there is some sort of profit share agreement between he and Dana, but I couldn't tell you any specifics. Heck, they haven't cut *my* check yet."

"You were selling books, right?"

Lynn's head motions safely in a circle committing to neither no nor yes. "The autographed copies were paid for by cash and by a card reader linked to a PayPal account — *those* proceeds go directly to me. The ones sold by the arena gets paid to the church and then the church cuts me a check." Lynn throws back another swig of the bottled water and she hears the detective say, *Impressive.* Lynn lowers the bottle and wraps her arms over her exposed midsection. "Thank you," Lynn says, guardedly.

"I meant the ring," her engagement ring sitting on the table.

"Oh, the ring," relief and embarrassment blends inside of Lynn.

"Don't get me wrong, that is not to say that you *aren't* impressive." The detective says, as he resettles in his seat. "Looking at you, I can't help being jealous of the pastor; he's a very lucky man, investigation aside."

"Wait a minute." Lynn tilts her ear toward her house guest. "This investigation… This isn't about D'mitri?"

Detective Claude's face tremors no. He watches Lynn swat her mouth with a hand. The detective leans forward and looks up as if Lynn's distress is a fly ball he is attempting to catch. "Please, Miss Cummings. It's really not that bad. May I call you Lynn?" She just stares bewildered. Claude continues, "Trust me, Lynn, even *if* there's any wrong doing on your fiancé's part, if he cooperates, we're giving full immunity. That's the deal we're offering to every pastor who got caught up in this ring."

Lynn feels dizzy like she'd been spun around and set back down on her couch. *Her* fiancé, the born-again virgin, the man whose eyes shine with boyish zeal, as it turns out, is a part of some criminal ring, or at least has his hands dipped in things warranting investigation. The verbal agreement made over a ring slipped onto her finger may as well have been a fruit loop. "Can you please just tell me what's happening?"

Long before that spring day at the barbershop, First Baptist held a three-day financial seminar facilitated by a proposed hundred-million-dollar hedge fund manager and financial guru. Victor Dante Westermann who is on a supposed financial crusade, targeting southern, and mostly, black churches on a mission to, "empower God's people through financial stewardship." Westermann's crusade had been two years ongoing, his reputation far preceding him when Levi, on his annual revival assignment, saw the poster sized checks with his own eyes, and returned from Tuscaloosa, Alabama, insisting that First Baptist invite Westermann to host the weekend seminar there.

According to Detective Claude, when the market dropped due to the recession, the Security Exchange Commission started receiving hundreds of complaints about a hedge fund, MAC Investment Group, not registered with the SEC. The investigation verified that MAC Investment Group is no more than an elaborate Ponzi scheme and they have yet to track down the architect. The investigation into the churches, Detective Claude assures, is just their way of following the bread crumbs, and that church leaders would only come under fire if clear evidence showed they were privy to the fraud. The detective is surprised that the uncovering of this Ponzi scheme isn't already all over the news.

The detective asks Lynn to call her if she notices anything suspicious and leaves her with his card.

Lynn doesn't know what think or to do next. She looks at the engagement ring on her finger. Stewart, in all likelihood, is innocent; the detective even said so. Lynn picks up her cell phone and makes a call to her future husband.

That morning, while Winnie, the church secretary, dug for her keys, her face tossed upward, puzzled. The door's glass yields no reflection. There is no glass. Diamond sized shards glitter the floor inside. Quietly, Winnie backs away, fear blasting inside of her like a gong.

After getting the frantic call, Pastor Stewart steps on the gas pedal, speeding, his tie half noosed. He slides his Camry into the parking lot, long-steps to his secretary and grips her shoulders, a flash gesture of comfort, before hurrying to the door with Winnie following as she tells the harrowing story. Stewart snakes his arm in through the door's empty pane; the light switch does nothing. "They cut the power somehow. That's why the alarm didn't trigger." He goes further in and calls out, "They got the hard drives." He comes out and freezes suddenly, a new nightmare springing up around him, "The bank!" The church's credit union is only a hundred feet down the walkway.

"Bank's fine," Winnie replies. "I checked already."

Stewart mopes in a circle, fists on his hips, his suit peeled open. "*Why!*" He explodes. Why on this day or why this church, why him.

"Why?" Winnie's question mocks his. "Something like this must not come as a shock to you, pastor. If you're in the will of God, you're in the way of Satan. That old deceiver has hardened some hearts against you. Some want to believe you're a crook." The word crook shoots up Stewart's spine, but his face refuses all emotion like a nobleman at a duel, slapped with a leather glove.

Winnie is more upset than he is. "Pray I don't find out who did this. I'll strangle 'em myself!" She goes off, her eyes going cattle wild. Stewart tries to interject, but she rants over him. "For eighty-five years, this church was the size of a corner store, and in fifteen years, you turned it into this-this mountain." Stewart shakes his head in disagreement.

His secretary, a quarter century his senior, is shocked by his naivety. "And you're standing there shaking your head with the door glass busted out and police on the way?"

Stewart would have explained that he disagrees with her anger, not her views, but his compass dial stops on that one word. "Police. You called the police?"

Her mouth utters *yes*, unsure of what it confirms.

Stewart's hand runs back over his head. "You know where we are, and who the sheriff is." A Klan outpost is rumored to be just miles past the county's furthest traffic light. The Sheriff is believed to be head of that outpost and his officers supposedly make up half their membership. Crimes in this area's black neighborhoods go unreported not because of a social code against snitching, but since, often the citizen reporting the crime is the one interrogated and coerced into guilty pleas for the crime they report.

"Oh, quit it, pastor," Winnie dismissed. "It is 2009–"

"What will we tell them?" He quizzes. Stewart folds his arms, a hand climbing out of the fold to pinch his chin. "What do you supposed this break in is all about?"

"Information. They took the hard drives. I guess it has something to do with the investment thing, I suppose," Winnie says with a shoulder hop.

Stewart positions himself directly in front of her. "Don't suppose anything. Not to *this* police force. We haven't talked to the robbers to know their motives, and we don't guess either. We can't give them probable cause to point the finger at us."

Two policemen arrive. The flat-faced, lazy eyed officer carrying a kit, slides on latex gloves. The muscular officer with a hunter's glare comes in furious, red faced, barking at the staff who had wandered into the office to look around. "Everybody out! Out, out, out! Right now! This is a crime scene boys and girls!" They can't leave fast enough to satisfy the man. He runs in, barking; employees run out, slipping on glass. "What do you think this is, a fish fry? This building belongs to the county until our work is done!"

Winnie, pantomimes her apologies to Stewart while being hustled out.

The gloved officer with the flat face dusts for prints while the freckled hulk with the hunter's glare conducts the interviews, recording on clipboard, his pen whipping like a seismograph needle as he asks questions concerning Stewart's time of arrival, if he witnessed anyone driving away, or any suspicious persons days leading up to this break-in. The less answers Stewart provides, the more cynical the officer's questions turns. "Suppose why they didn't touch the petty cash safe, but took the hard drives?"

Stewart replies, "I don't suppose anything sir."

The officer turns more cynical. "Banging somebody's wife? Child porn on your hard drive?"

"Child what! This is a Baptist church, not Catholic."

The staff waits outside until the police has swabbed for prints and collected their evidence. As soon as the police is gone, the lights flicker back on. Power is restored and next, Stewart looks to restore normalcy to the atmosphere. His exuberant smile reappears, displaying like a dental prop.

He leans in on a staff huddle where they are pressuring Levi, his second in command, to close the office and send them home for the day. Stewart slips them an idiom, "The day you leave your hardhat is the day Satan drops the anvil." He leaves them, confident that he had given them God's game plan for victory, but what they received is the queue to get back to work, no recovery time from the shakeup.

With no computers, everything must be handwritten. Efficiency rolls back twenty years. Within the hour pens stop writing, notepads thin down to the cardboard backing or so it seems. Stewart takes no excuses. He makes a display of breaking a pencil and handing an end to each plaintiff. "Losers find excuses. Winners find ways."

"Tell me who finds pencil sharpeners, then," the employee with the back end of the pencil asks.

Stewart calls on everyone to cover the phones while the secretary runs to the office supply store. Stewart's schedule is on a stolen hard drive so his appointments are like surprise parties in reverse.

Stewart has lunch delivered to keep everyone on site, huddled together in the midst of crisis. He thanks the staff for their resilience, before closing himself in his office. He'd forgotten to check and see if something else was taken.

His journal isn't in his bottom drawer, so he pulls all drawers like table hockey handles. His journal is gone. He swings out from behind the desk, ready to storm out front, questions loaded, but he notices that the hand reaching for the door knob, and his other hand, flutter like they did after Bianca's fake gun shot in the basement of the arena. He focuses on breathing, playing his lungs like an instrument, expanding and collapsing. He can't go out front and be seen in his present state, so he searches the office again for his journal.

Out front, the staff hears crashing sounds, their wowed eyes swim left in the direction of Stewart's office.

Outside, the parking lot attendants are blindsided by the distress call on their hips, bursting through radio static, although they're dressed like security. They dash down the hallway. Stewart's office spits out Deacon Bailey who hit the opposite wall and points back into the room that spat him out. "Pastor done lost it!"

The patrol looks in. One guard, stout and hairy, the other, tall and slender. The staff barricades behind them at the door. The stout one eases toward the center of the room, assessing the damage. Nothing stands on its feet. The tall metal file cabinet lay on its side. The couch leans up against the wall, tall as a man. The debris field shows that Stewart is pumping adrenaline. Stewart straddles his lopped over oak desk like a child on a rocking horse, his eyes as wild as cornered vermin. "Somebody stole my journal!" Stewart holds an unsheathed drawer in one hand.

"That's so, pastor?" The stout one has the calm of a hostage negotiator. Every muscle in his face smiles except for his eyes which darts between pastor and the drawer in his hand, a bludgeoning weapon if he were to start bucking again. "You rest a while, pastor. Let us he'p. You shouldn't be carryin' on like this. Ain't you the head of this here church?" He pronounces church like choych.

"You got somebody else in mind?" Stewart's reply is aimed at everyone in the doorway. He turns defensive, the only emotional gear available to him.

"Can't nobody hold a light to you, pastor. It ain't about that. What I'm saying to you is that the *head* of the church can't lose *his* head, amen?"

Aubrey, the church's web master, a hundred and forty pounds wet, scoots into the office, chased by terrified gasps. "If it's in here; we'll find it," he says while he takes a b-line to the counseling sofa, drops it on all fours and digs into the cushions.

The slim security guard draws his stick and pokes up at ceiling panels, asking, "This ledger: is it… incriminating?"

Stewart's glare could've dropped him. "You could only incriminate a criminal. Do I look like one to you?"

The lanky officer pushes his glasses up on his nose, "Sir… I suppose not, sir."

The staff pools into the office, a search party minus the lanterns and hounds. The pastor wrings his hands, his compass restoring. "No. It's nothing incriminating. It has nothing to do with church business. It's my personal journal." He apologizes continually as they search around him. He tries to make odds of his behavior, the ram-shackled office, "I guess… I felt so violated."

Winnie goes for the only item she sees undisturbed in the room: his robe hanging on its brass hanger. She digs into the large pocket and comes out with the book. "Might this be what you were looking for, pastor?"

He hugs the book like a child rescued from a well, and then he hugs the woman who found it. "I'm sorry, *so* sorry everyone." He buckles under the wave of relief.

Winnie hugs the pastor and corrects him, "You are *not* sorry. However, we accept your apology."

He shoos everyone out of his office, laughing, dismissing all concerns about his well-being, but after the incident, Stewart is not himself. He looks downtrodden, like he'd worked fields all the live-long day, yet it is just noon. They talk him into leaving early.

As Stewart exits the building, he looks down at his hands, so the microphone in his face surprises him. He is ambushed in the church parking lot by a rabid reporter asking about the investigation, the conman, implicating Stewart in his own break-in, throwing around jargon like allegations, accountability, and allegedly this; allegedly that. Stewart brushes past the microphone, with no comment.

He speeds off in his car, heading for the hospital because something has jarred inside of him; the fault-slip of continental plates in his chest, quaking. His breathing constricts as if python coils are lapped around his chest. He notices that he had left his phone in his car that morning in his hurry to get to the crime scene. There are five missed calls from Lynn, but he can't make his fitful hands return her call.

He careens into the nearest hospital's emergency drop. He trots in and drops on the front desk, exhausted, the oddest of places to steal a power nap. He says, feebly, "I'm having a heart attack."

They strap him on the gurney and muzzle him with an oxygen mask. Three nurses bus him back through large double doors, barking out orders in foreign tongue, cardio this and coronary that. Their jargon confuses him. To one nurse, his confusion looks like pain. She asks, "Getting worse?"

Stewart replies, "Actually it's getting better."

Suddenly the three nurses around the gurney, two male, one female, all lock eyes. Something about their training, their knowing intersects on the pastor's response.

The doctor checks the waiting room to report to the family. *Family* is two stone faced men in suits; church family. Associate Pastor Levi and Head Deacon Bailey are the first to arrive. They sit in the waiting room, one with his head down, the other punching dents into his derby hat, a doo-wop band stranded at a bus station, duped by the group's manager. At the sound of the pastor's name, they bob up from their chairs, Levi greeting the doctor with a handshake and a teethy smile. "Give it to me straight, doc," his grizzly voice boomerangs around the waiting room. The doctor takes the handshake and walks with it, guiding them swiftly down the hall, multi-tasking the courtesy escort to the patient's room along with the prognosis.

The doctor's report has them stumbling into the room, snickering fist over mouth where they find Stewart sitting upright at the foot of his bed, watching sports news. Levi gives his head a noogie, their laughter energized by their great relief, "A *panic* attack?"

"*Anxiety* attack," Stewart corrects.

"Man, we thought you was through-dealing," Deacon Bailey says.

The doctor leaves them with one final instruction. "Two weeks off for the big guy. Doctor's orders."

"We'll see to it doc," Bailey assures.

"How am I to build a school while laid up?"

Levi's excitement washes out like a painting doused with water. He has bad news for Stewart, but doesn't want to give him another panic attack. Catfish and Rudy Ginyard had already decided how to use the heart attack, along with the break-in, to their advantage.

Lynn can't reach Stewart by phone, which frustrates her at first, but she later realizes it is better not to give him news of the investigation while he is at church. Lynn has a lunch meeting already with Gayle, the lawyer, to discuss the future of the Fair Wage Transparency Bill, but Lynn also brings up Stewart's situation, seeking legal advice. Gayle has a lot to say on the issue but summarizes that Stewart shouldn't even worry about jail time, but he should worry about the damage a case like this can do to his reputation.

By the time their meeting is done, Stewart still isn't answering his phone, so Lynn carries on with her day. She retrieves her luggage case from her car trunk, extends the handle and starts her route to restock her books.

On her way to the hospital gift shop, she sees Stewart's car parked in the emergency bay, with the hazard lights on, but she dismisses it; it's not Dana's car, her thought having nothing to do with the look of the vehicle, just a feeling that the investigation is already enough, that God had already filled their quota of earthly troubles, but as Lynn closes in, she notices the wooden cross hanging from the rearview mirror; the front plate airbrushed with *He Lives*.

She rushes into the emergency room, aimless, fumbling with her briefcase, stuttering and pointing back in the direction of the parked car outside, too frazzled to state her concern. She can't shake the thought that her future husband lay dying in a sterile white room without her. Head Deacon Bailey, hurrying with Stewart's car keys to move the vehicle to a proper park, spots Lynn and shouts, "Room 412."

Lynn's face holds back tears like a levy, "Is he ok?"

"You ain't know? He had a lil ole panic attack. He good, sis."

With Bailey gone, Stewart and Levi are alone, Stewart sitting on the end of his hospital bed in a patient's apron and monitor wires patched to his forearms. Levi is seated in a chair next to the sink, their faces pointed at the television set in the room's upper corner.

Levi says, casually, "Must've been really upset about that diary. Look like a tornado hit your office."

Stewart, still fixed on the television, grimaces from a bitter swallow. "It wadn't so much the journal. Had a similar episode about a month ago, so it's been brewing it seems—"

"—Had that diary for a while, huh… How far back *does* it go?"

Stewart's head swings from the television to his associate pastor, detecting salt in the man's question. "Why do you ask?"

"Because of you: a man won't tear up his office over nothing. And since when has a man's black book been an innocent thing?"

"The only thing black about that book is its cover."

"I ain't fixin' to tap dance around the subject witchya bruh," Levi points at Stewart with five fingertips. "I shouldn't even *have* to ask; the truth is a volunteer, not a draftee. Anyhow, I'll shoot it to ya like this: I know with ninety-nine, point nine, nine percent certainty that my daughter is mine, but that doesn't mean I was the only one stirring the pot."

Stewart gasps. "Didn't we already have this conversation a long time ago?"

"Doesn't new evidence re-open cold cases?"

"What evidence?"

"For starters, after that blowup with Bianca when I asked if she would've been your first, you left me hanging. You could've left it at that, but no, maybe got to wondering *why* I asked, so you had to come back later with a cover up – talking 'bout it was Savannah – telling me that lie. That bull-dagger never laid down with you, so if not her, *who*?"

Stewart's brows are as tangled as Levi's theory. "Listen to yourself, man. A suspicious mind makes its own evidence. You assume what I told you is a lie just because it's unlikely. You can turn on the news and see that we're often dumfounded by truth."

"But I ain't talking about no news, brotha; I'm talking about my wife… Did you ever, in your life, lay with my wife? I'm talkin' *prior* to my being stationed back here, knowing you would never admit to after."

Stewart feels the jitters again; he runs his hands back and forward on his thighs. "Lee. Nothing happened."

Levi stands up and points. "That is a yes or no question, but you'd rather complicate things."

Stewart's gasps. The machine he is connected to, beeps faster.

Levi still presses the issue. "Sure, you answered the question before, but what's funny, is *how* you answer it the exact same way every time: *nothing happened.* That response makes me believe that, subconsciously, you're pointing to an event where something *did* happen, which you have resigned to write-off as nothing. So don't tell me that nothing happened. Tell me what *did* happen and let *me* judge if it's nothing."

Stewart stares at the man, dumfounded at how he could draw so many conclusions out of mere word phrasing.

This is how Lynn sees the two men when she enters the room. Stewart with that dumfounded look, the electrocardiogram beeping like crazy, Levi looking intense, leaning forward like an interrogator. Lynn pulls up in front of Stewart and starts kissing him on his lips, cheek, forehead. She then studies the fast beeping machine. "Is that normal?"

Levi falls back in his seat, his head shaking at the machine like it's a lie detector.

"It's been doing that off and on," Stewart says.

Lynn squeezes him tight. "I saw your car… the hazard lights were blinking and I…"

Lynn had come to comfort Stewart but he ends up comforting her. "I'm ok, baby. It's ok."

"I love you so much, Dana," she starts pecking his face again. He wouldn't meet her emotionally; he seems invulnerable, but then Lynn looks up and around and realizes why. Bailey has returned with a group who stands watching them.

They have yet to marry and already Lynn gets a glimpse of what crisis looks like in the life of a pastor: crowded. They are all watching, Bailey, Nay, Catfish, Rudy, all thrown by the sound of the name Dana, like they'd forgotten that Stewart had a first name.

Levi, clear of anger, says, "Doc says your *Dana* here's going on a little vacation: two whole weeks."

Catfish interrupts. "A month," he calls, like he is bidding at an auction. "We don't want him coming back at eighty percent. We want him back full strength."

Stewart leans outside of Lynn's embrace, eyeing Levi and then Catfish, "You're crazy, Lee, if you think I'm sitting out two weeks. And *you're* out of your mind, Otto, if you're thinking a month. We've got a school to build."

Catfish's hands goes up as if he's held at gunpoint. "Don't kill the messenger. Levi'll preach three Sundays and we're bringing Lamar in one Sunday 'fore we get back to the usual rotation."

"Lamar!"

Catfish lights up like a bulb, "You catch on quick, don't you?"

Lynn drapes her arm around her fiancé, and places one hand on his chest, protecting him. "Don't get yourself too worked up, Dana; it's not good for you." Next Lynn flashes a look at Catfish. "Can you all discuss this some other time?" She closes the front of Stewart's paper apron hiding the wires on his chest.

"I'll do you one better," Catfish proposes. "I won't discuss it at all."

"Lynn," Stewart says, as if she'd just spilled something. "I can speak for myself ok, babe."

Nay laughs and then covers her mouth. Lynn cut her eyes at Nay, but had second thoughts about responding.

The hospital says they'd keep Stewart for a few hours for observation. They had given him a shot that is supposed to keep his blood pressure low, but he is not allowed to drive himself, so Lynn has to stay; she would've stayed regardless.

Chapter 19

Levi arrives at Bianca's door with his derby hat tilted down, to avoid being noticed. Her welcoming smile makes him smile. "Surprised you're here this late."

"Today ain't no regular day."

"So, Pastor Stupid's laid up in the hospital, I hear," Bianca says.

"Nothing wrong with that boy. Not until the day he finds out that I'm taking back my pulpit." No sooner than Levi takes off his suit and flings it over the back of the couch, he smells pecan pie, his favorite. He becomes a boy again, absent minded enough to wander into a single woman's kitchen and come back with a slice of her pecan pie on a saucer. Bianca sits with her legs crossed, her skirt riding up, exposing her own brown slice between the top of her black thigh-high stocking and the hem of her short skirt. Her arm is draped across the couch, inviting her guest. Levi totally misses the drape of her arm when he sits, as he pulls the fork slowly from his mouth, savoring the bite.

"So, Stewart's returning when?"

"In a month, but that don't worry me. The fool think we're building that school. He'll have a heart attack for real when we break him the bad news."

"Don't feel bad for him either," Bianca commands. "You're the rightful pastor of this church, never forget that."

"Feel *bad*? For what? I never plotted against him; I've been loyal, until he showed himself, trying to get that gal behind the pulpit. Like I said: ya cross me when ya cross the word."

"So, it's because he believes in woman pastors?"

Levi can't answer right away, his head shakes no until the swallow frees his mouth. "Never seen one of those in my life; I'd sooner cross paths with a unicorn." Bianca's cheeks slacken in disapproval, so Levi clarifies, "Don't get me wrong, women are equal in the eyes of *God*, but her role in the *church* is… different. That's why that woman of his – he set her up too high. Someone's got to bring her back down. That's why, in hindsight, I'm glad that Nay was on her behind at rehearsals that time, and there'll be more where that came from, just sit back and watch."

Bianca slides closer and clasps two hands over the post of Levi's shoulder. "One thing your wife must realize: it makes her look like a bully if she goes after Lynn. She should learn to instigate Lynn to come after *her*."

The words *your wife* echoes like The Tell-Tale Heart. Bianca is close enough for Levi to get a whiff of her mint breath. If Levi were hooked up to an electrocardiogram *his* monitor would be going haywire like Stewart's. "At the hospital, I asked him, straight out, had he and Nay ever laid together…"

"Uh, uh…" Bianca is on edge, hanging on his words.

"… And you should've seen how his blood pressure went up when I asks him; that EKG monitor got to actin' up and beeping like a pin ball machine."

Bianca raises a finger, "What more evidence do you need?"

Levi takes the last bite and slides the saucer on the table.

Slyly, Bianca asks, "Like my pie?" She slides her arm behind him over the couch back.

Levi doesn't notice the arm around him. He asks, "You tight with Lynn right? I'm gone need you to be my ears and eyes."

Bianca wipes his mouth with a folded napkin. He let her. "How can I win your trust? I *know* about laying and waiting for opportunity," she says, her own opportunity to exact revenge against Nay for exposing her to Stewart, is opening up at that very moment. "You can't shoot and miss. No one can know the assassin's identity until after it's done. I know about pitting enemies against one another and keeping my hands clean. I know about secrets; many will go with me to my grave." She kisses his lips and retreats shamefully.

Levi's eyes fall closed, unable to look at her. "You *know* I'm a married man, Bianca. You *know* we ain't supposed to be doing this."

"That's when it's the best."

Levi opens his eyes, the only movement he could muster; he is trapped in her web: the pecan pie, the cleavage staring at him, her lips parting, her intoxicating words as she mounts him and runs her fingers back over his ears and scalp. "I can be much more than your ears. More than your eyes." She takes his glasses and put them on herself. He inhales her perfume, paralyzing like a neurotoxin. He tries to talk Bianca out of it but she ignores him. She digs into his zipper, then cut her eyes and smiles as a sign of approval for what she finds there. She teases it like a snake charmer and quickly quit the game. Bianca lowers over him shimmying down and sits like a hen roosting, her skirt bunched up on her waist like a cummerbund. Levi's head goes back in a large sigh from the heat coming down over him and the chill rising up his spine. Bianca snatches him by the shirt collars like he owes her. She hovers over him, eye to eye just out of kissing range. They begin riding a carousel to the music of desperate kisses, panting, his grunts, her moans, the ruffle of clothes flowered open but still on, and the leather couch groaning under them like it hurt. They stop altogether, listening, concentrating, teasing the moment, their faces shocked with pleasure at this roller coaster's arresting peak, before the next exhilarating dive. The man's leg snaps out like a switchblade and kicks the living room table. They take it to her bedroom to finish.

Levi lay there out of breath; Bianca, satisfied and playful like a kitten. Levi turns away from her, shy and hung over with guilt. She spoons him, what an odd twist, Levi thinks. Her chin rests on his shoulder where she peeks down at him. "How'd you like it?"

Five adjectives come to him and he discards each one; none of them does her performance any justice. His most memorable experience before her, drops to a distant second.

Bianca giggles, rolls away from him, fiddling with something on the nightstand and rolls back. Levi stays still; Bianca keeps on talking.

Levi listens, but he is not listening to her. He is listening for what is beyond the door. He hears, not sound, but a *presence* like a child's listening in on the man who is stone serious in the open, being playful with his mother behind closed doors. Levi's mind is taking him places he doesn't want to go; he needs to leave. Levi wonders; does he need a reason? Could he coldly announce his departure and start putting on his clothes? He doesn't know how extramarital affairs works, but on second thought, he does. His childhood, in review, is a satire on extramarital affairs.

Bianca could feel him working himself up to leave, so she helps him, "I know better than to want what I can't have. I want the part of you that's available to me, not a minute more." She picks up his paw, the one wearing the watch. "You're cutting into *her* time, so you need to hurry home. Don't worry about me. You've already given me what I wanted," she assures, as she watches the man get up and go to the bathroom to rinse her smell off of him.

Levi returns to the bedroom, buttoning his shirt. Bianca stands in front of her dresser, her back to him, but she watches him in the mirror. Levi gazes back with a smirk, studying things he could not study at home: her perfectly bald body, her perky thirty-year-old buttocks, not sagging under its own weight nor dimpled in its girth; she raises her hands to bundle her ponytail and Levi sees evidence of ribs. He is entranced by the strange-ness of her; the blue contacts eyeing him as she pops chewing gum, the bleached face in the mirror, two shades lighter than the buttocks outside the mirror.

He is now in the role of philandering pastor, a dark visitor in this apartment of impeccable cleanliness, scented with the aroma of pecan pie. There is no child in the picture, except for the youthful self he projects there. Bianca's apartment feels more like home than the one he must hurry to.

When Levi arrives home, Nay has no questions waiting for him. It is nine o'clock at night, unusual for Levi, but this is no usual night; Stewart is in the hospital. Nay hasn't had concerns about another woman in so long she'd stopped fact-checking. Nay is wearing her house robe, slippers and bandana, thumbing through sales papers. She rises to hug him, basic formality. Levi sits down across from her, his legs crossed, sporting that look of absolute dominion that Nay prays everyday not to show up. He asks, "Do you know why the caged bird sings?" He doesn't know himself. He's never read Maya Angelo, but in his ruthless swagger he'd make even the great laureate's words obey his will.

Nay flips the page of her magazine. "Lee, you smell like a woman. Who you been hugging?"

"I had a long talk with good ole Stew," the explanation for his whereabouts. "He started singing. Told me everything – in so many words."

Nay feels the dark cloud looming, the accusation he's held over her head for years. "If he told you everything, it must've been mighty quiet. How many times I got to tell you: *nothing happened*. So, don't start that mess tonight."

Levi's mind is deceptive. After leaving another woman's bed, his mind prevents him from realizing that he's transposing his guilt onto his wife; he believes that his accusation is as real as the lines in his hands. "What is nothing? Huh? Gimme the details."

"Here's what you do, Lee. Go back out that door, and come back in here like you got sense."

"You got until the time I get up out of this chair to answer me."

"Put your hands on me, and where you gon' sleep? I ain't up for that tonight." Nay turns front and center on the couch, ready to drive him back with her powerful legs if he approaches.

Levi laughs, his brow reaching in delight.

"Laugh today. Tomorrow you'll be *lying* about how scratches got on your face. No free licks tonight; it's gon' cost you. And that's on everything I love." Nay knows standing her ground could go either way, take him to the height of his wrath, or successfully deter him.

Levi feints like he'd get up and Nay's legs goes up, coiled to kick. They hear their daughter's keys grinding in the lock. College is out, she's home for the summer, in and out like a boarder. Levi tries to act normal, but botches the attempt. He is too glad to see Heather, so it raises her suspicion. Nay keeps her head down in her coupon paper.

Heather knows. She hugs her father then calls her mother, "You busy ma?" Their code, Heather's offering of asylum.

Nay is all too willing. The two head to Heather's room to talk about nothing, to huddle in the safety of teamwork, their community of two.

Levi, a goofball for his daughter, jokes, "So it's a girl thing?" He walks behind them, wanting in. Heather's room door closes in Levi's face. Levi's hands flop to his sides. "So, it's like that, huh?"

The room door would stay closed until morning. Nay laying sleepless in her daughter's bed, her marriage under review, playing out on ceilings and walls. She was fifteen and Levi twenty-six at the time of their first kiss. She knew the age difference was inappropriate, but was unaware how her little ideas of love was so easily coaxed by a man who had much more life experience than her; Nay was unaware that she was being groomed. When Levi deployed, Nay thought she'd die, but years later when he was reassigned in town at Fort Jackson base, returning to the ministry at First Baptist, she was old enough and wise enough to see him as the rapist he was.

Nay was the young Pastor Stewart's girlfriend. Nay and Stewart grieved Fiona's death together and it brought them closer. A year of friendship themed around the loss of Fiona began forming its own identity. They were dating only a few months when Levi returned and a conversation between the two men took place, Stewart coming away knowing that Nay was not the virgin she claimed to be. Stewart stressed to Nay during their teary breakup that her virginity was not the deal breaker; it was the deceit.

With Stewart out of the way, Levi tried relentlessly to win Nay's heart, visiting Nay at her campus job at Benedict University, hanging out at her hangout spots among a much younger crowd, but not under the pretense of courtship. Nay thought Levi was doing penance by giving her gifts and cash for her to hang out with her friends. He'd tag along anywhere just to be in the same room with her, for as long as Nay could tolerate the sight of him, for as long as he could weather her cold treatment. Nay's friends would chastise her for being so cruel to him when he was so generous to her. She never met him in isolation until one evening when he said it was the only way he'd give her the money she needed. That day, Levi broke down in tears, on his knees before her. Nay found herself comforting him out of some general sense of pity, but there they were again, together in the depths of human emotion, and they kissed in such a way that it snowballed into sex that, given their age, is considered consensual, but because of their history, perhaps not. Nay vowed never to take money from him, nor speak to Levi again. He was the same predator, using a different device of control; where he once used the advantage of experience, he later used money.

Nay kept to her word not to speak to him again, until her period was late and a home pregnancy test told her why. Heather was growing inside of her. The next time she spoke to Levi was at her parents' house, after they had called him there. Nay cried at the center of them all. Her parents thought they were a new couple. They had no clue their involvement went back to Chardonnay's tenth-grade year. They urged the couple to go on and do what God would have them do. Nay dropped out of college and the two married.

Heather's back is to Nay, but she knows her mother is awake. She turns over to show that she is awake too. "I'm not going back," Heather says in a low voice.

Nay couldn't have been hearing these words come from the daughter she sacrificed her own education for, "What, you don't like that *particular* school, and want to choose another one? Best believe you're going back to *some* school, cause no-school is not an option."

"Don't say it's not an option, ma, when you know it is."

"My situation was different."

"He'll kill you. And if it happens while I'm off at school, unable to protect you, how could I go on living with myself?"

Nay holds her child. She can't believe this turnaround. She quit her education for her daughter's sake, but never to be repaid, never as a license for the daughter sacrificing her education for her. Together, they weep in the dark, mother and daughter.

Chapter 20

Lynn had assured the doctor and the leaders present at Stewart's bedside that she would spend more time over at Stewart's home to watch over her ailing fiancé. It begins that night with his release from the hospital. Lynn drives him home. She doesn't mention her meeting with the investigator for fear of giving Stewart another panic attack, but the subject comes up all on its own when they arrive at Stewart's home and settle into the couch in time for the nightly news, where they air the video of Stewart being chased by the reporter.

The feed looks damaging. A startled Stewart's shoulders scrunch upward, his neck downward, as if trying to hide his head like a turtle. Realizing his head is still exposed, Stewart then evades the reporter with a few jerky changes of direction. The reporter and cameraman chase; the scene rattling from the unsteady camera capturing Stewart running away to his car.

Finally, the out-of-breath reporter concludes that the pastor's pompous flight, "… is indicative of a man who believes he can literally *run* from accountability."

Stewart pouts, "Ain't no doggone accountability. I was running because I was having a heart attack, for all I knew–"

Lynn shushes Stewart; there is more. Back to the studio, the news anchor shuffles a stack of papers and switches to a report that ties Westermann's financial seminar to one of the largest megachurches in the country, pastored by Bishop Freddie Farr. They post a most unflattering photo of the Jheri Curl-wearing overweight pastor. They air snippets of interviews with members who lost much of their retirements to the scheme. In an unsettling coincidence, like Pastor Stewart, Bishop Freddie Farr's administrative office was also broken into and had the hard drives stolen. They show a clip of Farr endorsing Westermann at the pulpit during worship.

Lynn asks, "Did you endorse Westermann like that?"

Stewart's eyes slice, as he returns, "You should know me better than that, Lynn."

"Did you, or the church, receive any profit?"

"No. Levi and the trustees wanted to, but I brought in Deacon Bacon's son who is a lawyer and he advised not to allow any exchange of money during that weekend."

"I talked with Gayle today. She's a lawyer," Lynn says. "Legally, you shouldn't have anything to worry about."

Stewart replies, "Of that, I was already sure."

"The FBI isn't so sure, though."

Stewart twitches upright, viewing Lynn side-eyed like an alert squirrel. "What you talkin 'bout, Lynn?"

Lynn tells Stewart about her interview with the investigator, but Stewart loses interest halfway through the telling. He seems impregnable, as if he's behind a door marked in lamb's blood, assured that the wrath would pass over him.

Stewart pops in a DVD recording of the financial seminar; he fast forwards to the disclosures he gave verbally and has additional disclaimers handed out in a packet to all attendees.

Lynn says, "That's good and all, but don't you think it's a bit much for the church to give financial guidance in the first place?"

Stewart explains by fast forwarding again, to where he explains how, with the many funerals he's eulogized, he is tired of seeing family squabble over estates because the deceased hadn't handled their affairs; this: Stewart says from the pulpit, as ushers pass out blank copies of last will and testaments. This is the one thing, above all, that Stewart wants them to take away, that without a will, a life of hard work's accumulation would matriculate evenly among siblings without respect to stewardship. He talks of probate court enforced sales, estates going for pennies on the dollar; the land and home, which accrues value, gets split three, five, seven different ways to surviving heirs. The responsible child who alters their lives to care for the ailing parent getting equal share with the black sheep of the family who contributed nothing.

The congregation is up on their feet, fanning their pastor as if he's on fire. Stewart decides to get rid of the microphone before he *really starts preaching*.

Westermann takes over to deliver the seminar's introductory speech. His spit-shined bald head catches the glare from the recessed lighting; a life-sized wooden cross decorates the wall behind him. He's tall, slender and impeccably clean in his crisp blue suit. He makes himself out to be some sort of agent infiltrating Wall Street, infiltrating whiteness, now returning to his people to bring back their secrets.

He piggy backs off of Stewart's message, how last wills and testaments or the lack thereof, is bleeding wealth out of the community. "By the time this seminar is over," Westermann says, "you will also understand how it is directly related to our disintegrating neighborhoods and schools. Rich folks know the difference; they think like owners. For much of our history in America, we didn't even own our*selves*, so culturally, we struggle *owning* our destiny; *massa* owned our destiny. When you don't think like owners, you describe your plight by using – what I call – the accusatory they. We say *they* won't promote us on our jobs; *they* setup our schools to fail. They won't give you a chance." Westermann pauses to let the term wash over his listeners. "The *accusatory they* points to those who own destiny, and it keeps you at their mercy; it *wants* better, but it is void of any personal obligation to *make* it better; it begs *them* to do right by us. We need to take that accusatory *they*," he pinches the air and twists it. "And turn it into a *responsive we*. The *responsive we* says enough is enough; it is a call to action; it gets things done. The day we turn our *they-s* into *we-s*, is the day we finally break the chains of slavery." He stops and scans, wide-eyed. "Did someone say slavery is distant history? Did someone look down at their ankles and wonder *what chains?* Westermann points at his head and says, "Our ancestors shed blood to break the chains from around our bodies, but it's on *us* to break the chains from around our *minds!*"

"Oh, he's good," Lynn appraises. "He's *really* good."

Stewart points the remote control and turns the TV off. "Smooth as a pimp, ain't it?"

Lynn puts on her professor hat, analyzing Westermann's speech. "He may be a crook, but I can still set that aside and appreciate the brilliance of his rhetoric. Don't you see, Dana? The congregation loves him because he removes the moral netting white America cast over the black community in suggesting laziness, careless, a culture of handouts. Westermann is handing them better reasons: barred access, a fixed game, weighted dice, generational hypnosis – that their situation is not their fault. They accept Westermann under the relief of him lifting black guilt from their consciousness. Like Moses to Mt. Sanai, he's been to Wall Street and back, returning with the blueprint to life." Lynn pauses, realizing she hasn't heard any feedback from Stewart, so she nudges him. "Don't you see how he's exploiting our connection to slavery?"

Stewart's only interest in the analytical breakdown is stopping it in its tracks. He cuts his eye. "Look who's talking."

Lynn draws back, tensed to strike, "What do you mean, 'look who's talking?'"

Stewart shrugs, "I'm just saying… your speech in the park: the Right to Work divide versus the Mason Dixon line. Then, your Women's Day speech covering Exodus, Moses freeing his people from slavery… So, how is the pot calling the kettle black?"

Lynn is at a loss for words for a few beats. She then shoves Stewart who falls over on the couch laughing.

Lynn studies him like she might now do worse. One side of her brow raises. "Am I laughing?"

Stewart is all teeth with his palms up. "I know you ain't mad, Lynn? You can't take a joke?"

"You compare me to a crook and I'm supposed to–" Lynn quits with a teeth suck and goes off stomping down the hallway to the shower.

Chapter 21

The last time Stewart was planning a wedding, his fiancé died. She was at the fitting for her wedding dress when she forgot how to speak and then fell backward into the mirror, shattering it. Doctors believed she was having twenty mini-seizures an hour. They run an MRI that showed the cause, an inoperable brain tumor the size of a ping-pong ball near the brain stem. The wedding was cancelled. They sent Fiona home with a stack of prescriptions, one to deal with the seizures and the others to deal with all the side effects of the first prescription. They sent her home to die with her family, no one knowing the day or hour. Stewart asked to go ahead with the wedding anyway, as a way to celebrate Fiona while she's living rather than just a funeral to celebrate her in death, but her parents wouldn't allow it. They agreed that the line, *until death do us part* would sound insensitive with the cloud of death already looming.

Nearly two decades later, the thought of planning another wedding makes Stewart sick. Maybe it's him who doesn't survive the wedding now, considering his recent emergency room visit.

With school still out, Lynn has all day to tend to her fiancé. Using a home blood pressure monitor Lynn bought from the pharmacy, she checks his blood pressure three times a day, as the doctor ordered.

They spend their days in front of the television, taking walks and enjoying lunch and dinner dates, knowing once Stewart returns to work, he would be too busy to have this much quality time together. Daily, Lynn flips through wedding magazines and surfs websites, often brining the open magazine to Stewart and pointing out the options, all of which, Stewart seems to have no hard opinions.

With all the time together, they notice a change in their relationship. The playfulness really began one morning when Lynn broke the ice. Stewart comes to the stove at breakfast where Lynn hands him his plate of pancakes and as he walks away with his plate, Lynn runs the spatula handle gently up the crack of his butt. Stewart jumps with his arms flailing. His breakfast plate goes airborne, the stuck pancake peeling off the ceiling a few seconds after the breaking plate. Lynn pounds the counter, cry-laughing. Stewart's outrage breaks into a smile and then a chuckle, and when it really hits Stewart how he must've looked, he rears back laughing, chest out like a rooster, his full throttle laughter also crowing like one.

They become playful all the time. They make googly eyes at worship with Levi preaching. Stewart stops worrying about the attacks on his ministry; he embraces the month off and plans to come back preaching with fire and building the Christian Academy. They sit next to each other in bible study class, also facilitated by Levi. Lynn keeps eyeing Stewart while he struggles to keep a straight face. When no one is looking, she snatches his notebook and Stewart fumbles to catch a falling pen. The couple straighten up stiff, snorting from suppressed laughter. Levi eyes them over the rim of his glasses, "You two a'ight?"

One day, walking down the main hallway, Stewart snatches Lynn into a conference room and they start kissing madly until they realize they are not alone. Old Deacon Ike clears his throat and the couple scurries out of the room like burglars, Stewart throwing back a hurried, "My bad Deek." They speed around the corner, backs to a wall, panting and giggling like delinquent minors.

The two love birds can't get out of church without hearing the question, "When is the wedding date?" The two would turn coy and shrug.

On the car ride back from Stewart's follow-up doctor's appointment, Stewart, looking directly over the steering wheel at the road, says, "What are we waiting for?"

Lynn looks at the red traffic light, then back at Stewart. "What do you mean?"

"The wedding," says Stewart.

Lynn sighs. "Well, we don't have enough time to have a wedding before the semester in August. And definitely not *during* the semester."

"Ok Miss Saving Yourself," Stewart smiles. "You wanna save y'self well into next year?"

A giggling Lynn reaches over and pinches his cheek with the words, "If you're hard up for sex, darling, just say that."

"I'm good." Stewart's fist raps his chest in masculine self-assurance. "Besides," Stewart adds. "I don't understand all this talk about the semester. The *semester*… I'm not about to have my first lady, my wife, working."

Lynn's eyes widen and blinks rapidly under this epiphany; the freedom she'll gain, the purpose she'll lose. "But…"

"But what?"

"Dana…" Lynn swivels to him. "Teaching isn't just a job; it's what I do."

"But you don't have to be slave to it… Or do you prefer 40- and 50-hour work weeks? You can *teach* Women's Bible study for forty hours a *month*. You can spend more time writing."

"But Nay's got women's bible study. She seems to love it, although she doesn't know what the heck she's doing. I doubt she'll just step aside."

"In due time, I believe I can talk her out of it."

"And in the meantime?"

"Trust me, the church will keep their new first lady busy enough."

Lynn asks, "So what wedding date do you suggest."

"Now."

Lynn's eyes go lazy with ridicule.

Since there would be no semester to worry about, they decide right then and there to have the wedding in late August; in a month and a half.

Chapter 22

The day before Stewart's return from his imposed month-long stint, Levi delivers a shady sermon. It's his last sermon before returning to the normal preaching rotation, so Levi is determined to leave a lasting impression. He even gives up his decade old robe for a new one. Levi is adorned in what looks like a white Cardinal robe with gold trimmings, gold, decorative crucifixes on each breast and sleeves as wide as buckets. Stewart and Lynn exchange sly looks over Levi's fancy new threads.

Levi preaches about the state of preaching in general, but the traits he references has someone very specific in mind. Levi's carefully worded setups and punch lines about "modern day preachers" makes Stewart itch under his collar. Levi refers to some modern-day preachers as nothing more than glorified fund raisers. This, the man says just weeks after Stewart ran the most successful and improbable fund raiser in First Baptist's history. Levi's next ambiguous dig puts Stewart's entire legacy under question.

Levi, in an effort to break down why the modern church is so confused – why so many in the faith follow false prophets – explains, "Because you crown them based on material success. Because they can build buildings you call them a man of God." Levi removes his glasses, un-holsters the microphone, and paces while mumbling to himself. "*Naw, they ain't ready for that Levi,*" he says, knowing the congregation would egg him on, antsy to hear the word. "Let me take it back a little bit," says Levi, as he pats his forehead with a handkerchief. "Y'all know about the housing boom, right? Housing boom is an improper term, you see… It was a *lending* boom." Levi then asks a question in third person, "Why are you talking about some lending boom from God's pulpit, pastor?" He then answers his own question, "Because the God *I* know encompasses all things; therefore, a man of God must search the face of all things in order to search the face of God!" His head shakes, his hands fly out, his large sleeves flap like wings. The trustees, who are scattered across the front of the church, are up cheering on their native son. The deacons, many of them Ginyards, are up in unison like children instigating a playground fight. Levi continues, "*Lending* boom – not a housing boom. Banks lent money for mortgages, surely, but businesses also got a record number of loans. Churches had their hands in the cookie jar too. Take a drive in any direction and you'll see churches that were not in existence fifteen years ago. Why? Did God suddenly start calling more preachers? Or was it the banks shelling out construction loans like candy? So, when you have people judging the effectiveness of a pastor by his building, one can say that the lending boom helped elevate many a false prophets!"

Stewart uncrosses his legs like he's about to get up and protest. The next time Stewart's hands come together is in prayer; he can't applaud insults clearly aimed at him. After the sermon, Levi tries avoiding Stewart, but Stewart catches up to him in the banquet, where Levi is surrounded by his brethren. Stewart breaks in on the circle, ignoring Levi's handshake offer. Stewart says, "You must be really feeling yourself right about now, huh Lee?"

Levi checks around, wondering to whom Stewart directs the aggressive tone. Then Levi leans in, his head shaking no, and with a singsong delivery, he says, "I ain't trying to walk in your shoes, brotha… but I ain't trying to *shine* 'em neither."

On the drive home, Stewart enlightens Lynn of his brief conversation with Levi. "This fool take me for somebody to play with, but Imma *show* him better than I can tell him."

Lynn glances and says, "Using the pulpit for competition?"

Stewart, spooling the steering wheel through his hands, says, "I use the pulpit how God would have me use it. Responding to Levi would only give Levi power."

Lynn says, "About Levi…" She was beginning to tell Stewart about the day Levi tried to intimidate her near the ladies' room, but remembers Stewart's anxiety since the break-in, and doesn't want to give the man another attack.

Stewart looks over. "What about Levi?"

Lynn adlibs, "Oh, it's just that I can't help but feel like you and Levi are now enemies because of me."

"None of this is your fault," Stewart says, as if that's that.

They remain quite for a spell. Lynn remembers, "Oh I forgot to tell you, Dana, that the cake maker says that the cake you chose, has to be assembled on site – which means they'll need to use the banquet – which also means they'll be in the way of the caterers."

Stewart shrugs. "Choose another cake, any cake, I don't care."

Lynn gazes out the passenger window at the sunbathed town floating by as if on a conveyor belt.

Stewart reaches over and takes her hand. "When I say I don't care, Lynn, I mean that the only thing I care about is you. Everything else is irrelevant."

"Same goes for me, hon. It wasn't that. I was just thinking. What a time to become first lady. Leadership is divided right now."

Stewart can do no more than apologize and squeeze her hand, assuring Lynn that everything will be alright. The remainder of the drive goes in silence, with each resigned to their thoughts.

They arrive at Stewart's home, and soon as Lynn's purse drops on the kitchen counter. "First lady," Lynn says with a sigh.

Stewart eyes her with concern. "You' still on that?"

"Am I even built for this? First ladies in many of the churches I've attended are nothing more than trophy wives."

Stewart, who is in the kitchen hunting for a snack, turns from inside the refrigerator door. "*Trophy* wife!" His face tenses with humor and confusion like it's the most ridiculous thing he's ever heard.

"Jeez, Dana, do you have to rebuke it so harshly?"

Stewart recognizes the catch-twenty-two: saying she's *not* a trophy wife insults her looks, but agreeing that she *is* a trophy wife insults her intellect. "Lynn… You're the most beautiful woman I ever laid eyes on."

Lynn gives a warm-hearted smile. "Isn't that what you're supposed to say?"

"But I must say," Stewart adds. "…you don't *dress* like a trophy wife. It's just not in you to be that superficial, but me – as a man – I want to adorn you *like* a trophy wife."

"You don't like my clothes?"

Stewart leaves the refrigerator with a quart carton of milk and something wrapped in foil. "When we're married your presentation reflects on me. The linen, the wooden bracelets and string necklaces… I just don't know… I'll put it this way: on sight, I want folks to see how I cherish you."

"So, to make sure that I represent you properly, I'd have to spend an hour in the mirror before leaving the house?"

Stewart begins to see the trap he is headed to and stops short of it, "No, babe. Be you. Just take into account my desire. My hope is that we can meet at least halfway."

"Give me an example, hon. Who am I to emulate?"

"Look no further than Nay. All her stuff is designer."

Lynn says, "If that's the case, I don't see you wearing Givenchy or Valentino suits… You drive a Camry… How are you representing me?"

"Say what? Girl you done bumped yo head? Look," Stewart waves his hands. "Forget the brand names. All I'm saying is that every time Nay steps out the house she's on point."

"*Nay?* Nay…" Both times Stewart confirms with nods. Lynn gathers her hands. "Whatever comes out of her mouth ruins that beautiful face of hers."

"She got that body though." Stewart says, after biting into a slice of pound cake wrapped in foil.

Lynn gets up. "You call that a body?" Lynn sets her hands on the thin waist that she works so hard to maintain. "Big ole fanny tossing side to side when she walks…" Lynn imitates Nay's butt-tossing walk, and the way Stewart laughs makes her stop and cut her eye at him. Stewart's crumbly mouth and the poundcake in Stewart's hand, helps Lynn remember the day they came in for measurements, with Nay taunting and strutting about how Stewart likes *cake*.

Stewart notices Lynn cutting her eye. "What," he says, with a shrug.

"Nothing," says Lynn. "It's nothing."

Her silence for the rest of the night says it's something. Lynn tries to play it off. Stewart, to avoid an uncomfortable conversation, pretends not to notice the attitude change – how every conversation is initiated by him, and how her responses are short and distant. Even when Lynn smiles or laughs, her happy expression is like a mask, the eyes behind it registering something deeper than jealousy. Lynn feels it in her spirit that something has happened between Nay and Stewart, her husband to be.

Chapter 23

On the day of the wedding, Lynn is kept at a secret location known only to her seamstress, the makeup artist, the wedding planner and her mother. She arrives in the limousine with the seamstress behind her, flattening out the train of her gown. Lynn's stepfather is already in tears as he hooks her arm and stands with her in front of the large oak door, waiting for the music.

An antique organ cranks out the tune. The double doors of the largest church in the city opens for her. Lynn would forever remember this thrill of walking into a room as the afternoon's prize. An audience of dignified men and women all smile at her. They blow kisses and shed tears. Her mother chokes up with pride.

Stewart waits at the altar in a pearl white suit, ugly-crying as he watches Lynn walk down the aisle. Stewart buckles with gratitude. He has to be held up by a groomsman.

The most memorable moment comes via the ring bearer, Stewart's six-year-old nephew, who hooks one finger into a nostril, thoroughly picking his nose, confused as to why everyone laughs.

The wedding is vintage. It is everything Lynn wished for as a little girl, and then it is everything she'd denied ever wanting again after a tragic first marriage.

After the reception, the limousine takes them straight to the private air strip, Stewart still in his tux and Lynn in her wedding gown, per Lynn's request. She wants to be carried over the threshold in her wedding gown. They have a plane to themselves. During the flight, the two can't keep their hands off of each other, they kiss and giggle the whole way. They look down and marvel at the clouds and the world below reduced to a patchwork of color. They land at a Martha's Vineyard grass airstrip where they're shuttled to the bed and breakfast.

The two are antsy with anticipation as they follow the concierge who shows them the layout of the resort and the amenities; the two, copping feels behind the guide's back, but straighten to attention the moment the concierge looks back.

They are grateful to have waited; the months long tease is about to end. Stewart loads the luggage in the room while Lynn waits outside. He then carries her across the threshold, Lynn's legs draped over Stewart's forearm, the two kiss like the world is ending when, in fact, it is their new beginning.

This time Lynn is *carried* over the threshold rather than *shoved*. This time Lynn knows what the commitment of marriage means, and what a man of God is. The icing on the blessing is having found one so handsome and strong. Stewart back-kicks the door closed, not to be opened again until morning.

For months, they've abstained patiently, but now they're so anxious, the next few minutes seem intolerable, and yet they're careful to approach it slowly, tenderly, spiritually. Tears roll down the face of each, yet they giggle as they struggle to get Lynn out of her gown.

Lynn digs her nails into Stewart's back as he lowers over her. Stewart whispers, "You okay?" Lynn places her hands on the sides of his face and pulls his lips to her, which feeds him into her body; their marriage suddenly consummated.

Stewart is grateful. God has truly been good. Above all blessings, his greatest is Lynn, his spiritual twin, so bold in her love of God. He rears back to let himself look at her, more beauty than eyes can capture. Stewart beams, just thinking about their sheer unlikelihood; how they've ended up here on an island off of Cape Cod at a bed and breakfast not far from where Pilgrims landed centuries ago, Stewart, now, inexplicably handling the same beautiful legs that caught his eye one sunny day at the barber.

Overflowing with gratitude, Stewarts speaks her new name, "Mrs. Evelyn Stewart."

Afterwards they lay there, husband and wife, kissing and smiling, their small talk meaning nothing. The fool wants to know if he was good enough. Lynn, gazing from their shared pillow, taps his nose with her fingertip, saying, "Dude… There's no way I'm only your second." Nothing Stewart could say would make Lynn believe otherwise; his performance made it fact.

Their honeymoon is a two-week slice of paradise. They rent bikes to explore the island's hamlets; they eat at different restaurants every day, the most memorable spot being the Black Dog Bakery. They worship together at a church in Vineyard Haven. They sit at the edge of the Aquinnah Cliffs, watching the relentless waves crash over the rocks like a repetitive glitch in the universe. They discuss their future, their shared life now laid out as sure as the ocean before them.

They've had their phones off during the entire two week honeymoon. When they return on Friday night, they are allowed to check their messages.

Lynn gets a message from D'mitri bearing great news; *Don't Pray For Love* has been nominated for multiple awards. Lynn is then shocked to find a message from Nay, asking Lynn to speak at the annual domestic violence luncheon, which isn't even the most crucial part of the message.

Lynn runs to Stewart with the phone in her hand and on speaker. He listens as Nay apologizes to Lynn for the altercation at rehearsals.

Lynn says, "Now watch this."

Nay sighs heavily and says, *I'd rather us be friends. You seem to have a genuine concern for me, Lynn, and I appreciate that. It's important that we get along because our husbands can't. Whatever mess they go through, Levi brings it home and I have to hear it. Well…* Nay sighs again and says, *Anyway, call me after the honeymoon. Smooches.*

Lynn says to her husband, "'Genuine concern for me?' She's talking about that time I questioned her at the banquet."

Stewart rubs his chin. "You sure? I don't know, Lynn."

"You heard it just like I did. She's reaching out. She needs a lifeline."

Stewart's head shakes. "I don't know about all that Lynn."

"You don't have to know. *I* know."

"Do me a favor," says Stewart. "Don't force it like you did last time at the banquet. Just hold on until the domestic violence luncheon, that way the subject has a chance to come up naturally."

"So…" Lynn sighs. "I imagine the most effective way to get through to her would be to tell her about my situation–"

"–No!" Stewart checks the bass in his voice. "I mean… people don't need to know that. When you get into stuff like that, it begins to reflect on me. They're already trying to force me out, I don't want to give them another reason."

"Ok," Lynn decides not to fight him on it. They still have the weekend to squeeze out the last drip of honeymoon romance, before Stewart returns to the office. The semester would've already begun, but now Lynn, rather Mrs. Stewart, can sleep in, focus on moving and the sale of her condo. They had enough lovemaking at Martha's Vineyard to make up for all the agony of celibate dating, but Stewart wants to break-in their marriage bed, to announce themselves in this dwelling, to make it officially theirs. "Whaddaya say," asks Stewart.

Lynn raises a brow as if accepting a dare. "You ain't said nothin' but a word."

The morning after, Lynn wakes first, while Stewart remains twitching in his sleep. Lynn lay there blinking; her pillowed face turned to the glass door.

Her eyes begin adjusting in the gray, low lit morning, depth perception deferring shadow to light, and suddenly, Lynn realizes that she's looking at a young fawn unusually close to the house. In the background, its flock treks from the pond's edge back to the forest beyond the backyard. Slowly, Lynn crawls out of bed. The young deer approaches. Lynn is down on the floor, laying the length of the glass door. The fawn tenses at the sight of man, but since Lynn is down, the threat doesn't take. It seems interested, its wet nose pulsing, unaware that Lynn's scent is blocked by the glass between them. It can only see, with its sorrowful brown orbs peeking through slits in sleek fur. It seems to pity Lynn; it seems to think she's injured since she's down and not raised up on her hind legs like other humans. Back by the forest edge, the mother spots its young. The sound of the mother's hoofs bolting makes the fawn leap off in reflexive flight.

Lynn looks back, chin to shoulder, and sees Stewart watching, his gait, shimmering and expectant as if he'd just had his fortune told. Lynn, lit with amazement, asks, "Did you see?"

He saw, from behind, the image of his wife's body lying across the wood floor, shellacked in pre-dawn light, with an innocent, twitching fawn lowering to study her. Stewart figures the image is so iconic, so blessed, that it's God announcing the blessing of a child.

Chapter 24

After Stewart leaves the office on Monday, Deacon Bailey comes by his home to bring him up to speed, and explain why, on Sunday, upon his return to worship, and then on Monday at his return to the church campus, why Stewart didn't feel the outpouring of welcome he'd expected.

Lynn, being the woman of the house, asks the men if they'd like refreshments. Bailey nods, "Sure, sis, whatever you bring."

Lynn drops off some apple juice for the men and then returns to the kitchen. Lynn cuts sour dough loaf into triangles and drizzles them with olive oil before sliding them into the oven. She takes out a container of store-bought hummus, rough chopped sprigs of basil, adds it to the hummus along with grated parmesan, and hot sauce, one of her favorite treats adopted from singlehood. While stirring in the ingredients and waiting on the bread to bake rigid enough to withstand dipping, her ears hone in on the living room discussion.

Bailey has a lot to say about Levi. "The brother done flipped the script, you hear me? He so lowdown he'd have to look up to a snake. The investigation is looking bad, pastor, *real* bad. And Levi, he up there pretend like he's defending you, when all he's doing is stirring the pot." Bailey describes some of the shots Levi has taken from the pulpit during Stewart's honeymoon. Deacon Bailey even impersonates Levi's slow snicker, "'Heh, heh, heh, I promise y'all, ole Stew idn't in hiding; he's out there at Martha's Vineyard having the time of his life; he ain't got y'all to think about heh, heh, heh … 'Soon as our fearless leader's *private jet* hit the tarmac, he'll get right to sorting things out, heh, heh, heh…'" He gives the impression that Stewart owns a private jet, when really, Stewart only chartered one. Bailey switches back to himself. "They're putting it all on *you* man."

"How could they? When I didn't want the seminar in the first place. *They* twisted my arm. So, what did I do? I brought in the lawyer who pumped the brakes on the whole thing or it would've been much worse than it is."

"*I* know that, pastor. *You* know that. Levi and the trustees know that. But *members* don't know that. They don't know how power is divided. All they see is you."

Stewart counters, "But even so, I did *not* endorse Westermann."

"But you let him speak at the pulpit though."

"*And?* The pulpit ain't nothing but a wooden podium."

"That's the way *I* feel about it, but when you turn on the TV and see Cornell West weighing in on Farr's scandal, saying that the invitation to the pulpit *is* endorsement, then people are going to take that and run with it."

Lynn's returns with the hors divers. "Careful, they're still hot." Lynn is satisfied with how they'd turned out. She mills around long enough for the reviews. Bailey gives her two thumbs up.

Lynn then says to Stewart, "You can say the pulpit is just a podium all you want. Obviously it's more than just a podium if they'd bar a whole gender from it."

Stewart and Bailey seem caught off guard by her input; there is a noticeable glitch before Bailey agrees, "I know that's right, sis."

Lynn retreats to the kitchen, wondering if they thought she'd overstepped her boundary, as if she's the help in her own home. She grew upset at being made to feel like her mother, serving her husband and his company, expected to interrupt only to check for refills, not for her opinion; *sight unseen*. Lynn's thoughts are turning vile. To prevent marching back to the living room and flipping over the plate of crouton and dip, Lynn contrives counter terrorist thoughts, like, maybe they are surprised by *what* she said rather than the fact that she spoke at all. While feeling around for a peaceful theme, Lynn somehow lands on facts: no one asked her to get refreshments; she volunteered so naturally, so happily, to expend her effort for their comfort. She chose the kitchen and is now feeling soiled by the experience.

She listens in again as she pulls a bottled water out of the refrigerator. Bailey says, out of the three hundred or so members who lost their investments, forty of them organized and are now threatening a lawsuit.

"Lawsuit," Stewart repeats.

"Yup, by forty members," Bailey confirms. "And Levi out front, cuttin' a fool. He did a sermon, last – no – two Sundays ago where he's making this lawsuit out to be prophecy. Using the number forty, he connected First Baptist's troubles to Israel's forty years in wilderness, and Noah's forty days and nights to cleanse the wicked. You know me, I don't make too much noise, but I *had* to say something. I told him like this, I said: 'ain't prophecies told in advance? Alls you talking about is What's Happening Now: *that* ain't prophecy; that's a sitcom.'"

Stewart seems thoroughly pleased, "You said that?"

Bailey admits, "That last part came to me later, but yeah."

Sight unseen walks in, sits down next to her husband, and tosses her bottle cap on the table like a poker chip. "Even if Levi told it in advance, he'd still be wrong. Forty *people* in the lawsuit deals in quantity, therefore, forty is just a number. Only in terms of *time,* is God marking a transformation, as in Noah's forty *days and nights*, or Israel's forty *years* surviving on manna, Jesus fasted forty *days and nights*, and a woman's pregnancy term is forty *weeks...*"

Stewart's head shakes with pride. He grabs Lynn's hand and kisses it. Lynn fights the idea that his affection is pet-like.

Bailey points, "First lady be *on point*, ain't it?" Bailey crosses his legs and asks, "So, when you taking over Women's Bible study? I tell ya, that Nay don't know what the heck she be talkin' about."

"Ain't that the truth," Lynn agrees, but then backtracks. "But what do you mean *when?*"

Bailey thumbs at Stewart, "Oh, this fool ain't tell you? Traditionally, the first lady facilitates bible study. Nay out – you in, simple as that." Bailey, observes how the couple becomes quiet. Bailey gives a look as if he'd just stepped in mud.

Lynn turns a facetious smile to Stewart, "You hear the deacon, babe? Nay out, I'm in; simple as that."

Stewart stammers, "That's what I had in mind, but I know we'll be so busy moving–"

"–And?" She awaits a better excuse.

"The other thing: you may not know yet, but you're pregnant."

Deacon Bailey's eyes go ablaze, ready to congratulate, but Lynn waves him off, explaining, "He's been saying that all weekend, just because a young deer walked right up to me."

Bailey giggles nervously, unsure if he's in the midst of an argument waiting to happen. Bailey asks, "First Lady… did I get pastor in trouble?"

Stewart comes right in on the bumper of the comment. "Ain't nobody in trouble."

After Head Deacon Bailey leaves, Lynn questions Stewart on the matter, though playfully throwing around the word *bruh* as Stewart did while talking to Bailey. "What's up with that bruh? You told me you had to *convince* Nay to step down, bruh?"

Stewart says, "But I've got something much bigger than bible study in mind for you. I didn't want to say it in front of Bailey just yet, but when the Academy is built, I want you to be the director."

"My thing is literature. The *bible* is literature."

Stewart says, "Ok, if it's bible study you want, it's bible study you get."

Lynn studies him for a moment. "Why are you acting like that?"

"Like what?"

Lynn takes a deep breath. "One thing about you that I marvel at, is how you can come into a group of people and tell them all what to do. I cringe when *I* have to tell another adult what to do, but you? You do it like it's nothing. You don't even study their reaction. You just point here, point there, and say 'you do this,' and 'hey *you* go there and do that.' You never even hesitate – *except* for when it comes to Nay."

Stewart smiles, paternally, saying, "What you observe, Lynn, is one hundred percent accurate. I do hesitate when it comes to Nay, but it's not just Nay. I've come to realize that I'm that way when it comes to anyone who had been a part of this church before I became pastor. It's like they've already bonded with a different me, so with them, I just…"

"Say no more," Lynn says. "I totally get it. Actually, I'm tempted to let Nay keep bible study for a while because it's probably good for her, considering what she's going through at home."

Stewart looks on, dead-faced.

"I know you don't believe me, love; you don't have to say it. I wanna get her to open up to me, I just don't know how."

"Very tactfully, Lynn. That's how," Stewart says. "Very tactfully. You wanna be sure, before you get between husband and wife."

"Tactfully, I'll give you that, but definitely. Something has to be done. She can't do it alone, Dana. It's psychological. She's trapped in the maze of her abuser's mind; she needs someone to lead her out. If someone didn't do it for me, way back when, I wouldn't be here today. That's a fact."

Chapter 25

They call a meeting with the lawyer and the forty members, hoping to reach a settlement. Stewart is glad to be, finally, putting the investment scandal issue to bed. He, Levi and two trustees, armed with their lawyer, Attorney Reuben Belfast, rendezvous in the parking garage at the opposing attorney's office. Attorney Belfast is old and dated, his graying hair greased back under his brim. His pinstripe suit looks like a Harlem Renaissance throwback.

They meet at the office of Attorney Latria Lyons, all of five feet tall with a stylish combover and pigtail bang.

Four, of the forty plaintiffs, enter the room. Mrs. Lyons announces, "My clients, the Boughtknights (Jeffery and Gwendolyn) and the McLevins (Lucinda and Pierce)… Welcome." The two couples walk in somberly, as if entering a wake.

Catfish boasts, "Let's get it crackin'." He points to the foot of the conference table, "See that gentleman over yonder? That's our lawyer."

Mrs. Lyons rolls her eyes. "This should be interesting; an accident lawyer?"

Belfast removes his brown shades, "Worst accident you'll ever be in, going against me."

Mrs. Lyons rubs her hands as she addresses the room. "Let us all keep at the forefront of our discussions today, the fact we all have the same goal: a swift resolution, so that we can all get on with our lives. The men and women here on the plaintiff's side of this matter are still very much in allegiance with First Baptist Church and they abhor the negative media attention as much as you do. So let us keep those common themes in mind during our negotiations today and I assure you, we can come to a resolution that will be satisfactory on all sides. Attorney Belfast?"

The man looks surprised by this formality. He gets up, buttoning his suit and clearing his throat. "Yeah, yeah… Big words for the little bird," he smirks as Mrs. Lyons gasps. "When you say resolution, you's talking 'bout a dollar amount, am I right?" Belfast bows slightly to the left and the right checking with both sides.

Mrs. Lyons closes her eyes. "You're making a big mistake, Mr. Belfast, if you think throwing out figures is going to solve anything. Money settles nothing if neither side is heard – or if there is no true reconciliation."

"What you want is for *your* side to embellish their damages, telling how much they suffered and for our side to sit here and listen. Thing is: didn't nobody bring no violins, Mrs. Lyons. The disclosures were given at the financial seminar. These members acted outside of the advice of the church and *only* the media – not wrongdoing – has provided you a seat at the negotiating table, so please, spare us the Fairy Godmother bit. We are here because the media *wants* the head of a black leader to roll and we *don't* want that to happen. End of story."

The biggest head of all, Catfish, hooks his finger in his shirt collar. "*Whose* head?"

Rudy adds, "Whoever stick his head out there to be chopped."

Catfish points at Stewart's head. "That'll be his. It'll roll nicely. Got a nice roundness to it. We ain't too crazy about him no-how."

Attorney Latria Lyons sighs at the madness, drained like a chemo patient. "This is the tone *you* set Mr. Belfast. Will you please do the honors?"

Attorney Belfast raps his ring finger against the table. "Gentlemen! Gentlemen!"

Jeffrey Boughtknight, however, is determined to get his word in, "You all brought that conman in and let him run his mouth about God, faith, stewardship, and all this – *right* from the pulpit like he's laying out the will of God for us. *Now* you wanna hide behind disclosures? C'mon, now."

Catfish is all over the man. "Since when you care about the word of God? All them years you ain't eem *seen* the inside of a church until sickness hauled you in." Catfish turns to the other gentlemen on his side of the table, explaining, "Ole Jeff here used to toot powder with them boys down there in West Hell (a nickname for West Columbia). Out of the forty people suing us, this the best y'all got to represent the group? This ole coke-head can't say a word to me."

Mrs. Boughtknight jumps in. "Coke-head or not–" laughter burst at the wife confirming her husband's addiction. All defendants laugh but Stewart who palms his face in agony. Mrs. Boughtknight restarts, "My husband worked all his life, put us up in a house, and built a nest egg for our retirement only to be taken by you crooks? I will *not* spend my old age as a Wal-Mart greeter, to keep up with the rising cost of medication."

The lawyers quiet them again, Reuben Belfast adding, "Calm down, y'all. Especially you Mr. Otto."

Catfish points at himself, "*Me?*"

"Yes you."

Mrs. Lyons announces, "This is not how it works… You will all be called upon, and I assure you everyone will have their say."

Stewart, who had held his face in his hands for the duration of the back and forth, imparts, "As Mrs. Lyons stated earlier, we all want the same thing–"

"–Say what now?" Catfish interrupts. "Just because we're sitting on the same side of this table don't mean we want the same thing, pastor. *We* want to save our church. *You* wanna save your ass." Catfish, the one supposedly silenced, shows palms. "I just wanted to put that out there, once and for all. You won't hear another peep out of me."

Mrs. McLevin, an Olive Oyl thin, seventy-year-old post office retiree, says, "Obviously we won't get anywhere with this one (Catfish) in the room. I vote that he be removed so we can get on with this."

"If he go; *we* go," threatens, Rudy and Levi.

Again, Catfish jumps into the fray, addressing their lawyer, "If I can't talk up for myself, *you* better cuss her out *for* me. Or what're we paying you for?"

Even the lawyers throw their hands up in despair as insults are lobbed from one side of the table to the other. Stewart is the lone voice of reason but to no avail. Rudy calls Stewart out. "To hell with you Stew. You're the sole damned reason we're here."

They'd sunken too low to recover. They yell about nest eggs being crushed under Armani shoes; knives twisted in backs. The one insult that cancels any chance for negotiation is Levi blaming the members for not having the sense God gave a Billy-goat. On that note, the room empties.

In the parking garage, tempers fly, Ginyard on Ginyard. Catfish lashes out at Levi, calling him spineless. Stewart steps up for Levi and goes after Catfish, but Levi stops him, his stiff hand wiggling in rejection. "Don't think you can stick up for me and suddenly we boys again, naw nigga. It's time for a change, and *I'm* that change."

Tires squeal and engines race to the street level exit. Stewart is left abandoned and alone.

Lynn helps Nay make tablescapes for the domestic violence ministry's annual luncheon for the coming Saturday.

They fill glass vases with glazed, purple pebbles, and tying them with purple ribbons, for domestic violence awareness. They unbox velvet roses from last year and dust them off. They form little candy arrangements in mesh, tied by a ribbon to be stored away until Saturday. Nay says, "We'll be set. That morning all we'll have to do is come in, boom, boom, boom and we done." Nay adds, "This is going to be *so* pretty."

Lynn says. "If *we* were going at it like our husbands, folks would call *us* catty."

"Ain't that the truth. So, what's the term for men?"

Lynn shrugs. "Do they even have one?"

"They meticulous about *our* flaws though. They take the time to name each one... Thirsty is the word they use now, for a woman who's desperate for a man–" Nay raises a finger, "–and *speaking* of Bianca..."

The two cut eyes at each other and let loose, weakening with laughter. A high five clenches and becomes a brace for them to keep from falling over each other.

Nay, recovering from well spent laughter, says, "I threw that out there just to see if you'd catch it... You're alright, Lynn," Nay spies from her periphery.

Lynn says, "The thing about Bianca, though, is that she isn't necessarily thirsty for a man; she thirsty for a pastor."

"*Now* you're talking," Nay's head bobs in agreement. "I'm trying to work up to letting you in on it, when you already know."

Lynn realizes she just told on herself, that she knows what Nay told Stewart, in confidence. "I forgot that I wasn't *supposed* to know."

"No, Lynn, honey. I would've thought something was wrong if you *didn't* know. Husbands and wives shouldn't keep no secrets." Nay goes over to the bin for more vases, pebbles, and velvet roses. Nay does a silent count of the tablescapes. "Heck, me and you, we're almost done." Nay looks over at Lynn and says, "How's the speech coming along; I know I called you on short notice."

"Actually, I'll be recycling a ten-minute, domestic violence speech I gave at the Chicks Before Cocks protest in 2005."

Nay's face shrivels in scorn. "*Lawd*, that mouth..."

"Not penises, Nay. Chickens. Remember when the Judiciary Committee *tabled* the criminal domestic violence bill but, in the same session, *passed* the felony cockfighting bill? – As if chickens are more important than women?"

"Well, as long as we in church, say chicken fighting. You know how you like to get footloose like you did at rehearsals that time." They chuckle together and then Nay cuts an eye at Lynn and says, "You didn't back down, thought."

"Not that I stood a chance. It's just that there's no real fear of a woman after many occasions being beaten unconscious by a man."

Nay's hand half raises to cover her mouth. "Aw naw, Lynn."

"The thing is, he wasn't that bad man. He was loyal, he was soft spoken, he was romantic... most days. Other days it was like being trapped in a small space with a raging bull. No matter how good I was to him, I couldn't keep that evil twin from showing up."

"Tell me about it," Nay says, accidentally.

Lynn's eyes widen. "So you know what I'm talking about?"

Nay looks down like a child. "Lynn..." Nay sighs. She's fighting tears.

Lynn takes Nay's hands and sits her down at the table. "Talk to me, Nay. No one can do this alone."

Nay opens her mouth to speak but the sound of a cell phone ring comes out. It's her phone. She checks it. "It's Levi. I have to take this." The phone rings again in Nay's hand.

"Ignore it," says Lynn. "Ignore it and talk to me."

Nay's eyes widen. "If you anything, Lynn, you should know that I *have* to take this."

Lynn's phone rings. "Stewart," she says. Nay answers her phone and wanders away for the conversation, so Lynn answers her call. "Bad timing, hon."

Nay heads to the exit, waving. "See ya at bible study, Lynn."

"Never mind," Lynn says to Stewart.

Stewart sounds like he's standing in the middle of traffic. He is clearly frustrated, fuming about the trustees and Levi. Lynn is afraid he'd suffer another anxiety attack. "Breathe," Lynn suggests. "Are you ok?" His health is her first concern.

Stewart calms down and begins to explain, although his telling of the negotiations sounds like a comedy skit. It's too wild. Negotiations crashed and burned too quickly.

After ending the call with Stewart, Lynn makes a call to Gayle to help making sense of it. Lynn tries to call Stewart back to give Gayle's assessment of what took place, but she can't get a hold of him.

Stewart and Lynn phone tag throughout the day. They aren't face to face until they run into each other on the way to bible study; Lynn, to women's bible study and Stewart to men's. They stop in the same little used hallway where Bianca punched Stewart in the mouth. Lynn asks, "Did you get my message?"

Stewart nods. "So just how certain is your lawyer friend about the trustees sabotaging the negotiations?"

"A hundred percent certain, love. That lawyer, Belfast, he's a nobody. The whole negotiation is smoke and mirrors. The *last* thing these trustees want, is for the bad press to let up. It reflects badly on the church, but worse on *you.*"

"I get that, but why go through all the trouble of staging meeting? Couldn't they have simply declined the negotiations and gotten the same result?"

Lynn's head shakes no well before Stewart finishes. "They want you thinking that they're handling everything on the legal front, so you'll feel like you won't have to get your own lawyer. They're just holding the rug, waiting to snatch it out from under you. Remember, I told you to get a lawyer, babe? You're taking all the heat for this investment thing, when it was their idea. *You* should be the one suing *them* for damage to your reputation."

Stewart scratches the back of his neck and looks away. "Damages… In the form of what, money? What good is money if I'm no longer the pastor? If I'm gone, they'll never break ground on the Christian academy."

Lynn grips his shoulders, training his attention on her. "Bottom line, we can't just lean on them. We have to do something."

Stewart looks at her as if gazing upon a child's drawing, so darling in how badly it mimics reality. "We…" He reaches to touch Lynn's face.

She dodges the hand. "What is that?"

Stewart's hand withers back to him. "What's is what?"

Lynn looks at him with a dare in her eyes. "You weren't trying to patronize me just now, were you? I hope not."

Stewart's tensed up fret, swaps for abhorrence. "Look, you know I didn't mean it that way. And I've got too many problems to be tiptoeing around my own wife."

Lynn is ready to unload on Stewart when a group enters the hallway. She flashes claws and teeth, but then smiles and waves for the passersby.

Stewart uses the opportunity to tap his watch, showing that he's running late for men's bible study for which he now must facilitate.

"So, you're leaving?" Lynn's disbelief takes on a fiendish, jack o'lantern smile, but then she folds her arms and then says, "Go." As if to see if he actually would.

Before taking off, Stewart kisses Lynn, but their disagreement is far from over.

After bible study, Stewart and Lynn return home for their first big argument. Stewart can't get over how one word has them arguing well into the night. Lynn keeps asserting that it is not *what* he said, but *how* he said it, and the timing, coming right after his quick dismissal of her advice to get a lawyer. Stewart's disposition made it clear that he doesn't see her as a teammate – not even a Batman's Robin or Sherlock's Watson. Their argument even confirms it when Stewart says he doesn't want Lynn battling alongside him, going head-to-head with Levi and the trustees; he wants to protect her. "Protect *me?*" Lynn calls time out to set the record straight. "Me? When I'm used to going head-to-head with senators; me, who'd rally in small towns, up against gun toting intimidators? Pu-lease!"

Lynn is disappointed at such a blow-up so soon in their marriage. They agree not to go to bed angry, so they manufacture a truce, but days later they're still feeling the effects of the argument. Each night Stewart slips out of bed to write in his journal. They speak only out of necessity, but with such caution and humility that Stewart unscrewing the lid on a jar of relish for Lynn is like the signing of a treaty.

Because their argument replays for days in Lynn's mind, she is sure the same is happening in Stewart's mind. Lynn analyzes their finger pointing, their trap questions and one-line zingers. Like a gold miner panning silt, Lynn pans insults in search for ores of substance; rinsing away the, *if you would wipe the evil out of your eye you would see...* now revealed the information on the back end. … *that this has nothing to do with respect, it's that I love you enough to protect you because they'll come after you too…* Lynn now sees chivalry and valor: his love language. He doesn't question her capability; he is hashing out culpability. In the mind of a tradition-oriented Baptist preacher, the role of protector is no joint venture; the role is *his*. However, in Lynn's view, nothing could help them know love more than battling side by side, sharing foxholes, shielding one another and, together, advancing on the enemy. She knows no other way to achieve the kind of love bond most sought after.

When Stewart rejected her question saying, *I don't have to explain myself to you…* In the moment he proved his arrogance, but Lynn, later, listens to the part she tuned out… *ever since we were dating, I've been trying to cure your doubt with my love, and that hasn't worked, so what good would words do now?* He is offended that he is so easily accused without figuring the checks and balances, that she'd accused him on something as brief as a strummed chord of emotion.

Two days after the blowup, Lynn wants reconciliation, but she isn't sure if her husband is ready. He still avoids eye contact. Lynn spends most of her time in the bedroom, her bordered nation, and Stewart sticks to his own sovereign nation, The Republic of Couch.

Lynn, however, begins to understand her husband's clockwork, and she begins feeling closer to him, regardless of their physical distance. He hates to be judged or blamed – not for fear accountability, but because he, himself, is slow to point the finger. He nearly did, that day at end of their argument when he said, *as if* you *walk on water… but have I lashed out at* you *for* your *mistakes?* Lynn couldn't think of any blemishes on her record. When she challenged, *what mistakes have I made?* Stewart had walked away.

His retreat seemed to prove that there were none, but Lynn is later reminded of her mistake when she wakes in the middle of the night and finds Stewart asleep on the couch with his journal wide open on his lap. She stands over him, reading, upside down, the record of her crime, in cursive handwriting, *Maybe she didn't think highly enough of me to tell me, in advance, that she was mar-ried before* ... Her secrecy hurt his feelings, yet he never spoke of it, not even in retaliation.

Lynn, stands over her sleeping husband, the desires of his heart, literally an open book where she reads how the man so humbly pleads with God to kindly honor one small request: to bless their marriage with conception, preferably by Christmas... *if it be Your will.* This makes Lynn smile.

Next, Lynn reads something that makes her cry. *Lord help me win my wife's deepest affections; help me be the husband You would have for her.*

Chapter 26

Lynn and Nay are early. Nay appraises Lynn. "Well, well… Look who's dressed to be blessed. Fancy folks don't ask what you're wearing they ask *who* you're wearing."

Lynn smiles. "Couldn't even tell you. All I know is the shoes. It's Monolo."

"Okay Monolos!" Nay give's Lynn a high-five. "Somebody got to spend that money, child. Lord knows that cheapskate Stewart won't spend it on himself."

They talk at length about fashion and the expectations for the day. They make quick work of setting the tables. Together they check in on the banquet staff; the entree preparation is on schedule.

Each time Lynn tries to rehash their conversation about abuse, Nay pretends to be distracted, and once the big, flowery hats begin filing through the entrance, Nay has all the distraction she needs.

The women turn out in force for the annual domestic violence luncheon; so many shades of brown, so many different renditions of beauty that beauty itself is reinvented with each entrance. Grace is dialed up to one hundred, as if the event were practice for the luncheons they'd have later in heaven.

Bianca starts the festivities with a solo a cappella that stirs their spirits. Someone's granddaughter does a ballet piece to Kirk Franklin's *Imagine Me* that leaves them beaming; the young lady still dancing in their hearts well after her performance.

Four speakers would take the podium: a DV survivor helped by the ministry; Nay, for opening and closing remarks and to introduce the featured speaker, Linda Nance, a local radio personality now open about her bout with domestic violence.

Lynn has just a ten minute speech which is supposed to be just background noise while the attendees are being served; however, Lynn's speech turns out to be the highlight of the event. Lynn's four-year-old protest speech is originally the response to Criminal Domestic Violence Bill opposer, Rep. Altman's salty response to a female reporter who questioned his stance on the bill. First Altman calls Susan Gorman's question dumb and poses a question of his own, which did nothing but parade his own ignorance, as thick as his southern drawl. "… tell me what self-respecting woman is going back around someone who beats them."

Unlike four years prior, Lynn's speech isn't a rushed project at a rushed protest, blindsided by the unexpected tabling of the bill.

The arc of Lynn's speech goes from political to personal. She starts by saying that Altman's question isn't a question, that it is devoid of curiosity, that it swaps the legislative burden for a personal one, a moral one, placing the solution squarely on the shoulders of the victims.

"The bill eventually passed, thank God," Lynn says to her audience. "But what puzzles me is that, in a state where – going back as far as domestic violence became a statistic – we've continually ranked worst in the nation when it comes to women dying at the hands of her abuser, yet this pip-squeak, Altman, had the gall to spit on the victims and still sits comfortably in his house seat?" Lynn draws applause like she'd just swung her bat and cracked a base hit.

Lynn refuses to entertain the element of self-respect. "What I know is that women are not the question *and* the answer. It's a human issue; bigotry *makes* it a gender issue… Women who stay, stay for the same reason that women who leave, leave: fear. Cemeteries are populated with women dead today *because* they left." One woman, hit with the vision of her alternate ending, cries out *Amen*. Lynn says, "The abuser will warn you: 'If you leave me, I will hunt you down, and I will kill you.' He may threaten to execute your children right at your feet." *Preach*, they call out. *Shame the devil.*

"… In some cases, you stay because you grew up in a household where something *abnormal* like abuse became *your* normal. You stay now because you've already stayed as a child when leaving was *not* even an option. Sure, you know better as an adult. But what you didn't know is that you were shaped by that abuse; it has its fingerprints all over you. *You* couldn't see it. But *someone* saw it, didn't they?" Lynn nods as surely as she knows the sky is blue. Her audience knows where she is going and they are confident, now, that Lynn could captain the journey. "Make no mistake. You were handpicked by the abuser." Half of the women stand with some outlet of emotion, arms swinging, thanking Jesus for this spiritual confirmation. "An abuser has the nose of a blood hound. He'll sniff you out. He'll patiently win your love and your loyalty unto him, until you're ripe for ambush. The first time, you write it off as just an aberration, he begs his way back into your heart but at the same time you're already pregnant with fear, a fear that, over time, he would nurture and grow inside of you, but they want to blame *you?*"

In closing, Lynn informs them that now in the present day, the house is trying to revise the bill and strike down the mandatory sentencing, which could put victims at greater risk. Lynn calls on them to use the power of protest and the power of their vote to challenge the proposed changes. Lynn tries to hand the microphone over, but Nay is in no condition to take over and introduce the main speaker. Nay is hugging herself with tears streaming down her face, her head shaking no, while she's repeating no, down in her throat. "Mm-mm, Mm-mm." Nay seems ready to testify. Lynn extends the microphone, but Nay rejects it, still, saying, "Mm-mm… Mm-mm… Hold me Jesus… Hold me Jesus."

Lynn continues, now adlibbing, speaking to the heart of every survivor by speaking to Nay's heart. "Not everyone is threatened with death. Not everyone stays to save their life. Some stay because we think we could fix him. Can I get a witness? You study your abuser. You learn to see the rage coming a mile away, and you successfully head it off *most* of the times, amen? When your savvy fails and you find yourself dabbing your cut lip, or icing your eye, you think it's *your* fault – that maybe if you'd done something differently... You thought you were making progress, but that progress is nothing more than a trick of the devil. The pathology of violence, in the abuser's mind, is degenerative; power satisfied by nothing but *more* power. Eventually, he doesn't even need a reason to raise his hand. He'll slap the taste out of your mouth and then *make* up a reason won't he?" Lynn's fire spreads throughout her audience.

"All too often... you're not ready to leave until you can predict your own death!" Three women cry out. Lynn, pauses and then repeats the statement to recapture her rhythm of speech. "All too often you leave when you can predict your own death... when you find yourself pulling a friend or family member aside and say to them, 'If anything ever happens to me...'" Lynn doesn't have to finish the statement. Hands go up in witness, but also like roll-call, for the fact that they are, by the grace of God, still here. Nay, gazing forward, glassy eyed, studies the images Lynn brings back to be revised under this truth.

Bianca, who can't understand the creed that connects these surviving women, understands how to serve them with her voice. She goes off the program and comforts them with *A Mighty Long Way*, in a mournful key.

When Nay is finally ready to take over, it is apparent that something inside of her has risen up to be accounted for, but Nay doesn't speak on it.

The keynote speaker's speech doesn't rise to the level of Lynn's, but afterwards, it's Linda Nance, the local celebrity they surround for facetime and autographs. Lynn hangs around waiting on an opportunity to talk to Nay again and possibly get her to open up.

Lynn notices the church mother named Mavis, looking directly at her, and shaking her head in disapproval...? Or pity...? Lynn doesn't spend a second studying the church mother they call crazy, regardless of Mavis looking quite regal this afternoon, with her neat dreadlocks spilling out of her lily-white church hat. Mavis looks like a retired model whose aging favoring the smugness of her beauty. Mavis walks over, her smile loaded with riddles. "You almost did it," Mavis says.

Lynn, ready with denial asks, "Did what?"

Mavis leans in. "You almost *told* on yourself."

To the degree that Mavis leans forward, Lynn leans back, already writing this off as nonsense coming from the woman that Lynn once spotted in church laughing and making a sexual gesture, her pointer finger jabbing the circle of the ok sign. "What are you talking about, Mavis?"

"I'm talking about what you're *not* talking about."

"If you have a question, *do* ask. I'm an open book."

"With blank pages."

Lynn gives a slow, measured, "Okay…"

"Your husband needs your help."

"He doesn't want my help."

"To a man's ears, *offering* help is no different than telling him he's screwing up; he'll deny it. So don't wait on his permission."

"What kind of help do you mean?"

"The seven dwarfs (the trustees) plan to remove him in the beginning of 2010, when First Baptist turns a hundred. He was their guy as long as we were growing, but we're no longer growing. Wanna know what kept him up on that pulpit?"

Lynn, confused, hasn't the wit to form a guess.

"Us: the congregation, thriving ministries, our tithes. Even the love offering is like poll numbers, an approval rating for the pastor. This last love offering…" Mavis's head shakes. "… it taught the Ginyards that they could get rid of Stewart without too much of an uproar. That's why Stewart wants so badly to build that school, which reminds me: they're gonna block the money Stewart raised for that school, so he *can't* build."

"What do you mean? *We* raised that money."

"When they're good and ready, they're using that money for their own plans."

"How would *you* know?"

"From their wives, who, by the way ain't so keen on seeing Stewart go. I, for one, will do all that I can to keep him where he is. You, on the other hand, need to start building some loyalty around here, which means you've got to be real with folks."

"Excuse me," says Lynn. "I'm *not* real?"

"You're hiding," says Mavis. "*Are* you a survivor of domestic violence?"

"If I were hiding, you wouldn't have known to ask."

"If you *weren't* hiding, you would've answered yes. You're too calculating; that's why people don't care much for you."

Lynn laughs. "People like me just fine, Mavis."

"Do they like you or do they like the attention that the first lady brings *them?* If you and Nay are so close why didn't she warn you of the Ginyards' plan to block the academy? People keep you in the dark about things when they think you're a bit high on yourself."

Lynn, a tower of resistance, replies. "People, or just you?"

"I'm no hater. And I wouldn't ask you to do what I wouldn't." Mavis takes a deep breath and says, "What do you know about me?"

Lynn cringes. "You did time in prison."

"For what?"

"For cutting a man's face."

"Why?"

"Because…"

"Say it."

"… He raped you, I heard, and then he fell asleep…" Lynn is noticeably uncomfortable.

"I did more time than he did. I would've walked Scot free had I cut his face *while* being raped. They said when I slid out from under him and went to my purse for my box cutter, that was premeditation. Now he's got a scar across his face, blind in one eye, though."

"That's what I heard," Lynn says.

"On any given day, there's about a hundred people I can call them up, and they will go with me behind those prison bars and sup with murderers and minister unto them. Why? Because people won't fight *for* you until they know you have fight *in* you. People see this wacky ole lady and they don't think much of me, but once they know that I *was* an orphan; that I *was* homeless; that I *was* an addict, and that life had already buried me, but I crawled up out of that grave, that's instant respect. Your present blessings – author, professor, fairytale marriage, first lady – does not inspire like you think. Inspiration comes from the *distance* between where you are now and from where you've come. Come clean, Lynn. What are you afraid of?"

Lynn ponders it and replies, earnestly, "It's not that I'm afraid. It's that I was married to my abuser. I can't put that out there that the pastor's wife was married before. I know it's not a big deal at most churches, but it seems to be a big deal at this church."

"I see," says Mavis. "I just hope you see." Mavis turns to go.

Lynn stops her. "See what?"

Mavis looks back. "That without you, everything that Stewart has worked for over the years will be for naught."

Mavis goes on to congregate with the other women. Lynn looks around for Nay and she's nowhere to be found.

When Lynn returns home, before she realizes it, she and her husband are talking like normal. He'd returned from the barber with nothing else to do on a beautiful Saturday afternoon. The early autumn feels like a mild extension of summer. They go for a walk along the pond where they catch up on the few days they were not speaking. Out of nowhere, Lynn says, "I talked to Mavis today."

Stewart smirks. "What'd *she* have to say?"

"I'm still trying to figure out. She's so random."

Stewart looks out over the placid pond, his eyes fixed on something. "Mavis is too devious to be random."

"Devious… Is that what she is?"

"In her own way. So how was the luncheon?"

"It was beautiful. Our speaker, Linda Nance, was outstanding."

"I heard *you* stole the show." He slides his hand around her waist and they stop to kiss on the stout wooden bridge arched over the middle of the pond. Stewart backs against the rail. Stewart holds her shoulders and apologizes, safe in their embrace to admit wrongdoing and expect amnesty. "You were right about me. In that moment, I was frustrated; I didn't want to hear anything. So, it made it seem as if I didn't value your opinion. Nothing personal. Sometimes I don't even wanna listen to God."

"It wasn't all you, love. I overreacted."

"I gave you something to overreact to."

"I love you so much, Dana." Lynn remembers the line in his journal where he asks God to help him be a better husband and she melts right there in his arms, but then she looks up and says, "I'm ovulating."

Without further ado, they hurry along the twenty yard walk back to their home.

After lovemaking, Lynn lies on her back, holding her legs up by the back of her thighs, to aid conception.

Their conversation plays out on the ceiling. Stewart, wanting in on a secret, asks, "What's this I hear about women's bible study the other night? Is there a thing between you and Nay?"

Lynn's brow lowers, "I wouldn't call it a thing. She believed that Magdalene is a repentant prostitute and I corrected her."

"I often wonder how that misconception still hangs around in a day and age where everyone can read."

Lynn's head turns on her stationary body, flat on its back. "Shows you how many people actually read the bible. Most people just hopscotch through the scriptures yet believe they're qualified to facilitate bible study."

"I think people are reading the bible, but their minds are already shaped by what they've been told, so what they read falls in line."

"Anyway, we stopped class for only a few minutes to straighten it out, but I wouldn't call it a thing." Lynn stops as if she is piecing something together on the ceiling. "Now that I think about it... Nay did come back with a rebuttal this morning. This time, not over Mary's identity, but that although she isn't *that* particular prostitute who anointed the feet of Jesus, but that she is a prostitute, nonetheless."

"How'd you respond to that?"

"Is this a quiz?"

Stewart smiles, his raised brow wrinkling his forehead as he pleads the fifth.

"She insists that Magdalene is a prostitute because Jesus cast seven demons out of her, which is the only fact that came out of Nay's mouth. Everything else is pure imagination: she assumed that those seven demons *had* to have been the seven deadly sins, which includes the demon of lust, which *had* to mean that she was a prostitute. My *students* can come up with a better argument than that, yet this is who teaches bible study?"

"She sounds like her husband. It's not that she doesn't comprehend. On some things, people don't trouble themselves with evidence. Right or wrong, they're going to stand in *their* truth, instead of *the* truth." Stewart observes something in Lynn that makes him ask, "What's that look?"

"How do you know what took place at women's bible study when there's nothing but women there? Which woman told you?" Lynn fights a smile, but fully expects to be humored with an explanation.

"Last I checked, women talk to their husbands. I heard it from a man." They rub noses and kiss. "Not much of anything goes on without me knowing."

"So, you know what the trustees are doing?"

"What have you heard?"

"They're seizing the money set aside for the academy."

Stewart looks up, alert. "Where'd you hear that?"

"Mavis."

Stewart's head sinks in the pillow, as if the source alone validates the claim. "I'd rather she bring it to me. I don't want you troubled with this stuff."

"Bring it to you, why? So, you can hide it from me?"

"You don't need the stress. We're trying to conceive." Stewart gazes at her pillowed face and says, "I love that you're so concerned about me that you'll go to whatever lengths to support me–"

"–And it's sweet, how you want to protect me." Lynn palms his chest to halt any further explanation from her husband, the future father of her child.

A Pimp In The Pulpit

Chapter 27

Lynn gets a call from federal agent Claude. The man says he has good news but he also has questions. Following Mavis's advice, Lynn doesn't ask Stewart's permission. In secret, Lynn goes to the local FBI office which crawls with agents wearing gun holsters over business casual attire. She's escorted from the receptionist area to Agent Claude's office, which is merely a cubicle littered with sticky notes and a calendar. After the greeting, Lynn hands over the seminar DVD, saying, "This video was removed from the church's digital library, so I wasn't sure if you'd seen it or not. This is where my husband gave all the disclosures, verbally and in writing–"

"–I've seen it," Claude waves. "You can keep it. Actually, your husband's church is now clear of any possible charges. Our investigation shows that First Baptist did it the right way. That's the good news."

"So, the forty litigants suing the church should no longer be a problem, right?"

"The FBI director here will do a press conference in the coming weeks. That alone should get that lawsuit dropped." Lynn sighs relief. Agent Claude leans back in his chair and says, "The bureau was never looking to book religious leaders while Wall Street killed the economy and gets a bailout. The focus was always on catching the real bad guy, Westermann."

"So, what else is there?"

"I've got something for you to see." He opens a window on his computer screen and presses the triangle play button on a grainy surveillance video of a car, which he freeze-frames and zooms in. "Familiar?"

Lynn squints. "That's Levi's car. Levi is the assistant pastor."

"This surveillance was taken from a business near the church on the night of the robbery. He's coming and going within minutes of the security alarm being disabled."

"So, it was Levi who burglarized his own church?!" Lynn's face tingles. Not only is the man abusing his wife, he's undermining her husband and the entire ministry. "Can I have a copy – I mean, is that allowed?"

"It's not," Claude says. "Plus, this simple larceny is not a federal crime, and we won't forward this to local police until the case on Westermann is closed."

"They'll have my husband removed by then, Claude. I need that video now."

"Sounds like this video means a lot to you." Claude ponders for a moment and says, "I can give you a copy of this video, but I'll need something from you in return."

"What could you possibly want from me?"

The man licks his lips and says, "I need you to peek into Pastor Stewart's journal."

"No," Lynn says. "I will not betray him like that."

Claude replies, "What if what's contained in his journal would show that he's betrayed you?"

"Nice try," says Lynn. "I have no such concerns about my husband. Even if I did, I would simply let the truth come to light. I'm not going through his journal. No one should have that kind of access to another person's innermost thoughts. You're investigators. Do your jobs. Don't ask me to do it for you."

Agent Claude sighs heavily and says, "Problem is, paranoid fugitives are the hardest to catch, and this guy, Westermann is quite the specimen. For example, he had no reason to think that we were tracking his cell phone, but just in case we were, he thought he should use it to throw us off. His cell phone would fall off the grid and then, hours later, ping a tower halfway across the country, which is consistent with flight, an airplane flying above the towers and then pinging cell towers upon touching down. We checked airport transactions and surveillance and I'm telling you; we were convinced that either the man is a ghost, or that he was getting help." Claude leans in and whispers, "Here's what he is doing: he is actually mailing his cell phone from city to city to private mailbox establishments. Once the package is delivered and it is placed in that metal one-square-foot box, it would lose signal again. Westermann goes through all of that without even knowing whether we were tracking him or not."

"But you *were*."

"We can't count on him getting sloppy is what I'm saying."

"Why are we whispering?"

"Because I'm the only one who knows this."

"Why would you keep something like that secret?"

"Because," he says. "No one knows just how big this case is—"

"*Tell* them, then. Won't you need all the help you can get to catch him?" Lynn looks around like she might flag down the nearest agent.

"No!" The detective dips and glances around conspicuously. "They'll bog this case down in bureaucracy and protocol. Want to know how I found out what he is doing?"

"Looks like you're about to tell me anyhow."

"Everyone else was looking at passenger flight records. I'm smart enough to know that those aren't the only planes in the air. I looked up FedEx flight times and matched it perfectly." Claude points at his temple. "*That's* real detective work. It doesn't take a room full of people. We've been one city behind this guy all along. *That's* what we're up against. So, in order to catch him, I'll have to be just as paranoid as he is. With that being said," Claude leans back, crosses his legs and holds the ankle. "I have to follow every possible lead, including Stewart's journal."

"There's nothing there. It's all personal stuff."

"I'm convinced there's more than that," Claude says, while rubbing his hands. Do you know why Pastor Stewart was rushed to the E.R. after the break-in?"

Lynn's voice cracks and she clears her throat. "Police were there… reporters… He was shaken up."

"Mrs. Stewart, I interviewed almost everyone who was there that morning, and in one way or another, they all said pretty much the same thing: he was ok when he thought it was only the hard drive that was stolen, but when he thought that his *journal* was stolen, that's what set him off."

"Why is this the first time I'm hearing this?"

"I can't speak for those who didn't tell you. Wouldn't *you* tell a friend about her fiancé or husband if you had a concern like that?"

"I would."

"But what if you're more loyal to the husband? Would you *then* tell the wife?" Claude takes her silence as a no, and that her eyes are now opening. "In total I've interviewed almost a hundred people at your church. It's so hard to get people to give straight answers, so I just let them talk and I take notes even as they tell me things I don't care to know. Stories vary, somewhat, but when it comes to some of the more tenured members who knew Pastor Stewart from way back, they say some pretty interesting things."

"As far as what… women?"

Claude sighs helplessly. "I've divulged too much already."

"*You* brought this up, and now leaving me hanging like this?" Lynn stands up to leave. "This was a total waste of my time."

"Not a total waste." Claude grabs her hand, holding her there while pressing the zip drive into her palm. "Do yourself a favor and check his journal. Go all the way back to around '91, and you might find some surprising things–" Lynn tries to snatch away but Claude tightens the grip on her hand. "–Also, do *me* a solid and check around the time of the financial seminars for any lead to Westermann."

Lynn had arrived with the intent to help Stewart. Lynn walks out, regretful now for the internal conflict she has created for herself on multiple levels. She's in the dark concerning something about her husband – something dark enough that people thought it worthy to be shared with a federal investigator, and as long as Lynn has been a part of this church, solidifying friendships, not one person has thought enough about her, to pull her aside and tell her what many already know, Nay included.

The discussion with Agent Claude reinforces what Mavis said, that people don't care very much for Lynn. These are people Lynn must now face, knowing that everyone roaming the halls of First Baptist church is more loyal to her husband than they are to her, and will lie to her to protect him.

At home on the living room couch, Lynn sits next to Stewart with a laptop open, the video on the screen. Stewart stares. Lynn says, "Now, I know how you want me to stay out of things, and how you want to protect me and all, honey, but look at what I was able to uncover."

Stewart watches silently until the end and then he says, "Damn Levi."

"Isn't that enough to get him thrown out?"

"What you're really asking is: is it enough to get his very own brethren to vote him out? No. It's not even enough for police to charge him with anything."

"But at least you know."

Stewart doesn't offer a reply.

"What," says Lynn. "It's better than not knowing."

Stewart says, "I told you I don't want you involved with this stuff and you went behind my back?"

"The agent reached out to me."

"And you went to him without telling me," says Stewart. "Me not wanting people coming after you is more than about just protecting you. It's also to protect them and myself. Because I don't know what lengths I would go through to protect you."

Stewart and Lynn had just made up and again they're at odds.

The next morning Stewart tries to confront Levi about the video.

At least Judas had the decency to kiss Jesus when he betrayed him. Levi avoids Stewart. All day, Stewart had been asking the man if he had a minute to talk and Levi had offered nothing but excuses. He even takes a long lunch and returns just an hour before quitting time.

Stewart comes to the secretary smiling, as if he is turning a prank. He has her buzz Levi and tell him his wife wants to see him out front. When Levi comes out and spots Stewart, his eyes stretch to fill out the round frame of his glasses.

"Glad you're free," Stewart says. "Come have a word with me, brother."

Levi snaps his fingers at his forgetfulness. "Yeah I was just about to come see you." He follows a fast walking Stewart who let him in his office and closes the door behind him. Levi asks, "So what's this about?"

The video is paused on Stewart's laptop on the desk. "That's precisely, brother, what I wanna ask you. What's *this* about?"

Levi claims ignorance, "I don't know; you tell me."

It is like one of those ambush, substance abuse interventions, the exposing family member versus the denying addict. "This is a surveillance video from nearby. This is the night of the break-in. Stewart hits play. "This places you at the scene."

Nonchalantly, Levi says, "Looks to me like it places me on the highway out there; not at the *scene.*"

"What else were you doing out this late, around the same time that the alarm system was disabled?"

"Snuck out for a late night snack. I get it in however I can."

"So you parked and got out of your car, for what?"

"To take a walk," Levi says. "If you think they can charge me on that alone, you're dumber than I thought. Maybe that's enough for them to issue a search warrant to see what they could find. Even if I had those hard drives, it wouldn't be within twenty miles away or below ground. I know you want someone to go down with you, but it won't be me." Levi giggles and shakes his head. "Nice video though."

A grand smile spread on Stewart's face. "Didn't you know? The investigation is over. They found no wrong doing."

"I wasn't talking about the investigation."

Stewart sits on the desk and closes the laptop. "Let's say this isn't enough to bring charges against you. It's enough for people to question whether you should be allowed to preach at this pulpit. What if, during announcements, this shows up on the large monitor?"

"Do it. I encourage you."

"It shouldn't surprise me that you would break into the church. They say you did it back in 1980 when the church burned down."

"I was only thirteen then. Was you even born?"

"Funny how quickly you knew exactly how old you were when the church burned down."

"Math's my best subject. I'm not admitting to anything, but what *if* that were true, and I'm still here, that ought to tell you that you're in a church full of Ginyards, *run* by Ginyards, the truth is what *we* make it. You don't run nothing here like you think – *you* nor your lil' hussy wife."

Stewart gets off his desk, and stands with an angled glare. "What you say about my wife!"

Nay is actually on campus looking for Levi. The secretary directs her to Stewart's office. She walks in right at the point where Levi is backing down with his hands up. "It don't need to be all that brother."

Stewart steps forward, "*Say* it again and watch me beat the *brakes* off of you!"

Nay jumps between them, and Stewart stands down. Nay escorts Levi out of the office and they go home.

Later that night, Nay wouldn't let Levi hear the end of it. Even as she's clearing the dinner plates, she keeps it going. "Mm-hm… Quick to put your hands on a woman, but when it comes to a *man* it's a totally different story."

Levi works a toothpick between his teeth, ignoring her.

"Good Lord saw fit to order my steps just in time to see you cowering like a lil bitch."

"I ain't wanna hurt that boy. I've been trained to kill. Soldier on a civilian ain't no fair fight."

"You call me bitch like it's my *name* in this house. But today we sees who *is* the bitch." She then mocks him. "C'mon Stew. Why it gotta be all that?"

"I didn't say no c'mon Stew. You're making that up." Levi gets up and heads for the living room.

Nay is right on his heels, heckling. "You are who I *thought* you were: a big coward." Nay knows she's pressing her luck, but it feels good to put him on the defensive for once. "How you call yourself a man and won't fight a man?"

Levi turns around with no threat in his eyes; he is in agreement. "Why *would* I fight a man? Men hit hard. Here, lemme show you." He belts Nay in the stomach. She feels the very shape of his fist and knuckles boring into her gut. Her gut spasm doubles her over and forces the wind out of her. Surprisingly her dinner doesn't hurl forth. Her scream is no more than a deflating hiss, no air from which to draw sound. She withers slowly to the floor, balling into a fetal position around that ballooning migraine in her middle, to contain it, to keep it from growing exponentially inside of her and splitting her at the seams.

Chapter 28

Bianca makes the travel arrangements to the annual Homer award ceremony in Atlanta. She invites Nay, so they can carpool in her Cadillac Escalade. "Riding in style" as Bianca so enthusiastically put it, "with *two* first ladies!"

Girl power is the theme. The trip starts with gospel in the sound system, and changes to R and B by the time they hit I-95. It's Mary J. Blige, Erica Badu, Angie Stone, Jill Scott, black women anthems ongoing, as the yellow sun broke through morning and follow them to Atlanta. They arrive well before check-in so they can bond over some shopping at Lenox Mall. They talk about any and everything as they go in and out of dressing rooms.

Nay holds two blouses on their hangers, trading in front of her, "Which one?" For the first time, deferring to Lynn.

"I've seen you with a Kors bag that'll go perfect with the maroon dress."

Nay nods at Lynn, surprised at her shopping prowess. "I'll have to take you shopping with me more often."

Lynn and Nay are more like old friends and Bianca the third leg. When Nay comes out in a mustard body dress, viewing her butt in the three-way mirror, Bianca touches Lynn so she could see her shaking head. "That don't make no kinda sense do it?"

Nay sasses, "Don't worry 'bout what God gave me, honey; study what He gave you."

Lynn adds, "Booty sticks back so far, got me looking for hind legs."

The trio laugh in the back of the store, each stopping to eye each other and then go on another round of giggles. Nay, wiping tears carefully around her glued lashes, says, "I ain't know you was a fool like that, Lynn."

Bianca adds, in regards her friend, "You ain't know?"

Bianca spots someone she knows through the store glass, a fellow actress also in town for the award ceremony. Bianca goes out the store and runs the woman down.

Lynn and Nay are a party of two for the time being, Lynn now posing in the mirror when Nay comments, "Here girl, have some of this gut off of me. You can afford to carry a little more and still be straight."

Lynn smiles and keeps turning in the mirror.

"That Pastor Stewart is a lucky man, yes he is."

"Thank you," Lynn says. "Shame we've been knowing each other all this time and just now getting around to shopping to-gether."

"Ain't had nothing to do with no getting around to it. I just couldn't stand your ass." Lynn stiffens at the swear coming from an associate pastor's wife. Nay adds, "I had you figured all wrong, though. You *must* be alright if you can be friends with your husband's ex."

"She's such people, how can ya not like her?"

Nay's eyes stretch, "She like to play clueless, but that chick stay up to something – *always* plottin'."

Lynn, under distrusting eyes, replies, "Seriously?"

Nay crosses her legs and blinks away, good as any verbal con-firmation, and then she changes subjects. "So, what're we gonna to do about our men, girl? I've been waiting on their thing to blow over but it's only gotten worse."

Lynn wonders if Nay knows about the surveillance on Levi. "I try to talk to him, but you know how men are. Stewart's feel-ings are hurt; Levi's feelings are hurt. But for some reason, men feel like they have to convert their hurt into anger so that it comes out looking manly. Before long, they'll be back like normal without a peep of apology."

"Not this time – I don't think." Nay digs in her purse for gum and offers Lynn a stick. "What's Stew planning on doing with that video?"

Lynn both shrugs and frowns, as if she had nothing more than this answer, "My husband… He puts his energy into advancing his own causes, not blocking someone else's."

"He got Joe Friday on the board of directors for the academy, now, ain't it?"

They're up at the register, Lynn paying for a skirt. After they leave the counter, Lynn throws an arm around Nay's broad shoulders. "No offense, Nay, but I prefer to leave church business at church. This is Atlanta. Let's just enjoy ourselves."

They're back at the hotel getting ready for the event when Nay tries, again, to pump Lynn for information. Lynn is seated, in her slip and bra, in front of the dresser mirror, smoothing in her foundation. Nay, in a turquoise bathrobe, comes out of the master suite into Bianca's and Lynn's quarters and sits on the edge of Lynn's queen bed; Bianca's shower-singing coming in muffled through the walls. Nay's face is bare and refreshed, no interest in her eyes as she makes small talk about the award ceremony just hours away, and then she changes the subject. "Know what, Lynn. I know you said you don't want to talk about it, so don't talk. But I'm going to say this." Lynn doesn't turn. She holds eye contact through the mirror. "We need to get these two men together somehow and help them work things out. You see, my husband is different from your husband. Things bother him real bad, *real* bad. When his mind is working on a problem too long, his thinking gets warped. He'll come up with things that'll make me go '*what?*'" Nay's face prunes. "Normal people don't think that way, Lee. He keeps saying things and ya think he's playing, but when he keeps harping on the same thing over and over… You know that saying: as a man thinketh; a man doeth."

Bianca comes out of the bathroom in her robe and shower cap and a look like she'd just walked in on something. "What're y'all talking about?"

Even though Lynn and Nay assure her it is nothing, the question mark stays with Bianca.

D'mitri picks them up from their Hilton suite in a stretch Hummer. D'mitri lowers their expectations in regards to the likelihood of bringing home any awards. The white world has done nothing but look down over their glasses at him, murder him in their column reviews and snub him at awards. That's why he shows up in the stretch hummer and tailored suits, he said, to brandish the tangible success than they cannot deny, since he once was, and is now again, grossing more than any other theatre company in this lower quarter of the country. Bianca is nominated for best vocals; Lynn is nominated for best adaptation; D'mitri is nominated for best director; the entire cast is nominated for Best Play.

Before exiting the limo, D'mitri says to them, "If we *do* win anything, when you go up there, don't act too grateful. Don't let them think they have the power to validate you."

The Boisfeuillet Jones Atlanta Civic Center is all suits and gowns like a symphony concert. The Nubian foursome is not to be mistaken for the help; they stride in like ambassadors during the social half-hour where they locate the rest of the cast and mingle, D'mitri, steering them to jovial greetings with colleagues, and holds them back while issuing competitive nods at rivals.

When the lights lower and their categories are called, they all lock hands. Bianca wins best vocalist, which is the least of the surprises; she's won it before. No one's expectations is lower than Lynn's; she braces herself for the letdown, a rejection letter in person; denial by calling a name not hers. *Real people* love her writing, real people have bought her book off of the shelves at a high enough clip to provide a legitimate second stream of income. Award committees and the gate keepers of the publishing world are *not* real people.

When the winner for best script is called, Lynn claps, unfazed, until D'mitri, Nay, and Bianca alert her that the name called was hers, before it changed: *Evelyn Cummings*. Lynn turns left and right; waves of strange faces look to her with applause. Lynn walks up to the stage on Bambi legs, covering her mouth as she goes to the podium. She has no speech prepared so she speaks from her heart, first thanking, "the one and only God through whom all things we are able." She talks about *Don't Pray for Love* being one of the four self-published novels to her name that she hauled around to gift shops, beauty salons, book fair events and homegrown book stores in Columbia, SC. She goes into the theme, which is all about acceptance. She announces that in the book version, Miriam dies, and then she explains that the character Miriam is all of her previously rejected books, wandering aimlessly, looking to be taken in, and that there's no inspiration more powerful than acceptance. She addresses the awards committee, in closing, thanking their recognition and appreciating *their* acceptance. When she returns to her seat, Nay's head flicks at Lynn, saying, "Look at you… Forever up on somebody's stage."

D'mitri is the one who had asked them not to act grateful, yet when his name is called for best director, he breaks down and feels his face as if he can't believe it's happening. He feels his pockets like a smoker searching for a lighter, pulls out a wrinkled acceptance speech, but forgets how to read. He stumbles through an off the cuff rant of pure, unabated gratitude, and he thanks too many people.

The biggest award, Best Play, goes to some little-known North Carolina theatre company for their one-word French title. D'mitri looks over at their three crystal statues and sees the award committee's political maneuver. With those three awards, the committee purchased their right to give the most prestigious award to a company less deserving and retain the perception of fairness – it's what D'mitri has to believe in order to keep that anti-establishment chip on his shoulder, the driving force behind his success.

Afterwards, they congregate in a ballroom area where there is an open bar and a mellow playing live band. Strangers seemingly wander into their circle to congratulate them. Lynn is treated like an unofficial valedictorian. They compliment her eloquent speech. They offer Lynn business cards and D'mitri shields her. "She's mine, thank you very much." He sees their first collaboration together as the beginning of more in the future.

Lynn and Nay, knowing no one outside of the *Don't Pray for Love* cast, stick together. They find themselves apart from Bianca who had gone to a group of people ten feet away, so Lynn asks, "What were you saying earlier? It sounded like you were worried."

"It's Lee. Reality gets away from him, sometimes." Nay glows with an idea. "You know what? It might serve Levi good if Stewart turns in that video. That just might be the thing to wake him up."

Lynn looks over at Nay who doesn't look back. "This sounds dangerous, Nay. What *has* he been going on and on about?"

"*Now* you want to talk about church business... All I'm telling you is to keep your eyes open and be careful because–" Nay quit the conversation because she sees Bianca approaching.

Bianca split the two, her arms around their waists. "What are y'all talking about? Be careful of what?"

Lynn nearly drops her glass. "You heard that? From way over there, with all this noise...?"

Bianca bites her bottom lip as if she's holding back her unfiltered first words; she starts over, "Since y'all are talking about being careful, and I can't be included in the discussion, I'd be inclined to think you were talking about being careful of me." Bianca's head swerves to one and then the other, her blue contacts and thick lashes condemning each. Lynn and Nay huddle around Bianca to reassure her, but Bianca isn't buying it. "Nay you're *my* friend. Lynn, you're *my* friend, but you're hardly friends with each other. What can you two have to discuss without me?"

Nay gets front and center with her. "And what's the difference between us and you? We're married. This married folk conversation; you wouldn't get it."

Bianca nods blankly, "Okay… So *that's* how it is, huh?"

"That's how it's gon' be until you find you a husband."

"I already have."

Lynn glances curiously at Bianca and then Nay. Nay explains, "Her imaginary boyfriend."

"My very *real* boyfriend who I'm keeping under wraps."

"How you know he's gone marry you? Where your ring at?"

"We're already married in spirit. But as it is in heaven it *shall* be done on earth."

Nay closes her eyes and shakes her head. When her eyes open again, she observes that the population is shrinking. "What y'all wanna do after this? Where're all the spots at Bianca? Ain't this your old stomping ground?"

Bianca names the clubs she *would've* gone to, but she doesn't want to, now that she's found love. She's thirty now, she said and fixed to be married and settled.

Where they ended up for the night is right where D'mitri's stretch Hummer picked them up: their hotel. The hotel bar is their last-ditch effort to add a little spice to the night. They're the only ones occupying stools, sipping soda and daring each other to get an actual drink.

Bianca starts them off with a round of lemon drop shots. Nay names the bartender Charlie and asks for another round, on her. The bartender watches these church ladies' eyes go liquid after just a couple drinks.

Nay says, "Your husband, good ole Stew? Used to drink hard; that man had a problem. That's why he won't drink a drop today. He's scared to go backwards."

"I've heard him allude to that," Lynn says, blinking slowly. "But nothing specific."

Bianca adds, "*You* knew him back then, Nay. Enlighten the woman."

Nay shrugs, "Hey, I wadn't around him all like that. All I know is that he wasn't a drinker until after Fiona died."

Bianca leans across the bar to look past Lynn and at Nay. "But weren't you and Fiona best friends though? I would imagine you had to be around, in some way."

"I said, he wadn't a drinker until after Fiona *died*. How am I best friends with a dead chick?"

"So, after Fiona died, you and Stewart suddenly *stopped* being friends? I imagine you two would mourn her together."

"Heifer, what you trying to say? If I wadn't drunk I'd slap them blue contacts *off* your eyes and *on* Lynn's."

The three go hysterical with laughter. Lynn spreads out over the bar, eyes shut, squealing. The other two stooges are no better: Nay's laughter rears back, wide open, while Bianca pounds the bar top insisting, again and again saying Nay is so stupid. "*Lawd* that woman a fool ain't she?"

They are three women dressed in body length, pricey gowns and heels, with no nightlife other than this one, at a hotel bar at ten o'clock at night.

Bianca stops and points at Nay – behind Nay. A gentleman stands with the sturdiness of a retired athlete, his muscles shaping his sweater into a mold. He has a thinking man's face and a mustache, thick like black foam, spreading with his smile. Nay looks him up and down, dumfounded with either shock, admiration, or both. He tells the bartender to buy the ladies another around and then says to Nay, "I didn't see your ring until I got right up on you. My eyes were on something else," he giggles. They all know what he means: her behind, swallowing the whole top of her stool. "Have a drink on me anyway, just for looking so divine."

Neither Lynn, nor Bianca had ever heard Nay issue such a giggle so girlish and free. Nay says, "Thank you Mister Handsome."

"Henry Thompson." He gives his hand and then pulls Nay's handshake into his lips. Nay recoils, giggling. "Ooh, that tickles." She checks the other two to see how they are reacting to her, and then she points at Bianca. "*She's* the single one at this bar."

The gentleman looks her way, as if he'd walk over, but Bianca stops him. "Actually, I *am* spoken for."

The man then bid adieu. Alone, Bianca may have entertained the man's company, but she can't give Nay anything to bring back to her husband, the two on each side of Lynn, faithful to the same man.

On the way to up to the room, Nay and Bianca fuss playfully. Lynn is their audience of one and their mediator. Suddenly Nay put Bianca on hold with one finger, and turns her playful chastisement to Lynn, "That reminds me, Miss Lynn?"

"Me?"

"Yes *you*... Before I forget, lemme have a word with you, cause I got to give this to ya while it's hot," her teeth chomps on the word hot. "You gone stop trying to correct me during bible study."

Lynn could tell by Bianca's expression that this confrontation is planned, and that Nay wouldn't be joking for long. Lynn pretends right along with Nay, half hoping, that this really is all fun and games. "I promise to stop correcting you, if *you* promise to stop being wrong."

"Broad please. You know how to *sound* right, but you don't be right." It is still fun and games as they spill out of the elevator, and debate all the way down the hall, but it turns serious the moment they enter their suite. Nay comes in, searching for her bible. They're debating over the term helpmeet, which Lynn corrected Nay's interpretation of woman being subordinate to man, and suggested more of a partnership. During their last women's bible study class, Lynn had quoted the International Standard version of Genesis 2:18, *I will make the woman to be an authority corresponding to him.*

Nay returns to the joint suite empty handed. "While man is busy naming all the animals and being given dominion over them, where is woman?"

Lynn answers, "*Dominion*, over animals... strong word for a zookeeper. There is no ah-ha moment that Adam needed a companion. God first made animals of both genders, so the *construct* of male and female was already roaming the earth on four feet, and flying in the firmament, prior to Adam."

Nay says, "Ooh, I wish I had a bible, so I can shame the devil."

"It's a hotel," says Lynn. "There's always a bible." Lynn goes to the nightstand and sure enough, finds one.

Nay doesn't want it. "If helpmeet means what you say it means, don't you think they would've made that clear?"

"You're reading words that are four hundred years old, Nay; meanings change. Even ten years ago a tweet was none other than the sound a bird makes, but now it refers to social media. It is made clear in the Hebrew text. It's when it was translated into English when men started this play on words." Lynn broke down the Hebrew translations, "The Hebrew word for help is *ezer*, to save or rescue and the Hebrew word for meet is *k'enegdo*, meaning, corresponding to. Can't you see this manifest in the world? How often are wayward men saved by a praying woman?"

Bianca is floored, "How do you *know* all this!"

Lynn replies, "It's not about knowing. It's about removing the veil that's been placed over our eyes."

Nay's arms are still folded against everything Lynn is saying. "Don't pay her no mind, Bianca. She's so convinced of what she thinks, that it comes off as truth. This is the bible my momma and daddy lived by; the book they raised me by. You think I'm gonna let you sit up here and call my momma and daddy liars!" Nay steps closer, arms unfolded, fists balled.

Lynn studies her, looking as if she notices something curiously familiar. "You were waiting for a reason weren't you? I wouldn't give you one, so you had to create one. Why plot with Satan? You know I mean no insult to your parents, whom I never met. But because I am a child of God, I'd curse his name if I fear any man. So, you go ahead and fashion whatever reasons you need and do whatever you want, but make no mistake whose child it is that you raise your hand against."

Bianca let out a little squeal of praise, in awe of Lynn's courage and wisdom, "Ooh, Lord Jesus."

Nay, seeing no fear there to devour, stands not knowing what to say or do.

"Let me show you something," Lynn says. She gets the bible and narrates as she turns the pages. "When it comes to gender, translations four hundred years ago turns quite ambiguous, around the time King James commissioned his edition in 1610. At the time, Shakespeare is forty-six years old." Lynn turns to 46th Psalms and asks Bianca, "Count forty-six words down." Bianca counted forty-six words down and stops on *shake*. Now count forty-six words backwards from the end of the 46th Psalm, ignoring Shē-'läh because it's not an actual word." Bianca counts forty-six words aloud and when she stops on *spear;* she then solves the riddle, "Shakespeare." Bianca covers her mouth, shocked at the discovery. Bianca offers Nay the bible to see for herself.

Nay, visibly defeated, says, "If you are a believer in the word of God, you must know that the word cannot be changed."

"*Meaning* is preserved, but word choice can play on perception, it can open the door to alternate interpretations."

"We can debate all day long, but you better heed what I told you from the jump: *interrupt* my class again," Nay warns. "I can show you better than I can tell you." Nay retreats to her end of the suite, closing the dividing door behind her. Lynn and Bianca overhear Nay venting on the phone, most likely to Levi, and then her venting turns into explaining. Lynn eavesdrops, but can't get a bead on Nay's words. Bianca refuses to spy with her, so Lynn quit and they sit and talk from the islands of their separate beds.

When Nay shows her face again, Bianca is in the bathroom. Nay stands in the doorway, "I'm catching the devil getting this zipper." Lynn turns to her, but does not approach. Nay laughs, "Girl, are you going to help me or not?" Lynn reads this as Nay's brand of apology, of canceling threats issued in the heat of argument. Lynn approaches Nay's rear. Nay says, "*Just* unfasten the hitch. *Don't* zip it all the way down."

But it is too late. Lynn had peeled the dress down like an ear of corn and sees a purple bruises the circumference of a grapefruit. Nay spins around angry, holding the front of her dress to her bosom. "Didn't I tell you *not* to zip..." but her anger drains in the face of Lynn's shock. Nay explains, "Actually, I forgot that was there… That ain't nothing girl… I fell." Nay sounds programmed, her lifeless giggle, pulled by back-string.

Nay pauses and sighs, realizing she now has no choice but to admit. Nay says that Levi hit her in the back with a cold can of soda, that he wound-up and stepped into the throw like a baseball pitcher.

Bianca having heard Nay's raised voice calls from inside the bathroom. "Everything alright?"

She gets no response. When she comes out, Lynn and Nay are sitting on the bed, their four hands joined in Nay's lap, Lynn, consoling the giant. They are talking about Levi, Lynn saying, "He's not worth it, Nay. He's a just a man like anyone else."

There is something Bianca doesn't like about this picture, the two huddled outside of her presence. Something she detests about Lynn's words, talking down about a man of God. Bianca says, "Hold up, Lynn. I'm not going to have you talking about *my* pastor like that. He's not some Joe off the street. He wins souls for Christ."

Nay, sniffling with her head down, tells Lynn, "She don't know."

"What don't I know? Are you leaving him?"

Lynn catches a glimpse of what looks like hope in Bianca's eyes, which Lynn quickly smothers. "No. She's not leaving him – unfortunately. He's been beating her for years."

Bianca sits on the other bed, the news percolating through her while listening to Lynn tell Nay about her worth and how the life God wants for her doesn't include her living in fear.

Nay replies, "God don't give nobody burdens they can't bear."

Lynn's head goes back and her eyes close. "Tell that to the many women looking up at the ceiling of their caskets. All burdens ain't God's."

Bianca becomes infuriated inside, but she speaks softly. "You two don't have the slightest clue." Two sets of eyes put her on trial. "Y'all sitting here blaming Levi; it's not him."

Lynn, holding Nay, feels her tense, but Nay relaxes and says, "Lawd help her if I get up off this bed."

"He been to war. It's Post Traumatic Stress Disorder. Y'all looking to condemn him when *he's* the one in need of help."

Lynn counters, "If that's the case, Nay needs safety while he *gets* help, then."

"Go on and leave your man. Follow up what this chick's talking 'bout."

Lynn had prepared her legs to leap in the way of Nay's attack, but there's no attack. Nay gazes in the mirror, her glassy-eyed self, staring back. "It went away for years. It came back in 2005 – and even then it was two, maybe three incidents in a year at most."

Lynn says, "Months between incidents, but I bet you walk on egg shells every day. The *threat* of violence is the psychological fist pounding you every day."

"Have I thought about leaving? Of course, I've thought about leaving. I didn't just jump into my life; I live it every day, so all your suggestions, I've considered a hundred times, already." Nay stops and shut her wet eyes, concentrating, going deep inside of herself. Her eyes open and she is sailing into her past. "I was fifteen. And that near thirty-year-old man, Levi, was my first. I was always weary of men eyeing my body and counting down to my eighteenth birthday. Levi didn't see my body. He only saw my smile, and he would do anything to get me to smile even more just so he could see it. He was the pastor's son. He acted as my protector. That's how he got in my heart. He said, 'Love is old enough to remember when age didn't matter.' He was going off to Kuwait. This was *after* Desert Storm," Nay directs at Bianca. "But there was still scattered conflict. In case he was killed in action, he handed me two unsealed letters: one, a request to his family to have me speak at his funeral; the other was the eulogy he wanted me to read, telling everyone he and I were in love. I felt so stupid when I found out later that he was stationed in a non-combat zone and was safer there in Kuwait than I was here at home. I was a damn fool." Nay cracks an embarrassed smile.

Lynn can't smile nor agree. "You were not a fool, Nay. You were a raped girl." It explains Nay's behavior, the quick temper and the intimidation are the resonances of trauma; the girl inside of her, fixated on reclaiming her power.

Nay continues her story, placing herself years later in college, having her share of exposure to young men, who seemed to have Attention Deficit Disorder when it comes to love, so when Levi re-stationed home, he was able to lure her with his steadfast attention and money.

"I never even *seen* him angry until *after* we were married. He never hit me until the second year."

Bianca displays her disinterest by flipping through a hotel brochure. Every now and then, she'd lift her head to stare, watching them like misbehaving children as they make a monster of Levi, *her* lover, *her* man. Although Levi would always remind Bianca that he would never leave Nay, Bianca knows that Levi is only reminding *himself*, only because her love has a way of making him forget. Bianca, flipping pages, speaks to the brochure. "The monster is not him; it is an unwelcomed guest *inside* of him – but what do I know? I'm just the only therapist in the room."

"I've *had* it with this bitch!" Nay springs up quick as lightening, almost too quick for Lynn, who scrambles to derail her. "Move Lynn," Nay commands.

Bianca runs to the door, but cancels her escape when she sees Lynn blocking Nay. Bianca grins impishly, "What'd I do? All I said was—"

"—You shouldn't say a damn thing! If you're so much of a therapist, you should know when to shut the hell up and listen. You're settin' up here tellin' *me* about *my* damn husband? Get out my *way*, Lynn. I'm fin'na beat this bitch up and down every floor of this hotel."

Bianca's eyes pierce, "Not long ago, I was holding you back from Lynn and now she's holding you back from me. *You're* the problem. If Levi is beating you, it's because you *need* to get beat!"

"*Keep* talking, Bianca, thinking Lynn can hold me back." Nay twitches at Lynn. "Get out of my *way*, girl. I ain't gonna ask you again."

Lynn is fronting Nay clamping her wrists, begging Nay, "Let it go. It's not worth it."

"Lynn, I'm telling you–" Before wasting another word, Nay brings her arms up through Lynn's and slowly pry them apart, just to show Lynn her strength. Once freed, she then orders, "Now, move before I move you mys*elf*."

Bianca opens the door, ready to run.

Lynn says, "Get it over with, Nay. I've got two cheeks."

"I ain't got no qualms with you, Lynn, but I swear, if you force my hand, your two cheeks is just the beginning." Nay flinches at Lynn. On reflex, Lynn's eyes clamp shut as she awaits her pummeling. Instead of pummeling her, Nay snatches Lynn up like a manikin and hurls her like a shot-put. Bianca's wild eyes follows Lynn's flight clear over one bed and onto the other.

Bianca bolts. Nay takes off after Bianca, chasing her only halfway down the carpeted hallway before realizing she should turn back and check on Lynn. When Nay returns to the room, Lynn is up, but still looking at where she'd been versus where she stands, wondering how she'd gotten there. Nay apologizes and Lynn forgives her.

By morning, Lynn and Nay try to blame the alcohol, but Bianca can't write off what happened. Something had broken between herself and Nay that Bianca swears would never be fixed again. She doesn't speak to Nay and hardly to Lynn. She catches a cab to a rental car dealer and drives home solo.

When Lynn returns home, she doesn't tell Stewart about the abuse; she keeps Nay's secret. It's Nay's choice on how she plans to manage her escape, and she'll need to know she has loyal people behind her to help her when she's out on her own. Lynn does, however, tell Stewart one thing: that on the ride back, Nay confided that Levi is the true facilitator of women's bible study. He outlines the lesson plans and emphasis of teaching. Nay is nothing more than her abuser's mouthpiece.

Chapter 29

Levi realizes he's in trouble when, at worship service, Bianca can't keep her eyes off of him. With Nay by his side, Bianca doesn't come near, but her distant stare shines competitively. Her smile offers something, or rather it let-on that it hides something that's dying to be asked. Levi sees the beginning of disaster, her dropping hints and acting out publicly, like she did with Stewart, but Levi figures it's time he show Bianca the difference Stewart and himself.

Using the element of surprise, he pops up unannounced at Bianca's apartment, but still she is prepared; the house clean and a meal prepared.

Bianca wears a kaki long skirt, and blouse scrolled up on her forearms, her beauty fresh without makeup.

As Levi enters, Bianca says, "Thought you could catch me slipping, huh? I'm always ready." She tells Levi that she never loafs around in pajamas, or with her hair undone during hours of the day that Levi *might* drop by unannounced. This level of dedication seems pathological. Levi has come to scare Bianca, but it's Bianca who scares him. Levi sits like a first-time visitor, wondering what he'd gotten himself into. Bianca sits next to him, tickling his ear, but he isn't in the mood for play. "How was the trip," Levi asks.

Bianca tells him everything, starting with how suspiciously close Nay and Lynn seemed all weekend, how Nay flirted with a man at the hotel bar, offering her hand to kiss and then giggling like a school girl. Levi rubs his brow under the stress. Bianca adds, "She's gonna leave you, Levi. She's letting Lynn fill her head with things."

"Lynn! That ole nappy headed pica ninny!"

Bianca gets a King James Bible. She explains Lynn's interpretation of gender through Genesis. "She said the animals were made before man, right… So those animals were both male and female animals, so therefore, even before God made Adam from clay, the construct of both genders were already here." Next Bianca flips through the bible and shows him the codex of Shakespeare's name in Psalms 46.

Levi raises a finger. "She pissin' me off. She's twisting the word, you see? She gonna get dealt with right along with Stewart."

Bianca then grows still and saddened like death's messenger. "Lynn found a bruise on Nay's back. How'd it get there?"

"How'd *she* say it got there?" Bianca lowers her gaze and Levi knows his wife has outed him. Absolute denial would only make him look like more guilty, so he tries a different approach. "Why are *you* so concerned? Are you worried about your*self*?"

"Why wouldn't I?"

"What you have to understand is that you and Nay are two very different women."

"How so?"

"I don't have to explain myself to you. Follow up your buddies, if that's what you wanna do." Levi springs up and paces in the direction of the kitchen.

Bianca follows; arms folded. "I'm asking *you*."

Levi turns in the kitchen's entryway, his arms bracing outward as if he is holding up the house. "But why are you asking though? You *know* my wife. You *know* that woman's biggety… manipulative – if my fist is a gun, she's the one turning it on herself and pulling the trigger. She hurts me worse than I'll ever hurt her. You side with her because *her* scar is visible."

Bianca places her hands on her hips and says, "Baby, you'd better know whose side I'm on. I defended you, Levi. They were making you out to be a monster and I set them straight. I said,

'I will not let you talk about my pastor that way.' I told Lynn – her man-hating behind–"

"–*Man* hating!"

"So, I told her *and* Nay, 'y'all so quick to blame Levi when it's not even him. It's his PTSD.'"

Levi's head nods, going with it. "Right… right…"

"So, you see… I'm on your side even when your wife isn't – I mean, how is it that the *other* woman has to defend a husband against his wife's judgment? Something's not right about that. A first lady is supposed to hold the pastor up, not tear him down."

Levi's head shakes.

"And then Nay had the nerve to try to fight me. Lynn had to hold her back," says Bianca. "She just don't know I can destroy her anytime I want."

Levi erupts. "Say what! Destroy her?"

Bianca raises her hands in plea. "That's not how I meant it, Levi."

Levi comes forward. "Are you sure? Is that why you're suddenly throwing shade from all the way across the room?"

"No. Levi." Bianca says, backing away. Before her back hits the wall, she wheels away. "Gone now, Levi."

"See, you think I'm Stewart. Naw." Levi pounds his chest. "Naw, I'm a grown ass man. I don't play. You think you can tip Nay off, or put doubt in her head… I'll put my fist upside yours."

Bianca stamps her feet, rooting herself to the spot. "Dammit, do it, Mr. Big and Bad! And watch me destroy *you!* The moment you put your thing in me, you surrendered your fate. *I* now control the fate of – not only your marriage, but your fate as a pastor." There's a stare down, Bianca awaiting a rebuttal that never comes; Levi is disarmed and speechless, his mind working to regather his troops.

Bianca smiles warmly and says, "The atmosphere between us, Levi, is so much freer and tender when I pretend to be the clueless dame and we're under this illusion that we're feeling our way through things together. But since you're laying out your terms, here's mine: pretty soon, either *you* end your marriage or I do it for you."

"That's not possible. I don't believe in divorce, Bianca."

"I'm so sorry, Levi, that you came into this expecting a long term sidepiece like your mother was to your father." Bianca's head shakes, "Not me. I am a first lady – through and through. Sadly, it's not a position where you can get a degree and apply for the job. You have to be chosen. So, I'm forcing you to choose, Levi. From day one, that's always been my play."

Levi throws a hand up in dismay, wanders away and flops on the couch. Finally, he says, "Since we're laying out terms, Bianca, you listen to me good. I want you to stop taking your birth control pills."

Now Bianca is the one who's rendered speechless.

Chapter 30

A more solidly established couple would laugh at the type of arguments Stewart and Lynn is having, how they react to every little thing as if it sets the table for the rest of their married lives, so every issue weighs ten times more than it should, and nothing trivial.

Lynn also blames the scandal. She has yet to know what their marriage looks like out from under that dark cloud. The FBI's press release announces that First Baptist Church is no longer suspected of wrong doing, yet the forty litigants stick to their guns for lack of another target to sue. The only sure-fire way to free Stewart of scrutiny is to find Westermann.

The detective calls Lynn one day. She could tell by the fatigue in the detective's phone voice how the case is wearing him down. He'd been spun around so many times he's dizzy, and desperate for information. He asks Lynn if she ever looked into Stewart's journal. He had to take his ear away from the phone for the blasting that comes through. Lynn and her husband may have drawn lines in the sand, but there are boundaries that Lynn would not cross even to help her husband.

At church, people stop coming forward. Usually, after each sermon, Stewart would have at least four or five join the church, which is already a down number, but even *that* dwindled to where he'd be lucky to have one come to confess.

Even though the church is no longer a focus of the federal investigation, his reputation has already been sullied. The pastor must add more members than the church sheds, so in that respect, Stewart is failing.

Stewart stays true, not using the pulpit for self-promotion, but he is approaching the boarder. He says, to his congregation, that they are under attack, that Satan has set out wolves in sheep's clothing to lurk among them. He has to prepare them, for Satan would try to lure them out of the flock. Stewart points out Satan's identifying traits, like he's on The Most Wanted List, composite sketches being drawn. Stewart peers through the window of Genesis, and asks, "Who is Satan, really? In a word, how would you describe him?" Pastor Stewart trots down the auburn steps soliciting responses. Interactive preaching is more than off script; it is out of character. The answers members sling at him varied from antagonizer to imposter, Lucifer and to the obvious: a snake.

Stewart trots back up to the podium, smirking, a magician pulling from the hat, "He's a conspiracy theorist." He watches the notion reverberate through the pews. "People say the devil is a liar; I slightly disagree." Stewart gets his expected response, for the congregation to gasp, at an apparent defense of Satan. "No one is fooled by a known liar. You tune him out, soon as he opens his mouth. The devil deals in *facts*. He'll show you only the facts that support his case; he'll muddy the facts that undo his case. He'll deceive you in regards to the *implications* of said facts. Here in the garden of Eden..." Stewart's finger jabs the open bible on the podium. "The serpent *did not lie* in that the fruit would make them Godlike in knowledge, but he omitted the consequences: death, suffering, the mortal curse... Conspiracy theorist," Stewart pounds. "They have but one purpose: to distract you from *God's* purpose, to recruit allies to their own dark causes, with no regard to what it would cost you. They want *you* to dwell in the mess *they* dwell in. They want *you* to hate who *they* hate."

His lone highlight, when he really gets the church going for about five minutes is when he said he is concerned about First Baptist's morale. He broke down ministry as the mechanism to pass on the seeds of Godliness into the unsaved who would germinate that seed out into their environments as witnesses to God's goodness, and by this process, ultimately bring more people into the bosom of God. "*That's* the common theme in everything we do," Stewart says, pacing, while looking down, a bead of sweat by his sideburn. "The icing on the cake is that, in doing so, we build treasures in heaven, waiting until we get there. Amen?" He pats his face with a napkin. "Say you're working the soup kitchen, feeding the hungry with a glad heart, ministering unto them, building God's kingdom. Say, a fellow in ministry pulls you aside and shares some negative findings about your church and suddenly you're feeling somewhat down about the work you do." He is in front of the pulpit, two fists held in front, as if holding the bars of a cage. "Couldn't you just muster a fake smile and go back to ministering *just* like you were doing before?" The congregation's applause affirmed yes, but their pastor's head shakes no. "No matter how bright a smile shows on your face, if you heart is filled with negativity, you cannot go back to doing what you were doing before. Before: with gladness – not just on your face – but *in your heart* – you were filling the kingdom. But with gladness on your face and *not* in your heart, you're not filling the kingdom; you're just filling bowls with soup!" The message washes over the congregation. The opportunistic band jumps in with a quick scat, and hundreds dance and praise.

He sticks the landing with a brief summary, letting them know that *Purpose* is tone deaf to negativity. *Faith*, he said, allows obedience despite circumstances. "Brothers and sisters in Christ, if you do not protect the gladness in your heart, not only do you surrender *your* victory; you surrender God's victory. Safeguard the gladness in your hearts," he insists. "Because without gladness in your heart, all you do in Christ is for naught."

They love the sermon, but no one budges for the call to discipleship. Stewart keeps pressing the issue, asking those who have not a church home; those who have a church home but visiting because your spirit hasn't fed. He walks in front of the altar from end-to-end arms out waiting to receive, asking *Will you come? Will you come?* He carries altar call for so long, Stewart begins to look desperate.

After service, back at home, Lynn can see the hurt on Stewart's face. She feels so sorry for Stewart she wants to comfort him but they haven't been getting along.

The holiday season is rolling in fast. Lynn learned, while knee deep in November, that the first lady, traditionally, heads the annual Sponsor a Family Christmas charity. Of all people, Nay is the messenger, tapping her watch face, telling Lynn she needs to get it together. Lynn answers jokingly, but also with slight snare, "You kept bible study. You may as well keep that too."

But Lynn goes ahead faithfully. She watches her rented storage room filled with donations of bicycles, baby dolls, and electronics. She gives the adopted families a four hour a day, three day a week window for pick up at a discreet offsite storage unit where gifts were grouped and labeled. Bianca assists her. She brings a quartet from her teen choir to sing Christmas carols as the parents, almost unanimously single mothers, arrive to pick up the items on their Christmas wish lists. The first to arrive is a single mother named Joy wearing custodial scrubs and a boyish Mohawk, frosted with red die. "This is so much better than last year," Joy says, as she hugs Lynn. "Last year was done all out in the open like it is a pageant for the poor."

Lynn, sending inquiring eyes at Bianca, finds her brazen confirmation waiting. Bianca adds, "The *last* first lady did it to glorify self. *This* first lady glorifies God." Bianca does a comical, Aunt Esther *Ha Glory* praise that makes them all laugh.

Joy, in her fading laughter, says. "You don't do people like that. People go through stuff – some more than others. *I'm* guilty of that, as you can see I'm here another year, but regardless, people still want to hold onto their pride. And you made that easy, Mrs. Stewart." Joy hugs Lynn in a true Christmas moment, the quartet singing Noel behind them.

Lynn holds the girl out at arm's length, a smiling examination. Throughout all of her years of ministry and non-profits helping women, Lynn immediately knows how to reach her. Custodial work obviously is not her career of choice; there is something holding her back. "What's on your record," Lynn asks.

Joy flinches at first, but she can't accept their gifts and tell the woman to mind her business, but something else about Lynn tells her she can't lie either. "Bad checks."

"Why is it still on your record? That's easily expunged."

"Never looked into it," she shrugs in shame.

"Aren't you worth it?" Lynn gives her a moment to respond, but she doesn't. "What's stopping you from stepping into a better life? God's word shows you that you *are* deserving, that whatever your past, He forgives. His forgiveness helps us forgive ourselves."

Joy's head drops and shakes, like she is about to give a reason why this God thing won't work. "I've been meaning to be saved, I just can't walk down that aisle."

"Come to church Sunday. I will find you and I will walk with you."

Bianca can't believe what's happening. From her stool, she sits locked in awe like a coming of age for the woman with the title of first lady now becoming one. She gathers herself to help Lynn and Joy load the little Subaru hatchback with all the items on her children's wish list, but after the woman drives off, Bianca's shock switches on again. "What was that," Bianca asks, hands on hips. "You don't even know her."

"It's not about knowing her; it's about knowing scripture."

"I didn't hear any scriptures."

"Because that would be too impersonal."

"*Nay* would've treated her like a beggar and then talk trash about her when she left."

"And you would've been right there sniggling with her," Lynn laughs.

Bianca's head goes bobbling away, pleading the fifth, but darts back, quizzing, "So when are you taking over bible study?"

Lynn avoids the question by busying herself with the second arrival. All week, Lynn has been sacked with hugs. They are grateful for her humble soul, even more so because she's a celebrity among them. Some know Lynn from her activism where they had rallied behind her speeches. Some bring their copies of Lynn's novels to be autographed. They show Lynn selfies from the play at the Colonial Life Arena. What surprises Lynn is that many seem star struck, as if they'd have a lot to say if she wasn't standing before them in the flesh, making them nervous. They accredit Lynn's Women's day speech with planting a resilient seed, still growing, threatening to break through the crust of their weary worn lives.

Throughout the days spent handing out gifts from the storage unit, Lynn pulls many of them aside in hushed conversation where Bianca sees them come away changed.

Bianca wouldn't let Lynn off the hook in regards to women's bible study. On the final day, two days before Christmas, as Lynn sweeps out the storage unit, Bianca goes for it again, "This big ole church and only a few women in women's bible study? The co-ed bible study has more women than the women's bible study class! Because Nay runs them off. She doesn't know what she's doing."

Finally, Lynn gives a reason. "It's Levi's lessons. Nay is just his mouthpiece."

This fact jogs Bianca back but she surges forward. "How would you know?" Lynn goes back to sweeping the concrete floor, all the gifts now gone. Bianca trails her with more questions, "At least during women's bible study, when Nay comes out of her mouth wrong, you would stand up and correct her. You don't even do that no more."

Lynn buckles under the pressure to share what Nay confided. "On the way back from Atlanta, Nay said that whenever I pointed out the errors in Levi's lesson, he'd punish her for losing the argument."

"Wrong can't win against right."

"I asked Nay, 'Why do you have to tell your husband everything?' Nay says she never tells. She believes Levi has a spy in the class; she believes that the spy is you."

Bianca falls away in disbelief, huffing, all manner of denial catches in her throat. "So, what do *you* believe?"

This quiz has little to do with belief. The question put their friendship squarely on a scale to see if it could outweigh reason. "I can't tell you what I believe because I don't jump to conclusions. I'm not sold that you are that person. However, I do believe that how you were defending Levi in that hotel suite, in the face of his battered wife, is inappropriate. So, when I look at that, it certainly makes me feel like I wouldn't put it past you."

Bianca looks away and digs in her ear. "She's playing you," Bianca says, as she spots the broom in Lynn's hand, the fact so clear it turns comical. "Got you out here doing all the grunt work of the first lady while she hoards the spotlight."

"If it's alright with *me*, then it's alright."

Bianca tries again. "Why do you think she was so adamant about going with us to Atlanta?"

"That was *your* idea."

"No, it wasn't. Is Nay nominated for any awards? *No*. But she just *had* to go. You think it is by chance that she asked *you* to unzip her? She found out about what *you* went through, so she's using that to seduce you and keep you exactly where *she* wants you," she says while taking a lasting look at the broom in Lynn's hand.

"Bianca, what you're saying is crazy. How'd she get the bruise? Do you know how hard it would be to self-inflict a bruise on your back? Besides, from the first time I laid eyes on Nay I knew her situation. Atlanta just confirmed it."

Bianca goes blurry with gloom. "You know what…" A hand goes up as if pressing against an imaginary pane of glass, holding Lynn at bay, and steadying herself. "If only you know what that woman has done to me…" Her lips crumples; she can't withstand the telling. Her head only rattles to rid itself of the trauma.

Lynn figures Nay must've done more than be Stewart's informant. "*Tell* me, Bianca. What did she do to you that is so bad, and why didn't you end the friendship *then?*"

"She was never really my friend and she's not your friend either," Bianca says. She reaches into her purse and pulls out a picture and holds it to her breast. "When you first showed up at this church, Nay gave me this picture. She wanted me to show it to you. I wouldn't do it because I knew it would be for the wrong reason." What the picture did is let Bianca know, for sure, that there was no future in pursuing Stewart, as long as there is a woman walking this earth who looks just like the woman his grieving has so memorialized that he could only love someone who reminds him of her.

She hands the picture over to Lynn who sees her teenage self. "Where did she get this?"

"That's not you in the picture; it's Fiona."

"My God," Lynn says as she stares in disbelief.

Bianca dips to make eye contact. "Nay gave me this picture because she wanted to hurt you. She wanted to make you feel irrelevant."

Lynn asks, "But why? Why would she want to hurt me when she didn't even know me?"

Bianca pivots to leave with these words: "She didn't know you. She only knew whose arm you was on." Bianca walks away deaf, as if she doesn't hear Lynn calling after her, wanting more of an explanation.

Lynn doesn't chase Bianca. Lynn turns around with slumped shoulders looking back into the empty storage room with her broom in hand. Lynn comes to terms with the fact that she's being played by Nay, the one person whose life Lynn is trying to save. Lynn noticed ever since the day that Nay had pretended to lose her keys that Nay's jealousy is aroused when it comes to Stewart. And *Stewart*... Lynn looks at the photo again and her belly stirs so badly that she presses it with a hand. The resemblance is so close it makes Lynn think back to her wedding day, in her gown; when Stewart removed her veil and gazed at her with tears in his eyes, as if his prayers were finally answered. Lynn now wonders who were those tears really for? Who was Dana really marrying?

Chapter 31

*I*t's the days before Christmas, where Lynn's family and her in-laws are coming together for the newly-weds' first Christmas, and Lynn had been so busy with the sponsor a family ministry, she still hasn't gotten any groceries. Since Lynn desperately wants the holiday dinner to be a success, she pulls herself together and makes no mention of the picture of Fiona. Lynn rummages through the refrigerator and cabinets to compile her late shopping list for the Christmas feast.

"The meal's already taken care of," Stewart hollers from the living room.

Lynn turns in the refrigerator door to face him.

"Sophia's having her staff cater it." Sophia, the banquet's executive chef.

Lynn is offended at the idea of her Christmas feast coming out of another woman's kitchen, even if her kitchen is also the church's. "But this is our first Christmas together."

"I know." Stewart pulls her out of the cool refrigerator door and into the warmth of his arms. "It's too much work. Every Christmas we used to let mom slave in the kitchen the night before and when it was time to open gifts, she'd be operating on fumes, nodding off on her chair. I don't want that for you. I don't want that for us. I want you alive during the festivities." Lynn thinks, If this is his way of saving his family from her cooking, he smoothed it over the right way. Lynn couldn't even form a rebuttal.

For Lynn, holding her peace about Fiona's picture feels like, perhaps, a smoker suppressing the urge; it starts getting bigger. Lynn spends so much time in prayer and in private conversations with herself that by the arrival of Christmas day, she's fully present with her husband and their guests: Lynn's mother, stepfather, her two step brothers and their three children, and then there is Stewart's parents, his twin sister, Drea, her husband Milt and their two children, their three-year-old being the star of the show.

Although the dinner is catered, there's still much work to do. The wives, Lynn and Drea, Dana's twin sister, fill the oven, set the tables. The mothers try to take over the kitchen on pure instinct, but Lynn and Drea politely, and respectfully escort them out, the torch not passed but confiscated by the daughters.

Lynn enjoys Drea's company. She is, after all, the female version of her husband. Out of the blurry corner of Lynn's eyes, Drea *is* Stewart, the same iced tea color, the lower strain of her talking voice, a candied version of Dana's. Even with so much time and distance, half the country between them since college, their mannerisms are the same, as if they'd practiced together in the mirror.

Drea and Lynn, both English professors, spend less time working and more time discussing literature. Drea mentions that she had published an analytical essay that won a Scribner award where she proposed Braham Stoker's Dracula as "… much darker than an exploitation on the fears of ultra-conservative Victorian society, but that it is a dark satire on homosexuality. I go as far to say that the work is a coded tablet for the hidden subculture of homosexuality during the Victorian era, to which he (Stoker) was allegedly immersed."

"We'd be such good friends if you lived here," Lynn says.

"Best," Drea corrects.

But Lynn notices something, in her mannerism just like she would've noticed in her own husband if *he* were holding back. Lynn asks, "You were about to say something?"

Drea goes blank as if she were caught.

Lynn filled in Drea's blank, "Are you planning on moving back here?"

Drea raises her head; spying, guardedly over her nostrils. "Depends… That's *all* I'm allowed to say." Drea's shared secret makes Lynn feel officially apart of the family. Finding nothing left to do in the kitchen, they join the others.

The grandfathers, who had long since escaped out to the porch and surprised each other with their private flasks, now return jolly. Stewart's mother notices first, "There's a whole lot of Christmas spirit out there on that porch idn't?"

Dorothy agrees, her man, Leon, in trouble too. "Sho is."

All the locals make for home around six in the evening. Drea and her family stay because they won't fly back until Monday morning.

Christmas dinner was a success and since there is nothing that could be done after the fact to undo that success, Lynn shows Stewart the picture. They're in the bedroom, turning in for the night when Lynn holds the picture next to her face, asking for an explanation.

Stewart looks like he'd seen a ghost. "Where'd you get that?"

"Where I got this is the least of your worries, right now."

"It's a picture of Fiona, but I'm sure you already know that. What are you really asking?"

"Ever since I started going to First Baptist, people would ask me if I'm related to the Foshays; *this* is why."

Stewart's arms flops. "What if I had pictures of *your* exes? Wouldn't I find brothers six feet tall, brown skin? All this means is that you're my type, physically. Personality-wise, there's no pair on earth more different than you and Fiona."

"This goes beyond matching profiles, and you know it. Even *I* mistook her for myself. Were you pursuing *me*, or were you pursuing Fiona's ghost? You have this fixation. Bianca says it's called Prolonged Subconscious Grieving."

Hurriedly, Stewart gets out of bed and heads for the door.

Lynn, with her arms out, holding an imaginary tray stacked with accountability that Stewart is abandoning, says, "Where do you think you're going?"

He stops in the doorway, sneering back. "I'm coming back with something that'll make you and Bianca – your little quack psychologist – go back to the drawing board." Stewart waltzes back into the room with the large photo album that his mother left behind. He crawls into the bed and sits up next to Lynn who looks on, silently, dismissively. Stewart stops to his mother's high school graduation picture and drops the heavy book on Lynn's lap. Even in the old yellowed photo, Lynn sees herself with a muted smile, in a cap and gown, a tassel by her ear. Stewart flips through his parents' wedding photos from before he is born, and to white bordered birthday Polaroids from a time when Stewart's mother still thought of herself as sexy. Stewart flips the pages, compiling evidence upon evidence; he stops and taunts, "Are you sure it's a prolonged sub-surface what-ya-ma-call-it?"

Lynn is still dumfounded by her resemblance to Mrs. Stewart's younger version. Lynn smiles, bashfully. "You got me… I'm speechless."

"Good." Stewart places his hands on her body and kisses her, but pulls back when he feels dead lips.

"Really?"

Stewart frowns. "Really what…"

Lynn's eyes widen in mach terror. "You're trying to get some, after showing me how I look like your mother?"

Since Stewart's twin and her family's flight doesn't leave until Monday, they attend worship on Sunday, sitting with Lynn, Stewart up at the pulpit. At the start of Stewart's sermon, he takes the time to get them to stand and be acknowledged on no merit other than being his kin flown in from Connecticut.

Lynn finds Joy in the congregation. Joy sees her but turns away as if she didn't. After the sermon when Stewart announces that the door of the church is open, Joy looks down and doesn't budge. Lynn gets up and goes to her, bypassing the deacon who mistakenly thought she was one coming to confess. Lynn walks Joy to the altar. More women that Lynn encountered during the sponsor a family drive, sees Lynn escorting Joy to the altar and it gives them the courage to come forward and be saved. After they come out from filling out their information slips, to stand before the congregation, Lynn stands behind each one. Stewart let each of them say a few words and they each give a glowing report for the first lady, the wind at their sails.

When the microphone comes to Joy, she confirms the crucifixion, the resurrection, and accepts discipleship, but dodges the microphone when offered the opportunity to testify, so Stewart gives the microphone to Lynn, the young lady's intercessor.

Lynn throws an arm around Joy and squeezes her as she speaks into the microphone. "My friend, Joy, here… I felt her spirit even before she told me her name," Lynn says to the congregation. "What kept Joy from coming forward for so long is: she felt unworthy of God's forgiveness. Truly, it's hard to fathom God's forgiveness in a world where man won't give you a second chance; it's man who'll deny you a loan due to credit history; man, who'll deny you a job due to criminal background; man, who'll deny you health insurance due to a preexisting condition." The congregation vouches for her with handclaps and amens. "God, however… He wipes your slate clean, just like *that*," Lynn snaps her fingers. "The sad thing is, there are many, right now, sitting in their pews who should be running up to this altar." Lynn steps out in front of Joy and addresses the congregation. Stewart's eyes bulge in surprise, as if he isn't sure this is allowed. "Yes: you're ashamed of things you've done, but in the spirit, there's no one holding it against you but you." Two and then four more come forward, one in tears, but the first lady isn't done. "Some of you stay put because coming forward feels like you're being outed when really you're no different than the person seated next to you. Just by show of hands. Have you ever done something so bad that if you were to tell me what you did, I would look at you like you were a lowdown, dirty dog?" Many hands go up, which cancels out the fear of being judged. Lynn is prepared to offer, to those who still need reconciliation to come forward, but they're coming already.

Six, eleven, fourteen men and women come forward. Stewart motions hurriedly for the deacons to corral them in. Stewart realizes that this isn't some random inspiration; Lynn is deliberately helping him. Stewart shakes in amazement at Lynn, the woman he has chosen for his wife, as if he is just then realizing just how blessed he really is.

Chapter 32

On the third Wednesday in January, the first women's bible study of 2010, Nay begins her first installment of a six part, Back to Basics series. Even Nay's attire, a turtle neck, dress pants, and flats, seems to have gone back to basics. By this time, Nay had agreed that after the six-part, six-month series, women's bible study would be handed over to Lynn. By then, however, Levi and the Ginyards expect to have Stewart removed, so Lynn would never have the chance to take over the class, so there would be no passing of the Women's Bible Study baton.

The New Year gives the class an attendance boost, twenty-four women, up from eighteen. Lynn is surprised that Bianca is up front when she isn't speaking to Nay, and according to Bianca, she never will again.

Lynn sits next to a newcomer, a young lady no more than twenty-two who is showing off a new engagement ring from her New Years' eve proposal. The straight-haired young lady is now attending women's bible study for direction on the higher call of marriage. She keeps smiling at Lynn, not knowing how to break the ice, but Lynn recognizes her spirit. The young lady wants a mentor. As the class settles in, Lynn is chatting with the young lady, when they're all startled by Nay whacking the easel board with a wooden rod.

"It's a new year," Nay announces. "A time for reflection. I look at the church today and see how far off track we are. I know God's looking down at us shaking His head like what in the world do they think they're doing." She calls on her amen corner to back her up. "Am I right Deaconess Rainey? Tell me I'm lying, Miss Paulette." Classic Nay posturing, calling on her united front of Ginyard women. Anyone who challenges Nay also challenges them.

"Why the back-to-basics theme?" Nay answers her own question by saying, "There's too many ideas brought into the church to appease man but it ain't word. "Even phrases we speak forth *like* it's scripture but they're really not. For instance, 'You take one step God takes two,' *that* ain't in the bible. 'Hell, hath no fury like a woman scorned,' *that* ain't scripture – you see some things got to be torn down and then built back up again. Can't slop mortar over bad bricks? We're bringing the world into the church, when we're supposed to be taking the church out into the world, amen?"

Lynn looks next to her and the astute young lady is taking notes. Nay orders the class to turn to the scripture she'll be examining. Lynn is well aware that Nay is nothing more than a mouthpiece for Levi, so Lynn immediately knows how an abuser would interpret Peter 3:7. Lynn has heard this scripture a thousand times from her own abusive ex-husband.

Lynn's stomach feels ill, like it's full of soft butter. Nay reads:

Likewise, ye husbands, dwell with them according to knowledge, giving honor unto the wife, as unto the weaker vessel, and as being heirs together of the grace of the life; that your prayers be not hindered.

Nay takes a strut across the front of the class stopping on the torque of her hip. "Now. One of the main problems in the church is we got men who don't know how to be men, and we have women who don't know how to be women. Let's deal with this term, here, for a little bit: weaker vessel. As you can see, it ain't *my* words. You're looking at it right there in the text. We are all vessels unto God. Vessels through which the God spirit flows."

Lynn could tolerate Nay's drill sergeant bit, marching around the front of the room, swatting the easel board with her wooden wand, but this… Before Lynn knows it, she's standing. Lynn stands but doesn't say a word.

Nay gives a side-eye, "Everything alright, Lynn?"

She'd promised never to correct Nay again in women's bible study because somehow information gets back to Levi, and he beats her for not winning the debate. Unable to set the record straight, nor sit through an abuser's interpretation of Peter 3:7, Lynn gathers her notebook and pulls her purse over her shoulder.

Lynn then stamps out of the room. Nay announces her departure like comedy house M.C. "Put your hands together for Lynn, everybody." Only her Ginyard corner applauds.

Lynn speed-walks down the hall, fuming; her repetitive heel click echoing off the walls, driving a deepening hypnotic rage, taking her back to a time where she believed the exact interpretation Nay is making. It's the mentality that allowed Lynn to marry an abusive boyfriend rather than leave him.

Lynn throws the exit door open and speed-walks down the concrete walkway, passing the front of the banquet where Lynn remembers the impressionable young lady that was sitting next to her, taking notes. With the young lady in mind, Lynn spins around.

She goes into the banquet, drops her purse and notebook on a white clothed table, grabs two vases and comes storming back into the women's bible study class. The women see the vases and clear out of the way, moving desks scraping the floor. Nay shuffles back defensively, welcoming the fight, saying, "C'mon heifer. That's what I want you to do."

Lynn, instead of going for Nay, goes in front of the class and holds up the two vases as props. "Let me explain to you what that term weaker vessel means!"

Nay flags down the whole ordeal. "Uh, uh chick, this *my* class."

"Oh really? We both know whose class it *really* is." Half the class is standing, wading like a double-Dutch turn, ready to jump in if the two starts swinging.

Nay yells, "You think because you're married to the pastor you can do whatever you want?" Her Ginyard cronies back her up. *Girl sit yo'self down. She ain't nobody.*

"If I ain't nobody *you* ain't nobody," Lynn says. "Can't sink people you share a boat with. I didn't become first lady, nor you deaconesses by no other merit than who you married."

Nay points at Lynn but speaks to the class, "Does this sound like a woman who's *for* the church? She the devil. She one of them feminists."

"I'll *tell* you who I am," Lynn turns to the class. "I'm a survivor of domestic violence. The man who'd given me a broken rib and a fractured orbital bone used to tell me that *I* was the lesser vessel. Years after I escaped with my life, that same man, later, murdered his common law wife and her two children, and then turned the gun on himself." Lynn grows still and her eyes close to shut tears in.

Her all-woman audience is in shock; they assumed Lynn always had a charmed life, never thinking that among her many titles, first lady, author, playwright… is also DV survivor.

Nay pats Lynn's back. "And we thank you for that testimony, sugar. Now you can go ahead and sit ya behind back down." The women side with Lynn who's shaken; they trash Nay for her cruelty. *Girl, don't do that, Nay. You're wrong for that.*

The young, newly engaged woman stands, her hands out, waving toward the vases as if doing magic on them, "What were you saying about the vases, first lady? Continue!" The other women join her, urging Lynn to continue. Apologetically Lynn says, "Nay, I didn't mean for this."

Nay looks Lynn up and down, then looks at the women that makes up her class. "That's who y'all want. That's who y'all got." Then Nay marches out, her four Ginyard cronies tailing her.

Lynn picks up the vases again and has them turn to second Kings, the story of Elijah and the widow's oil. "What does vessel mean here?" The class answers, unanimously, *a container.*

"Vessel means same thing in Peter 3:7, only the type of container it refers to is the human body." Lynn continues, "Let's say the tin vase is the male vessel and the glass vase is the female vessel. Say if I add water to these vases. Is water in *this* vessel more valuable than the water in *this* vessel? No! Such is the living water – the spirit of God that dwells with a man or within a woman." Lynn poses another question, "Will the water in the male vessel quench thirst any better than the water in the female vessel?" The class is all over the answer. *No suh! Amen!* "Such is the *living* water contained in a male or female vessel: equal substance, but held in different vessels; different bodies." Lynn then holds both containers out in front of her. "But if I *drop* these vases, the female vessel (the glass vase) would be the one to break, right? *This* is what *lesser* vessel refers to. It is not a spiritual comparison; it is a physical one. So, when Peter says, *giving honor to the wife*, he's telling husbands *not* to use his physical advantage, but rather to *dwell according to knowledge*. The husband must appeal to the wife. He can't intimidate you, in the name of God, while the very act of intimidation is against the word of God. And *that* is the proper interpretation of Peter chapter three, verse seven."

As if Lynn's explanation has a foul odor, noses wrinkle in their epiphanies, which is the best reaction a facilitator could want. Bent faces show bent minds.

Lynn relaxes and takes the time to apologize for barging in earlier. With no script or lesson planned in advance, Lynn begins taking questions, some questions personal, about her domestic violence experience and some questions scriptural. One woman puts her head down in the bible, flipping pages. She doesn't raise her hand, but begins reading out aloud, a heckler in the crowd. "A man ought not cover his head, since he is the image and glory of God; but woman is the glory of man. For man did not come from woman, but woman from man."

Lynn fixes her eyes on the woman and says. "Man came from dirt; therefore do we worship dirt? How did Jesus come to this earth? Perfection came by way of God and a woman. Man had nothing to do with Him. Does that answer your question?" Lynn waits long enough for a response then continues. "That came from first Corinthians. Do you know who was the author of first Corinthians? Paul. The same disciple who said three times he asked God to take a thorn out of his spirit. So, when I read Paul it makes me wonder what that thorn is, considering he's so hard on women – no pun intended."

It takes a second to wash over them and suddenly *hard on*, takes on a new meaning. They cover their mouth and look around. One woman says, "Ooh, child first lady, you a mess!"

They begin requesting topics for the next class. Lynn asks, "What do you mean next class?" They agree that they're tired of hearing Nay's topics of: "Submissiveness," one woman says. "Surrendering," says another. One by one, they add to the list, "– back bending, child bearing, child *rear*ing, body shaming, mouth shutting–"

"–Ok, ok, I get it," says Lynn. Now that Lynn has stood up to Nay, the class doesn't want her back. Lynn had expected Bianca to be excited, since she now despises Nay, but Bianca is as quiet as a mouse.

When class is over, Bianca leaves without a word. She calls Levi to report what had happened. She then goes straight home, and waits on Levi.

Night is falling by the time Levi arrives. Levi sits in Bianca's den on a brisk and grey evening, a purring wind outside. Huddled over her smartphone, they listen to the recording. After Lynn's hostile takeover of women's bible study, Bianca had activated a voice recording app on her phone. She and Levi listen without interruption, only Levi's head shaking in misery, or at times, his eyes wide open in horror for what he's hearing.

Bianca, the undercover agent, fast forwards to Lynn's take on Paul. It takes a moment for the play on words to wash over Levi, as it did the class. "Hard-on," Levi objects. "Turn it off. I done heard enough."

Bianca says, "See what I tell you?"

Levi's head shakes. "Ain't no way. She gots to go."

Bianca asks, "But who's supposed to take over? You hear them ladies. They for sure don't want Nay back. And traditionally the first lady–"

"Tradition hell!" Levi pounds the coffee table. "We don't even have to oust Lynn, we just got to oust Stew, and it is done. She mo' dangerous than him. Call her what ya want: lobbyist, feminist, activist... She the devil. First Baptist is infiltrated by the devil!"

Carefully, Bianca interjects. "But what she said about the weaker vessel – I mean – how is she wrong, though?"

"She pour a little honey in their ear and they're ready to jump right in the fires of hell."

Bianca smiles a little to soften her reply. "Forgive me Pastor Levi, but that still don't explain where she was wrong."

Levi would've slapped his wife for far less. With Bianca he's gentle, he cheeses a little, "See, you have to read the whole bible – can't go with bits and pieces. In chapter two it says that wives should submit to their husbands as Christ submit to the cross."

Bianca's eyebrows go uneven.

Levi pinches her cheek. "Actually, it's an awesome thing because if the husband is any real man, submitting to him gets you everything you desire anyway."

Bianca, in ridicule, folds her arms and scrunches her lips.

Levi kisses her scrunched lips and he then makes a phone call to have a meeting with the board about Lynn's takeover of Women's Bible Study and the salacious things she's uttered before the flock. Levi never takes the phone from his ear again, but for a moment to kiss Bianca good bye and then leaves in a hurry for an emergency meeting.

Chapter 33

Levi plays dumb. He waits to see how long it would take Nay to inform him that she is no longer facilitating women's bible study; weeks goes by. Levi is still helping Nay with Bible study lessons that would never take place. Finally, Levi asks her, "Are you sure *you're* teaching the class on Wednesday?"

Nay backs away in fear. She knew he'd find out eventually, but she couldn't bring herself to tell him. Some taboo of self-preservation wouldn't let her say and bring immediate harm, although she knows the punishment would be more severe when Levi learned through other means. "I can't do it no more Lee." Nay says, creeping backwards.

Levi, creeps forward. "You can't do *what* no more?"

"Women's Bible study."

"Why are you walking away from me? I'm not going to hit you." He reaches a hand out to her.

Nay still doesn't trust him, but she takes the hand out of obedience and then braces for the knee to her stomach or the forearm to her throat. "I would've kept on doing the class anyway, but *they* want Lynn. She's a college professor; I'm no match for her."

Levi's head shakes, advance sorrow for what he'll do to her. "You didn't listen."

"No darling, I'm telling you, I listened, but it wasn't up to me." She could see Levi calculating her punishment behind his eyes.

"*Are* you facilitating women's bible study Wednesday?"

"No."

"Therefore, you didn't listen."

"They all agree that *your* interpretation is wrong. I tried to reason with them, but one up against twenty? C'mon, Lee."

"You should've had them flip back to where it says *wives be in subjection to your husbands…?* Did you point that out to them?"

"You keep leaving things out, Levi. Right after that it says, about the husband, that, *if any obey not the word, they also may, without the word, be won by the conversation of the wives,*" something Nay feels like she is doing in that moment.

Levi carries the verse further, "… While they behold your chaste conversation coupled with fear!"

Nay doesn't cower. "But fear doesn't mean that I should be in terror of you beating me down, Levi. Fear means that I speak and act with a reverence towards God."

Levi rises up at Nay, but surprisingly, she doesn't flinch. Standing on the word, she stands taller. "After that class, Levi, I kept studying First Peter from beginning to end, wondering what I could've said different, and I now know first Peter like the like the back of my hand. You can sit up here and try to twist things all you want, but I know it for mys*elf.*"

Levi snatches Nay by the arm, deferring to strength over knowledge. He pulls her to the bookshelf to get a bible. Nay, asks, but does not plead, for him to stop squeezing her arm. He then pulls her to the kitchen, opens the bible to First Peter, chapter two and drops the book on the counter, "Now read!"

"I already know what it says, Lee."

"I ain't asks you what you know! I said read!"

Nay picks up the bible to read, but Levi forces the book down on the counter. He switches on the spine lamp to shine directly on the book. "Read from right there under that lamp… And keep going to chapter three verse one." He pushes her head close to the text like forcing a pup's nose in its mistake. He let up enough for her to read, and while Nay reads, he uses the other hand to loosen his zipper and lift the back of Nay's dress. And then Nay knows what he is doing. She fights him, to no avail. She begs, as he bore inside of her. Levi smashes her face down harder on the open bible and holds her there with the one hand, raping her with her face in the ink of God's word. By the time he shudders and convulses inside of her, Nay's fight has left. Her soul has left her lying limp over the kitchen counter, an empty vessel.

Levi chides, "Did I tell you to stop reading?" He pounds Nay in the middle of her back. Nay is so deeply entranced she doesn't feel the blow. Even Levi is spooked, how she lay prostrate over the kitchen counter, as lifeless as a corpse. Her face lay on God's word like an open-eyed death, her tears bleeding sideways across her face, spotting the pages of The Holy Bible.

Chapter 34

With Lynn now at the helm, women's bible study explodes. They nearly outgrow the classroom. Chairs are brought in to accommodate the crowd. Lynn is dumbfounded, wondering what caused the boom: her taking over, or Nay's departure. The bible study explosion becomes a popular topic with her husband. Even non-members and the unsaved were invited to the class by enthusiastic members who had witnessed the first class.

Lynn bet on everything but herself, saying that it must've been an influx from New Year's resolutions, but Stewart counter claims that the first class of the new year had already happened and not even half as many participants came. "The reason is you, babe." Stewart is staring at the television, half engaged, but then her silence makes him turn to her. Lynn sits next to him Indian style with the ottoman pulled up to the couch as her work surface with an open bible and a spiral notebook where she mines scripture for her next class. Lynn ignores her husband, but he keeps talking. Stewart says, "When you speak about the word of God you're so sure of it, you'll make even an atheist hang his head and apologize." Stewart observes how Lynn drifts, how she sinks below her own surface. Stewart asks, "What are you thinking about? Every time I talk about your gift, you zone out on me. Where does your mind go off to?"

Lynn gets up and goes to the kitchen for no apparent reason.

Stewart isn't letting her off the hook this time. He sends his voice after her. "I saw it the first day we met in the barbershop, the way you commanded the floor. How they all bowed when you preached the word."

She comes back with a cup of yogurt, shoveling a mound of yogurt into her mouth and pulling out a leveled spoon. She sits on Stewart, her back, a wall in front of his face, blocking his television view. "I wasn't preaching; I was *analyzing* the word. There's a difference."

"You sure do analyze with fire and conviction, then," Stewart says to her back. He peers around her to get a look at her face.

Again, Lynn slips into a daydream. Not quite out of her trance, Lynn says, "The word on you is that you'd find any reason to promote a woman. What's up with that?"

Stewart's eyes stretch. "I *don't* do that. God's business is too important to play favorites."

"The investment scandal isn't the thing that got the trustees bearing down on you; it is you trying to get me behind the pulpit instead of the lectern that did it." They go quiet for a beat and then Lynn starts again. "Was Drea ever interested in preaching?"

Stewart sighs and shakes his head. He thinks Lynn is avoiding the subject again, but he answers anyway. "We were into everything together. What I liked, she liked and vice versa. We were on the debate team, ministers in teen ministry. I tried to convince her to enroll in seminary with me, not just out of the anxiety of separating with my twin; she was actually really good. But back then – and even now – women pastors struggle with empty pews and even receive death threats while, up north, Oprah became the first black female television host and Vanessa Williams the first black Miss America, so she felt she could find a better life up there."

"Tell me this," Lynn stares him down. "Do you think maybe you fight to create opportunities for women in ministry because of the opportunity your sister didn't have?"

Although Stewart had just told her otherwise, he now entertains this reason, out of preference; honoring his twin sister sounds somewhat heroic. "Maybe… Maybe…"

Nay is nowhere to be found, not even at worship on Sunday. Levi announces that his wife is under the weather, recovering from a bout with the flu, and although she is now getting around like her usual self, she is staying home as a self-imposed quarantine.

Lynn's gut feeling tells her Nay is dealing with something worse than the flu. Just thinking about the women's bible study takeover, Lynn breathes heavy with guilt for, undoubtedly, spurring who knows what level of abuse inflicted upon Nay.

At altar call, the front of the church is lined up with visitors, mostly women, bringing their membership to First Baptist. When the microphone is passed their way, they mention the first lady's class as the reason they'd come forward. Lynn's women's bible study class is helping Stewart like she predicted.

All along Lynn is racked with worry, though. After service she tries calling Nay, but Nay would not answer, which is understandable because she is probably upset at Lynn and ignored her number. Lynn seeks out Bianca, but her search is interrupted by Catfish, the mouth piece for the controlling board, his huge mascot head turning on his neck as Lynn hurries by. He calls Lynn to him and offers a handshake, saying, "I just want you to know that the work you're doing here isn't going unnoticed."

Lynn, wide-eyed, gives hurried nods and then continues her search for Bianca. Lynn calls her but gets no answer. Lynn goes outside and bumps into Mavis. "You got a minute?"

"Girl you must've read my mind," Mavis says.

They find privacy in the sanctuary that just disgorged a few thousand well-dressed people. The sanctuary is deserted and soundless. They sit middle column, back row. "Have you heard from Nay?"

Mavis answers, "Yeah. Why?"

"Is she alright?"

Mavis nods, "She's alright as far as I can tell over the phone. Why, did you hear something?"

"No, actually," Lynn says. "Maybe I'm just... I don't know..."

Mavis touches Lynn's arm to quiet her. "Let me tell you a story, Lynn." First Mavis asks Lynn what year it is.

Lynn droops forward at the question's absurdity. "2010, I would hope."

"And do you know the year that a couple farmers by the name of Tully and Henry Ginyard founded this church? 1910."

"This is the year of the one hundredth anniversary. Everyone knows that."

"Right…" Mavis gathers herself and clears her throat for storytelling. "When I was young, the original church had expanded a good bit, but it wasn't far off from its original form, that is, until 1980 when it burned down. I remember the hand clapping gettin' it like rain; we'd get to stompin' that ole wood floor like a percussion instrument. Didn't have no band. Praising and making music was one in the same. I also remember Emma. People don't talk about her much nowadays."

Lynn starts snapping her fingers to coax her memory. "Emma, Emma… I've heard someone speak of her."

Mavis says, "Emma is the reason those niggers burnt down the old church." Only the bad word echoes in the sanctuary. "Forgive me Lord." Mavis's hand reaches in the direction of the large cross over the choir section. Mavis explains, "Pastor Blake Ginyard was the pastor before Levi's father. When they needed a pastor, they called Blake down from New York and he came with his wife, Emma. People thought she was uppity. She wasn't uppity; she was educated. It was quite rare, then, to be a black woman and have a doctorate. She was gorgeous, smart, and yet personable. They say she could insult you so eloquently, it wouldn't sink in until the next day. In time, people warmed up to her because every time she opened her mouth – whether at women's bible study or praying during worship… *Every* time she opened her mouth, out flew the holy ghost. With the little platforms available to her, she outshined her own husband, but Blake didn't mind; he bragged about his wife. It was the *other* Ginyard men who couldn't stand her. When Blake's health started taking a turn for the worse, he got some folks together behind the idea of his wife taking over as pastor because no one wanted Levi's father, Sinclair Pappy Ginyard, who was a hard drinker and a known wife-beater with side-babies, one being Levi. Rem Blake up and died, and his dying wish was to have his wife preach the following Sunday. Word has it that there was a vote. The vote was in Emma's favor. Pappy was furious. He stormed into the meeting with a gun. Thankfully, no one was hurt. Pappy was so insecure about them letting Emma preach just this one sermon, he feared they would use it as leverage to make her the pastor instead of himself. Blake passed away on a Friday, but come Sunday morning, for Emma to preach, they find the church burnt to a crisp. They had hoisted up a cross on the lawn to make it look like the Klan, but come to find out young Levi was held out of school because of a burn on his hand. Yup: Pappy and them took that boy along. Made *him* do it because if he was their future. He needed to understand what being a Ginyard was all about."

Lynn sits silent, letting everything sink in and then she asks, "What happened to Emma? Is she still around?"

"She is a northerner to her heart, didn't much like the south. Her husband was dead, church was burnt to rubble. She sold their land and moved back up north." Mavis stops and waves her hands, smudging out the derailment of her story and gets back on track. "Listen to what I'm telling you, though. You're dealing with a man who has burned a church; this church. There ain't no God in him. Even his wife can't talk to him, said the man's unreachable, said he's liked to kill somebody. And *you*, Lynn, is public enemy number one."

Lynn who had been once before marked by death, doesn't blink. "What do you expect me to do; tremble with fear? I hid from God's calling all my life; sat in the back pews, containing my praise, kept his word hostage in my heart. Looking back, that *was* death when you love the Lord like I do. I didn't realize it, fully, until taking over women's bible study. The true joy of the Lord is sharing Him. And now, I refuse to dim the God in me for fear of *no* man."

Mavis is already awaiting her turn, hands on hips. "I ain't telling you sit on God. I'm telling you to keep your eyes peeled.

A snake can't outrun any warm-blooded thing it seeks to eat, but snake doesn't rely on speed, it rely on ambush."

Mavis's warning is never clearer than a few days later when Lynn suspects Levi of stalking her.

Lynn arrives at her appointment at the church daycare. The administrators thought it would be a good idea to, at least once a month, have a naptime story read by the first lady. When Lynn walks into the daycare, the children mob her, showing her their coloring pictures and one showing off his cartwheel. The daycare staff round them up on bean bags and mats and Lynn reads a story from a stool.

Levi enters. While Lynn reads, he lingers in the kitchen, looming behind the service window. Lynn is nervous, but she holds it together. By the time she snaps the book closed, the kids are either drowsy or napping already. Lynn quickly, but quietly hugs one staff member, asks that one to deliver her goodbyes to the others. Hurriedly, Lynn sneaks out.

After the door closes behind her, Lynn hears the door open and close again, and then she hears footsteps paced faster than hers. Lynn is heading down the hallway toward the administrative building, en route to Stewart's office. "First lady," Levi calls. Lynn keeps walking, with every intention of ignoring him. Levi yells, "First lady!"

Lynn stops and spins, letting out an irritated, "*Yes*, Levi."

He says nothing until he catches up, face to face. "I think it's time we have a little talk."

"About?"

Levi glances around for privacy, but he could tell Lynn's feet are planted, not willing to venture behind closed doors. "First let me say that I think you are good for this church." Lynn goes flaccid with disbelief as she listens to Levi. "I *used* to think you were taking advantage of Stewart, you know, with him risking everything on that play, and the hasty marriage. But now I've seen for myself that you're one of God's best and brightest."

Lynn finds his words disarming, but she is still skeptical, as if he were a street hustler selling hot merchandise. "Why are you telling me this?"

"I ain't all *good*, but what I want you to know about me is that I ain't all *bad* either. I came first to tell you that this church has big plans, and from what you've shown us, we'd like to sell you on being part of those big plans. We'll explain further, in due time, but in the meantime, first lady, I want to warn you about the company you keep." Levi touches her shoulder to help her out of the way of passersby, then they're both leaning against the wall, facing each other.

Lynn nearly died when his hand touched her shoulder, even in politeness. Lynn flushes a calming sigh and says, "Before you go any further, Levi, do you realize how odd this is for me?" Lynn peers around for listeners. "Isn't it you who insulted me after my women's day speech – flinched at me, even? We both know that you broke into the church and took the hard drives. You mention the company I keep? No one had to *tell* me those things."

"You don't have the slightest clue do you?" Levi smiles with all of his teeth. "Let's say if I *were* the one who broke into his office, I could give a rat's rear-end about a hard drive. I would've been after his journal. We were being investigated and if his journal is taken for evidence it may have revealed information that could tear my family apart."

Lynn remembers the detective telling her how statements he'd taken points to Stewart's panic attack being triggered by the missing journal. "What information?"

"Your so-called friends haven't told you yet?"

"Will *you* do the honors please?" Lynn stops her foot from tapping.

"They all have history with your husband. You know about Bianca, but did you know about Mavis? You got Mavis singing in your ear when she's the reason why we put cameras in the pastors' offices." Lynn rocks inside at the thought of what Mavis could've done to warrant cameras. Levi then backtracks, "Back when I was deployed, I had to help people who looked just like the ones who were out to put a bullet in me, so I learned how to study and differentiate nuances in people because my life depended on knowing the difference between those who might mean me good and those who might mean me harm. And I've never seen that ability so lacking in a person until I met you. Mavis wants you to hate me, Bianca wants you to *hate* Nay, and Nay wants you to *love* Nay. If they cared about you, they wouldn't withhold secrets from you."

Lynn's hands flop at her side in frustration. "You keep talking about these secrets. Ok, you told me something about Mavis. What else?"

Levi glances to both sides and says, "I'll put it like this: you're busy trying to make Stewart a father when he already is one. I'm raising Stewart's child like she's my own. So, again, if I *were* to break into the church, I would've been looking for that journal, so that information would never go public, and Heather would always know *me* as her father." Lynn is lost, like a child without an Easter speech. Levi waves a hand and says, "That's all I'm gone say." He marches toward the door. He pops the rectangle door handle with the side of his fist and walks through the door.

Lynn refuses to collapse until the door closes behind Levi. She then withers down on one knee. A deaconess notices and tries to help Lynn find whatever she is looking for down there, but when Lynn looks up, glazed over and disoriented, the deaconess knows something is wrong. She sits Lynn down in the prayer room and gets her a soda. Lynn tells her not to tell her husband. She decides not to visit Stewart, knowing she would turn his office into a crime scene.

As Lynn is in her car, exiting the parking lot, Nay is driving in, their two heads rotating in their driver's side windows as they pass. Lynn is too consumed with anger to stop and lower her window to speak. In that brief moment in passing, however, Lynn recognizes that ghostly look, a hollowed self, like her own mirror reflections after having her pride, courage, and dignity beaten out of her and be left with only the base remnants of humanity intact. That look tells Lynn that Levi has taken the abuse to a new level, but what Lynn must do now doesn't allow her time to stop for Nay. She speeds home to search for Stewart's journal – to find out for herself what Nay, Bianca, and Mavis won't tell her.

Lynn finds Stewart's journal in his study. She flips to the beginning and sees only a few years back, but Heather is eighteen. There must be other journals, she thinks. She opens a chest and flings its contents back over her shoulder. She goes in and out of rooms disgorging drawers. In his closet, she finds a stack of journals in a shoebox, and another stack in another shoebox, and so on.

Lynn spends the rest of the day flipping through and studying them. She learns how to locate the significant moments; the writing seems rushed, frantic. He writes in larger paragraphs, long, run-on sentences scrunching against the margins. She finds the incident with Mavis. Mavis didn't have "a history" with Stewart, as Levi put it. There was never a relationship. It was one-time episode of crazy Mavis, a woman who has spent years in a barred cage, had taken crazy to new heights. It was during a time when Stewart was heartbroken, when Savannah had finally confessed that she was a lesbian. Stewart's handwriting looks frustrated, the ink lines thicker from pressure on the pen, dimpling the back of the pages. He couldn't accept that Savannah's same-sex desires were more than just phantom heart flutters because Stewart was convinced that she lived on his love, when in reality, his love was her prison. Lynn flips through months of constant, crazed writing, a sign of depression. He wrote that, Mavis, among others, were getting on his case, saying that he wasn't being himself, that even his fiery preaching was reduced to a flicker. Mavis was so thoroughly disappointed with Stewart that she came to his office to set him straight. She bashed Stewart for being so down over a woman and assured him that every woman has the same thing Savannah has, and, while in her seat, Mavis lifted her dress and spread her legs to show him the evidence.

Lynn becomes nauseated. She flips back to where Stewart's journaling began, after Fiona's death. Lynn browses through dated pages of Stewart's young thoughts expressing anger at

God for calling Fiona home early. He was a brand-new pastor making regular trips to place flowers at the grave of the only love he thought was assigned to him. The other prevailing concern of his early twenties, were about his frustrations trying to promote change in the ministry when there were elders standing in his way, fighting tooth and nail for their long-standing traditions. Stewart mentioned a drinking problem. He drank from cases of wine bought for the wedding that never happened.

Nay's name starts showing up often. Nay was Fiona's sassy best friend, so when Fiona died, Nay bore the loss as hard as Stewart. Stewart and Nay bonded over this common grief. They leaned one another, one always finding strength where the other faltered. Nay learned that Stewart's grief and spiritual conflict, was deeper than he led on. Nay found out about the drinking and she did what any good Christian would do for a friend; more than just pray. She distracted him by keeping him on the phone, and during their phone conversations, if she suspected him of boozing, she'd come over and keep watch.

Later they realized that their time together was no longer about Fiona nor his drinking, that they had formed their own nucleus. Nay realized this sooner than Stewart did, and she showed him, one evening, with a kiss on the cheek that begged for his lips; he obliged. They broke away, ashamed and bewildered but then they repeated the act.

Lynn realizes that this is what Bianca was hinting at while at the hotel bar in Atlanta. Back then, Bianca wasn't a member at the time, but she perhaps finds out through other means. Lynn flips pages, scanning for clues, looking for evidence that Nay and Stewart dated officially.

Lynn spots the word *naked* and hones in on that paragraph. Stewart wrote that he woke up to the aroma of breakfast, wondering how he'd ended up in his bed half-naked, when his last memory placed him in the living room, fully clothed. He found Nay in the kitchen dumping eggs out of the pan. He asked if there was anything done the night before that couldn't be undone. She "played stupid," Stewart wrote. Nay was so disgusted with him for drinking himself unconscious, she punished him with her refusal to answer. She said, *If you wadn't blind off that wine, maybe you'd know.*

Stewart wrote that he later finds his pissed pants in the hamper and figured maybe *that* explained why he was half dressed, that maybe Nay did nothing more than help him out of his soiled clothes.

Stewart then began writing about Levi's return to finish out his enlistment at Ft. Jackson. Levi, more than a decade Stewart's senior, came to Stewart with his hat in his hand, asking Stewart to gracefully bow out of the relationship with Nay. Levi told Stewart that he'd already laid claim to Nay, in the eyes of God. Levi didn't mention the year, nor did Stewart think to inquire. Stewart ended the relationship with Nay simply because she had lied about being a virgin. When Nay was pregnant and scheduled to marry, she *then* expressed to Stewart, referring to that night, saying, *Nothing happened.*

Lynn is so deep in the journals that she loses track of time. She doesn't look up until she hears Stewart's car pull up in the driveway. She grabs an armload of the journals and runs back to the closet, hurrying to put them back in the shoeboxes like she found them.

Stewart comes through the door ducking. Lynn throws pillows and cups at him. A bug-eyed Stewart slips and slides in his church shoes, boogying as he ducks and dodges everything thrown at him. "Hey, Lynn… What the… Girl?"

Lynn yells, "You son of a bitch!" She sends lamps and chairs airborne punctuating his crimes, "You had a thing with Nay!" Her key chain dots Stewart's forehead. "I become friends with Nay and you never thought to *tell* me?" A coffee mug misses badly. She looks for more things to throw, still yelling. "I should've known since the day Monique did our measurements. That big ole wildebeest, switching her hips, talking about, 'I knowed that man long time, *long* time,'" Lynn mocks. "She said you're not into cookies; you're into *cakes!*" Lynn comes at Stewart, this time with her hands. Stewart wheels around to evade her. "Cookies and cakes? Babe! You done lost your mind!"

Lynn picks up the mug she'd missed with and winds up to throw. Stewart balls into a defensive shell, but Lynn lobs the mug the opposite direction, further into the kitchen. "You didn't even tell me about Bianca until you *had* to! Who *else?* Is there more?"

"No."

"Are you *sure?*"

"Yes."

Lynn, now in the kitchen grabs a bottle of dishwashing liquid. "Liar! Or did you forget about *Mavis!*" Lynn hurls the dishwashing liquid.

"*Ma*-vis?" The name turns grotesque in Stewart's mouth.

"Yes Mavis."

"Oh *that?* She flashed me once. She was trying to make a point, that's all."

"You didn't tell me. I had to find out; that's my point!" Lynn opens the freezer, and throws few ice cubes at him, and then she stops and shakes her head.

Stewart is still apprehensive about approaching her. Stewart scans the damage, like a mini tornado had been there. "Who have you been talking to?"

Lynn pump-fakes with a box of frozen broccoli. "You're letting another man raise your child?!"

Stewart's hand goes forward like a crossing guard signaling stop. "Hold your tongue, Lynn. Don't play like that, now."

Lynn cocks back her weapon, squinting at him. "*What* did you just say to me? Watch me take this frozen box of broccoli and bat your head down that hallway."

Stewart steps forward, despite her threat. "Look, you've done enough. Can we talk now?"

"Did you and Nay have sex?"

"Nothing happened between me and Nay."

"That's what *she* told you, isn't it?"

"I know I ain't no *daddy*. There ain't no such thing as a fourteen-month pregnancy term."

"So, you're not a daddy but you did have sex with Nay."

"I already answered you. It's like you'd rather hold it against me anyway."

Lynn steps forward, her chin leading her. "You just said there's no such thing as a fourteen month pregnancy term, right? Fourteen months from what, huh? Just be straight with me, Dana." Lynn's tears starts running faster, her mouth trembling. "Tell me what I don't know to ask."

Stewart takes a deep breath and rubs his head. "Fourteen months from… Honestly I don't know what… One night I was drunk. Nay spent the night. I woke up naked. I asked her if anything happened… I asked her on multiple occasions and she refused to tell me if anything happened or not. I don't know why… It messed with me so bad that I never picked up another drink since."

Lynn doubles over the kitchen counter and lowers her face in her stack of forearms. She jolts like it's a fit of hiccups, but it's something else. Some energy cranks inside of her that does not crank out tears. She begins wheezing, churn style. Stewart worries, but he's unsure if trying to comfort her would still draw her wrath. Lynn lifts her head to sit upright and there's a display of pearly whites. Stewart looks on confused, like a dog awaking to find himself neutered. Lynn laughs herself out of breath, her eyes clench, and there's even a snort. Still laughing, she staggers, in mirth, toward the littered living room, sliding Stewart aside like a coat on a hanger, as she walks past him. Lynn laughs herself to tears, and then she closes her eyes and shakes her head, the laughter gone; the tears still falling.

Chapter 35

They aren't speaking again, for the most part. They spend most of their time divided by walls, in their own silence, grinding their axes, until one is inspired to march across borders and strike.

In the morning, the two take their turns at the coffee pot; one going in after the other clears the kitchen. Lynn fills her mug, but this time doesn't take it into the bedroom. She invades Stewart's territory. She stretches her legs out on the couch without a word. They both study the television, intent on silence. Stewart sighs and then re-adjusted himself in his recliner. Lynn says, "Wanna know what I think?" She *knows*, actually, from reading his journal.

Stewart's head rotates like a toy action figure.

"I think you choose women for ministry as a way to choose them for yourself."

Stewart looks at his wife like she is a stock falling. "The more we resort to this kind of divisiveness, the more commonplace it becomes in our marriage."

With a two-handed grip on her mug, Lynn takes a sip. "Cute," she says. "You say *we*, as a way to tell *me* I'm in the wrong. Ok then, *we* need to be more forthcoming in our dealings with the opposite sex, outside the marriage."

A phone call cuts Stewart off before he can reply. Lynn sips her coffee and pretends to be uninterested in Stewart's phone call. Stewart covers the mouth-end and asks, "Hey Lynn. You got time for a meeting?"

Lynn lowers her cup. "Meeting?"

"The trustees. They wanna see us."

"Us…?"

Lynn and Stewart arrive together to go before First Baptist's governing board. Nay, backed by Levi, had submitted a grievance against the pastor and first lady. The tables are arranged in a U shape, Catfish at the head. His power comes from his absence of conscience, his ability to package and sell their selfish ambitions as justice.

Stewart and Lynn sits at the bottom chairs, the feet of the U, where their mischief has landed them, apart from each other, facing each other, a breakaway smile from each conveys that they could put away differences and team against this wretched bunch of Ginyards.

Stewart sighs at their posturing, the shuffling of meaningless papers, the looking down over glasses, throat clearing, watch checking, and roll call, to make things seem official, as if they could not quickly scan the room and see all persons present.

Catfish, stretching his eyes behind his glasses, expresses that the pastor and first lady were called together for what is reported as a coordinated bullying effort against Levi, the associate pastor, and his wife, Nay.

Before he could finish the sentence, Lynn is stepping on his tongue. "Nay? Calling someone a bully? Get outta here."

He reads the complaints waged against them, citing how Lynn threatened Nay with a vase and Stewart threatened Levi in his office. They say Lynn's incident with the vases had many witnesses who were able to clear her. But Stewart's incident had only two witnesses, which happens to be both complainants, corroborating against him.

Catfish shuffles his papers, and cites another indictment. "I hear, Lynn, that you walk a fine line in your bible study class. Among other things, you made a reference to Apostle Paul that makes even *me* blush. I offer you the floor to explain yourself."

Lynn has no papers to shuffle, just her empty hands to look up from. "I simply said that his teachings were hard on women.

I didn't realize how it sounded until I saw the reaction from the class. Knowing what most people think about Paul, I clarified that there is no pun intended."

"If you could, please, explain to us what most people think about Paul?"

Lynn glances across at Stewart who had bends slightly forward, as if to raise an objection, request a recess, but this is not courtroom. He waits for disaster as Lynn answers, "Paul was the most outspoken of the Apostles about his fleshly desires, but he never names it. The 'thorn' in his spirit could be lust for women, or even men. Who knows?"

Stewart mashes his face with his hand. The board buzzes, like they are calling for her arrest, but Catfish reels them in. "Fools... All she's saying is that she doesn't know. Her style is to speak in a provocative way. Aren't you all provoked?" They look around at themselves, guilty. "She's been provoking sinners right up to the altar of this church. In the last couple months, she's brought in more members than anyone here; *you* included," his eyes bulge at Pastor Stewart, the one most accountable for growing membership. Catfish closes the folder on Lynn, and asks another question, apparently off the record. "In your political realm, do you support abortion?"

Lynn shoots back, "Do you support me slapping the hell outta you?" Catfish is amused. Lynn catches a corner glimpse of Stewart nearly fainting at her response but she ignores him. "Our organization doesn't even *partner* with organizations that support abortion. We do, however, feel some kind of way about any legislation giving the hand of the law reach into the body. Funny how the law only takes aim at *our* bodies. But if there comes a day when legislation takes aim at *your* rectum, I'd protest just as hard on the behalf of men."

The Ginyard men pause and check with each other before bursting with laughter. This woman's entertainment alone is worth the meeting.

Catfish let Lynn go free. "I'll say again that we appreciate the work you're doing, but you'll do well to watch that tongue of yours."

Catfish dismisses Lynn. As she's leaving, eyes turn to Stewart. Lynn, outside, roams nearby wringing her hands, hoping the best for her husband, although they haven't been speaking.

The topic changes to the investment scandal. Stewart watches as they pretend like they haven't awaited this moment for years now, where the pastor who says he's more powerful than their pen, who spoke openly against their plans to franchise the ministry, who campaigned for, and propped up women whenever he could, and flaunted their success as if he were using their ministry to make a spiritual statement aimed against everything they stand for. Stewart could've withstood this investment scandal four years back when members were still marveling in their growth, how First Baptist grew ministries and buildings like wild mushrooms, but in the last few years of losing membership like a slow drip, and hadn't put a door knob on the church, all Stewart had given them is a financial scandal and, as Catfish reminds them, a fraternizing incident with the teen choir leader, Bianca. Pastor Stewart is losing the people's confidence that he'd built over the previous fifteen years and stands now, a shell of himself, subject to this assembly's authority. Ready for his fate, Stewart appraises his executioners, the Ginyard clan, their dominant traits showing up in each one, their wide noses, stump necks, and deep-set eyes staring at him, judging him, wincing fake pains over their decision, as if their decision hadn't already been made prior to this meeting.

In ten minutes, Stewarts comes out of the meeting speed-walking right past Lynn as if he doesn't see her. Stewart seems possessed. Lynn trots after him, wondering if he is still the pastor; if she is still the first lady.

He doesn't even see Lynn until he's getting in his car and Lynn gets in the passenger side. Lynn asks, "What happened?"

Stewart puts the car in gear and says, "I'm suspended."

"For–"

"–A month."

Lynn caresses his hand. "I'm sorry," she says, but is otherwise speechless.

Stewart grinds his teeth. "So, during that month suspension, they're gonna have a blind vote to see whether I'm out for good. You and I already know what it's gonna be. The only way out of this mess is to catch Westermann," says Stewart. "So, who's the detective that gave you the video on Levi? Got a business card?"

Lynn reaches into her purse and hands it over. "Do you know something?"

Stewart sighs, "I don't know if it's something, but I remember one time overhearing Westermann on his cell phone. He was talking about money wires to a gentleman named Carlos Fuentes."

"You remember a name you overheard from that long ago?"

"Only because that's the name of one of my sister's favorite authors."

Lynn thinks about not asking but changes her mind. "How come you didn't mention it when they questioned you?"

"I was advised by a lawyer, Deacon Bacon's son, not to say anything. Once you give a statement, you become material to the investigation, which is not a good place to be in."

Lynn asks, "When are we going to see the investigator?"

Stewart gives her an evil look and says, "No, Lynn. You need to stay in your lane. That's what's got me in this mess, right now."

It's the last words spoken between each other that day; they stop speaking again.

Chapter 36

In the morning, Stewart is regretful. He realizes he had gone too far. There are many mirrors he could use to string his tie, but he chooses the mirror on the dresser in front of their bed. He knows Lynn is pretending to sleep, so he talks to her anyway. "I just wanna say I'm sorry, Lynn. None of this is your fault, I was just… upset. That's all."

"It doesn't take you that long to tie a tie."

"I couldn't leave this house with that on my conscience. I couldn't go on having you thinking that what I said had any resemblance to the truth."

Lynn twists around enough to beam angry eyes. "Believe me, after all I've learned, almost nothing you say to me can be taken as truth." On that note, Stewart marches out.

By midmorning, Lynn finally checks her phone and finds four missed calls, half were from Stewart. The other half is from a number she doesn't recognize. She checks the messages and learns that the calls were from Catfish, saying it's urgent that they meet.

Even after what Stewart said the day before about staying in her lane, Lynn returns Catfish's call and agrees to meet, thinking that she could, in some way be of help to her husband. She put the address in her navigator and it leads her to a decaying shopping center with a local tax filing business, a to-go Chinese restaurant, and a beauty supply store, keeping the property afloat. The suite number for the address is to a gutted shop, the front wearing purple tint. Whatever the place was, it had been long closed for business. Catfish and Rudy get out of their car and hurry to meet Lynn, "Afternoon," They say. Catfish has a key, which he uses to unlock the door and they all walk in together, Lynn asking, "What *is* this?"

Rudy takes over as the presenter, his arms spread. "*This* is going to be the location of your new bible study class. Won't take us but a week to renovate it. You've outgrown that room y'all are in."

"House my *what?*"

Catfish swells with pride. "Your class has outgrown two rooms already; you need the space. I'm the one who came up with this idea."

Lynn grabs her head with both hands and smooths her crinkly hair back. She suspects a setup. "And how will they know that the class location's changed? And when is this supposed to start? And what's with that giant grin on your face, Rudy?"

Rudy asks Catfish. "Should I tell her now?"

"May as well go on 'head."

"This is happening faster than we anticipated. We had to rush you down here to let you know before everything went down."

"Before what went down?"

"With your husband, I'm saying."

Lynn's eyes pinch closed and her head shakes.

"You know the TV program on in the early morning? The ratings are at the bottom, right now, but we still got some months left on that contract."

Lynn's heart races. She's out of breath as if she's breathing for two people. "Forgive me, Rudy, but you've lost me. On the one hand you're talking about women's bible study and on the next, you're talking about some television deal? What does one have to do with the other?"

Catfish takes over. "We want to use the remaining months on that TV contract to air your women's bible study classes instead of your husband's sermons."

Lynn backs away, her head shaking no.

They rush alongside her, each flanking an arm, trying to calm her down. "Let's talk a while. You hongry? The place next door got the best honey wings in town. Let's get you some wings."

Lynn is swept up in their encouragement and suddenly she is standing in the rundown Chinese restaurant with wood paneled walls and two wobbly tables. they sit Lynn down at the table next to the row of gumball machines and then hustle the clerk to get them some tea, which they hurriedly set down a large Styrofoam cup in front of Lynn. Nerves had run her mouth dry. Lynn draws from the straw like she hadn't drunk in days.

She says, "I've never heard of someone airing bible study on T.V."

"Oh, yeah," Catfish remembers. "About that. That ain't exactly for bible study. That's your church. You're the pastor, but this is like a trial run. They're letting us do a month-to-month lease."

"What!" Lynn nearly faints, but she doesn't. She hides her face behind her hands.

Rudy and Catfish look at each other and back to Lynn. "We can get you a better venue," Rudy says. Catfish shushes him with an elbow.

"But you don't even allow women behind the pulpit."

"Because First Baptist ain't our church; it's in our care. We'll be the founders of *this* church, so we'll do what we want. Listen to me, Lynn. Don't say nothing. Just listen because you're giving all this reaction on only half the information. There's more."

Catfish takes over and says they would lease, and potentially, buy the old Coliseum downtown, the old, vacant basketball arena, for a new sanctuary. He heads off all her objections, "We know the university still owns the building and they're even holding classes in the bottom levels, but they don't hold classes on Sunday though, do they?" Based on Lynn's television ratings, they'll know if the plan to make a new ministry out of Coliseum would be viable. "We've been looking for someone new and fresh, and we come to the conclusion that ain't nobody newer or fresher than you. So, we choose *you*, we're just waiting on you to choose us."

Lynn is swirling in everything, no thought holding still long enough for her to speak on, except for one thing, and it is humorous how they'd missed one crucial detail. "I've never been to seminary. Have you thought about that?"

"Yup. One is not required to go to seminary to pastor a church, but if you must, we can pay for that out of our scholarship fund. Only takes a year of online classes." They set down the to go box of wings and rice in front of Lynn and when the steam rises, the smell makes Lynn sick to her stomach. She closes the box. She is afraid that if she speaks, she'll hurl, so she sits there listening to the two, and watching them chew with their mouths open, devouring their wings to the bone like hyenas.

They've studied churches that have become mega churches overnight, and determined that they all had one thing in common: the most successful pastors have the ability minister to women. *Men* tend put off religion until marriage. It's the wife who ushers him into the church.

Lynn pinches her nose to avoid the smell and in a nasally voice, says, "Are you implying that the woman is the spiritual leader?"

They stammer, defensively, Catfish clarifying, "No. Women are drawn to the security of God's covering, and the beautiful language of the word. Men are drawn to the *principles* of the word. He's better at *applying* the word."

"If so, why does he outpace women twenty to one when it comes to crime? Doesn't sound like they're doing such a good job of applying the word, to me."

Catfish rebuttals, "That's because Satan, in order to destroy the family, he goes after the head. You cut off the head and the body will fall. The survival rates, teen pregnancy, and graduation rates of our youth is much improved with the father in the home."

Lynn eyes Catfish as if she had his body bag unzipped and waiting. "How about when the mother is *not* in the home? Did you look up *that* statistic? How can you frame that success around the just the father when mother's there too? Why not *two-parent* households versus *one-parent* households? *Two-incomes* can afford safer neighborhoods and better schools, right? Doesn't two voices discipline better than one – two hearts love more than one – two sets of eyes keep watch better than one set?" Lynn's erect finger wags next to her temple. "You try to make something spiritual out of something logistical. In your bigotry you adorn the man with your laurel wreath when it's clearly not his size. Woman's place is by his side and not in his shadow!" Lynn comes to, seeing them wince back from their tables and she realizes, only then, how she has berated the men who just offered her a coliseum. Her rant, Lynn assumes, has cancelled the negotiations.

They two Ginyard men stare from a bubble of silence, which Catfish pops with his hand chopping forward hatchet style. "*That's* what I'm talking 'bout, right there!" The man celebrates like he'd dropped a royal flush on a poker table. Lynn's insight and passion exemplifies perfectly why she is their choice in the first place.

"If I were to accept – and that's a big if – how does my husband fit in?"

"He sure as hell don't fit in at First Baptist. You can have him. He can be *your* first lady, I guess," they laugh.

They give Lynn three weeks to decide.

Chapter 37

The detective arrives at Stewart's home, but Stewart is running late. On a day that Lynn, surprisingly, has nothing to do, she is more surprised by the knock at the door. She answers the door, pinching the top of her housecoat. When she questions Claude, he answers with his own question, "He didn't tell you?"

Stewart had made no mention, which is not odd, since conversation is down to a bare minimum. They had found safety in silence; closed mouths can't inflict harm. Rationale is just now seeping up through the façade of anger, and what may have happened twenty years ago between Stewart and Nay is no longer important, nor was it ever. His past is no more relevant than her past of having been married before. They are just getting around to resuming the habit of daily conversation, venting about their day, dealing in light topics to circumvent arguing, avoiding the heavier topics of conversation. Lynn remembers trying to tell her husband about the meeting with Catfish and Rudy, but mumbled stupid and then cancelled with a quick *never mind*. Likewise, Stewart had failed to mention what came of his meeting with the detective.

Claude takes a landline phone out of a bag and hooks it into their wall jack. "That lead? Mr. Fuentes? Turned out to be gold. All along we were monitoring *cell phone* towers. Through *him* we learned that the bastard's using a satellite phone, which led us to another fake identify he's taken on."

Lynn notices a locked briefcase that she assumes is full of cash. Lynn frowns at the thing. "I hope you're not expecting my husband to deliver this."

Claude looks up from looping the cord into his hand. "I wouldn't go through with it if I didn't think it was safe."

"How is it safe with my husband delivering a briefcase with you and ten or more agents waiting with guns drawn? What if *Westermann* has a gun? Dana's in the crossfire."

"There won't be ten agents; only me."

Lynn eyes him. "That doesn't sound right."

"In this case, less is more. We've profiled this guy; he's not violent at all."

Lynn flicks open the briefcase and Claude hurries over to confiscate the case of banded hundred-dollar bills. Lynn, speaking under her wrinkled nose, says, "This money stinks."

"It was bribe money hidden in a meat freezer," he says, pride sneaking its way into his cheek. He places the briefcase out of arm's reach.

More than the money doesn't smell right to Lynn. "Do your superiors know what you're doing – holding bribe money, using my husband for bait?"

"*He* came to me. He said this is the only way to save his ministry."

"And that is enough for you to go rogue?"

"I doubt Westermann will even show up, Lynn." Claude stops everything to explain how important this arrest would be, detailing how The SEC and FBI were being criticized even after capturing Madoff because not only was he just one man, but that he had went decades unchecked, and how the country was upset about Wall Street using taxpayers' bailout to pay executives millions in bonuses for nearly collapsing the American economy.

Lynn throws her arms out and let them flop. "I don't care about that. Tell me about you and my husband. Tell me how this is ok."

"We have to do this under the radar; it's the only way. By the time commands go up and down the chain we'll lose Westermann due to all the bullshit bureaucracy."

"That bureaucracy is what's going to keep my husband safe. Curtailing that bureaucracy also puts your career at risk, so tell me why would you risk your career?"

The detective is getting agitated. "Why don't you talk to your husband when he gets here? His opinion *ought* to matter, because if not for him you'd still be that underappreciated teacher, carting your books all over town." Lynn blanches at how the detective has turned on her. She observes, like a tiff with a friend, where you let them let you have it, just to learn what they really think of you. The detective adds, "It is *his* influence that sold out that arena, which sent you into orbit. You can sit up here and act like you're some success story, but you didn't pack a coliseum nor win any award because you suddenly became a better writer; it is all him."

Lynn crosses her legs and lines him up in her sights. She knows what an attack out of anger looks like; this is an attack out of fear. "You say I'm only worried about what I want? What do *you* want?" He glances at her bare crossed legs coming out of her housecoat. Lynn clarifies, "You bring a briefcase of bribe money into my home that is literally dirty money and you're throwing around insults? I have a mind to call the office in the morning and let your superiors in on your little plan."

"If I tell you the real reason, will you promise to not make that call?"

"That would be foolish. I can only guarantee, that if you do *not* tell me that I will call for sure."

His index finger turns on himself. "*I'm* the one who unraveled this case. *I'm* the one who didn't treat it like just another file on the caseload, and I kept working the case even after I had to transfer it to another office. They don't get to swoop in on my detective work and take all the credit. This case is *my* sold-out arena. This could put *me* into orbit. Do you know about Marty Beale?"

"Who is he?" Her three words come out like one.

"For forty something years, he was just another guy – until he quietly took down one of the largest insider trading rings ever. He wrote books; became an expert analyst on TV; started his own corporate investigative firm; got a younger wife… Here's the thing, see: he was never the genius he made himself to be. Years later we find out that he received an anonymous tip that pretty much handed him the case." Claude pauses and says, "*I'm* just a guy too. But if cracking this case allows me to sell the idea that I'm some demigod walking among men, I'm going to treat this opportunity like it's my lottery ticket."

"You may want to lower those expectations a bit. Does it really matter how slippery Westermann is, how savvy your detective work? This is just *one* conman – not a ring of conmen like the guy you're patterning after."

They hear Stewart's car pull up in the driveway. "But this one man? Westermann? Has dirt on thirty to fifty men."

Lynn's head rises up with a silent *ah*.

"You see: When the markets were nose-diving, fear drove investors to cash out. Westermann couldn't keep cashing everyone out because the profits he reported weren't real, so, in hopes to keep the scheme going, he tried to raise the money by investing with legitimate brokers. But here's the thing: knowingly transacting funds from an illegal enterprise constitutes laundering. I know those investors knew by how recklessly they invested Westermann's money, ignoring stop-loss mitigation, which is punishable in itself. We got Madoff who is the biggest fish in history, but still, he's only one fish. What America needs is to be able to turn on the evening news and see thirty clean cut brokers hauled off in the patty wagon. Whoever's responsible for their arrests will gain a reputation they could make a nice easy living off of."

Stewart closes the door behind him to announce his arrival.

Claude, soliciting his help, asks, "Please have a word with your wife." Claude has no idea how difficult that simple task would be, given the climate of their marriage.

Stewart glances at the detective and then to his wife, alone with a man in their home, her housecoat split up to the thigh of her crossed legs. Stewart replies, "Not until she makes herself decent." Lynn pinches her housecoat closed, gets up, and marches down the hallway. Lynn doesn't show her face again for as long as the detective is there.

After Stewart and the detective takes an hour to execute phase one of their plan, Stewart comes to the bedroom to check on Lynn and finds her fully dressed her curves hugged by a lavender Argyle sweater dress; she's fully made up, her lips candy red, her freed twists falling around her shoulders. There is a yawning briefcase on the bed that Lynn is filling with clothes.

"Babe, what are you doing, babe?"

"What does it look like I'm doing?"

Stewart's heart drops. He's prepared to grovel at her feet, but she seems so cold, in her in her exquisite beauty, that she'd likely step on his back on the way out. "What are you *doing*, Lynn…"

She wouldn't have looked if not for hearing the break in his voice. This hour or so while her husband consorted with the detective, she had prepared for precisely that question. "If I can't have peace in *this* situation, I'll make a situation where I can."

Lynn throws another item in the luggage case. Desperately, Stewart yells, "*Stop* it, will you!"

"I'm not ending this marriage, but there are levels of marriage I'm willing accept. I'm going to my mother's."

Stewart flashes distress. "Have you called your mother?" Her head shakes no. "*Don't,*" he jumps.

Her head shakes no again, but meaning something different: she must. "I will *not* be dismissed as if I'm your child." She then models her body dress, "Am I *decent* enough for you now?"

Stewart encourages the thrashing. "Let me have it, Lynn. Get it all off of your chest. I deserve it."

Lynn looks at him ridiculously like he's a circus clown at a funeral. "You don't want to hear what I have to say, or you'll *help* me pack." She throws a rolled bundle of socks in the open luggage.Stewart squats on the edge of the bed, ready to dive on the luggage like a live grenade. Lynn asks, "If you're really worried about saving this marriage, don't go through with this briefcase mess. Or is the ministry the only thing you give a damn about?"

Stewart hears his wife's anger laced in hurt feelings. He softens his reply, like words spoken at the side of a hospice bed, talking the loved one out of dying. "That's not true, Lynn. No matter how good it sounds, babe, it's just not true."

"What is it that would make you do something like this, then?" Lynn stamps. "And do *not* tell me that God's putting you up to this. God certainly has a way of telling you what you want to hear." Lynn breezes past him to her nightstand for tissue. Stewart's eyes, slits in his face, are all over her dress. From his seat on the bed Stewart reaches out and places his hands on the handles of her hips which are level with his face. He pulls her into him. Without looking, he knows her tears are streaming, he places his face to her abdomen and whispers, "I need you." And again, "I need you, Lynn." He stands and holds her tight, Lynn leans away from him. His face chased hers left and right until she gives up the chase and their eyes lock in the middle, their noses sniffing around that moment where the bottom could fall out from under bitterness and they'd find themselves tangled in passion. He kisses her candy red lips, no pulse there. She turns away, eyes holding tears. Stewart's hands fall to her buttocks his fingers sinking into her plush pillow. A fatal mistake; *needing* her takes on new meaning. Her eyes widen, glassy and violated. She wiggles away from him. "Pig," she spat. She goes back to packing, remembering, aloud, her reasons why. "*Now* you're ready to talk. After you're through torturing me."

"You tortured me too." He shrinks away from his answer, realizing how she'd hear it: tortured him with sex. In her mind, sex is knee-high to communication, and any counter debate is pure perversity. Stewart tries a different angle, "Have you asked yourself if this is what God would have you do? Even for a few days? Husband and wife leave their parents and cleave unto each other – not the other way around."

Lynn laughs like she is genuinely amused. Stewart laughs too, if that were the appropriate thing, anything to keep her from leaving. Lynn says, "If you would look outside of yourself, you'd see what God is saying."

"What do you mean baby? Tell me."

Lynn's head tilts to mean that's precisely what he doesn't want. "This is First Baptist's hundredth year isn't it?" Stewart gives a quick *yup* just to hurry her along. "This is also the fortieth year since the church was burned down to keep Emma, a woman, out of the pulpit, right? You would *see* that if you weren't so busy scribbling in your notebook authoring yourself at the center of everything. God doesn't make mistakes. Maybe His plans for this church doesn't include you!"

Stewart can't follow where she's going with this. He can't guess who else, besides him. "Do you really think God wants Levi at the head of this church?"

"Why would you even mention Levi and God in the same sentence," Lynn says. "You know the word. You know how God works in numbers. It's forty years since a woman was slated to get behind the pulpit. Forty is transformation. Maybe God's got his eyes on a woman."

"What woman?" Stewart watches her from the corner of his eye, fearing her answer.

"They offered me a church."

Stewart, who'd just sat down springs up again. "*Who* offered you a church?"

"They want to air my bible study classes on TV instead of your sermons."

Stewart never knew betrayal until now. "So… how long have you been consorting with my enemies?"

Villain and victim swap vessels. Lynn now struggles to explain to Stewart, a tear slipping off her chin. "It's not like I went behind your back; we weren't speaking."

He looks down like his heart has tumbled out the cage of his chest and fallen. "*Sure,* you didn't." Stewart walks, solemnly, out of the room and closes the door behind him. Lynn takes one step after him but not one more. She needs to go through with her decision to go, or no threat from here on out would be taken seriously.

She hears glass crashing and what sounds like a frightful yell, out front. Lynn goes for the door, but as soon as her hand touches the metal of the doorknob she hears feet running past the door so fast there had to have been two pairs. She's seen candid video clips of deer crashing through glass plate doors finding themselves trapped in a maze with only the instinct buck its way out. She opens the door wide enough for one peering eye. At the end of the hallway, their side door flings open, her husband, framed by the doorway, sprinting, head up, heels flicking back. Lynn tears after him, screaming his name. She hit the grass like she's shot out of the side of the house into a bitter dusk, cold enough that breath billows steam. Her husband climbs on the guard rail of the small, stocky bridge. His head turns on his shoulders looking at her momentarily. He's sharply three dimensional against a cartoon sky, the sun, a pink gumball smeared across the horizon, the distant trees are frozen black smoke in the distance. Lynn's scream *Nooo* trembles as her feet pedals the ground, her arms pumping. Her husband leaps off the rail feet first. And then Lynn climbs up on the rail and jumps, her lavender Prada dress lifting against the gumball sky. Stewart bobs up. Lynn plunges, the cold stinging like porcupine quills, the bubbles, small and tight, under the dark water feels like swimming in a large pool of root beer. She comes up, looking around and yelling for her husband. He comes up behind her. She spins around and they embraced as first order of business, but then Lynn pounds his chest, yelling at him for scaring her half to death, and they embrace again, their teeth chattering in the cold, as they fuss at each other, Lynn yelling at Stewart for jumping in and Stewart yelling at her for jumping after him, but they leave the pond holding each other on the walk back to the house.

Stewart feeds the fireplace. Lynn rests on her side on the velvet chase, Stewart sits on the floor at Lynn's feet, both watching the crackling fire in linen robes, sipping warm cider, talking as if they'd just woke from the same nightmare, making sense of the dream. Stewart says, "Honestly I don't know why I did it… But you coming after me…" He pauses to gather himself. "Somehow helps me know that this marriage is real."

Lynn reaches down and takes his hand in agreement.

"You've got a bible study class tomorrow. I don't think you should drive two hours to your mother's and–"

"–I'm not." Lynn yawns. She's struggling to keep her head lifted; she's dozing off to sleep; Stewart isn't far behind.

"*Were* you really going to your mother's house?"

"Yes…" They're talking out of their head, sleep drunk. "Dana?"

"Yes?"

"I'm going to turn down their offer."

"Lynn… Whatever you want to do, I'll support you… Lynn?"

"Yes?"

"I'm still going through with the sting."

"Promise me you'll back out the moment you feel unsafe."

"I love you."

"I love you too."

Chapter 38

*I*n all their years of marriage, abuse finally shows up at church. While passing Lynn's women's bible study class, Levi sees the crowd backed up at the entrance like a clogged drain, and he becomes enraged. He calls Nay, saying they need to talk. He leads Nay to the administrative building after hours. Nay questions Levi as he jiggles with his keys and then disarms the alarm. Nay enters his office full of sass, refusing to acknowledge him directly and examining her nails as he fusses, knowing she could get away with the attitude because he would never attack her at church. Without looking, Levi reaches back over his shoulder, unsheathes a book from the shelf behind him and launches it at Nay's insolence. Nay ducks; the book misses by an inch, close enough to catch the book's breeze carrying the smell of pages. Nay pops up from her chair, shocked, asking her husband if he'd lost his mind, but that vampire-ish, blood-thirsty look confirms that Levi is, in fact, out of his mind. Nay leaps for the door; he blocks her. He squeezes her jaw and runs her back into the opposite wall, evil running through him like electric currents. They are alone in the administrative building; Levi has all the privacy he needs.

On pure adrenaline, Nay places the heel of her palm under Levi's chin and drives *him* back, trying, with all of her might, to un-lid him. Her strength surprises Levi. He has to let go of his grip on her and use both hands to pry his wife's palm from under his chin. Nay can't match his strength; her arms and shoulders knot and burn as Levi slowly, but surely, frees himself. The lock of hands slip against each other and clears space between them – a space that Nay uses to punt Levi in the groin, which sounds like a flag whip, his pant-scrunch raising the bottom hem above his church socks, revealing ashy shins. His eyes bulge, his mouth shrinks to a small O on his face and he tips over like a cut tree. Nay flees the scene, speed walking in heels, checking back over her shoulder, but realizes that her purse with her car keys and her cell phone is left behind in the office with Levi. She can't turn back. If she finds him recovered, he'd strangle her to an inch of her life.

When Levi regains the ability to walk, he lurks the hallways, stopping for no one, peeking in dark rooms and flipping on lights. He checks the ladies' rooms and then women's bible study, but oddly, the classroom that was being stuffed with women is now empty. He goes to old retired church, which was turned into the ministries building and his search is interrupted by a woman's voice coming from the retired sanctuary of worship. He pushes through the double doors and finds women lined up on the old pews like birds on power lines. Levi targets Lynn at a pulpit that is retired, but a pulpit nonetheless. Levi blasts, "What in the *hell* do you think you're doing?" He marches toward the front.

Lynn could've respectfully explained that even the biggest room couldn't hold her class, but Lynn, ducking into the microphone, meets fire with fire. "This is *women's* bible study, Levi. Either you're confused about *where* you are or *what* you are."

"Retired or not, this is still a pulpit." Anger gives Levi tunnel vision, like the sights of a sniper rifle; he only sees his target, Lynn, so he walks right past Nay who is hunched down in a pew.

Women peel out of their seats to run get help. As Levi approaches, the front row lifts and creates a barrier between Levi and Lynn. There is no pushing or shoving, only the women setting themselves up as human posts and Levi dodging and slipping past each one.

Stewart appears trotting, flanked by the two women who had alerted him. Stewart enters the old sanctuary to find Levi arguing face to face with Lynn. As Stewart scurries up the steps, he yells, "You're messin' with the *wrong* one now!" He steps in front of Levi, shielding Lynn behind him and barks, "*Say* another word to my wife! Give me a reason to *drag* your sorry behind!"

Levi doesn't back down in front of the audience. They stare down like prize fighters at a weigh-in. Levi grins, "Who do you think you're you fooling, Pastor Stupid? Bet you ain't never killed so much as a *yard* chicken in your life. I've rung the necks of *men* twice your worth."

Men from the bible study rush the stage, elbows swimming over shoulders to pry the two pastors apart. Security arrives, scanning for an angle to engage the riot. Levi keeps yelling, above the commotion, "Where's my wife! Where's my wife!" She has his medication he says; he needs his medication, he implores. "Where! Is! My! Wife!" They only know where Nay had been, but in the commotion, no one saw where she went.

They cancel men's bible study. Stewart goes back to the men's bible study room and can't find his keys. Nearly everyone searches for one of two things: Nay and Stewart's keys, never guessing the two might be in the same place.

Stewart knows he didn't leave his keys in his ignition because he'd used his keys in the building, but as the other possibilities are eliminated, they keep urging him to check, so finally, he goes out to the parking lot.

The key is dangling in the ignition. Stewart thought the keys might be locked in, but the door gives. And then Stewart thinks he's hearing voices, a whisper from the backseat saying, "Pastor, is that you?"

Nay lay on the back floor between the seats, covered with the windshield, sun visor.

"What on earth are you doing, Nay? Everybody's looking for you." Stewart drops in the seat and pulls the key.

She peeks out from under her cover with a finger to her lips. "Shhh… I need you to get me out of here. Levi's really lost it this time."

Next, Stewart shushes Nay, and hops out of the car to divert someone from approaching. Nay goes stone-faced when she hears who Stewart greets, "Hey *Lynn,* baby." He dangles the keys. "I left it in the car after all."

Lynn doesn't notice how badly telegraphed Stewart sounds. She shut him up by pressing her lips against his, raising on tip-toe, their first kiss in weeks. She pauses for words; she points back toward the building. "*That…*" how he'd rushed in the old sanctuary like a hero and defended her. "… was *so* sexy." Stewart turns bashful. She wipes the lipstick off of his lips. They have a short conversation about bible study. Women's bible study is still on, so Lynn has to get back, but before going, she plants a hand on his chest, lowers her head like she is prophesying. "Tonight…" Even the writer can't find words to describe what would take place. "You're not even ready for what's about to take place tonight," she says, as the hand slides down his body and she turns to walk away.

Hurriedly, Stewart gets in the car and drives away. Nay feels the car moving, the sunlight winding in the car during Stewart's three-point turn. She sits up when she feels that they're on the highway.

A frustrated Stewart asks, "Why didn't you just drive off with my car and call me later?"

"I'm going to need a place to stay for a couple days and I don't have any money for a hotel because Levi's got my purse."

"But you've got family."

"I'm not fixin' to have them niggers in my business."

Nay's large, bare calf, steps between the front seats. Stewart leans to clear space. For a moment he is face to face with her pumpkin rump. When she drops in the seat, her dress rides up so badly, revealing the shadow of her buttocks, and the trim of her underwear, Stewart wonders if she'd done it on purpose. The car drifts and Stewart swerves back in line.

Nay does a double-take. "Got a problem with your eyes?" She lifts up so her dress could fall.

Stewart stiffens like a professional chauffer; his eyes fixed on driving. "Why not call the police?"

"Because they don't care until *after* we're busted up."

"Would you have called them even *then?*"

Nay ignores the question. "I hope you figured out for your-self that Levi put me up to that complaint against you and your wife. Otherwise, I would've never done that."

Stewart just nods, his eyes never leaving the road. She directs him to the opposite edge of the city where buildings thin out. He stops at a cash machine, gives Nay three hundred dollars, the most the machine could give out in a day. Next, they find a hotel. Stewart sits in the driveway, head bent over the steering wheel, thinking how Lynn would kill him if she finds out that he is at a hotel with Nay.

Nay goes in. Stewart, from outside, peers into the hotel watching Nay transact at the counter; he eagerly awaits the o.k. signal, but Nay returns upset. "They say they need a card on file, or they won't do it." Stewart gives Nay his card and she replies, "Do I look like a man? They'll think I stole this card. Come on in here. Lynn will understand. Matter fact, I'll call her myself."

"No!" Stewart's force startles Nay. She doesn't know she is the topic of arguments in Stewart's marriage. "Why did you have to take *my* keys," Stewart pouts.

"Because I didn't have time to choose. Your keys was right there."

Stewart goes in with her. Once they scan his card, he hands Nay the plastic room keys and wishes her well, but Nay starts breaking down. The situation is getting real. She'd be alone in a hotel room, a carpeted solitary confinement with nothing famil-iar but fear and loneliness. This is no subdued whimper; her whole face is dimpled in misery, she sounds hoarse when she says, "Levi raped me." Nay collapses forward. Stewart catches her in his arms, patting her back as she let loose, bawling on his shoulder. People swerve around them with their luggage, but not without concerned stares. Stewart peaks out of the embrace, feeling unnervingly visible, being that he's the most recognizable pastor in the metropolitan Bible belt. Stewart can't leave Nay alone in that condition, but he doesn't want to be seen, so he ushers her into the elevator and they both face front, afraid to look at each other, the elevator door closing like a kimono on the worst pair imaginable, a battered woman and a fallen pastor, their shared past at the center of their separate marital issues.

When Lynn comes back from bible study she hears Stewart in the shower. Stewart is scrubbing himself like he had stubborn stains all over him. Lynn steps out of her clothes, looking to fulfill her parking-lot prophesy. She joins him behind the steamy glass. Before long, Lynn is calling his name with her hand smearing down the foggy glass door.

Afterwards they lay together in bed, Lynn on his broad, peppered chest. They lay in shame for denying themselves this pleasure for drifting apart over the weeks. Lovemaking now solidifies their bond three times the usual, and makes them wise. They confess their blunders, take back words – neither letting the other accept blame, but setting it squarely on their own shoulders. They promise to never slip back into darkness and to now see virtues over flaws, likenesses over differences, to bear their love like Christ's cross, but not alone. Silence falls again when they run out of declarations. Lynn lifts her head and says, "Nay never turned up, but her car is still there at church, even after bible study was over."

"She's at a hotel."

Lynn freezes, slow to interrogate or accuse, but awaiting an explanation.

"I found her hiding in my car. That's how my keys went missing. Levi attacked her at church–"

"*No…*" Lynn aches.

"When she ran from Levi she left her purse, keys, wallet..."

Suspicion clears, leaving only concern for Nay. "Is she hurt?"

"She's ok." Lynn shoves herself up and sits on the end of the bed, ready to jump into action for the woman who had made the formal complaint against her and her husband, and for that, Stewart admires Lynn. "I love you, baby," he says.

Lynn blushes. "I love you too… But which hotel?"

Stewart, watching the crease at the bend of her thighs, her hips spread at the sides of her folded waist, a visual he isn't ready to part with. He grabs her hand. "Nay's fine."

Instead of going, Lynn calls. Lynn paces the bedroom as they patched her through to Nay's room and they have a conversation where Nay assures that she is alright. Lynn urges her not to contact Levi.

Once Lynn's conscious is clear, she rolls back into bed in the enclosure of Stewart's arms. Stewart says, "I hand off the briefcase on Saturday."

Lynn pulls away, but not enough force to leave his embrace.

Stewart kisses her forehead, her nose, her trembling lips. "If anything happens to me, I want you to preach on Sunday in my place. So, you'll need to have a sermon ready."

Lynn's head shakes. Thoughts of him dying are not welcome in her mind or in their shared bed – not moments after finding their legs in this new marriage.

"There's a lot of folks still loyal to me," Stewart says. "They'll make sure that if I'm not there to preach, Levi won't. It'll be you." He kisses Lynn's hand. "If his thing with the detective *doesn't* work – worst case scenario – I still come out ok… I'll be finished as pastor of First Baptist, but ok. As far as Levi: when the truth breaks, he'll be hung right alongside of me."

She could notify the FBI of Claude's plan and guarantee Dana's safety, but he might never forgive her. Lynn remembers Dana's willingness to support her even if she'd accept the trustees' offer and that solves her dilemma; she'd have to support him, without interference, but she plans to pray harder than she ever has in her life.

The next day, Lynn rounds up a few women she knows to be true soldiers in Christ who will aid discreetly without raising an eyebrow in judgment or spreading gossip, and they go to the hotel to check on Nay. They could not convince Nay to leave Levi for good. Nay says she'd hide out at the hotel for a few days until she had Levi eating out of her hands, and then she'd return home. By then Nay had only contacted family members to notify them that she's fine, but without disclosing her location.

Levi spread the word that his wife had had an "episode" and that she is in a private facility; folks assume he means, psychiatric facility. He asks everyone to respect their privacy and assures that Nay would be back soon.

By Saturday, Nay feels like she has Levi "eating out of her hands," so to speak, so she feels ready for reconciliation. Nay would've never left that hotel with Levi if she knew what Levi found out at the front desk.

Levi had forgotten the room number so went to the front desk and asks the clerk to look up his wife's name. There is no Chardonnay Ginyard in the system. Levi thinks maybe he's at wrong hotel. He begins to describe his wife, her dimensions and her short honey badger hair. The clerk remembers hearing something about a woman fitting the description. She was in the lobby crying on the shoulder of a pastor. She asks, "Aren't you a pastor?"

"Yes."

The clerk types information in her computer, studies the screen and says, "That'll be room number 418 Pastor Stewart."

Levi nearly faints. Going up the elevator, he takes deep breaths to calm his nerves, to pull off an affront that everything's ok.

Nay agrees to take Levi back because he promised to go to the Veterans Administration Hospital for a psychological evaluation. The man agrees to go immediately, without hesitation, they only need to go home in order to change cars and for him to gather his insulin and blood pressure medications in case they admit him to inpatient therapy.

Nay waits in their living room until Levi returns with his things. Nay turns towards the door to lead him out, but he tackles her from behind. From the force of the tackle, Nay's face hit the front door and she is knocked unconscious before she could scream. Levi takes a syringe out of his bag, draws from a vile of insulin and injects his wife to keep her groggy and weak even after gaining consciousness.

Nay comes to, feeling the gravitational pull of an elephant. She struggles to keep her head lifted; her vision shifts like a kaleidoscope. She hears her husband's voice, coaching her,

"There you go. That's a good girl." And then he slaps her. Her head swings to the side and stays, too heavy to re-center. She clenches and stretches her eyes, but her focus is shot. Everything outside the circumference of a quarter is blurry.

Levi questions her over and over. "Why is Stewart checking you into a hotel? Did you and Stewart have sex?"

Nay is aware just enough to utter that one, automatic response, "Nothing happened."

Levi bites the first knuckle on his fist, thinking. "You know what… I always imagined we would go as a couple. I lose it. Choke you out for too long, maybe, unable to revive you. I would not have been able to live with myself. I would've gotten you all dressed up, lay your corpse in the bed, and I would crawl in with you and turn a pistol to my head. That's what I *thought*…" He watches Nay's eyes roll forward in her hanging head, struggling to align with his. "I thought I wouldn't be able to live with myself because there would always be that question: what if she were telling the truth; what *if* nothing happen? But this changes everything. You, in a hotel room with Stew? You'll be a missing person's case forever. I know exactly how I'll get rid of your body."

Nay looks into Levi's eyes and knows that with every fiber of his being, he means what he says. Nay struggles to escape. She throws her weight and causes the chair to shove only few inches. Levi gives her another shot of insulin using it as a tranquilizer, and wipes the clear spit stringing from Nay's chin.

Levi knows time is of the essence, that in twenty-four hours, police would be all over her disappearance like ants; this Levi knows from the many times he'd studied the news, following details and timelines of missing persons investigations, knowing one day he might be the suspect in one.

Levi goes out to his truck and begins executing a plan that had lived in his developed over years in his mind. He uses all back roads, avoiding surveillance, now wiser of the mistake he made with the church break-in. He drives down an abandoned trail and stops at a dead end of thick brush. He loops a rope through the handle of a large basin packed with a tent and supplies, including the hydrochloric acid that he'll use to liquefy Nay's corpse. It would be nearly impossible to convict him without a body.

He pulls from over his shoulder, dragging the basin a mile deep into the forest pines. Levi pitches the camouflage tent in a clearing and under the cover of this tent, digs a hole deep enough for the large basin. The only thing missing is Nay, who is still tied up in their basement.

Levi has known these woods all his life. He's at a place that he knows would be clear of hunters and campers, because the only fishing hole for people and drinking hole for deer, dried up way back when Levi was a child, when dam construction choked the stream dry, but just in case, he decides not to submerge Nay in the acid bath during the day because the initial smell of burning flesh and hair could reach noses up to a half mile away. He planned to save her acid grave for the graveyard shift, so by morning, the stench would've dissipated to a large degree, and then within twenty-four hours, his wife of nearly twenty years, flesh, bone hair, teeth would become vapor blowing in the forest breeze.

This is the easy part. It is no crime having a basin in the ground with jugs of pool cleaner in the forest. Levi rests under the tent, sitting on the forest floor, the crispy top layer of dry leaves over earthen foliage as soft as a mat. The sun shines through the tent's split, the canopy of pines splaying its light in a prism of colorful, fading copies of the sun. Branch shadows reached for Levi like black, cryptic fingers. On one hand Levi feels like his heart could change, that he could go home and never return to this God forsaken place, leaving the pitched tent as an altar of redemption. Levi's head lowers between the arms hugging his knees, a beam of sunlight warms the back of his neck like the outstretched hand of God.

Nay is missing. It's a somber mood, in the prayer room, with Lynn, Mavis, and a few other prayer warriors gathered on behalf of Nay, waiting for police to arrive and take a report.

Their eyes, just opened from prayer, finds Bianca standing in the doorway, eyes full of tears. Bianca looks at them, tears falling, her voice cracking as she says, "I'm so ashamed of myself…" They huddle around Bianca, not one eye bat in judgement, as Bianca comes clean about her affair with Levi.

A Pimp In The Pulpit

Chapter 39

etective Claude and Stewart wait at Stewart's home. "Westermann should've called by now. He's not falling for it."

Stewart rebuttals, "But you said he was desperate for money. Where else is he going to get money from?"

Stewart's phone rings. He hurries to answer, thinking it's Westermann, but it is Lynn, calling from church, reporting that there's still no word of Nay. Stewart has to end the call abruptly because Westermann's call comes in on the dummy cell phone.

In short order, Westermann names the time and the general location, saving the exact location to throw off any possible ambush. Westermann urges Stewart to hurry and that he'll call back with further instructions.

The assignment is easy: simply drop off the briefcase of money. A GPS tracker stitched in the seams of the briefcase would do the rest. Once Westermann takes the money, Detective Claude could relax and let Stewart get to a safe distance, or even tail Westermann if necessary.

Stewart jumps in his car and goes on the move with Agent Claude tailing him. This is his chance to secure everything he'd been building over the last twenty years. This must work, Stewart thinks. He has a little insurance in his glove compartment the gun with blank ammo that Bianca left in his hands, that day after the play. Stewart takes the and tucks it in his belt at the base of his back.

Stewart gets another call from Westermann. Turn by turn, the man instructs Stewart by phone. He has Stewart driving around in circles. The detective figures Westermann is watching, maybe from the roof of a building, checking for a pattern in the traffic, to see if Stewart is being tailed by agents, so Detective Claude falls back.

When Westermann thinks it's safe, he directs Stewart where to park, and gives him the chain lock combination to a bicycle nearby. Still by phone, Westermann directs Stewart to ride the bike as fast as he can, down a busy, pedestrian sidewalk. Stewart does the best he can, with a phone to his ear and the briefcase hooked over the handlebar dangling and banging his knee.

Eyes wide open, wind streaming over his ears, Stewart has the presence of mind to peak up and sees a man on a cell phone, standing in the glass skywalk between the hotel and the parking garage; he has an eye on Westermann. Shortly, he guides Stewart to enter the hotel and gives him the room number. Stewart hurries up to the room and finds the door ajar.

After many deep breaths, still unable to calm the shaking of his hands, Stewart enters. Westermann greets him with a gun pointed at his head. Stewart's pores scream, but he does not. He raises his hands, inadvertently dropping he briefcase, then apologizes. With quick gun flicks, Westermann gives directions, telling him to close the door, pick up the briefcase, throw it on the bed, lock the deadbolt behind him.

The deadbolt is rigged with a pair of lock pliers, stripped of the metal grip, making it impossible to be unlocked by hand. He isn't looking to lock anyone out, but after the transaction, he plans to lock Stewart in.

The Victor Dante Westermann Stewart remembers looked refined and stately, but *this* Dante Westermann, or whatever his real name, looks rabid behind the gun. He wipes his forehead in a forearm sleeve and resumes his aim, the crevice of his laugh lines, bulldoggish under the immense pressure. A nervous twitch from the man's index finger could splatter Stewart's brains on the wall. What a way to learn, Stewart thinks while staring down the gun barrel, that criminal profiling isn't an exact science. The detective had said Westermann was no threat. Now, Stewart only wished he had listened to his wife.

On Levi's return from the forest, his phone blows up with calls and texts. He's in such a hurry; the roof of his truck nearly scrapes his rising garage door. He gives Nay another dose of insulin; shed his soiled clothes, showers and gets dressed.

Nay hadn't been in the basement half a day and already two officers pull up in his driveway. Levi, with his heartbeat drumming in his chest, pretends to be oblivious. "Is everything alright officers?"

The first thing they say, is, "This is not an investigation – at this point." They say they've come at the insistence of people who reported that there had been a domestic dispute a few days ago and now the whereabouts of the alleged victim is unknown. "Were just here to ask questions. Is it ok if my partner takes a look around outside?"

Levi obliges. The interviewing officer asks to come in. He interviews from the couch as the partner searches outside, looking for freshly overturned ground on the premises, or blood stains by the pool. When the other is done outside he comes in, asking, "Mind if I look around in here too?"

Levi goes on the defensive, "What is this? You think I have something to do with–"

"–I'll be forthcoming," the officer interrupts. "We do not have a search warrant, so you have every right to deny our request, but if you're that guarded about a sniff test, we may go ahead and get that search warrant and bring in the black light and swab kits."

"Don't make no difference to me," Levi says confidently, his hands, flipped. "… I have nothing to hide." The scout officer goes down hallways, looking but not going into rooms, while the interviewing officer continues the questioning. "So you *did* make contact with her today, but you say you had an argument in the car and you put her out of the car in Irmo near the Saluda Shoals Park, is that right?"

Levi confirms with a nod. "Feel free to check surveillance."

"I doubt we'd find surveillance in that area."

Levi sighs, "Seems like surveillance is everywhere nowadays."

"Unfortunately, not," the officer says.

Levi tries not to seem distracted by the searching officer who ventures into the kitchen. The man has no way of knowing that, behind, what looks like a pantry or closet door, is a staircase going down into a basement, but he seems intent on finding out.

Levi, needs a diversion, and his interviewer provides him the perfect opportunity when he says, "I must admit, Pastor Ginyard, it seems as if everyone's worried about your wife except you."

Levi stands up and turns belligerent, almost combative, pointing in the man's chest, ranting about their unwarranted suspicion, yelling what they *need* to be doing, and how much time they're wasting. The roaming officer comes out of the kitchen, away from the basement door and to the living room, ready to wrestle the combatant down, if necessary.

"I'm going to have to ask you to calm down sir," the interviewing officer demands.

"How are you two boy scouts interrogating *me* instead of the man who is screwing my wife behind my back?"

They perk up at word of an affair. It's a motive for Levi, but also implicates a second person of interest. "She was having an affair, you say? Gimme a name."

"Pastor Stewart. He was with my wife at a hotel last night. He checked into the room with his information but the hotel employees can vouch that wife was with him." Levi plops in his chair and pinches his nose bridge, sniffling and whining. "I forgave her. I picked her up from the hotel. That woman is my heart." Levi looks up with tear tracks and a trembling mouth. "I would *never* do anything to hurt her!"

While tending to Levi, the scouting officer has been away from the basement door for so long, he forgets to return there and continue the search; besides, they have a new, more interesting lead now, the pastor already in the news for the investment scandal.

They go chasing the new lead, leaving Levi with the phrase, "Time is of the essence." For Levi, that statement has never been truer than now.

Stewart pleads that there is no need for guns, and adds that he should be let go. "I kept my end of the deal. All I had to do is bring you the money."

Westermann's head tilts, his brows maddened. "If I were dropping off this large sum of money, as a loan, would I be in such a hurry to leave it behind? I don't think so," says Westermann. "*I* think, that I would spend some time with that person, gauge their motives, and if something about them told me I *might* not get my money back, I would then take up my briefcase and go. So, I find it awful peculiar, pastor, how you don't seem to give half a damn about this money."

Stewart, trembling with his hands up, replies. "The *only* thing I care about right now is *not* having a gun pointed at me." Stewart then smiles to try to endear, saying, "C'mon, man, there's no need for a gun up in here, man." Stewart thinks he's smiling, but his spread mouth is so strained with nerves, he appears to be taking a dump in his clothes. "At least don't *point* it at me brotha."

Dante Westermann orders Stewart to turn against the wall, and pats him down. Westermann confiscates Stewart's cell phone and resumes patting him down. In Westermann's search for wires, he finds the gun in the small of Stewart's back, tucked under his belt. "If there's no need for guns, why'd *you* bring one?"

"Because…" Stewart can't divulge the real answer; he'd brought the gun to detain Westermann in case he tries to change briefcases. The first order of business, after confiscating Stewart's gun, Westermann tosses his own briefcase on the bed and orders Stewart to fill it. Stewart begins transferring the bands of cash, each one the size of a brick. Westermann makes Stewart flick each cash bundle so he could see if there were any devices inside.

As Stewart packs the money, Westermann split the curtains for a bird's eye view on any possible police movement. "Did you come alone? If *not* you better tell me now, because if you lie to me, and they bust in this room, I will load your body with bullets, forcing them to kill me, because, to me, prison is death anyway. Now, if they *are* coming, and you tell me the truth, I'll show mercy to you, and turn my gun on *them*. In either scenario, it all ends the same way for me. You, however, can decide your fate. So, I ask you, did you come alone?"

"Yes," Stewart says quickly, fearing any hesitation would breed suspicion. Stewart continues packing the money, his nerves making him shiver as if he is packing ice.

Detective Claude thinks Stewart is taking too long. He must be in danger. Claude follows the briefcase's GPS signal to the hotel and down the hallway until he arrives at the room door that makes the handheld tracker go haywire. The detective knocks. A male voice asks, "Who is it?"

The detective replies, "Someone reported a disturbance coming from this room."

As the door handle turns, Agent Claude draws his gun. The man who opens the door is barebacked, with a large hairy belly. His arms raise at the sight of the gun. Claude lowers the gun and the man closes the door without hesitation. The problem with the tracker is that it only provides geographic, two-dimensional location, and cannot account for elevation. One of the rooms, stacked directly above this bottom floor, is the room with the briefcase, Stewart and Westermann – in who knows what predicament. Claude starts going up each floor level, checking each room directly above the room with the hairy orangutan in flip-flops.

Stewart looks up soberly from his work. "Of course, I came alone. The deal is between you and me. No one else."

"It's just that your deal is so foolish, I thought it might be a setup," Victor says from a sunlit profile, peering through the curtains. "So, you are really that naïve to think that once I'm home free with this briefcase, that I'd give a rat's ass about you?"

Stewart shows all the disappointment of a man losing a large briefcase of money. "I only hope that *when* they catch you, you'll be unarmed, so you can't force them to shoot you. That way you'll be locked away with a whole lot of time to think about what you've done. You'll be locked away with all the other thieves."

Westermann comes away from the window with a challenging stare. He takes a seat on the edge of the dresser, the gun hanging lazily out of his folded arms. "*You're* calling me a thief? With me, a lot of people cashed out their accounts and got back more money than they put in."

"Not everyone; just enough to keep them believing in your scheme."

"Pardon me, but, what portion do *you* give back? You're sitting pretty in a *mansion*, my brotha… Your own members can fall on hard times, become homeless, and all you give them is soup!?" The man giggles like a stoner. "I'd say that's *worse* than a Ponzi scheme; that's brainwashing."

"We offer something you can never give."

"And what might that be!"

"Salvation."

The man laughs out loud. "Don't you have to die for that! Your own *people* don't even believe in it. That's why you get only ten percent out of them, but I get fifty percent, nearly a hundred percent of their life savings, in some cases. So, what does that say about their faith? They had more faith in *me* than you – the so-called man of God."

Stewart feels somewhat relaxed, now, even with his life hanging in the balance. "Some folks may have given you nearly a hundred percent, but many *lost* a hundred percent too. Lies are always more enticing than the truth – always promising much reward out of little sacrifice. Everybody in the *church* ain't in *Christ*. People in Christ know that's not how God works. Out of my ten thousand members, you got – what – a measly few hundred people to fall for your scheme? So, I'd say that my members, in large, know what a man of God looks like. *I* certainly didn't endorse you; *I* didn't take any referral kickbacks or royalties–"

"–*You* were not told you could take a break from loading that money either." Westermann resets his aim at Stewart's head. "New rule. Only people with guns are allowed to speak."

Stewart finishes moving all the money from the FBI's briefcase to Westermann's briefcase. He latches it shut and backs away. Westermann removes the pliers from the deadbolt, sweeps up the briefcase by the handle and goes to the adjoining door, which he opens, and then pauses for parting words. "I feel nothing for most of those man-worshipping congregations, but I actually do feel bad that churches like yours, with effective ministries – churches that are doing it the right way – had to get got. Wish you luck, pastor," the man says, as he walks through the door to the adjoining room and locks it from the other side.

Stewart is trapped and his cell phone had been confiscated. He picks up the handle on the hotel phone but the line is dead. The phone cord is severed. Stewart throws himself at the door but the force nearly throws out his shoulder; he slides down the door, writhing in pain. Stewart goes out to the balcony thinking maybe he could leap to the neighboring balcony, but one look at that death drop changes his mind. He takes the mattress off the bed and stands it up against the door. He goes out on the balcony for a running start. He runs and launches himself with both feet first and hit below his mark. The bottom half of the door cracks and the top hinge splinters loose. Slowly, determinedly Stewart shimmies himself out into the on his belly. Hallway patrons clear, and run. Stewart runs down the hallway for the elevator, but as he waits for the elevator, he sees Westermann out of the window, crossing the glass skywalk from the hotel to the parking garage. Stewart takes the elevator down to the lobby and runs out into traffic, hands out, stopping cars. He runs to the parking garage exit, hoping to find Westermann's head behind a steering wheel where he could at least get his license plate number. He sees a motorcycle roaring down, hopping the pedestrian walkway around the arm gate, the helmeted rider steering with one hand and clutching a briefcase to his belly. "Westermann!" Without thinking Stewart sprints toward the speeding motorcycle, turning into the street.

Only after Stewart's next move would he look back on it and wonder the heck he was thinking. Stewart runs full sprint and dives on the biker. The front wheel jackknifes causing the bike to buck them into the air. The briefcase twirls and coughs up its contents.

Stewart and Westermann lay on the pavement, knocked senseless by the impact. The bike lay humming on its side. Pedestrians run to the scattered bands of cash. Westermann springs up and runs over with his gun pointed, sending them running and screaming. Stewart gets up and Westermann aims at him, and then comes after him, cursing. The moment Stewart gets to his feet, Westermann is upon him. He jams Stewart in the head with the gun butt. Stewart falls back against a parked car, setting off its alarm, his arms winged against the broadside of the car to stop his fall, one eye clenched in pain. He is sure his skull is split open, but he feels the side of his head and finds no blood.

Patrons in an apparel store and café peak out from their hiding places, thrilled and afraid, but recording on their phones. Westermann holds the gun on Stewart while he backpedals toward the scattered money, warding off onlookers, his stiff arm, swings the gun like a turning clock hand, targeting anything that moves, like a schizophrenic, convinced that the world, all at once, has turned on him. He holds them at bay with the gun as he collects the money. Stewart pushes off of the car, struggling to get his legs under him. Westermann swings his aim back to Stewart, who starts walking straight towards him, either on a death wish or he is disoriented from the head blow, but nevertheless closing in on Westermann, who can't back away from the money at his feet, but then he can't allow Stewart to get close enough to restrain him. Westermann yells, jerking the gun with each word. "Don't! Take! Another! Step!"

In the time it takes Westermann to say as much, Stewart has taken six steps, advancing like a war worn soldier. "No weapon formed against me shall prosper," Stewart announces.

Westermann points the gun, more convincingly, but Stewart is undeterred. Stewart is almost in arm's reach which forces Westermann's hand. The gunshot pops like God's whip. Birds perched on street signs and building tops scatter up into the sky. Everyone under the sound of the bang screams and ducks like a mass cakewalk. The echo cracks through the network of buildings.

At the sound of the shot, Stewart stops. His body had flinched, as if he were nudged in the chest. He pinches his shirt out from his body. It's a miracle that there's no hole in his shirt. Westermann can't believe he missed. Stewart resumes coming forward. Dante trots back, pulling the trigger again and again, until the gun only clicks because it's out of ammo. Stewart advances, still, mumbling a quick prayer asking forgiveness for what he'll do. Stewart punches the gunman squarely on the chin. The punch turns Westermann completely around, his leg giving away, and he drops as if corkscrewed into the ground.

City police converged on the scene flashing blue lights, shielding themselves behind open car doors and pointing real guns. Detective Claude runs up with his FBI badge raised.

Westermann is cuffed in the back of one squad car and Stewart is cuffed in the backseat of another, sitting for nearly an hour while police talk on their radios, talk to Detective Claude, talk to witnesses, and talk amongst themselves – talking to everyone but Pastor Stewart. Stewart in the back of the squad car behind rolled up windows sees, but can't hear Detective Claude outside pleading with the cops. Whatever argument Detective Claude tries to make, it fails. He eventually peers at Stewart in the car as his arms flap down at his sides as if to say, that there is nothing more he could do. An officer gets in the front seat, twists back towards Stewart, and reads his Miranda rights. Stewart interrupts, demanding to know why he is being arrested. The officer says, "We haven't charged you with anything *yet*, but, dude, you just had a gunfight over a pile of money and you expect us to let you walk?"

It is late Saturday, so regardless if they decide to drop the charges against Stewart, he'll be stuck in county jail for the weekend, since bond hearings resume on Monday.

They take Stewart downtown. He feels sick being among criminals who he'd readily lay hands on in prayer, but it is different being caged *with* gang bangers, Johns, and addicts still twitching, smelling like cigarettes and musk. They recognize Pastor Stewart from TV; they rib him for getting "caught up." They preach to *him* about things done in the dark coming to light, while Stewart sits comatosed on a steel bench.

Eventually, they bring Stewart out for interrogation. Stewart sits for about a half hour in a room by himself before a detective comes in, a small headed man in an oxford shirt tucked tightly over his round belly. The detective enters saying that he is not interested in the guns and the briefcase of money, saying that *that* case is one they'd leave up to the Feds.

Stewart slaps the table. "Why am I here, then?!"

The detective slaps a folder on the table holding statements from Levi, hotel clerks, and even Stewart's own wife. The officer peers across the table and asks, "Where is she?"

"Where's who?"

The detective had expected the perp to claim ignorance, "The same married woman you took up to the hotel room…" He slides a copy of the hotel receipt under his pointer finger. "Name here says Dana Stewart. Idn't that you, pastor?"

Chapter 40

Around nine o'clock at night, Bianca rings Levi's doorbell. She's dressed like an escort, in candy purple lipstick and a black, silky wig, hanging as straight as a waterfall opened around her face. She wears a long, gray fur that makes Levi wonder if she's naked underneath. He pulls her in, while peering outside. "What are you doing here?"

She recites, "You're not answering your phone."

"Have you given one thought as to why? Like I'm fixin to create phone records with the mistress on the day my wife went missing…"

Bianca opens a hand in front of his face and holds it there as she walks past him and goes further into the house. "You done started off way wrong. Way wrong."

"How?"

"I'll *tell* you when I get ready." Her neck swerves as she stamps one high heeled shoe.

Levi puts on this act of playing distraught. He sits in the recliner, telling, in painful detail, how he called Nay's relatives trying to locate her, and that he spent hours driving around town and turned up nothing.

Bianca says, "They got Pastor Stupid. That devil been busy all this time – got him with a briefcase of money… *And* guns…"

"That ain't the only thing they got him on. Did you know that he and Nay checked into a hotel together?"

Bianca sits on the arm of the recliner and looks down at him. "You must be fu-ri-ous," her purple lips shaping each syllable.

"I'll just leave it in the hands of the Lord."

"I'm pregnant," Bianca blurts. "That's why I just had to see you tonight."

Levi is too stressed to celebrate. "Believe me, baby, I'm celebrating on the inside."

"You're about to be a father again. They're fixin to vote Stewart out so you'll also be the head pastor. Got some good things going for you right now Levi. What about me? What's next for us?"

To Levi, it seems Bianca wants some verbal commitment that she'll be made his wife. "Nay ain't been missing a day and you come here with this mess already?"

"I'm pregnant *already*. Ain't I?"

Bianca plucks his hand off of her thigh and releases it like it's filthy. Her nose wrinkles. "I don't like your responses... I don't like your whole energy," she says with a hand fanning out in an arc.

"You want me to lie?"

"I *want* you to do right by me."

"We've gotta play it smart. But listen. There's never a doubt that you're gonna be my beautiful first lady." Levi sees how Bianca bathes in whatever brief imagination his promise produces inside of her mind.

Bianca comes out of her imagination and studies Levi. His brow goes uneven under her gaze. Bianca holds the stare. He smiles. She sighs, with her head shaking slowly. "You didn't harm Nay did you? Where is she?"

Levi stares at her, gauging her, and then he huffs. "You better gone down to the jailhouse and talk to Stew about that."

"Sounds all well and good, but actually..." Bianca's finger traces down Levi's nose bridge, as she says in a low, seductive voice. "I talked to Lynn, and apparently, the guns and the money they found Stewart with, was a part of a sting." Bianca gets up from the chair arm and paces. "He wasn't working with Westermann, he was taking the man down. There's a federal agent that can vouch for his whereabouts, so it couldn't have been Stewart."

Levi says, "They were in a hotel together. Maybe Nay threatened to ruin his marriage like you threatened me."

"I'm on your side, Levi." Praying hands meet at her lips, silencing her. Those praying hands then lower to aim at Levi. "Let me rephrase the question," she says with a vague smile. "Do you need my help? In any way? Yes or no?"

Levi's wife is tied up in the basement. As they speak, he wonders if the last shot he'd give Nay is wearing off by now, but he looks at Bianca quite plainly and says, "Look, I told you–"

"–Levi!" The back of one hand smacks the palm of the other hand. "Do you have a situation on your hands?"

She awaits an answer that Levi, for a few beats, refuses to give, but then he says, "Even if I tell you no, it's like telling you that I *do* have a situation, but that I'm handling myself. But I don't have a situation; your question does not apply."

They've arrived at a stalemate. Bianca breaks the intense silence with a sing-song, "Juuust checkin'." Bianca comes back to the recliner. Levi stands to meet her. They begin kissing. Bianca quickly pulls back, showing him it was only a good bye kiss. "Gotta go. Gotta play it smart – as you said – right?" Levi tries to convince her, with kisses, to stay, but Bianca keeps shuffling backwards toward the door, leading him until her back is against the door. Levi picks up one of her legs. Bianca sings, "Aw sookie, sookie, nah," as she grinds there. Then she laughs. "Naw for real Levi. This is not a good look."

Levi's head lowers between the fur, nosing around her breasts. "But who's looking?"

Bianca taps him, urgently. "You don't know?"

Levi stops. "Know what?"

"This house is being watched, baby."

"What!"

Bianca, eyes wide, says, "I lie to you not." Levi runs to the blinds as Bianca explains, "When I turned on Crestwood, I drove past a car that's just sitting there, idling. And on the other end of the street; there's another car. A guy sitting there. The car's interior lit up by the cell phone in his lap," says Bianca. "The cars: they just have that look about them, like they're unmarked."

Levi comes away from the blinds and back to Bianca. Although he was just begging her to stay, he now rushes Bianca out. "My goddamn wife missing and you comin to my house lookin' like a call girl!"

Bianca digs in her heels in front of the open door to explain, "Had I known that your house was being watched I wouldn't–"

"–Girl *getchyo*," Levi shoves her, and she sprawls down the front steps in six inch heels.

Bianca hurries to her car, and drives a good distance before the reality hits her, and she begins to break down. She snatches off her wig and tries to breath deep to stave off hyperventilation. She rests her head on the rim of the steering wheel to catch her breath. "My God… My God," Bianca cries. She didn't want to reveal her pregnancy to Levi just yet, but she told him in hopes that this new bond might help him open up to her, if there is anything to confess. Although he did not confess, Bianca heard something with her trained ear. She isn't sure of what she heard, but she knows, undoubtedly that whatever she heard is living. She heard a small, but constant scratch, which, she imagined, is either something tiny, like a mouse with a lot of life, or something big, like a person, but with only a little life left.

Once Bianca had heard the sound, she made up the lie about the house being watched, hoping to paralyze Levi with fear, to buy time for help to arrive, but before making the call to Lynn, Bianca takes a moment for herself to just cry. If Levi is capable of murder, then she's pregnant by a man who is no more a pastor than a garbageman. Being pregnant with a potential murderer's child, suffocates her.

After Bianca gets herself together, she calls Lynn who puts her on speakerphone where there's Lynn, Mavis, and a few other concerned women are at the sanctuary, praying for Lynn and Stewart but mostly praying for Nay. A crying Bianca begins, "Nay is alive. I think she's in the basement…" The women celebrate what they believe to be a confirmation of life, but they temper their celebration; there are more questions.

Mavis turns away from the group, getting out her own cell phone to call the police, ready to pass on their question and relay information as it comes from Bianca.

The other women huddle in over the phone asking for details. *You say you heard something? What'd you hear? Did you hear Nay's voice? What'd it sound like?*

By the end of Bianca's call, there remains more questions than answers. During Mavis's call, police informs her that they'd already thoroughly searched the house and there was no Nay on the premises; therefore, police refuse to return on account of someone hearing scratching sounds in the walls. Mavis pleads with them; she tries to remain calm but quickly unravels, "I'd beg to differ, sir. A woman's life is at stake. Say what? I'd Bet if it was one of *y'all*, you'd give a damn! You should rather not been born than to be so useless! Go crawl back in ya momma's pussy!"

They crowd Mavis to calm her, to shush her with that kind of language in the prayer room. Mavis's arms flail at them. "Oh, get the hell away from me." Mavis parts them down the middle as she marches outside for some fresh air.

In her wake, Lynn sighs and says, "Guess there's nothing we can do, now, but wait." Deaconess Bailey adds, "And pray."

Lynn, spending the night alone in their home for the first time, has a lot to pray for that night, first and foremost, for Nay's life. God is already in the process of answering her prayers about her husband. The news stations, stay with the most salacious route of the Stewart/Westermann story, pushing a *curse of greed* narrative where money turns crime allies against one another.

The narrative plays out differently on social media with cell phone videos going viral captioned *Miracle! Preacher-man walks through bullets!* The video shows Westermann firing multiple times, straight at Stewart's chest. The woman recording the video screams hysterically, as if she'd just witnessed a murder, but then she realizes Stewart is still walking, mumbling a prayer and marking himself with a crucifix, then flooring the crook with one punch. Stewart had no interest in the money scattered on the ground. The woman holding the camera, narrating, is nearly as captivating as the miracle, how her emotions come through so raw, grateful of having her faith affirmed in this way. She says, "For those of you who don't believe that there is a God... What do you have to say now?" No one knows the gun from the play, filled with blanks. Lynn doesn't know until Stewart calls her from county holding and explains.

Before Levi could carry out his plan, he needs to ensure he isn't being watched. He plans to keep Nay alive up to the moment before laying her in her acid grave, so if the authorities catch him before hand, or for some reason double back to search the property, they'd find Nay alive and the worst they can charge him with is kidnapping and intent. Since Bianca said his house was being watched, Levi wants to make sure that the watchmen are gone before he goes out in the thick of night, tailed by the authorities while his wife lay unconscious in the bed of his pickup truck.

He walks out into the night in a plaid lumberjack, his hands stuffed in kaki pockets. The wind, combing tree tops sounds like the gentle breath of a mountain ridge yawning over the town. Dipping wind swirls sending maple leaves, stiff as foil, skidding across the asphalt street. The moon is a perfect round hole-punch of halogen light stickered against the black sky. If the streets did have eyes, Levi wants them to see the gait of a distraught husband escaping the walls of his home, the constant reminder of his missing wife, so he droops his head down and doesn't swivel like a man who's up to something; his eyes work alone, rolling conspicuously, like loose marbles in the windows of his face.

He spots an interior light from a car in the distance, like Bianca said, but as Levi gets closer and shadows separate, he realizes that it is nothing more than a windshield reflection of the moon, speckled by the shadows of tree branches. He sees someone far off, walking towards him, but that too is just a street sign in the distance, Levi's own advancing giving the illusion of on-coming.

Levi's mind is playing tricks on him. He is almost certain that, at one point, he walks through the smell of cigarette smoke. For the first time, his neck cranes back, searching down the row of cars parked along the street for the small burning end of a cigarette. He even doubles back through that same stretch of sidewalk and the smell is gone.

His plan was to take Nay to the clearing in the woods and execute her tonight, but his paranoia grows. The darkness was supposed to work in his favor, but now, unable to assess his sur-roundings, the darkness works against him.

Chapter 41

Lynn arrives early for worship and goes up the chancel steps, claiming the clergy seat to the far left, the facing congregation's right. Reverend Bailey, Stewart's loyal ally, sits to her right to serve as her guardian protector. As the praise team sings down front, welcoming members' entrance with praise, Lynn sees men flinch at the sight her in the clergy seat; she sees gorgeous church hats flick up and take notice. It seems, to Lynn, that every watching eye studies her like an enigma and she suspects that every turned head looks away on purpose. They make it through morning prayers and the Apostle's creed recital without incident.

A deacon pries himself out of his seat and approaches Deacon Bailey, pamphlet in hand, pointing out that there is no layman speaker on the program; therefore, no exception for nonclergy sitting in a clergy seat. Reverend Bailey shakes the deacon's hand, while his other hand goes behind the deacon's back, patting him towards the deacon section from where he came. After that whispered conversation between church officers, the congregation seems to stir; they know something's up. Lynn imagines thoughts for the sea of members, perhaps charging her clergy seat to the misfortune that had befallen her husband, their pastor, having been taken into custody the day before, maybe first lady has an announcement for the congregation.

Deacons and church officers who spot Levi's arriving in the parking lot, run outside to meet him and alert him to what's going on inside. Levi, the pastor grieving his missing wife, walks up the other side of the chancel, kneels before the pastor's chair and prays with his forehead resting on his fist. Next, he wastes no time confronting Reverend Bailey and Lynn.

The congregation can't hear over the music, but they see it's no exchange of comradery, nor condolences for the missing wife or the jailed husband. They see Levi literally chewing them out, his head movement and strong words, chomping with all the thrusts and jerks of an attacking dog. His hand points to the floor and swipes across, marking an imaginary line that Lynn should not cross.

Bianca throws a brick through a window and climbs in. She expects an alarm, but Levi could not arm his home security system because Nay's movements might've triggered motion sensors. Bianca hears the feet of Nay's chair shuffling in the basement and she turns weak. Her plan last night worked; Nay is spared another day to allow this opportunity for rescue. Bianca opens the basement door and nearly falls down the steps for what she sees. Nay is bound to a chair with a busted face, the swollen eye trying its best to stretch along with the good eye as she screams behind her gag. Bianca's mind is so rattled she can't concentrate on walking, she stumbles over her feet, falls on all fours and crab-walks to Nay's chair. She uses a kitchen knife to cut ties from around Nay's wrists and ankles.

Nay wobbles up on weak legs, the first time her legs has straightened out nearly a day. She squeezes Bianca and sobs in gratitude, for being spared. Bianca taps out on Nay's shoulder, letting her know she is suffocating from the squeeze. They send up praises, a rushed Holy Ghost party, grateful of God's mercy. Bianca begs Nay's forgiveness for dismissing the abuse back in Atlanta. They scale the stair way. Nay rushes to the bathroom and then appears in the kitchen with her purse. She nabs a muffin, a carton of juice and she sticks a kitchen knife in her purse. Bianca yells for Nay to hurry so they could go down to the police station. Nay's head shakes no. "Uh, uh. We going to church!"

They speed off in the getaway car, heading for First Baptist. Bianca seems more distraught than her passenger, who had been tied and gagged. Bianca listens despondently as Nay tells how the man sedated her, how he planned to vaporize her corpse in hydrochloric acid. Nay takes Bianca's phone, dials 911, and yells at the operator, "Ya better get down here to First Baptist Church with the police *and* the ambulance for what I'm fixing to do."

For Bianca, there was never a question about saving Nay's life, but Bianca is saddened that she is carrying Levi's child with no chance of being a first lady because Levi would surely be in prison. Bianca remembers to text Lynn and let her know that they are on their way. Dreams of the ministry she and Levi were supposed to build together, now becomes the nightmare of reality: a psychopath's child in her belly. No pastor would want a single mother, she thinks, as she drives down the highway, the scenery rushing past, as if on a large conveyor belt, the wind whipping through the half-lowered window, as she barrels down the throat of the highway, listening to Nay describe how Levi planned to get rid of her dead body.

Lynn's confidence has diminished since the start of service. She feels childish to think she could pull off her husband's crazy plan, as if switching microphone feeds in the sound booth would force the congregation to accept whatever preacher holds the working mic, as if the Ginyard clan would sit idle and not descend upon her in seconds. Lynn keeps checking her phone, waiting on a text from Bianca that might never come, because Bianca wasn't sure if the sounds her ears picked up were actually human.

At the time for the preached word, Lynn feels like she is no more than dead weight on the visiting clergy chair. Levi goes up to preach and grabs the sides of the pulpit like handlebars, but his opening words fall on a dead microphone, shut off by the sound-booth as planned. Levi studies the microphone. There is a loud microphone blare through the microphone in Lynn's purse. The speakers also pick up the vibration Lynn's phone in her purse, buzzing because of the text from Bianca.

Lynn stands up with her microphone, the working microphone, and she raises her cell phone in celebration of the text from Bianca. Lynn speaks into the microphone. "Everyone I have an announcement to make. Nay has been found alive and well." By now Levi realizes who has the working microphone and comes after Lynn. Levi pretends to react positively to the news, raising both hands in victory, but quickly edging towards Lynn. Lynn hurries away, cross stepping sideways down the chancel steps, and hopping on each foot to pull off her high heels as Reverend Bailey gets in Levi's way. Lynn points at Levi, telling the congregation, "*Levi* man had her tied up in their basement."

Levi loses it. He throws Deacon Bailey on his back and runs after Lynn who runs toward the back of the church. Deacons and ushers converge on them but is confused about who to apprehend. Deacon Bacon and Deacon Latrell grab Lynn, one taking hold of each arm, lifting her kicking feet clear off the floor. Levi, to his surprise, is also restrained. Levi tries to negotiate his way out of the grasp of three deacons. Just then, Nay and Bianca come busting through the church doors. Lynn points, her distressed voice shrieking through the sound system. "Look! Look!"

The men let Lynn go; her treading feet hit the ground running. She runs toward Nay but Nay chooses a different aisle to run up. Nay screams as she runs full sprint. Members seem ready to hug her and celebrate her return until they see the kitchen knife drawn, and they scatter. The men detaining Levi scatter as Nay approaches. Levi decides not to run but to try to sweet talk Nay out of it. All the while Lynn has run up a different aisle, against the grain of well-dressed folks who scatter away, their mass screams sounding like a rollercoaster ride. Lynn gets to Levi before Nay does. She fronts him, providing a human shield for a killer. Levi cowers behind her. Lynn pleads, "Doesn't matter how evil Levi is. He's no threat to you in this moment. They'll put you away like they did Mavis. Don't do it, Nay! Think about your daughter."

While Nay pauses for just a moment. Mavis comes from behind and wrestles the knife out her hand, to Lynn's relief, which is only momentary when she sees that Mavis has only wrestled the knife away to try to stab Levi herself, screaming, "I don't mind going back!"

Levi clamps Lynn in a chokehold, and spins her shielding himself now from Mavis's raised knife, urging her. "Do it, Mavis! Do it!"

Mavis is beyond outrage; she's rabid. "Ole Billy goat! Umma gutchya like a fish." Mavis turns the knife sideways. Levi turns with Lynn in his grasp, all along Lynn is turning blue in the face from the chokehold. Mavis, looking for place to plunge the knife, raises it high. Levi lifts Lynn, tightening the chokehold. Lynn's eyes bulge in their sockets; her bare feet dangles.

At the same time that a pair of deacons grab Mavis from behind, Lynn flicks her leg back, catching Levi in the groin. The chokehold loosens, Lynn uses Levi's own weight as leverage and dumps the two-hundred-plus-pound man over her shoulder. No sooner than he hit the ground Lynn is on him with a chicken wing arm bar. Nay goes berserk, repeatedly kicking and stomping him, crying and drooling. Lynn lets go of the armbar. Levi struggles to get up. Mavis wrings loose and runs at Levi from behind, seeing the man on all fours and can't resist the urge. Mavis digs her foot into Levi's rump and he flops forward.

With the knife put away, the parking lot security closes in. They hoist him up by his shoulders, but the moment Levi's two feet touches the ground, he slips them and runs toward the exit, where Levi is met by police. He has no choice but to raise his hands and lie flat on his belly while they cuff him. All members watch as if they'd actually got dressed up this morning to be an audience to a man being hogtied by police.

Outside, they stuff Levi in a squad car. There is an ambulance for Nay, who they strap on a gurney and take in for dehydration.

Inside, the choir director orders the choir to sing to bring some calm to the situation. And they do. Distractedly, the congregation goes along. Bailey comes up to the pulpit with the working microphone to announce that the next voice they will hear after the choir selection will be none other than that of First Lady, Lynn Stewart.

Members are filing back in, needing the Holy Ghost more now because of the situation outside. They slowly crank up the praise, although quizzical looks steer around in all directions.

A hundred years since former slaves established this church and Lynn is set to be the first woman preach from the pulpit rather than the lectern.

Many of the deacons outside, loyal to Levi doesn't return to the sanctuary. Those inside do nothing to stop Lynn. Catfish is in the front row with his legs cross, eager to see what Lynn, their investment, is capable of.

After the song, Lynn comes up to the pulpit, to the surprise of one disgruntled elder who gets up and quotes first Timothy, saying that women should not teach or have authority over men. He makes an appeal to those around him and a few follow him out of the sanctuary in open mutiny. Women from Lynn's bible study class appeal for members to stay put, to witness the brilliance they'd become accustomed to. Still, Men leave in large numbers, some taking their family with them, refusing to drink of God's living water because of the vessel it's being poured out of.

Lynn just waits. She waits until things are settled down, and while she waits, this feeling of reassurance washes over her. She knows it's only a matter of time that everything would be back to normal; that her husband would be back behind this same pulpit; that he would be judged by his act of heroism, rather than the financial seminars error.

The moment Lynn touches the wood of the pulpit, she feels a charged jolt. She takes air into her nostrils, and knows that she was made for this, and that everything that has happened now was no mistake. Her only mistake was running from this call and that she is standing behind the pulpit, not by chance, but by transformation: forty years after the church burned the last time a woman was set to preach from the pulpit, also on the very day of the one-hundred-year anniversary of First Baptist's founding.

Lynn feels filled with a sense of belonging as she scans the congregation. With the full confidence of the Holy Spirit, she then delivers the word of God.

Epilogue

astor Stewart is released on Monday morning; no bond hearing necessary. No charges come of the incident. Stewart is regarded as a hero. The forty litigants now steer their civil case towards Westermann.

The day after being released, Stewart marches into the sanctuary, uttering not even a good morning; an axe in hand. He goes straight to the altar with the axe and begins chopping away at the lectern. People run in, to see what the noise is about. Women gather, while tears gather in their eyes. Stewart looks up and finds and audience. They begin applauding. Stewart calls Mavis out of the gathering and hands the axe over to Mavis, who gets right to chopping off a piece of the handle of the lectern and raises it in triumph. Mavis hands the axe to Nay. Nay hacks away her souvenir and passes the axe to Deacon Bailey's wife and so on, and so forth, until the lectern is fully cleaved away from God's altar.

Stewart preaches the next sermon from First Baptist's pulpit and he preaches them into the middle of the year, while Lynn preaches in the newly renovated office space, her sermons aired on television, her following growing like wildfire.

Instead of taking the Ginyard's offer to expand their ministry to the retired University of South Carolina coliseum, Lynn joins Stewart, who puts up his own money and cuts a deal to lease the coliseum. He and Lynn start their own ministry there as both husband and wife and as co-pastors.

Lynn does the honors of the first sermon at their new sanctuary and looking out over the audience, she sees many familiar faces that had left First Baptist.

After the sermon, she's joined onstage by her husband. They stand side by side, holding hands. They look over at each other and raise their hands in shared victory.

…About Bianca. Since the day she ran into the sanctuary with a knife-wielding Nay, no one had seen nor heard of her. Her car is gone. Her closet is empty, but she's left all of her furniture in her apartment. Bianca had only spoken to her parents, letting them know she'll be gone for a long time, but not to worry; she'll be ok.

As it turns out, all along, Bianca had her plan B, a pastor twenty years her senior, widowed just recently. The dirt hasn't even settled on his wife's grave while Bishop Simon Bonneau struts with a new pretty young thing on his arm before a congregation who still mourns their first lady.

Bianca and the bishop rush to marry, beating the baby bump to the altar. Bishop Simon Bonneau is a walnut colored man with his hair processed in a throwback style, slick as Nat King Cole himself. This man opens the veil of a bride in which he believes, that the secret child she carries, is his own.

Bianca seems so sincerely in love, smiling back awaiting the kiss to seal her lifelong dream of becoming a first lady. She'd wanted her wedding photos to be perfect, so she wears her blue contacts, and had gone a step further by dyeing her hair blonde. Leading up to the wedding, she'd been bleaching her skin more often, almost to the point where she now looks pale and sickly. Against her pale skin her lipstick is as bright as blood. She receives her kiss of marriage.

To The Reader:

Bianca's happy ending, however, isn't so happy nor is it an ending. Troubles do follow. To see a continuation of Bianca's story, check out Rod Palmer's fifth novel, *The Waymaker*.

This book is dedicated to my loving, courageous mother, Betty Palmer, a domestic violence survivor and a woman who personifies this scripture, "And let us not be weary in well doing; for in due season, we shall reap," (Galatians 6:9).

About The Author

Son of a carpenter and a nanny, Rod Palmer was born in a historic Gullah Geechie community in Charleston, SC. He received his degrees in creative writing and Afro studies at the University of South Carolina. Currently he resides in Europe where he is a dedicated husband and girl-dad, enjoys travel and writing the next novel.

His other works are:

A Pimp In The Pulpit
The Work-Husband Caper
The Harvest
Karma Wears Versace
KWV II: Man Eater
The Waymaker

www.ingramcontent.com/pod-product-compliance
Lightning Source LLC
Chambersburg PA
CBHW021344310726
48971CB00001B/284